The Sense of Paper

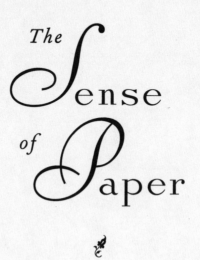

The *Sense* of *Paper*

TAYLOR HOLDEN

BANTAM BOOKS

New York   Toronto   London   Sydney   Auckland

THE SENSE OF PAPER
A Bantam Book / October 2006

Published by Bantam Dell
A Division of Random House, Inc.
New York, New York

This is a work of fiction. Names, characters, places, and incidents either are the product of
the author's imagination or are used fictitiously. Any resemblance to actual persons,
living or dead, events, or locales is entirely coincidental.

Page 179: Virginia Woolf quote from *Mrs. Dalloway*, foreword by Maureen
Howard. San Diego: Harvest/Harcourt Brace & Company, 1981, pp. 98, 147.

Page 250: Arthur Miller quote from *After the Fall* (1945). Taken from *The Penguin
International Thesaurus of Quotations*, Penguin Books, 1985, p. 51, ref. 77.3.

Page 304: Jean Giraudoux quote from: *The Madwoman of Chaillot* (1945), adapted
by Maurice Valency. Taken from *The Penguin International Thesaurus of Quotations*,
Penguin Books, 1985, p. 604, ref. 911.17.

Book design by Ellen Cipriano

Bantam Books is a registered trademark of Random House, Inc.,
and the colophon is a trademark of Random House, Inc.

Library of Congress Cataloging-in-Publication Data
Holden, Wendy, 1961–
     The sense of paper / Taylor Holden.
       p. cm.
     Novel.
     ISBN-13: 978-0-553-80394-5
     ISBN-10: 0-553-80394-8
     I. Title.

PR6108.O43S46 2006
823'.92—dc22

                                          2005056272

Printed in the United States of America
Published simultaneously in Canada

www.bantamdell.com

BVG   10 9 8 7 6 5 4 3 2 1

To my much-missed parents,
who gave me the confidence to follow my heart,
and to my friend Silk, who taught me
the meaning of truth

PAPER, rag, pulp, wood, newsprint, card, Bristol card, calendered paper, art paper, cartridge paper, India paper, carbon paper, tissue paper, crêpe paper, sugar paper, tracing paper, cellophane, papier-mâché, cardboard, pasteboard, millboard, strawboard, fiberboard, chipboard, hardboard, plasterboard, sheet, foolscap, quarto, imperial, quire, ream, notepaper.

Roget's Thesaurus

PAPER, a material made in thin sheets as an aqueous deposit from linen rags, esparto, wood pulp, or other form of cellulose, used for writing, printing, wrapping, and other purposes: extended to other materials of similar purpose or appearance, as to papyrus, rice paper, to the substance of which some wasps build their nests, to cardboard, and even tinfoil (silver paper): a piece of paper: a written or printed document or instrument, note, receipt, bill, bond, deed, etc: a newspaper: an essay or literary contribution, esp. one read before a society: a set of examination questions: paper money: paper-hanging for walls: a wrapping of paper: a quantity of anything wrapped in or attached to paper.

The Chambers Dictionary

The Sense of Paper

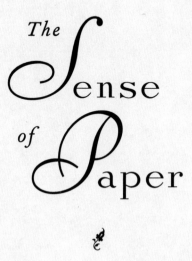

Pulp

A soft, wet, shapeless mass

derived from rags, wood, etc., used in

papermaking; poor quality or sensational writing

originally printed on rough paper;

the soft fleshy part of fruit; to reduce to pulp

1

Fragments of memory pierce her subconsciousness like shards of broken glass. Her body twitches convulsively in her sleep. Fear presses down on her chest, making it heave as she snatches for breath.

Bang. The cellar door is kicked in on its rusting hinges. A sweaty soldier lumbers toward her in the flickering torchlight. Behind him, others leer at her. His uneven teeth smirk beneath a wiry moustache as his left hand unzips his urine-stained trousers. A scream wells in her throat. Before she can utter a sound, his fat fingers, stinking of nicotine, are clamped across her mouth. His other hand drags her by her hair up the stone steps, scuffing her knees on every one.

Bang. Out in the pale moonlight, grubby hands reach for her, rending her clothing as she flails and twists away. A boot slams into her stomach, driving the air from her lungs. All she can smell is sweat, smoke, and semen. Fear gives her strength. Struggling in their grasp, she shouts: "*Novinar! Zurnalista!* Journalist!" Their laughter fills the spaces in her head as they manhandle her roughly toward a clearing in the woods. Throwing her facedown in the dirt, they press forward eagerly, one by one.

BANG. She is up on her feet somehow and running hard. Running for her life. Gasping for breath through torn, bleeding lips. Clawing at the red earth with broken fingernails as she slips. Heading for the road in the dark.

BANG. The truck appears from nowhere in the darkness. The roar of its horn stuns her as she whirls to face the sudden brutal glare of its headlights bearing down on her.

BANG. Inconceivable, searing pain. The sensation of flying effortlessly through the clear night sky, before landing on the ground with a sickening thud.

Oblivion.

A FULL FIFTEEN minutes under the shower's stinging hot jets usually dissolved the worst of the night. She'd already endured the first phase, vomiting into the toilet bowl until only yellow bile emerged as her cheek pressed against the cold white porcelain. This morning, purging was taking a lot longer. Charlie stood gripping the showerhead, neck arched, her mouth opening and closing as she allowed the steaming rivulets to cascade down her taut body. Inside her skull, her mind thrashed beyond her control, each involuntary reflex stirring up more mire from the depths of its murky pool.

Leaning into the water, relishing its cleansing power, she fought hard to focus. *Happier days.* That's it. Remember what it used to be like, a long time ago. Before. She swallowed hard to prevent the rising in her throat.

Angry with herself, she knew she could do it. Remember the times when being with a man felt good. Remember how it could be. How it once was, with Nick. Taking a shower together, his lips everywhere, his knowing, capable hands pulling her head back by her soapy hair. Their self-control almost lost as she dropped to her knees and sought him out with her mouth. *Before*. Good. That's it.

If she didn't hurry, she was going to be late. She had an important appointment and she'd already slept through the buzzing alarm. But she wasn't ready, not quite yet. Just a few minutes more and she'd be fine. Soap. Water. Heat. The scent of rosemary oil and geranium. Essential oils. Essential to her.

Soon, the stench of nicotine would be gone from the membrane in her nostrils. Soon, she'd be able to face the day.

2

THE SILENCE LAY HEAVY around them as he slid the key in the lock of the large, flat safe-deposit box. The stale air of the room deep within the bank vaults was filled with Alan's unique scent of varnish and linseed oil.

Far above them, the giant exhaust pipe of London belched in the summer heat. Fleets of taxis scuttled through the City like shiny black beetles, carrying their cargo home. Beneath the sizzling pavements, Charlie offered cool contrast in her lilac cotton sleeveless blouse and blue linen trousers.

Click. The key turned with surprising ease. Glancing up beneath a lock of greying hair, Alan invited her to open the box with an elegant gesture of his right hand.

His reverence was contagious. Lifting the lid and closing her eyes in anticipation, Charlie could almost believe that she was about to witness the unveiling of some ancient, mystical relic, in a time long before her own.

She could smell it before she saw it, a distinctive, crisp odour. She opened her eyes. There, partially wrapped in a waterproof covering and interleaved with acid-free tissue, lay the precious last sheets of Alan's beloved paper. Possibly the last of its kind in the world.

"So, this is it," she murmured.

"Yes." He nodded, a smile of pride curving his lips as he reached into the box to peel back the crinkly tissue.

They stared for a moment at the product of what would have amounted to several weeks of intensive labour. Crafted by hand using ancient techniques, this paper would have begun life as a dense pulp of linen matter floating in a vat of water, its mashed fibres interlocking to create its unique texture. Lifted by a fine sieve mould and slid onto damp felt, each sheet would have been draped over waxed horsehair ropes, then lifted high into shuttered lofts to air-dry. Left to cure for a month and glazed with a gelatine solution known as "size," each sheet would have been pressed and meticulously hand-polished with agate before being cut ready for use.

Two hundred years ago, only the finest artists or the wealthiest writers would have been able to afford such a prize. Those who could jealously guarded their meagre supplies. It was not just its rarity that made this paper so sought after. It was highly temperamental, absorbing and giving off moisture even after production. It had to be stored in a place that was not too hot or too cold, too damp or too dry, no more than twenty-five sheets at a time. Contact with certain woods or metals corrupted it.

Alan had originally kept much of his precious cache in specially crafted wooden map chests in his studio but, after a fire, he'd transferred what remained to the safety of the buttressed bowels of his bank. Inspired by its beauty, he considered this paper his talisman. Because of the chemicals used in modern manufacture, nothing like it would ever be produced again. And he believed that it had shaped him into the world-famous artist he had become.

Lifting the top sheet, he whispered, "You'll never understand how unique this is, until you see me working it."

Trembling a little, Charlie watched in silence as his hands peeled off the single sheet, its fragile edges crumbling slightly at his touch. Lifting it up to the light, he exposed the legendary watermark giving its origin, purpose, and manufacture, and the visible grid marks of the mould on its pitted surface.

"It was paper much like this, crafted in the same mill, which the great

Turner used as the foundation for some of his finest watercolours," he told her. "He depended on its whiteness and its rich, warm tones to let his colours shine through. Like me, he believed there was nothing to compare. And when I've used up this, my final hoard, it will be time."

"Time for what?" Charlie asked.

"Death, of course," Alan replied, a sad smile twisting the corner of his mouth.

TRAVELING BACK ALONG the Embankment in a taxi, Charlie felt suffocated by the stifling heat. The air seemed to be crackling with electricity and her hair felt hot and heavy on her neck. News bulletins from Iraq blared relentlessly from the cabdriver's radio, and she felt unable to catch her breath. Winding down the window, she sucked in oxygen greedily.

An unexpected text message, its sudden chirping breaking into her concentration, felt like a lifeline thrown out to the choppy waters of her mind. But the moment she replied, she felt, as she so often did, cross with herself for grabbing at it so eagerly.

By the time Charlie arrived home, she needed a drink. An ache thumped inside her head and her throat felt scratchy. Something about that final hour with Alan in the airless vault had unbalanced her carefully maintained equilibrium.

Closing her front door against the chaos of the city, she stood for a moment and savoured the cool tranquillity of her hallway, like a novice leaving the vulgar world behind her for the hush of the convent. Ignoring the junk mail on the doormat, she slipped off her sandals and padded softly across the floor of her apartment to throw wide the French windows to a small stone terrace.

Reaching for a glass, she wandered into the kitchen and opened the refrigerator door. All the shelves held were four bottles of wine, three of sparkling mineral water, and an unopened packet of Columbian coffee. Her fingers hovered between a pale Muscadet or an oaky Australian Chardonnay. She chose the Muscadet.

Within minutes, the cork had popped satisfyingly from the neck of the bottle and her glass was filled. Sipping its fresh, clean contents, she waited for the alcohol to soften the edges of her day as she wandered out onto the terrace. Inhaling the warm scent of the late summer roses that overran its raised brick borders, she could hear the hum of bees, deep within their velvety petals, collecting the last of the season's pollen. Looking down, she watched as one small furry insect, drunk on nectar, made his way unsteadily across the paving stones towards her bare feet. Only at the very last minute did it turn away.

Back inside, she glanced at the answering machine blinking on a side table, then reached instead for the stereo. She adjusted the volume until a familiar cello suite filled the air. Closing her eyes, she allowed the melancholy music to carry her, drifting back and forth. For several minutes, she stood like that, wrapped up in her secret self. When the movement ended, her eyelids fluttered open as if she'd just awakened from a long sleep.

Behind her, a mahogany bookcase dominated the room. Its shelves held the familiar companions she'd collected over the years, books on everything from fiction to food, fine art to military history. Garnered from secondhand shops, their battered covers were testament to the frequency with which they'd been read long before she'd bought them. Charlie knew and loved every one. She would often run her fingers across their backs, feeling the worn leather or cloth spines in turn. Sometimes she'd open them and flick through their pages absentmindedly, enjoying a word here or snippet of sentence there, relishing either a story she knew well, or the delicious anticipation of something yet to be enjoyed.

The mere touch of her hand on the paper of an unread book could excite her.

Hidden amongst her collection was *Road to Rajak: A Day in the Life of Kosovo* by Charlotte Hudson; a book which had taken her a year to write, one year further away from what had gone before. It had been described by one reviewer as "a moving and intensely humane portrait of one of Europe's most heinous and inhumane conflicts." Its widespread critical acclaim now felt as fragile to her as the cobweb that traced a silvery line along its back.

Pulling her mind back to the present, Charlie sank into the sofa's enveloping softness and pressed the button on her answering machine.

"Hi, it's Nick," said a voice she knew almost as well as her own. *"Just checking in. Sorry I haven't been in touch for a few weeks, but work's been manic. I'd love to catch up if you're free this evening. I'll try your mobile, but if I don't get through, give me a ring before you open your second bottle, okay?"*

Charlie arched an eyebrow and pressed her cool glass against the warm skin of her throat.

"Hello, Charlotte," said the next voice. *"Your father and I were wondering if you might be able to squeeze in a visit to us this weekend. You haven't been for nearly three weeks now and you know how much he looks forward to seeing you. Anyway, let me know, dear. Bye."*

The final voice was Nick's. *"Hi. Ignore my earlier call. You just replied to my text message. Thanks for the invite. Takeout sounds great. I'll pick it up on my way over. Hope Chinese is okay. See you about eight."*

Charlie glanced up at the old wooden clock her grandfather had left her and realised she didn't have much time. Gulping her wine, she hurried to the bathroom, scrubbing her face and hands vigorously with a nail-brush and a fresh bar of lemon soap. From the rows of hangers in her wardrobe, on which her clothes hung in precise colour sequence, she selected a plain white shirt and black linen trousers.

Methodically, she brushed out her thick brown hair before twisting it into a smooth French plait at the back of her neck. Examining her face, almost devoid of makeup, she smeared some balm across her lips. Pulling a tissue from the pretty pink papier-mâché box on her dressing table, she pressed her mouth carefully over its neatly folded edge.

By the time the doorbell rang a few minutes later, she was ready to face her husband.

3

*I*T WASN'T NICK'S FAULT. He'd only come because she'd invited him. The trouble was Charlie couldn't now remember why she'd suggested it in the first place.

Taking a deep breath and smoothing the creases in her trousers with the palms of her hands, she fixed a smile of welcome onto her face and opened the door. In sharp contrast to her freshness, Nick was decidedly sticky in his grey suit trousers and duck-egg-blue shirt, tie loose, jacket thrown casually over his shoulder. A six o'clock shadow made the skin above his chin look sallow. His fine blond hair was its usual unruly self, defiantly creeping over his collar, but his eyes, exactly the same colour as the shirt, smiled readily, and she relaxed a little.

As usual, he lingered a few seconds longer than necessary as he bent to kiss her cheek. She detected stale sweat, the grime of a London newspaper office and, recoiling slightly, an undertone of cigarette smoke.

"Come on in." Charlie stepped aside as he entered her hallway carrying a briefcase and two brown paper bags bulging with food. "Excuse the mess."

Nick wandered through to the bright kitchen and placed their supper on the spotless work surface. Everything around him appeared hard and white and gleaming. Reaching for plates so shiny he could see his own reflection in them he called over his shoulder, "What mess? You need a tetanus shot before you can eat in my kitchen."

As he lifted his arms, she noticed two circles of sweat staining his shirt and a button missing from his right cuff. He pulled out some chopsticks (for Charlie) and a knife and fork (for him).

"How's life?" Charlie asked.

"Crazy," Nick replied, prising the cardboard lid off a foil carton so that the steam danced around his face. "Complete crap today." Charlie winced as he plunged an unwashed finger into the carton and brought it up to his mouth, dripping with sauce.

"Really?" she asked, reaching for another glass. "Why? What happened?"

"Oh, the usual fuckups. Our lawyer in a complete lather over some legal warning we'd received on a Guantánamo Bay story. Wants the reporter involved sacked. It took me more than two hours to calm him down. Then, someone slapped an embargo on an exclusive we had about the latest shenanigans with Enron. Jake wanted to break the embargo but the city editor swore he'd quit if we did. Jake finally agreed to hold off until tomorrow morning, but only after I'd persuaded the powers-that-be at the Stock Exchange that they owed us one for doing so."

Wandering towards her, Nick took a full glass of wine from her extended hand and gulped appreciatively. "Actually," he added, rubbing his right temple with the heel of his palm, "I have a splitting headache. Do you have any aspirin?"

Charlie's expression faltered slightly but she didn't flinch. "No. I don't keep any pills."

Nick stared at her for a moment, then turned away. "Never mind. I'm sure the wine will do the trick."

"How's Miranda?" Charlie asked, changing the subject.

"Okay." Smirking, he added, "She's good for me."

"Good for a quick screw, you mean."

Her words hung in the air between them like a bad odour.

The muscles in Nick's jaw tightened but he refused to take the bait.

"So, how's the new book going?" he asked a little too loudly, crumpling the greasy paper bags into the bin and rummaging through a drawer for the napkins he knew she'd insist upon.

"Fine," Charlie replied, a little too quickly, watching his large frame prowling around her kitchen. She'd forgotten how small he made everything seem.

"That bad, eh?" He watched her closely. "I must say I always thought it an unlikely project for you. I mean, the history of art paper and its importance to J.M.W. Turner isn't exactly sexy, front-line stuff, is it?"

Charlie retreated to the sitting room. "Maybe not, but it's what I need right now. And actually, it's going okay. Really. Alan's been incredibly helpful."

Nick stopped what he was doing and stared at her. "Oh, it's Alan now, is it? I get it."

"No, Nick, you don't *get* anything," Charlie said crossly, moving a framed photograph of her grandfather half an inch to the left. "Of course we're on first-name terms. We're collaborating. We can hardly call each other Ms Hudson and Sir Alan Matheson the whole time, can we?"

Nick's face broke into a grin, the lines around his eyes and mouth forming deep crevasses. Damn him, she hated it when he did that. He caught her out almost every time. Reddening, she stepped away and turned down the music while he fussed around her little kitchen.

"You're not allowed to tease, Nick. Not today. It's been a long week and I've got to be up horribly early in the morning."

"To see *Alan* again, I suppose?"

She watched as he licked coconut milk from his thumb. "Maybe. Not that it would be any concern of yours."

"No, I don't suppose it is. Just as it's none of your concern who I'm screwing."

The CD came to an abrupt halt and there was a silence neither of them could remember how to fill. A vein began to twitch spasmodically beneath Charlie's left eye as she studied Nick's expression. Automatically, she pressed two fingers against it. She'd forgotten how cruel his face could become. Thankfully he was too far away to reach out and grab her by the throat. Their eyes locked; she felt a momentary pang of desire and wondered what he'd do if she reached up and kissed his mouth. Before she could find out, he'd pushed past her and out of the room.

When he returned from the bathroom minutes later, he found her standing in the patio garden, her arms wrapped tightly around herself. Through the cotton of her shirt, her shoulder blades jutted like the wings of a bird.

"Here, come and eat something." His voice was softer. As his fingertips brushed her arm, she registered, with complete detachment, that her nerve endings no longer issued any response. Taking her elbow, he led her gently to the table where everything was laid out, the lights dimmed and a candle lit.

That was the trouble with Nick. He knew her better than she knew herself. Inhaling deeply, she tried to focus on getting through the rest of the evening without picking a fight.

Keep swimming on the surface, Charlie told herself. *Don't go too deep.*

She felt Nick's eyes on her as the silence hung between them accusingly. There had been a time when such silences felt so natural, like a soft blanket wrapped around them, neither one needing to speak. But that was before.

Obviously nettled, Nick shoved a steaming dish of king prawns with spring onions and ginger towards her. "Try this." But as he did so, some of its contents slopped messily onto the table, and lay glistening.

Charlie dabbed at the mess with a napkin, irked by his clumsiness but more irritated at the ruination of the napkin. It was an especially pretty one, the finest tissue paper, feather-light and imprinted with a pretty Asian pheasant design in pink and gold on a pale blue background. It made a comforting rustling sound in her hands. She looked across at his, crumpled into a tight, irretrievable ball at the side of his plate, and frowned.

Reminding herself that Nick was her guest, she forced a smile. Waving at the food, she said, "Thanks for all this. I probably should have cooked you something."

"When was the last time you cooked a proper meal?" Nick snorted, derisively. Charlie couldn't help but shrug and laugh. It was years since she'd opened a recipe book, bought ingredients, and washed, diced, cut, and prepared something wholesome and delicious. Since she'd been living alone, she seemed to exist on wine and caffeine. She'd never been fat—"String Bean," her grandfather used to call her—but now her clothes hung from her frame and the wedding ring she wore out of habit swiveled loosely on her finger.

Secretly, she relished her thinness. It was the one area of her life over which she had full control.

"Come on, then," Nick urged impatiently, shoveling food between his lips. "I might not expect you to cook but I do expect you to eat some of it!" A tiny smear of sauce created a red crease in the corner of his mouth, like blood.

Charlie deftly extracted a prawn with her chopsticks and examined it silently, before nibbling at it, a tiny mouthful at a time.

"What's up?" Nick asked, slurping his wine noisily.

"Nothing."

"You're all right, then?" He ran his tongue experimentally around his teeth.

"Of course."

"Sleeping okay?"

"Uh-huh."

He stared at her, his mouth suddenly still. "So why does my sixth sense about you tell me something's wrong?"

"I can't imagine." She smiled, bracing herself for another tiny bite.

He waited, his heavily laden fork poised midair. His silence usually brought results.

Charlie felt a little pain in the pit of her stomach and set down her chopsticks. She drew back in her chair and let her hands slide from the table onto her lap. "Oh, it's nothing at all, Nick. Really." She sighed. "I'm just feeling a little vulnerable, I guess. I'm at that point in the book where I'm afraid I won't find enough material or the sanity I'll need to piece it all together."

Devouring his mouthful, Nick grimaced as food lodged in his throat.

"I don't know why you should even think that," he said hoarsely, gulping down more wine. "You're a better writer than half the journalists on my staff. You can do this book standing on your head."

"Can I?" Charlie asked. "But what if I can't, Nick? What if I really am burned out? Yes, I was a damn good journalist once, but then I lost my nerve. What can I claim to be now?" Even as she asked the question, she felt a sudden, stupid desire to cry.

Nick squeezed the bridge of his nose between his thumb and forefinger. "You don't have to claim to *be* anything, don't you see? If you insist, yes, okay, you're still here; you're alive. Against impossible odds. Isn't that good enough for you? Because it damn well should be!"

Reaching across the table, his hand stopped just short of hers. "Come on now, Charlie, of course you can do this." His tone was adamant. "You're one of the best. God knows, you lived and almost died for it. Just because you've become a 'civilian' doesn't mean to say you've lost what it takes. Your first book was brilliant. This one'll be *fine*. You have to keep believing that."

Charlie nodded bleakly. "I'm sorry. I'm sure you didn't come here tonight to hear all this. What would our therapist have said? If you don't want to know, don't ask. Well, I'm afraid you did ask."

Nick withdrew his hand and stabbed testily at a cube of chicken. "You're just having a small crisis of confidence. You'll be okay."

"I know," she said, full of sudden affection. "Sometimes I think I just need to hear you tell me."

Nick suddenly grabbed her wrist and stared hard into her face. Looking as if he wanted to hurt her the way she'd hurt him, he opened his mouth to speak but then snapped it shut. When he released her, they both studied the angry red mark he'd left behind.

"Oh, for Christ's sake," he snapped, "pick up those damn chopsticks and eat some of this bloody food before it gets cold!"

4

AN ACCIDENT OF TIMING had brought Charlie into contact with Sir Alan Matheson. A happenstance, her grandfather would have called it. It was a word she loved and one which had never been more appropriate than for her chance encounter with the nation's greatest living artist.

That blustery Saturday morning in May, Charlie had woken early after a fitful night and decided on a whim to restore her inner calm by wallowing in the magical surroundings of L. Cornelissen & Son. The definitive artists' supply shop was situated in Great Russell Street, in that genteel area called Bloomsbury, the literary centre of London and home to dozens of antiquarian bookshops. Founded in 1855, just four years after Turner's death, Cornelissen's was the place to which her grandfather would regularly journey from Kent to buy all his materials, ever since the legendary Lechertier, Barbe had closed its premises in Jermyn Street or it became too onerous for him to travel to the famous Sennelier's in Paris.

Pushing open the heavy green door of the bow-fronted establishment she knew so well, Charlie paused and allowed the reservoir of her memory to fill. The air was heady with painterly scents; she could feel herself being drawn back in time. The walls were lined, floor to ceiling, with dark oak shelves and drawers that spoke of the shop's Georgian past. The stripped wood floorboards were worn by the passage of feet, the ceiling lights pendulous and low.

Powdered pigments in every colour of the rainbow pierced the gloom. They stood legion in tall glass jars displayed with mathematical precision on the upper shelves. The lower shelves were crammed with fat pastel crayons, brushes of every size and length, tubes of watercolour and oil paint, pencils and wax crayons. Behind the counter, scores of numbered drawers concealed delicate wafers of gold leaf, along with sable brushes and every possible tool for gilding.

Deeper into the shop lay more slim wooden drawers. Each housed a veritable treasure trove of chalks, the mauves and pinks and greens and blues arranged according to the colour spectrum, their chalky residue staining the interior. Lacquers and varnishes of every description inhabited an entire corner, and on the farthest and highest shelves, tall glass jars hid all manner of intriguing delights: *Japan Wax; Fuller's Earth; Paraffin Wax; Gum Elan; Dragon's Blood; Lump Sanguine; Madder Root; Leaf Gelatine; Parchment Clippings; Isinglass; Lemon Shellac.* Each spoke of a time past, of the era of Turner, when artists would size and varnish their own paintings with the boiled-down residues of animal-hide parchment, or with isinglass, harvested from the air bladder of the highly prized sturgeon.

But it was the extraordinary range of papers for sale at Cornelissen's that always lured Charlie. They took up the remotest corner of the shop and represented the products of dozens of companies worldwide, from the modern-day Whatman's to Arjo Wiggins in Paris and Strathmore Artist Papers in Massachusetts, one of the first manufacturers in the United States. More familiar names like Winsor & Newton, Daler-Rowney, and Cotman were also available here; the papers Charlie would herself have purchased in blocks from her little art suppliers in Suffolk. The paper her grandfather had allowed her to use.

"Turner painted on anything he could lay his hands on," Granddad loved to tell Charlie, "even the greasy paper his cheese came wrapped in. The cheapest may not be the best, but it'll do for starters." Charlie smiled at the memory.

The range of handmade paper available in Cornelissen's was seductive. She could tell which ones were handmade from their "deckle edges," formed when a thin layer of the pulp creeps beneath that part of the mould known as the deckle. Such edges are found on all four sides of a handmade sheet, but on only the two opposite sides of a machine-made sheet. Once regarded as an imperfection and cut away, the deckle edge was now a sign of the finest quality.

Charlie fingered the various papers and lost herself to them. There was the Lana company, near Strasbourg, which had been making paper for over four centuries. She also liked the bright off-white paper made by the Zecchi family near Florence from one hundred per cent cotton rag, sized with pine-tree resin. And that of the Dordogne company Moulin de Larroque, which still produced a handmade linen paper called Ficelle. Carriage House Paper of Brooklyn, New York, offered a range of handmade products, including coloured speciality papers, crafted with an old mould and deckle from England.

Then there were the English papers. St Cuthbert's Mill in the Axe valley in Somerset, which had made fine papers for over two hundred and fifty years, produced Saunders Waterford paper, whose predecessor was the TH Saunders watercolour paper used by artists all over the world. St Cuthbert's also produced Bockingford paper from quality wood pulp. Another tiny West Country mill, this time on the outskirts of Exmoor, Devon, was the Two Rivers company. Annually, it manufactured two tons of cotton and flax heavyweight paper for the fine-art market.

There was even a paper called Turner's Blue Wove, one of several modern versions of papers originally manufactured in the late eighteenth century to the specific requirements of some of the world's greatest watercolourists. A company based in east London made this one by hand from cotton, its surface smooth and granular with the dull blue hue of an English winter sky.

There were also Indian papers, crafted from jute and khadi, the handspun cotton originally produced in the poorest villages under the auspices of Mahatma Gandhi. Charlie lifted them up and swore she could smell the heat and spices of Asia. Another Indian paper was made from banana fibre but smelt inexplicably of chocolate. A Nepalese product woven from vegetable fibre felt like papyrus to the touch. Japanese paper made from kozo fibre smelt of onions; Czech paper of cotton and flax from a mill founded when Elizabeth Tudor was Queen of England was comfortingly smooth.

Charlie's favourite paper was the astonishingly expensive Fabriano range. Rich and creamy white, it had exquisite names like Artistico and Medioevalis and a random woven texture that was crying out for paint. The company, she knew, specialised in chlorine-free, natural, combed cotton, which was made without whiteners or acid to preserve its integrity. At five pounds per sheet, it wasn't cheap, but she found herself inexplicably drawn to it and simply had to buy some.

Approaching the deep wooden counter, she tried to decide if the shaven-headed young man manning it would be able to answer the question nibbling like a mouse at the back of her mind.

"If J.M.W. Turner were alive today," she asked finally, "which of these papers do you think he might choose?"

"Not one of them!" a terse voice interjected behind her, as the assistant rolled her precious purchase and bound it with an elastic band. "They wouldn't have been nearly good enough."

Turning, Charlie found herself face to face with a tall, lean man in his fifties. His sharp nose rather dominated his face, making his eyes seem slightly too close together. His thick head of silvery hair was capricious, and his pronounced Adam's apple bobbed up and down in his throat when he swallowed.

Under his arm, he carried a rolled-up copy of the *Daily Telegraph*, bulging with weekend supplements.

"None of them?" she asked with surprise, gesturing at the colourful cornucopia of goods for sale. "What makes you say that?"

The man examined Charlie so critically while he considered his answer that she looked down at her body self-consciously. Casually dressed in a cream V-neck T-shirt and blue trousers, she wore a navy cardigan tied loosely around her shoulders. Her face carried no makeup and her hair with its natural kink was pulled back. Her green eyes, enhanced only by a light brushing of mascara, spoke, she knew, of experience beyond her years. And her hands, he would undoubtedly note, betrayed her. Chapped and scrubbed clean, the oval fingernails were devoid of polish. They could easily have belonged to someone much older.

"I'm Alan Matheson," he said by way of reply, extending his hand.

"Charlie Hudson," she replied, her small hand swamped by his. Then, faltering, she added, "Alan Matheson? The artist?"

The shop assistant gushed from behind her. "Sir Alan's one of our most valued customers. And one of the Tate's leading scholars on Turner. If you need to know anything about the papers the master might have used, then Sir Alan's your man."

Charlie almost laughed at her own good fortune. This embryo idea of hers, nestling deep within the bony cocoon of her skull, was eerily beginning to develop a strange life force all its own. "Then you are just the person I need to talk to," she conceded. Seeing the curiosity in his eyes, she risked more. "I wonder, Sir Alan...I know you're probably incredibly busy, but do you think you could possibly spare me a few minutes of your time? I really need to pick your brains."

Alan Matheson touched the newspaper tucked under his arm as if for reassurance, but was clearly intrigued. "Go on."

"Well, I'm a writer, and I've been toying with the idea of putting together some sort of book about Turner. My grandfather was a keen artist—nothing like you, of course, but he had a passion for Turner that I've inherited. I know there've been dozens of books about him; do you think there could be anything new and worthwhile to be said?"

"Perhaps," Alan replied, a new light behind his eyes.

"Really? Because what's been troubling me most is that there can't possibly be any aspect of this subject that hasn't already been fully explored."

"You have the answer in your hands." Alan pointed to her purchase.

"Sorry?"

"First, respect your paper!" he boomed, his body leaning slightly towards hers.

Involuntarily, Charlie pulled away. "Excuse me?"

"Those were Turner's words to any painter who asked him for advice. Far better than yet another tedious biography would be a book exploring the importance of the remarkable paper he used. Do you have any idea what was involved? Paper production is affected by everything from war and poverty to changes in fashion. The story of its creation and supply would make a book in itself. You only have to look around this shop to imagine what it might have been like in Turner's day."

Charlie could feel her heart soar. "Could I . . . ? I mean, would you . . . ? Listen, can I please buy you a coffee? There's a place just around the corner."

Without giving him a chance to change his mind, she led her new acquaintance out of the shop and into the café on Tottenham Court Road. There, she ordered two large cappuccinos and manoeuvred him into a quiet corner. They sat, side by side on a huge dog-bed sofa. Her knees tucked up under her, cradling her mug in her hand, she soaked up everything Sir Alan Matheson told her.

"This is kismet," he admitted, sipping at the froth and wiping his lips with his fingers. "I've been trying to persuade any number of my protégées to write a readable book on the history and importance of art paper for years, without success. If you're really serious about this, I'd be happy to help."

"You can start by telling me what you know."

There was an almost childlike wonder in the artist's eyes as he began to talk her through the complex processes and politics of the papermaking industry in preindustrial Britain. His encyclopaedic knowledge of Turner was impressive and his enthusiasm infectious. Charlie's initial cautiousness vanished as she suddenly found herself looking forward to mining the strata of this man's remarkable mind. Her face turned towards him, soaking up the sunny encouragement her pallid ego craved, she was also happy to note that, somewhere along the way, Sir Alan Matheson had abandoned his newspaper for good.

• • •

THE FOLLOWING MORNING, Charlie woke early, surprised at how happy she felt at the prospect of embarking on her new project. Her initial plan was to unearth all she could about the history of artists' papers, especially Turner's favoured medium, the watercolour paper Alan Matheson had told her about, which was created by a small Kentish company called J.W. Whatman. She had no idea if there would be enough new material to justify an entire book, but Alan had so fired her with excitement that she was determined to find out.

From the outset, Alan was true to his word. Within days of their brief encounter, a huge cardboard box arrived by courier at her London apartment. It was filled with books and academic papers on Turner, articles and pamphlets on art paper, and some scribbled notes of his own on how he thought her project might eventually be structured.

"I, for one," he wrote on a piece of headed notepaper, *"would pay good money for such a book if you were to decide to go ahead. Please don't hesitate to call if you think I can be of any further use."*

The notepaper helpfully listed the telephone numbers of his apartment in London and his country home in East Anglia. Charlie drew a soft breath of recognition when she saw that the area code was the same as that for her tiny Suffolk cottage, the bolt-hole she'd bought when she split up with Nick three years earlier. On further inquiry, she discovered that Sir Alan lived just a few miles away.

Kismet? Or happenstance? she wondered.

The more Charlie discovered about Sir Alan, the more delighted she was at her great good fortune in meeting him. Had she not bumped into him at Cornelissen's, she doubted if she would even have dared make a formal request for his professional advice. As an artist, he'd never been in higher demand. His works commanded stratospheric prices: high fives for a portrait, six figures for one of his celebrated landscapes. He'd been chosen by Buckingham Palace for a number of official commissions, most of which adorned the walls of the National Portrait Gallery. Three Mathesons hung at Number Ten, two in the White House. His calendar was filled for the next two years and yet, within a few weeks of their meeting, he was offering to postpone important, lucrative commissions to assist her with her modest project.

Paper Chase: The Importance of Paper to J. M. W. Turner, it was provisionally entitled. Her first departure from writing about war, and a subject she'd chosen herself rather than one that had chosen her. Preface by Sir Alan Matheson, K.B.E., R.A. Well, as soon as she plucked up the courage to ask him, that is. But Charlie instinctively felt that he might. Alan Matheson was, she decided, the sort of man who liked to act as a catalyst for other people's lives. Not for him the faltering social dance that people usually performed on a first encounter. He was someone who, if he took a shine to you, would do what he could and expect not much in return. His invaluable input would be just the impetus she needed for this book.

Very little had been written about art paper, Charlie quickly discovered. Aside from what Alan had sent her and some rather turgid books on the English papermaking industry, there seemed to be scant commercial competition.

Nigel Armstrong, her agent, thought he knew why.

"Are you out of your tiny mind?" he'd demanded, glaring at Charlie incredulously when she first broached the subject in his messy, book-lined office. "Do I have to remind you that you're already under contract to a publisher? You've probably spent half the advance for a follow-up to *Road to Rajak,* which is now five months overdue. What's all this nonsense about Turner, for pity's sake?"

Charlie argued her case passionately, trying to make Nigel understand, but falling short of explaining why she so badly needed to seek refuge in a past other than her own.

Sitting behind his desk, his sweaty face florid under his thinning hairline, the agent shook his head in open hostility. "You can't just walk away from everything you've done, everything you've been, on the basis of a single encounter in an art shop, even if it is with such a national icon," he scolded.

"It's not that simple!" Charlie cried, banging her fist so hard on his desk that his tea did a seismic shudder in its mug. "When I came back from Kosovo, I had no choice but to put everything down onto paper.

That took nearly all my strength, and now there's nothing left. I've told you, Nigel, I don't care if I have to hand the advance back. This isn't about the money."

Nigel raised an eyebrow.

"But with the right packaging," she went on, quoting Alan directly, "this book could have genuine commercial appeal. I mean, think about it: the story of an artistic genius and how he came to use a small English company to create some of the masterworks of all time. Can't you see it?"

Snorting, Nigel told her he couldn't see it at all. He'd already stuck his neck out for Ms Charlotte Hudson and this time she was asking too much. She knew he'd only taken her on in the first place as a favour to one of her colleagues, a former BBC foreign editor. "She's a real pro," the old man had promised him, but Nigel clearly had his doubts. He told her he'd have to cut her loose if this sort of irresponsible behaviour continued.

"Listen, Charlie. I know it's not been easy, but you need this next book to keep the momentum going. God knows we both need the money. And there's already cash on the table for it. Let's get this sequel out of the way first. Then you can write what the hell you like."

Despite his threats, Charlie wouldn't budge. Couldn't. She knew she was onto something; she hadn't felt this inspired in years, and she wasn't going to give in now. Under considerable sufferance, Nigel finally relented, managing to get a further postponement from her publishers and securing her what he described as "an insulting" advance from one of the art-based publishing houses. But he warned her, in his inimitable style, that *Paper Chase* would, in his view, be a "literary miscarriage."

Painfully aware of the stopwatch hand sweeping around inside her agent's head, Charlie instantly immersed herself in her research, spending long hours at the London Library, the British Museum, and the Tate Gallery. She brought the best of her journalistic powers to bear, delving into the background of Turner and his chosen materials with the skill and intensity of the first-class investigator she'd once been.

Time and again, she found the need to refer back to Alan, to ask his advice and unlock the vaults on his incredible memory. Time and again, she was surprised to find him willing to give her some of his valuable time—meeting her after he'd finished a long day in his studio, even taking her to the bank to retrieve some of his precious paper.

She knew she was using him quite unashamedly for her own professional advantage, but she found herself hoping, as the weeks went by, that he was gaining something from the collaboration, too, enjoying the fruition of a project so close to his heart. He certainly seemed to match her enthusiasm for it.

"Whenever you feel swamped, just stop and think for a moment what paper means to people," Alan told her one night in a little restaurant he favoured in Chinatown. "How ubiquitous it is in everyday life. A life without paper is almost impossible to contemplate. A material of paradoxes, it can be used and abused in a thousand ways and still be the same under its skin. The human mind still hasn't come up with all the ways it can be used. It can be waterproof or permeable, flammable or nonflammable. It can act as a barrier or a filter, be worn, carried, read, transparent or opaque. Yet, each sheet irrevocably decays and can be recycled.

"Paper is the embodiment of man's achievement, an entirely natural product strong enough to build with and yet as transient and flimsy as a tissue. So human in its faults and weaknesses, it exists only to have its purity despoiled."

Charlie sipped on her jasmine tea and silently pondered the images Alan was conjuring up.

"Just try to imagine how rare and unusual it once was," he went on, his eyes bright. "Cloths and rags were the only wrapping materials commonly available. Slates were used for writing on in schools; the largely illiterate populace existed without newspapers or letters or books, or only those produced on animal hides; and the common currency was metal coins, not notes. How stunningly innovative this fine new product must have appeared."

Charlie, her mind as fired as his, continued the thread. "And for young artists like Turner, those exquisite art papers which arrived in tied bundles from Italy and France and the Moorish lands must have seemed so exotic."

"Precisely! They would have been like manna from Heaven! They would have smelled different, felt different! Every precious sheet would count, every brushstroke would matter. Mistakes would have been disastrous, and each artist would have had to try to find ways to save the work and the paper it was painted on.

"Then came the Napoleonic Wars and all foreign imports stopped. Think of the panic as paper prices went through the roof and no one knew where to source new supplies. That's the moment when the British papermakers rose to the challenge. They needed to produce art papers of quality and beauty equal to those of their European counterparts. That was when Turner first discovered Whatman's. The rest, as they say, is history."

He was a consummate raconteur. Watching Alan's face as he walked her through history, Charlie was drawn into the vivid pictures he painted of life during Turner's time. He also had the impeccable manners she'd expect from the ultimate English gentleman—holding the door open for her, walking on the outside of the pavement, insisting on paying for drinks or dinner. A hand in the small of her back to help her into his car; a guiding touch of her elbow to lead her into a room; a peck on each cheek, European style, each time he bid her good night. There was the way he bobbed his head thoughtfully while listening to what she had to say, or how he touched her arm when pressing home a point. And when he smiled, deep laughter lines transformed his sharp features, gathering in wrinkles around his eyes and lifting the corners of his mouth. Best of all, Sir Alan Matheson was not in the slightest bit threatening to her—a factor helped by the fact that he was at least thirteen years her senior.

For the first time in years, in this man's company, Charlie sensed the slightest unraveling of the tight coil she had carefully curled herself into. She laughed more freely, felt easier in her own skin, and found herself looking forward to each new encounter. But she couldn't deny her secret fear that his attention to her and the slow unraveling it brought would lead to what she dreaded more than anything—the terrifying unshackling of her mind.

5

"I HAVE FOUND A new paper that pleases me," Charlie had Turner confide to his fellow artist Thomas Girtin when he first came across a sample of Whatman's as a young man. *"It may be devilish expensive, but the results are remarkable. I must urge you to try it."*

She had decided to structure her book in a way that she hoped would appeal to both the traditionalists and a more modern audience used to televised dramatisations and reconstructions. A technique she called "raising the dead," in which each key player was given a voice to make them flesh and blood in the mind of the reader.

The young John Ruskin, Victorian artist and thinker who defended Turner staunchly against his critics before and after the great master died, Charlie described as *"having the facial attributes of a rather sad Old English sheepdog, but with the same doggedness."* She pinned Turner's success squarely on Ruskin's shoulders and it was to him she gave credit for the artist's popularity.

James Whatman, the Kentish papermaker, may have been a much more ordinary mortal than his fellow characters but was nonetheless interesting. She planned to set him largely in his manor house, Vinters, sited next to his mill, assisted there by his wife, Susanna, who helped him run the business and who herself became independently renowned for her published housekeeping records.

At first Alan was vehemently against her idea. He argued that her book would no longer be considered one of value if she invented conversations among the protagonists. "You can't play around with history and put words into people's mouths. It just isn't done." But when he read some of her early drafts, to her delight, he changed his mind.

"I suppose it does no harm," he conceded. "And you're right, it certainly makes these characters come alive." Looking at her sideways, he added, thoughtfully, "I rather imagine you were once a very good journalist, Ms Hudson."

Charlie lowered her head and returned to her notes.

Inspired by her radical ideas for the book, Alan pronounced that he, too, would play around with the past and present.

"I'm going to demonstrate to you the true importance of Turner's paper by attempting to deconstruct one of his finest paintings, as an *hommage* to him. I shall use the finest paper I possess to show you how he painted. By taking one of his greatest oils and copying it in watercolour, I'm hoping that you'll be able to fully understand exactly how he worked. I believe the best of his paintings only really come to life on good paper, which gives it a nuance and depth canvas simply cannot."

"Which painting have you chosen?" Charlie asked, flattered.

"*Crossing the Brook*," Alan replied, showing her a copy of it in one of his glossy art books. "Described by one of Turner's biographers as—let me see, what did he say—'*A low valley receding gently out of the hills. A hint of distant sea. A young woman leans against a large block of stone in a shallow brook, her feet ankle-deep in water, and looks back at an unkempt dog which is loyally following her across the brook, bearing her hat in his mouth.*'"

"What made you choose that particular painting?"

"It is one of his most pastoral works. There's no raging fire, no epic subject like the fall of Carthage or the sinking of Venice. This is Turner copying a rural scene and expressing his feelings most simply. It shows his profound affection for the English countryside, to which he was largely confined because of foreign wars he didn't understand. Although he longed to go to Europe to paint, *Crossing the Brook* speaks to me of being home and coming home. Of finding contentment in your own surroundings."

"It looks more like a Constable than a Turner," Charlie commented, leaning forward to examine the painting's soft green trees and pale blue sky. "There are none of those later mad swirling vortices of cloud or light. This seems—well, quite *sane* by comparison."

Alan laughed. "All artists are a little bit mad, you know. Think about it. There's a direct link between art and madness. Just look at Dalí, Warhol, and Van Gogh. Creative endeavour requires an extremely vivid imagination, Charlie. Given free rein, that imagination can make an artist lose all touch with reality and start to believe in the fantastical worlds he creates. Demons drive him, and by his very nature, he cannot see what is real. Picasso once said that art is a lie which makes us realise the truth."

Alan turned once more to the picture he'd chosen. "The truth of *Crossing the Brook* is that wars may be raging elsewhere, but beauty and, most of all, peace from the madness can be found just around the corner, if you choose to look for it."

"But what made you think it was right for this project, and for me?"

"There was something about it," Alan replied, refusing to let her eyes slide from his. "The woman on her journey halfway across the brook—it seemed just perfect to me."

CHARLIE SAT A FEW feet away from Alan. As he started to prepare his paper, she watched the rope of tendons in his forearm flex each time he wielded his brushes. He was in surprisingly good shape for someone who, according to his entry in *Who's Who,* was approaching fifty-five. Slim and supple, he'd aged well and dressed stylishly. Even now, in his sloppiest cardigan and corduroy trousers, the cut of his clothes was unmistakably chic.

By contrast, the detritus of an artist's life lay all around him, here in his Suffolk studio. It had taken all of Charlie's willpower to resist the temptation to try to restore order. Every surface was littered with clutter—

twisted pieces of driftwood, shells of all shapes and sizes, bolts of brightly coloured cloth, Victorian bottles, their green glass thick and opaque; a bird's fragile skull, the bleached skeleton of a crab, pebbles, fading velvet ribbon and empty wine bottles, most of them covered in a fine layer of dust.

Arcane scents of turpentine and varnish filled the air. The polished pamment brick floor was splashed with paint, and the tools of Alan's craft—his brushes, palettes, chalks, and oils—lay jumbled on a trestle table a few feet from where he stood. An ancient chest occupied one corner of the room, its walnut veneer peeling with age. Its drawers were open; from them spilled scraps of canvas, paper, incomplete sketches, lengths of wood, and, Charlie couldn't help but notice, a black lace bra.

Her eyes strayed to the half-finished canvases and watercolours stacked against the walls. There were tantalising glimpses of sweeping English and foreign landscapes, historic buildings, and familiar faces of the great and the good. She knew she was privileged to have access to Alan's inner sanctum like this. Even his housekeeper, Mrs Reeder, was expressly forbidden from entering. Only his cats, Evalina and Georgiana—named after Turner's daughters—were permitted here. They sat together now, licking themselves drowsily on the worn rug near his feet, seemingly oblivious to their master's constant movement as he prepared his palette.

"Sir Alan?" a woman's voice called from just outside the door. It was the redoubtable Mrs Reeder, clearly reluctant to step farther inside.

"What is it?" he snapped impatiently.

"Telephone call," the disembodied voice replied. "It's Sarah, your ex-wife. She says it's urgent."

"It's always bloody urgent," Alan hissed under his breath, before meeting Charlie's gaze and giving her a pinched smile. Throwing his palette down, he wiped his hands on a stained rag and stalked moodily from the room.

Idly flicking through one of the dusty art books when he was gone, Charlie came across a plain brown envelope concealed within its pages. The envelope was marked "Cornwall, 1986" and contained some smudged charcoal sketches. Most of them featured a young girl, no more than eleven, kneeling by a rock pool, focusing intently on a shell, her hair like a curtain over her face. She was naked.

Charlie instantly remembered the sharp, salty smell of the sea, the sand ribbed like the roof of a dog's mouth, and her grandfather's silent presence, hunched over his easel nearby.

Every contour of the young girl's body had been lovingly drawn, from the moulded skin on her thighs, to her hands, their fingers reaching in wonderment for their prize. Her breasts, not yet fully developed, formed small, soft mounds upon her chest. Her flesh was pure and white. Unsullied. Like paper.

"Once a journalist, eh?" Alan's accusation flew at her from the doorway, making her gasp. "I wouldn't go digging too deeply around here if I were you," he added, his expression flickering. "You might not like what you find."

"I wasn't digging," she protested, rising to her feet, the sketches dangling in her hand. "They fell out of a book and I was admiring them. Who is she?"

In answer, Alan seized the sheets of paper and the envelope and tossed them in a drawer, slamming it shut. The sudden sound sent his two cats flying. "The daughter of someone I thought I knew," he replied with surprising coldness, before taking her arm and leading her towards the easel. "Now, where was I?"

Charlie watched the muscles in his jaw tighten and wondered whether it was the sketches she'd unearthed or the call from his ex-wife that had upset him so.

No MATTER HOW Charlie tried to ignore the Purcell that Alan was playing at full volume while she focused on some research reading, the haunting air of *Dido and Aeneas* kept insinuating itself into her thoughts. The opera based on the *Aeneid* had been a favourite of her grandfather's, something he'd play softly in his room late at night, the voices seeping through the walls and into her dreams.

"When I am laid in earth... remember me..." The tragic story of the lovelorn couple had stayed with her since her schooldays. When Aeneas was forced by the gods to set sail for bolder adventures, leaving his brokenhearted Queen of Carthage behind, Charlie had been unable to continue when her teacher asked her to read Dido's immortal lines aloud. Before she fell on Aeneas's sword, Dido said: *"I have lived my life and completed the course that Fortune has set before me, and now my great spirit will go beneath the Earth."* Charlie's classmates had ribbed her mercilessly for her tears, and she was embarrassed by her own sensitivity.

It was this particular weakness which was to cause her so much trouble later on. Not least when she was sent as a twenty-two-year-old reporter to cover the story of a gunman who went berserk in a sleepy English village on a sultry summer's afternoon. The young man had shot sixteen people dead before turning the gun on himself. Charlie spent six weeks at the coalface of that particular story. She'd watched dry-eyed as body after body was zipped into black plastic bags, or numbed relatives identified loved ones laid out with military precision on the scuffed floor of the village hall. One destroyed family after another poured their hearts out to her, as she furiously recorded their pain. Having covered every funeral and sat through "Abide with Me" countless times, she found herself at the packed memorial service, listening to the final rendition of that most melancholy of hymns.

Despite her best endeavours, tears spilled down her cheeks. By the end of the hymn she was weeping so openly that visiting journalists assumed her to be a grieving relative. Her shattered face was broadcast around the globe and unwittingly printed on the front pages of a dozen newspapers. Her editor was singularly unimpressed, however, and from that moment, Charlie vowed to keep any future tears to herself.

It was a vow that was harder to keep than she ever imagined, as her career path sent her time and again to the front line of human suffering. Storing her emotions away in a secret place inside her—a place where she held other, older secrets—she planned to face them all another day. While others cracked, Charlie managed to maintain her indifference, writing reports that moved her readers far more than her. By the time she reached Kosovo at the end of the 1990s, she was at the end of a treadmill that encompassed everything from Northern Ireland and Beirut to the fall of the Communist bloc, the Gulf War, Croatia, and Bosnia. Her tear ducts were, by then, dysfunctional. Which was probably just as well.

CHARLIE PULLED HERSELF back. She found her eyes wandering across the polished brick floor towards Alan Matheson's lean frame, towering over his easel like some bird of prey. Having applied blocks of colour with the largest paintbrush Charlie had ever seen, he now stood back and examined the effect on the opalescent layers of washes already laid down. So absorbed was he in his work, she doubted he even remembered she was there.

Standing in an angled shaft of light from the huge window cut into the tiled roof of his studio, he'd ground up his ancient Lerchertier, Barbe paints with a pestle and mortar. The finer he ground the rare pigments, the deeper the colour. For oil painting, he explained, he would add drops of amber-coloured linseed oil to the powder until it had the consistency of melted butter. But for watercolour, the medium was always gum arabic.

"Gum arabic is an aromatic resin extracted from certain kinds of acacia tree in the Sudan. It's also used in glue, and in incense, cosmetics, and cooking. Some people even take it as a herbal supplement."

"Really? What does it do?"

"It makes the pigments water soluble, enabling their insoluble particles to disperse over the surface of the paint evenly. The gum also increases the brilliancy of the colours. It gives them gloss, transparency, and depth. It slows the drying process and helps to control the spread of wet paint into wet paint."

Charlie laughed. "No, I mean, what is it supposed to do as a herbal supplement?"

"Oh, reduce inflammation, I believe. People take it as a drink to soothe anything from an upset stomach to a sore throat. And once again, it's entirely natural. As much a product of the earth as the fibres that made the cloth that were pulped to make the paper. Gum arabic is, quite literally, the glue that binds the work together."

Once ready, Alan's palette lay on a paint-flecked stepladder at his side. A nearby table was littered with rags and sponges, blotting paper, and an assortment of glass jars filled with water in which to dip his brushes. He'd checked and rechecked his materials with meticulous care, his fingers touching each item as he ticked them off a mental checklist.

But it was the paper with which he was most absorbed. The sheet he'd freed from the bank's safe-deposit box in her company two days earlier was taped onto a large wooden board, which, unusually, had a handle fixed to the back. Suddenly, he plunged the board into a huge half barrel filled with water by his feet, lifting it dripping back to his easel, before starting to apply different hues with the slightest dab of his wide badger brush.

The effect was astonishing. As water puddled around him, the chrome yellow, Prussian blue, or Mars red pigments he'd dripped onto the wet paper marbled and ran across it, seemingly completely out of control. As Alan's hands turned and tilted the paper, the colours magically merged and melded, creating a vibrant backdrop. To this, he explained, he could later add detail after much scrubbing and scraping, blotting and mottling. Either by stippling with a hard dry brush or by scratching at it with a knife, he'd attack the surface of the paper to give it even greater texture.

Charlie was mesmerised. Combined with water, the paint became mercurial and capricious, fleeing this way and that, running from its master. But with the lightest touch, the mere flick of a wrist, Alan had it completely back under his spell, harnessing its energy to stunning effect, allowing colour to seep into colour, watching as the paint lost its strength and became ever more submissive. The power he wielded seemed consummate. No matter how much the paint tried to run, there was no escape.

Forcing herself to look away, Charlie drew her legs up under her and rearranged the shabby tapestry cushions on the chaise longue. The worn green velvet chaise was the only place to sit comfortably among the debris. It had also been used as the centrepiece of a series of extraordinary paintings she'd chanced upon in a back room earlier that day.

A host of naked women, each one more striking than the last, had posed on the very same chaise, their bodies twisted into unusual shapes. There was one on all fours, her head thrown backwards in a deeply unnatural pose. Another sat, legs wide apart, her long red fingernails gouging crescent moons into the flesh of her thighs, her heavily made-up eyes cast downwards. A third woman, with ugly features and enormous, misshapen breasts, sat with both legs outstretched.

Charlie had examined the cruel paintings guiltily, her hands flicking through the unframed canvases. There was so much about them that was shocking that, at first, she wondered if they could have been painted by someone else. But as she ran her fingers lightly over the distinctively minimalist "AM" signature with its long, sloping letters, she knew she must be mistaken.

How many young women had lain naked across this chaise and had Alan's pale gaze probing every curve, every crevice and fold of skin as he'd painted them? How many had longed to succumb when he laid down his brushes and wiped his hands?

For a moment, Charlie allowed herself to imagine what it might be like to be touched by those long, paint-specked fingers. She envisioned him manipulating her limbs, manoeuvring them, twisting her torso so that the skin at her waist formed thin folds above the blunt curve of her hip, her muscles taut with strain.

Unbidden and without warning, memories of other twisted torsos, hideously disfigured, flickered on the screen inside her head. Mothers and babies, old men and women, their soft, unprotected flesh torn to shreds after a mortar bomb slammed into a crowded café in Bosnia; their lives snuffed out by men for whom brutality was the sole currency. She gulped back the images and shuddered as they trickled down coldly inside her.

Looking up, she found that Alan had wrenched his gaze from his work for the first time in several hours and fixed it upon her.

"Are you all right?"

"I just need some air," she heard herself lie. Uncurling her hands and placing her books on the floor with an iron control, she rose to her feet and headed self-consciously for the door. She could feel Alan's eyes boring into her as she passed him. She resisted the temptation to meet his stare.

6

OUTSIDE, IN THE still summer air, the smell of the earth rose up to meet her. Donning sunglasses to hide her eyes, she tied her cardigan around her waist, stepped across the courtyard, and wandered towards the open fields beyond the redbrick farmhouse. Stopping to stare at the dark silhouette of trees with the glimmer of sea beyond, she inhaled deeply and watched as a distant tractor ploughed the rich loamy soil of a recently harvested cornfield.

Overhead, a fighter jet from one of the local military bases growled as it wheeled and spun, glinting, in the sky. A pheasant disturbed by the noise flew up from a hedgerow, startling her with its raucous rattle. She watched it glide gracefully to land in the rough stubble on the other side of the field.

Drawing her arms around her, her breath more even now, she turned to examine Pear Tree Farm, the seventeenth-century property that was Alan Matheson's country home. Timber-framed with brick herringboned between its beams, it was a comfortingly familiar building, similar to many Suffolk longhouses. Beautifully furnished, elegantly appointed, and immaculately maintained, it seemed to suit its owner perfectly. Each room was painted one of the pale colours of the earth—terra-cotta, sand, or stone. The walls were lined with exquisite oils by the likes of Alfred

Munnings and Harry Becker, interspersed with personal portraits of Alan's beloved house in Italy. Beneath them stood sturdy pieces of seventeenth-century oak, coffers, tables, and dressers, each positioned to allow the natural light to illuminate the rich patina of the wood.

The front door opened onto a wide hallway of polished flagstones. A formal dining room and a magnificent oak-paneled drawing room were flanked by a wall of French windows leading onto a terrace. The central staircase, with carved mahogany balustrades, divided the drawing room from the hallway, rising from the floor before curling round on itself on either side to form a galleried landing.

Aside from the large farmhouse kitchen with its quarry-tiled floor, the secondary rooms at the back of the house weren't nearly so grand. Former servants' quarters, they were in fact quite shabby by comparison. This was clearly a property designed for a country gentleman who'd show his guests into his impressive principal rooms, leaving the lesser mortals to rooms unseen.

Alan's studio lay at the back of the house in what would have once been the old stable block, across a courtyard cobbled with rounded grey stones, gathered by hand centuries before from nearby Dunwich beach. Partially destroyed by a fire seven years ago, the studio had been lovingly rebuilt, and a wooden plaque bearing the name of the restorer and the date of its completion had been nailed to bricks the colour of rust.

The plants in the adjacent borders were looking faded now, but Charlie could tell—with the eye of the amateur gardener she'd only recently become—that beneath the late summer decay lay bulbs and seedlings that would emerge the following spring to fill the borders with vibrancy and light.

Her grandfather would have been able to identify every plant. It was he who'd so lovingly tended their suburban garden in Kent, secateurs in hand, a smile of contentment on his face as he pruned, clipped, and dead-headed. This plot was planted exactly as he'd have had it. Old roses and climbers at the back for height, herbaceous perennials in the centre, fragrant lavenders and lady's mantle spilling over the paths, ferns and hostas in the shady areas, herbs scattered randomly between. The old pear tree, which lent its name to the house, stood sentinel over the border, its gnarled branches dripping with fruit. Charlie watched the black and yellow wasps crawling over the golden skin of the ripening pears and backed slowly away.

Alan had nothing to do with the maintenance of this garden. He employed a number of staff, here, at his London flat, and at his house in Italy, to keep everything in order, orchestrating it all with the detachment that came from years of having hired help. The garden was the responsibility of Mr Reeder, his able, if ancient, caretaker, who lived in the cottage next door with his wife.

As a housekeeper, Mrs Reeder was not someone to be trifled with. With a thin, hard face that was difficult to date but a crooked body that betrayed her seventy-odd years, she'd looked Charlie up and down with a scowl when she'd first arrived.

"Will she be staying in the house?" she'd demanded of her employer, beige makeup caked in the corners of her mouth.

"No," Alan had replied with an easy smile, ignoring her tone. "Ms Hudson has a home of her own, not far away."

"Will she be staying for lunch, then?"

"Well, Charlie?" Alan asked, his eyes mischievous.

"That would be lovely . . . if it's not too much trouble."

"No trouble." Mrs Reeder sniffed, hitching up her bosom as Alan's eye winked at Charlie conspiratorially. She stalked back to the kitchen, a trail of indignation in her wake. "As long as you're not one of those vegetarians," she called over her shoulder. "Sir Alan likes his meat."

TURNING BACK TOWARDS the fields, Charlie walked. The day had begun with an early promise of heat, but this close to the sea, it hadn't quite delivered. Autumn, her favourite season, was waiting somewhere nearby. All too soon, the bitter east winds would tear the leaves from the trees and rain would pit the soft earth. Locked away in her little cottage smelling of apple-wood smoke, she'd be safe from the elements raging outside her windows, if not always from those battling it out in her head.

Each measured step across the field gave her new strength. Every pace away from her memories lifted her spirits. Suffolk, with its ever-changing contrasts of lights and darks, its lonely churches and endless sense of space, had a unique ability to heal her. It was truly an artist's paradise, as people often said.

She'd aspired to be an artist ever since she'd donned her plastic apron and daubed gaudy poster paints onto coloured pieces of cartridge paper as a child. Later, her grandfather had taught her the rudimentary skills, although, sadly, never to great effect. Giving up her own futile attempts in frustration, she'd sat next to him for hours while he worked, soaking up his presence as he focused his energy on the painting before him, his eyes a dazzling blue.

"This is what's important, Charlotte," he told her, long ago, in his throaty Scottish burr. She watched jealously as his hand moved effortlessly across the paper, creating beautiful images with magical swiftness. "Nothing else matters. War taught me that. We live and die and the earth or the sea swallows us whole and then we're gone. But if we're lucky, we can leave something beautiful behind." Sadly, his legacies had been locked away by Charlie's mother after he died. She couldn't bear to look at them, she'd claimed. Charlie had managed to steal a few favourite sketches but the rest were lost to her.

All she had left was the legacy of his respect for Joseph Mallord William Turner, which was immense. "His father was a common barber," he'd tell Charlie, unwittingly providing the commentary for her book thirty years into the future. "Had a little shop in Covent Garden where he sold his son's drawings for a few shillings each. I wonder if any of those early customers realised just how valuable those pictures would later become?"

Turner was, she'd since come to learn, a highly complex character. Short, stout, and brooding, with heavy features, his only real joy in life seemed to be his art. His gloominess had been shaped by the madness of his mother, who never recovered from the death of her only daughter. Seeking refuge in drawing, Turner was rarely seen without a pencil stump or piece of chalk in his hand. His father arranged for him to join the Royal

Academy at fifteen and thus embark on a career that was to change the world of art forever.

"When he first started out," Granddad told her, "he could only afford the cheapest brushes. Sometimes he even used wedges of stale bread as makeshift sponges. He loved to paint outdoors but whenever he was caught in a rain shower, his cheaper papers would 'fox' or fall apart. That's when he realised you get what you pay for."

After her grandfather's death, Charlie had packed away the water-colours and brushes he'd left her, never expecting to use them again. Instead, she turned her attentions to painting pictures of a different kind—covering paper with words instead of images. The compulsion to write, which had been with her since childhood, found fevered expression in her late teens and early twenties, and led her ultimately into the career that would show her the best and the worst of all that life had to offer.

She rediscovered her paints at the bottom of an old canvas rucksack only when she finally left Nick. Stacked beneath them was her cache of her grandfather's sketches. She knew every one by heart—the Kent and Sussex beaches, the country lanes with their hedgerows, the churches and historic buildings they'd visited together, she his ever-present, adoring companion.

Filling a glass jar with water and picking up her brushes on an impulse, she'd attempted to paint once more, hoping that some strange alchemy might have transferred her grandfather's talent to her after his death. Hours flew past, like the elusive clouds she was desperate to copy, as she lost herself completely in the process of creation, running watery paint into wet hues or dragging a dry brush across a colour-washed sky. But when she stood back to examine her work, it always seemed childlike and inept. Worse, she invariably found unpalatable similarities between the jagged trees and those she remembered from the deceptively pretty coun-tryside of Bosnia and Kosovo, places she desperately hoped not to revisit in her mind.

Anxiously daubing paint onto the paper to try to restore some order, she'd usually overwork it—ruining it further with too much colour or water. What she had intended as a pale pastel of a familiar rural idyll would become livid and sinister. Disfigured. Frustrated and angry, she would tear the sheet into a hundred pieces, pack up her easel, and head home.

And yet Suffolk slowly wove its magic. The nightmares that crept up from the bottom of the night had become less frequent. The doctors had patched her body, and, with fresh air and gentle exercise, the healing process had begun. Dragging her bad leg along the narrow sand and shingle beaches, she strained her eyes for the seals that occasionally popped their shiny grey heads above the foaming waves. A wherry with a blood-coloured sail might flash past, its cargo of holidaymakers waving despite the biting east winds. Children, their gaily coloured kites tugging at strings, would run by, giggling. She'd watch the fishermen coming into Southwold Harbour with their catch of dab or flounder, the lighthouse blinking its red light in the distance. She marveled at the mackerel-skin sunsets in their brilliant pinks and blues.

In Suffolk, she could breathe. Here there was none of that drowning feeling she'd come to experience on her last few trips abroad, no sense of the all-engulfing panic attacks which left her snatching great lungfuls of oxygen before the waves closed over her. Her adult life had been constantly ruled by time—deadlines, airport timetables, pressing appointments, and early morning alarm calls. But here, she unclipped her watch, slipped it into a drawer, and never wore it again.

"I'm going to live here," she'd announced to herself one day on the beach near Southwold, hugging her knees, fingers hooked over her toes as she stared at the sea crashing dramatically to shore. Almost before the ink was dry on the sale of the house she and Nick had bought in Blackheath— the home she'd never really known—she'd bought a small basement flat in east London and a cottage at Blythcove.

Rhubarb Cottage was one of the easternmost buildings on this part of the Suffolk coast, ever since the old town of Blythcove had been swallowed up by the waves. Redbrick, under a shaggy reed thatch, its upper windows set deep in the eaves, it looked rather like an old grey owl hunched defiantly two hundred yards from the cliff.

The estate agent warned Charlie she'd never get a mortgage. "The sea takes about thirty feet a year," he'd moaned ominously as he pushed the front door open against a mountain of junk mail. "At that rate, this'll be gone in twenty years." Charlie didn't care. It was all she could do to think beyond the next few months.

INHALING THE SALT of the sea, Charlie turned back towards Alan's studio, ready to face him again. She'd walk in as if nothing had happened, she told herself, wander past him, and slide the bolt on the door of the tiny bathroom at the back of the studio.

Reaching into her bag, she'd extract a virgin bar of lemon-scented soap, peel off its waxy paper, and scrub her hands until all traces of the Balkans and its bloodied dirt beneath her fingernails was gone. Dried with a paper towel, the soap would be carefully rewrapped, before Charlie quietly took her place back on the green velvet chaise longue and picked up her notes on Turner as if nothing at all had happened.

As she pulled open the studio door and stepped inside, she reflected with a small smile how far she'd come and how quickly she could now make the demons inside her head recede. Although—like the sea and Turner's mother's madness—Charlie couldn't help but fear the inevitability of their return.

7

"DID YOU KNOW Matheson had a daughter who killed herself six years ago?" Nick's question slammed into her ear like a runaway train down the telephone line, derailing her brain.

"Yes, of course," Charlie lied evenly, her hands plunged deep into the hot, soapy water of her kitchen sink as she balanced her cordless telephone precariously on her right shoulder.

"Oh... Well, doesn't it bother you?" Nick persisted.

"Not especially." Charlie fought to control the quiver in her throat and the tremble in her heart. Nothing in her carefully measured voice must give away how much Nick's news had shaken her. "Is that all you called to tell me?" she asked brusquely, eager to be rid of him. "That you've been digging around for some dirt on the first man I've been able to spend longer than a few hours with in years?"

"No... I just thought you ought to know, that's all."

"Why?" she asked, throwing a dishcloth angrily into the sink. Soap bubbles danced in the air around her like dandelion seeds.

"Because you should always know as much as you can about the people you're associating with, Charlie. It's important. I'm a journalist, remember? You are, too. Or at least you were, once." If he'd hoped for a response to his taunt, he was to be disappointed. After listening to her silence for a few seconds, he asked, "Did Matheson tell you about his daughter, then?"

"No."

"Well, who did?"

"I—I just found out."

"Does he ever talk about her?"

"No." Charlie's response came too quickly. She added, "Most people prefer not to exorcise their family ghosts in the presence of a relative stranger."

"Don't you think that's a little odd? I mean, from what you've told me, you're hardly strangers. You've been working together pretty intensively. You'd think he might have mentioned his only child, and the fact that she topped herself."

"No, Nick, I wouldn't," Charlie said, sharply. "You, of all people, should know why I wouldn't think that."

She hung up on him before he could reply.

AND SO IT was that Charlie found herself in the offices of her former newspaper late the following Sunday night when she knew it would be deserted. After sweet-talking an old ally, she began to rummage through the computer data banks and the few remaining files that hadn't yet been transferred to screen.

Her chief reason for being there, she persuaded herself, was to look up any articles of interest on Turner and the most recent exhibitions of his work. Several quickly emerged—including one fascinating report in *New Scientist* which claimed that many of Turner's famous sunsets were a direct result of an 1815 volcanic eruption on an island in the East Indies called Krakatoa, which had tinged the world's sky in brilliant hues. And she came across an interesting discourse on a touring exhibition on Turner, Whistler, and Monet, comparing the work of all three and extolling the influence Turner had over his two contemporaries. She printed both articles off and slipped copies into a cardboard file she'd brought along with her.

Typing in the name "Sir Alan Matheson" threw up more than two-and-a-half thousand matches and, impulsively, Charlie began to trawl through them one by one. "Once a journalist, eh?" Alan had sneered at her when he'd found her with those sketches of a girl in his studio. The sense of guilt she'd felt then returned with a vengeance now as she scanned the reviews of his commissions and works, underscoring her sense of betrayal to someone who'd shown her nothing but generosity and kindness.

The headline she'd been seeking charged at her from the computer screen like a bull elephant.

ROYAL ARTIST'S DAUGHTER'S SUICIDE
SIR ALAN MATHESON'S TROUBLED
ONLY CHILD FOUND DEAD.

Beneath was a photograph of Alan. One hand was raised against the flashing cameras, the other clasping that of an ashen-faced woman as he led her through the media throng. It was, the caption read, his wife, Sarah. In that image, that tiny square of glazed paper in which Alan had been captured for posterity, Charlie saw, or thought she could see, an expression of such contempt that it made her shiver.

Accompanying other reports on the suicide was another image, so striking that it took Charlie's breath away. It was an arty black-and-white photograph of Angela Matheson, taken close up, so that her head filled the frame. Straight blond hair fell like a pale curtain over one half of her face, veiling her right eye. The effect was to give an eerie impression of light and dark, as the rest of her youthful features remained partially in shadow. All that could be clearly seen, as bright and shiny as glass, was her left eye staring straight at the camera, and half of her full mouth, its lips lifted into a mocking smirk. Charlie stared at the eye staring up at her and, for a moment, lost herself in its inky blackness. Pushing back her swivel chair and walking blindly to the photocopier, she ran off several copies and watched, mesmerised, as Angela's image flew repeatedly into the paper tray.

In the three months Charlie had been working with Alan, he had never once mentioned this extraordinary-looking daughter. He'd volunteered very little about himself or his family. Then again, Charlie reminded herself, so had she.

Only once, at a restaurant in Notting Hill, had the subject ever come up.

"Do you have any children, Alan?" she'd asked him lightly after a spirited conversation about Turner's crass ineptitude as a son to his mother and as a largely absentee parent to his two daughters.

Alan had been about to take a slug of whisky from a tumbler; his glass froze midair. For an instant, Charlie saw something she didn't recognise steal across his face, but before she could identify it, he rearranged his features.

"No. No, I don't. Now, go on, read that bit to me again about what you wanted Turner to say about his father."

The only other time she'd seen him react like that, his shutters banging down with a resounding thud, was when he'd caught her with those sketches of the young girl. As then, she was given a sharp rebuke that their relationship was strictly professional and that his personal life wasn't up for discussion. Now, looking at the media hysteria over his daughter's suicide, she understood. It was surely too painful for him to speak of the troubled child who'd taken a massive overdose at a clinic when all the doctors and therapists had failed. No wonder he concealed his pain over what must have been a catastrophic series of events.

Taking copies of the cuttings and the photograph, Charlie read and reread the news reports, and pinned the photo of Angela to the corkboard on the wall behind her computer. No matter where she stood in the room, it seemed, the dead woman's eye tracked her. At various times of the day, and in different lights, Charlie thought she could see every emotion in it from arrogance to fear. Sometimes scorn, sometimes pain. Always a cool detachment. It was a face that cried out for further investigation, a photograph of such intrigue and power that Charlie found her gaze drawn to it time and again.

Torn between the guilt she felt at her thoughtless trampling over Alan's grief and an instinctive need to learn more, Charlie battled with herself privately for several days. Surely, he'd never know if she made a few discreet enquiries, she argued, just so she could be fully prepared if the subject ever came up. But what right did she have to pry? How horrified would she be if he delved into her past? And why did she feel such a fierce and immediate connection to this damaged young woman she'd never even met, who had been unable to pull out of her own emotional free fall?

The urge to know more gnawed in Charlie's head like a dog with a bone. At least if she knew all the facts about Angela, she reasoned, she would be able to come to her own conclusions about the circumstances behind the girl's tragic suicide. She might then also understand how pivotal or otherwise Alan's role in his daughter's life, and death, had been. She needed to know the truth beneath the lurid headlines. Charlie finally succumbed to her innate curiosity and sought the assistance of the best investigative reporter she knew.

Martin Seamark and Charlie went back a long way. Greyhound lean, with a shock of silver hair and nearly colourless eyes, Martin still looked good for his fifty-plus years, but after a few too many expense-account lunches, his stomach was starting to fold over his belt and the once sharp features of his face were beginning to blur.

"There are few surprises in Matheson's professional background," Martin told her over a designer coffee at Canary Wharf. Reading from his notebook, he reeled off much of what she already knew. "Family from Hampshire, only son of a senior British diplomat, Eton, then the Slade, worked briefly in advertising. His first big commission was for a portrait of Princess Margaret, commissioned by Lord Snowdon. From that moment on, he was made."

"That figures." Charlie nodded, as she stirred her soya milk latte. There was a silence and she looked up.

"It's his personal life that holds the most interest," Martin added. "That was hardly chronicled until his marriage, thirty years ago, to a former debutante, Sarah Hildon, ten years his senior. From then on, the young artist and his society wife were photographed at all the major events—touring Europe; arriving at the Monte Carlo rally for a reception by Grace Kelly; attending the wedding of Princess Anne; on the red carpet at the premiere of *One Flew Over the Cuckoo's Nest*."

In every photograph Martin slid across the table, Charlie's new mentor's expression was unreadable; as if he were bored senseless and merely attending each function out of duty. Sarah, by contrast—blond and quite beautiful—seemed permanently animated. Clad in a sequinned ball gown or designer trouser suit, she was usually pictured clinging to his arm, gazing up at him adoringly.

"Their presence at such events stopped abruptly with the arrival of their only child, Angela Mary, in 1976." Charlie thought back to the charcoal sketches she'd found in his studio, the little girl holding a shell in her hand marked "Cornwall, 1986." Could they have been of Angela? She'd have been about the right age. What could have turned such an innocent with a child's fascination for shells into a broken young woman so disillusioned with her life that she'd been determined to relinquish it?

"After Angela arrived on the scene, almost all the news stories relate solely to Alan again, to his growing stature in the art world, the critical acclaim, the lucrative commissions from around the globe, his travels alone, et cetera, et cetera." Martin fast-forwarded through his notes. "If his wife and daughter were mentioned, it was in passing, a brief reference to the death of Alan's titled father-in-law and the rumours about Sarah's massive inheritance."

"How massive is massive?"

"You know Prince Charles owns Cornwall?"

"Yes."

"Well, Sarah Matheson's father owned just about everything else."

"And Angela? What did you find out about Angela?"

Martin stared at her before answering. "Well, she had everything she could possibly have wanted. She attended the best English and Swiss schools, studied art in London and, with her father's encouragement, became a successful, if somewhat controversial, young artist. After her suicide, her mother suffered some sort of collapse. Sarah was admitted to a London clinic for alcohol and tranquiliser addiction. She and Matheson divorced shortly afterwards."

"Poor woman. She lost them both."

"She's rarely seen socially anymore."

"What about Sir Alan?"

"He filed for divorce and eight months later he was married again, to a woman almost twenty years his junior. You've probably heard of her, Diane Colvin, that waspish American art critic working for the *New York Times* who was supposed to have had an affair with the disgraced Lord Sanders. Her marriage to Alan Matheson lasted less than a year: it collapsed shortly after she became Lady Matheson. By all accounts, clever Diane returned triumphant to her homeland with the new title and a considerable chunk of her ex-husband's money."

"What about Alan?" Charlie pressed.

"Since his second divorce he's been pretty much playing the field. Everyone from supermodels to Booker Prize winners. The *Evening Standard* recently nominated him one of London's most eligible bachelors. Not bad for a man his age, eh? There's hope for me yet."

It was the obituaries that Martin handed Charlie which troubled her most. The *Daily Mirror* had run a near-libelous centre-page spread on Angela and the "unanswered questions" surrounding the twenty-four-year-old's death. The story was pulled after the first editions, when Sarah Matheson's lawyers slapped an injunction on the newspaper, but Martin had managed to unearth the original. The headline promised: *"The tortured young artist and her brilliant father: a special investigation."* The accompanying article claimed to have uncovered police "unease" about the suicide at the Norwich clinic and "revealed" that Sir Alan had been questioned three times by detectives following the discovery of his daughter's body.

Even the obituary in the *Daily Telegraph* had been spiky:

It was widely known amongst close friends of the family that Miss Matheson's relationship with her father had not always been smooth. Having inherited his artistic temperament, she often seemed to go out of her way to antagonise him. Her campaign against him culminated in arson. Police, called to investigate a fire at his Suffolk studio, concluded that Miss Matheson had started the blaze deliberately, while the balance of her mind was disturbed. No charges were ever brought, but the twenty-three-year-old was admitted to a psychiatric hospital six days later for treatment. A number of important works by the artist, including irreplaceable early sketches of Her Majesty the Queen Mother, were lost to the flames.

There was a faint smell of burning cinders whenever Alan lit the studio's potbellied stove, but he'd never divulged the cause of the blaze, never spoke of the deranged daughter with a box of matches and a jerry can full of petrol who'd deliberately sought to destroy it.

Had Angela stood there and watched the flames licking at her father's precious studio, laughing as she did so? What on earth could have possessed her to do such a thing? What was it about Alan's exquisitely executed paintings that had so threatened her? What dark despair led her to take her own life when it seemed she had everything, and so much more to look forward to? Charlie doubted she would ever know.

"Can I ask you something, Charlie?" Martin ventured, as he put away his notebook. "Why do you want to know all this stuff?"

Why did the mystery of the dead woman's life and death tug at her, colouring everything? Was it because she knew the power this suicide could so easily come to hold over her, if she allowed it? It was as deadly as a siren's call.

"Because it's important," Charlie replied. "Because it changes everything."

"Yes, but why so much interest in this girl who killed herself, Charlie? Who's Angela Matheson to you?"

Charlie thought for a moment before answering. Then she softly whispered, "The daughter of someone I thought I knew."

Rag

A torn, frayed, or worn piece of woven material;

one of the irregular scraps to which cloth is

reduced by wear and tear

8

$\mathscr{N}$ICK COULD SCARCELY concentrate on the morning's news conference. He said his piece about the wretched quality of reporting
from Baghdad and settled back into his chair, feet up on the table, to let
others have their say.

"Our reporters' hands are tied," his foreign editor argued valiantly.
"There's little they're allowed to see and when they do see something,
they're forbidden from reporting it. They're in a no-win situation."

Losing interest, and using the tip of the silver Parker pen Charlie had
given him as a birthday present, Nick stabbed repeatedly at the metal rings
that held the top of his notebook together. Meticulously fishing out the
tiny scraps of paper left behind by torn-off pages, the table around him
was soon littered with them. Like the droppings of a tiny bird.

He wished he'd handled his last telephone conversation with Charlie
more sensitively. What the hell did it matter if Alan Matheson had a
daughter who killed herself? It was none of his business. Charlie was his
wife in name only. His feelings on that particular subject had been bottled,
labeled, and put on a shelf long ago. Now he could only watch helplessly
from afar as she slipped further and further from his grasp.

Miranda would say that, if the truth were known, Charlie had been
out of his reach for years. One of the sharpest young reporters on his

staff, Miranda had a disconcertingly acute take on the breakdown of his marriage. Too cynical for her years, she had few romantic illusions about her lover's estranged wife.

"Your marriage was never going to work, with you tied to a desk in London and her permanently on foreigns," she'd told him bluntly just the night before, as she lay smoking a cigarette minutes after they'd finished their peculiarly clinical form of lovemaking.

As ever, his need for her had been urgent, and they'd never even made it to the bedroom. Their clothes strewn along the hallway, they'd fallen onto the hardwood floor, new bruises creeping over old. Winding her long red hair around his fist, he'd yanked back her head, his lips pressed hard against her throat. Pain and passion had, for him, become inextricably entwined.

"I mean, you lost her the minute you let her think she was Lois Lane," Miranda added flatly. "It might have worked if you'd gone with her, but as soon as her career took off, you were doomed."

Nick watched her inhale greedily from her cigarette; stared as the glowing strands of tobacco smouldered within the wafer of paper that trapped them in place. Reaching for it, he screwed it angrily into the floor, his eyes indicating his readiness to begin again. Miranda didn't know the half of it, despite her smugness. Anyway, it was her body he wanted, not her opinions.

But damn her, maybe she was right. Charlie had been in her element, gadding all over the world, chasing one story after another. Freed from the stifling control of her mother, relishing being an independent career woman following her own path at last, she'd risen to every challenge, physically and intellectually. Sometimes when he looked at her, Nick could scarcely believe she was his; the transformation had been so complete. Her letters home, written on flimsy blue airmail paper, scared him. *"I'm doing the job I always dreamed of,"* she'd write, in her looping handwriting. *"I never want this to end."*

Determined to be supportive, he made a point of always meeting her at the airport. Her eyes shining, she'd run to his arms and cling to him as if she'd never leave him again. They'd tumble into bed as soon as they got home, exploring each other hungrily. It was as if she wanted to give herself to him completely as a reward for waiting so patiently. Much as he hated her going, he ached for her return, knowing how exhilarating it would be. Sex was never better than on those long, hot nights.

"I love you, Nick Lambert," she'd say, rocking on the cradle of his hips. "I'm a damn fool to leave." Locked together, skin against skin, they'd rediscover forgotten pleasures. Sharing a shower together afterwards as part of their slow erotic ritual, desire would flame in them once again.

Catching up with friends, those who led humdrum lives tied by work, children, or duty, and who were always eager for a vicarious taste of her travels, Charlie would be picked over for stories of her latest trip. Like the carcass of a chicken, Nick reflected. Leaving him nothing but bleached bones.

"So there we were in this god-awful hotel in the middle of Belize City," she'd regale her audience, "when I was awoken in the dead of night by screams from the photographer next door. I sprinted into his room, hairbrush in hand in case I had to belt someone, and there he was, sitting bolt upright, shivering in his bed. 'What's wrong, Colin?' I asked. 'Rats!' he replied, white as a sheet. 'A whole family of them—eating the dead skin off my feet!' Needless to say, after that we stayed up all night, back to back, with the lights on."

Nick would watch this vibrant young woman holding court and wonder who she really was. Every now and again, she'd flash him such a smile of love and yearning that he thought he knew the answer. And each time she left him for another assignment, he tried not to ask himself what she was running from. Was it him? Or something else? Hadn't she once said she'd probably spend the rest of her life fleeing the memory of her grandfather's death?

She'd only once spoken of that loss. "I should have done more to help," she'd told Nick, drunkenly, late one night, her mascara bleeding. "I should have tried harder. I might even have become the artist he always hoped I'd be. If only I'd stuck it out at home a bit longer, I could have been with him . . . at the end." She never mentioned the old man again.

Nick pretended not to notice the subtle changes each time Charlie returned from an assignment. He made himself believe that she was just overtired or unsettled by jet lag when she was unable to sleep. Without comment, she packed the pills the doctor prescribed her and carried on, flying in and out of his life to cover disasters, train crashes, terrorist attacks, rapes, and murders.

Often, she'd be first on the scene, long before the emergency services had made things palatable for public view. Flashing her press card, she'd smile her way under the security cordon. With her near-photographic memory, she'd walk through the carnage, her green eyes registering scenes too grisly to be reported, taking a calm mental note of the things that could. Her informative and reasoned reporting brought her to the attention of the ambitious young editor and his powerful foreign editor.

"Why don't we test her on something farther afield?" the latter had suggested, and the former, keen to be seen promoting women—especially one as young and attractive as Charlie Hudson—readily agreed. He could see himself in the Round Room at Brookes's, smoking Havanas with the Foreign Secretary, smiling benignly as Charlie, fresh from some far-flung corner of the earth, reported personally from the front line. Yes, this would undoubtedly be another feather in his—as yet—unknighted cap.

From then on they deliberately took her down a new and more dangerous path—as one of the paper's busiest "firemen"—beginning with the endless conflicts in Northern Ireland, leading her through the bloody, violent collapse of Communism in Eastern Europe and into the inferno of the Lebanon. She covered the death throes of the ruthless feud between Iran and Iraq and the complex political machinations in Libya, and she earned the dubious distinction of being the longest-serving reporter in Baghdad during the first Gulf War.

Her turn on the Middle East treadmill lasted five years. She stepped into the shoes of a photojournalist who'd been blown up by a mortar attack on the Gaza Strip. He'd lasted three years. Few survived beyond that. They either died or burned out along the way. Charlie was well aware of the risks, but somehow believed she was immune.

"I'll be fine, Nick," she'd tried to reassure him, her ambition burning a hole into his brain. "You've always known this is what I wanted, and now we're in it together—a team. I'm much more careful than the rest—because I've got someone to come home to."

Secretly, Nick wondered how much of a team they really were. What exactly was his role, apart from fucking her senseless when she got home and pretending to anyone who asked that he and Charlie had the best of both worlds? Still, he waved her off each time, increasingly frightened of her ability to run towards places everyone else was running away from. He even made halfhearted offers to give up his well-plotted route to the editorship and join her, working freelance by her side.

"Don't be stupid," she replied, smiling. "You love your job, and besides, men are much more vulnerable; you could easily be mistaken for a sniper. I'll be fine. And the last thing I need is you to worry about as well. Anyway, I've got Carrie."

CARRIE KIDD WAS the closest Charlie had to a best friend. With her strawberry blond hair and freckles, rounded cheekbones, and never a trace of makeup, Carrie was a natural beauty. Gamine, forever in jeans, T-shirts, and caterpillar boots, she humped her camera gear around the world without a grumble. They'd started working together in Belfast soon after Charlie joined the *Tribune* and the two women were sent to cover a controversial IRA funeral.

"Down!" Charlie had screamed when she heard the first shot whistling past her ear and saw a Loyalist gunman waving a pistol wildly at mourners. The two women hit the sodden turf together, as those around them were felled. Charlie watched as the last breath gurgled noisily from a man who'd folded like water at her side. Her eyes locked onto his, she waited for the light in them to die before reaching out and tenderly sliding shut the lids. It was only afterwards she realised Carrie had been taking pictures all along.

In Londonderry later, Charlie spotted Carrie in a crowd of marchers, and, raising her hand, wandered towards her. Seconds later, a pipe bomb exploded beneath the car she'd just been leaning against, bantering with a young soldier. She was thrown to the ground by the blast, as shards of metal, glass, and nails sliced through the denim of her jeans and embedded themselves into her legs. Carrie's picture of Charlie's bloody injuries appeared on the front page of the *Tribune* the following morning. It couldn't publish the picture of what remained of the squaddie with the broad Geordie accent. The dead soldier's easy smile and mischievous blue eyes patrolled both women's dreams for months.

After that, they demanded each other on assignments, trusting no one else. Cocooned together, far from their loved ones, they developed a common sense of humour that bolstered them from the starker realities.

"Champagne, bananas, and chocolate," they'd promise each other as their must-have treats the moment they reached civilisation. Once they'd made it, they'd order room service, slump on Charlie's bed in terry-cloth dressing gowns, smelling of soap, their skin pink and wrinkled from the first hot bath either of them had enjoyed in weeks, and watch some weepy movie on television. They'd wake the next morning, heads thumping, surrounded by the detritus of their evening—candy wrappers, banana skins, empty champagne bottles, and dozens of soggy tissues.

"Next time," Charlie would call hoarsely from the bathroom as she splashed her face with icy water, "let's go easy on the bananas." The pair of them would collapse helplessly into fits of laughter, each one nursing a hangover they could have sold to science.

Loyal and fiercely protective of each other, Charlie and Carrie fended off the many male advances with an impenetrable barrier of friendship. Each considered the other her lucky charm. The newspaper that employed them accepted their unique relationship and happily shipped the photogenic pair off together, until the straitened picture desk budget began to preclude Carrie's involvement. After that, Charlie was forced to travel alone.

Despite Nick's insistence that he had a sixth sense about Charlie whenever she was somewhere dangerous, it was Carrie who first recognised that the job was becoming an addiction for Charlie. She'd seen what it was like, the unspoken but intense competition between fellow correspondents, each vying for the next "fix." The greatest coup was to gain access to a place no one else had managed to penetrate (usually with very good reason) and file the first breaking story. The fact that this meant Charlie was often there unarmed, without a visa or relevant authorisation, seemed to momentarily escape her.

Or maybe that was the attraction; Carrie never really knew. Charlie played with death, teased it into coming for her, and laughed when it narrowly missed. Mortality fascinated her like no one else Carrie had ever met. Long after the events in Northern Ireland, she'd come upon Charlie peering into the faces of the murdered and mutilated, staring into their milky eyes, as if searching for a glimpse of something only she wished to see. While everyone else recoiled from the grim details, Charlie would closely question witnesses and officials, personally attend postmortems and forensic examinations. Her copy was always achingly poignant, yet it revealed nothing of the courage it took to research it so deeply.

If Carrie knew the dangers Charlie was facing, Nick could only imagine them. Between them, they tried to protect and then warn her, forging a miserable alliance every time she left on assignment, both missing her for their own reasons. But Charlie refused to be protected. Hardening herself to the life she'd chosen, she was clearly intoxicated by its perils and paradoxes. She'd fallen head over heels in love with war, with the best and the worst it brought out in humanity. With the best and the worst it brought out in her. Nothing else could possibly compete.

NICK HEARD HIS name being called. Jake was glaring at him across the smoke-filled room, visibly irked by his lack of response to some question.

"Sorry, Jake." Nick cleared his throat, stalling for time. "I missed that."

"Obviously. At least do us the courtesy of pretending to be awake during morning conference, will you?"

"Okay, yeah. Sorry, what was the question?"

"Do you or do you not think Karima Ridgley should be the next reporter we send into Baghdad?" Jake repeated, scowling. Exasperation sharpened his tone.

"No," Nick replied flatly, wiping an imaginary speck of dirt from his polished black brogues.

"Why not?" Penny Shields protested, three seats away from him. "Karima's bloody good. And she did a great job for us in Kabul."

"She also did well on that Al-Qaeda investigation," Gary Noble reminded him.

"Yes, but she's married, isn't she?" Nick said quietly, twirling his pen between his fingers.

"What the fuck's that got to do with it?" Jake rasped.

"Everything," Nick said. Looking up defiantly, he added: "Bloody everything."

9

THERE WAS SOMETHING elemental about paper. For as long as Charlie could remember she'd been enthralled by its sensuous texture and distinctive scent. She'd never lost that sense of wonder when she opened her mother's pad of watermarked Basildon Bond or balanced the nib of a pen above a pristine sheet. Or the thrill of filling its blank spaces with words.

She'd kept notebooks as a child, scribbled poetry, plays, and short stories on handmade paper as a teenager, cherished a vellum-covered diary, written dozens of letters just for the joy of the paper. She'd even collected samples of wallpaper, cutting neat squares of embossed and patterned paper from cloth-bound books discarded by the decorator who repapered her parents' house, pasting them into a flimsy prised patchwork. But nothing, absolutely nothing, gave her more pleasure than using up all the spaces in one of her notebooks and reaching the final page. Not least, because it meant she could start writing again, very soon, in a brand-new book.

Every aspect of paper and papermaking intrigued her. She'd been a frequent visitor to the layout floor or "stone" at the newspaper, watching the massive rolls of paper feed through the presses and emerge on the other side with her report across the front page. She loved nothing more than to wander into a bookshop and flick through the hardbacks, or finger handmade wrapping paper speckled with oatmeal or dried petals. She spent a fortune on greeting cards and paper napkins. She hoarded rolls of paper for wrapping gifts, and favoured certain newspapers over others just for their texture and smell. But, until the Turner project, she'd never before had to place the entire process of papermaking in its proper historical context.

Her chosen guide for this aspect of the book on Alan's recommendation was, arguably, one of the best in the business. Lori Hunter was a respected paper historian at one of the more eminent Cambridge colleges.

Charlie liked Lori the minute she set eyes on her. A willowy blonde with alabaster skin and a ready smile, Lori was the epitome of an intelligent, articulate professional. She was also extremely beautiful and—for a moment—Charlie found herself a little dazzled.

"Tell me how I can help," Lori urged, the first time they met in the brightly lit café in the vaulted bowels of the university. She smelled nice— Eternity, unless Charlie was mistaken—a perfume Carrie wore on special occasions.

"I need your expertise. As I mentioned in my e-mail, I'm researching a book on Turner and his papers and I want to learn everything I can about how paper developed in Britain."

Lori Hunter beamed at her. "It'll be my very great pleasure. I've cleared my appointment book for at least an hour, so let's get started."

Carrying her cup of decaffeinated cappuccino with an enviably steady hand, the historian led Charlie to an impressive book-lined office. Seated in a battered leather armchair opposite a desk that looked as if it should belong to a cigar-smoking chairman of the board, Charlie found herself wondering how petite Lori fared in such a bastion of the British establishment.

"Ask away," Lori invited, perching on the edge of the desk and somehow drinking from her cup without leaving a trace of foam on her top lip. Charlie couldn't help but notice her long, lean legs and the way her short black skirt slid up her thigh just enough to reveal the top of her stockings. This was clearly a pose she often adopted.

"Well, I know that all paper originates from plant matter. I know, too, that it was first created in China two thousand years ago, probably after someone noticed how wasps build their nests by chewing wood until it's a pulp." Taking out a pen and notebook in a show of efficiency, Charlie added: "I know that its name is derived from the papyrus which was used by ancient Egyptians, Romans, and Greeks, but I need to understand more about its evolution here in England. My specific interest lies in the fine-art and writing papers of the early nineteenth century. The sort of papers that would have been available in Turner's day."

"Okay." Lori nodded, standing and reaching for a large book with a black-and-white cover. Sitting back on the desk edge, she recrossed her shapely legs and opened the book's creamy white pages.

"As you so rightly said, all paper is derived from cellulose fibre," she said, "and began in China with the boiling and beating to pulp of bast— the inner bark of trees such as the mulberry and lime. Leaf fibres and seed hair from cotton were also used. In the eighth century, the process moved, via the silk routes and war, from the Far East to India and the Middle East and from there on to Europe. Chinese prisoners of war taught their captors the secret art of papermaking, known as "white craft," using everything from fine bamboo and flax to old fishing nets. These new paper products far surpassed what was previously available—parchment and vellum made from animal skins."

Charlie wrote the words "whitecraft" together, as if they were one. Beneath it, she wrote the word "witchcraft?"

"In thirteenth-century Italy, the papermakers of Fabriano and Amalfi perfected the techniques of papermaking. They added gelatine as a sizing to stop paints and inks from running into the paper. They enlisted water power, using mills, and invented complicated presses and delicate wire moulds. By comparison, the English papermaking industry was quite late developing, starting tentatively in the late fifteenth century. But we were leaps and bounds ahead of many other countries. The fledgling nation of America only started making paper in earnest when the Europeans settled there in the eighteenth century."

Charlie scribbled away, while Lori continued.

"It was the Europeans who truly embraced the idea of using recycled fibres from waste clothing, instead of starting from scratch with raw materials. The landed gentry had the best-quality linens and were urged to preserve their waste rags. In the seventeenth century, the government passed a series of laws decreeing that the dead should be buried only in woollen garments, so as to free up linen for papermaking and stop it 'corrupting in the grave.' The law also put an end to grave robbers who dug up bodies just to strip them of the linen they could then sell. Such practices were widely believed to have started the Great Plague. When linen became scarce during the Napoleonic Wars with France, such was the demand for paper that hemp fibres from old ropes, sailcloth, sacking, straw, cotton, and even trimmings of old books were used instead."

Charlie was incredulous. "I knew about the different cloth but I didn't know they used old books." She wrote furiously, her shorthand squiggles and symbols flying across the page. She could already envision a scene where James Whatman or one of the papermaker's predecessors balked at the destruction of what would have been such a precious commodity.

"Of course, old books didn't make great paper," Lori conceded. "They were made into cheap wrappings, such as the cartridge papers used by the army to wrap gunpowder in the Napoleonic Wars, hence the name 'cartridge.' Only the finest white rags could make the purest white paper, and even then it had a distinctly creamy hue."

Charlie shook her head. It was nothing short of a miracle that the stunning range of papers used by Turner and other great artists was crafted from such humble materials. Witchcraft indeed.

"What did they do with all the linen once they'd collected it?"

"That's where the rag cutters came in." Lori swiveled the book round on the desk to show Charlie a sepia photograph of a room full of women and children, sitting by huge mounds of cloth. Their lifeless expressions were those of people without hope. Charlie had seen that look a hundred times before, in a dozen countries. Her heart went out to them.

"These women had a most unenviable job. The clothing they sifted through stank, was rank with lice, and carried airborne infections in its dust. People didn't discard clothes in those days until the items were well past their best. Often the garments came from corpses. The rag cutters examined and cut about a hundredweight and a half of rags per ten-hour working day, for which they earned, on average, ten pence."

Charlie tried to imagine how these women and children must have lived, what poverty had forced them into such appalling work. She recalled seeing young families scrabbling over the fetid rubbish dumps in some of the cities she'd visited. She'd had to hold a scarf to her nostrils while filthy infants sat naked amidst rotting vegetation, picking up maggoty scraps and cramming them into their mouths.

"The air was thick with dust and disease," Lori told her. "Every piece of cloth had to be checked for quality and colour. Buttons, laces, and seams were removed before the cloth was cut into tiny squares and sorted into as many as fifty categories. One missed button or unemptied pocket could blight a whole batch of paper, producing thousands of tiny particles that would disfigure every sheet. Dark flecks in a sheet of brown paper often came from overlooked tar on old ropes." She showed Charlie some samples of paper rejected for such imperfections.

"What happened to the rags once they were cut?"

"They were placed in enormous vats filled with water and left to ferment for six weeks until they were too hot to handle. Sometimes they were so well rotted that clumps of mushrooms sprouted on top."

"Edible mushrooms?"

"Probably not, but I'm sure if they were, the resourceful workers would have harvested them to supplement what must have been an appallingly meagre diet."

"How sad."

"The fermented rags were crushed, ground, and beaten in great threshing machines fitted with metal bars, or, later, in stamping machines that pounded them with vast wooden hammers. The trick was to try to tease the individual fibres out to be as long as possible, so as to allow them to entangle better later."

"And then the pulp would be poured into a vat of water to float on the surface and fished out with a mould or sieve?"

"That's right." Lori finished her coffee and placed the cup gently back onto its saucer. "The vat man would slip his wire mould underneath the pulp and lift it up, leaving any excess water to drain through the wire." Reaching for an old wire mould on a nearby shelf, she showed Charlie how each maker's unique watermark was stitched by tiny metal threads to the wire mesh to leave an impression in the pulp. "The interlocked fibres left dripping on the surface would be turned out onto large slabs of felt by someone called the couch squirt. Once they relinquished their water, they'd bond together. The greater the bonding, the stronger the sheet."

"Sounds tricky."

"It required a great deal of skill and expertise. Air bubbles had to be dispersed, corners straightened, and the mould held firmly in place so as not to slip and leave a scar on the finished paper. It was hot, thirsty work, and the vat men were allowed to drink their fill from an enormous keg of beer brought daily onto the factory floor."

Lori showed Charlie a photo of florid-faced men, their shirts soaked with sweat, gulping thirstily from huge wooden tankards. Behind them rose a large vat, the pale pulp floating on the surface clearly visible.

"After that the sheets would be dried and pressed?"

"That's right, but it was an extremely precise process, done in special drying lofts. Paper dried improperly or too quickly buckled or cockled when water was applied to it later. It was up to the layman to take the moist sheets of paper off the felt at just the right time."

Charlie quickly turned a page of her notebook and continued writing, as Lori waited for her to finish. "This is great," she said, looking up and smiling. "Just the sort of detail I needed. So, who was producing the best white paper at the time?"

"By the early 1800s, there were more than four hundred mills in Britain, such was the demand. Turner would have had a pretty wide choice."

"What about the Turkey Mill run by the Whatman family in Kent?"

"That was one of the most prolific and innovative mills. At peak production, around ten reams of paper could be produced every day, more than five thousand sheets. Whatman's produced the largest handmade paper in Europe, the Antiquarian, at thirty-one by fifty-three inches. Previously, the size of the paper had always been determined by the stretch of the vat man's arms, but Whatman devised a special wooden contraption on pulleys to lower the mould into the vat."

"Were any other mills making such fine paper?"

"Oh, yes. There was fierce competition."

"What about modern papers? How do they compare?"

Lori sighed. "Generally speaking, they bear little or no comparison. The whole papermaking process was mechanised by the end of the nineteenth century, and quality suffered. Modern papers are usually machine-made from cotton pulp or wood, sized with chemicals, and artificially dried. I'm afraid it shows."

Charlie reached into her briefcase and withdrew a small square of Alan's vintage paper. "What about this? It's Whatman's, probably made in about 1947, before they completely shut down their handmade operation."

Lori held the sheet in her hands as tenderly as if it were a tiny bird and walked to the sash window that dominated one wall of her office. Light fell across her face, illuminating her fine profile. Holding the paper up, she examined it closely. "This is true rag paper and quite a prize, if only for its very collectible watermark," she said, turning. Just as the bright sunlight had allowed her to see through the paper, it now shone through her white cotton blouse, silhouetting her body beneath it like a watermark. Charlie noticed for the first time that she wasn't wearing a bra.

"Really rather special, I'd say. There's not much of this vintage paper left anymore. Where did you find it?"

"It belongs to Sir Alan Matheson," Charlie confided. "But, tell me, would this particular example have been up to Turner's standards?"

"Sir Alan? You know him?"

"Yes. He's helping me with this book."

Lori gave a thin smile, and turned back towards the window. "So you know him well, then?"

"Yes. Of course." Charlie sensed something more. "And you?"

Turning back to face Charlie, Lori faltered. "If you must know, we had a brief affair."

"Oh. I see...."

"It was only for a month or so, and it stopped as suddenly as it began. I've not heard a word from him since. It's been over a year now."

"I'm sorry, I didn't know.... It was Alan who recommended you, actually."

"Really?" Lori looked surprised.

There was something Charlie couldn't quite identify in her eyes. Need? Desire? Or fear?

"What did he say?"

"He said you were one of the best in the business," Charlie told her honestly. "He also said you were very kind."

"He did?" Lori's eyebrows formed a perfect arch across her forehead.

"Yes." Charlie, feeling suddenly protective of Alan, snapped her notebook shut and put it away. "He did."

"I suppose he means because of Angela. She worked with me here for a while, you know, learning the trade, so to speak."

"Angela did?" Charlie replied, her gaze steady. "When was that?"

"The year before she...before she died. She was an excellent student."

"Was she?"

"Yes, she was unlike almost anybody else I've ever met. She wanted to know everything. She soaked up information like a sponge, hardly even taking notes. Her approach might have been a little scattergun and she rarely stopped talking—words just seemed to pour out of her, and not all of them the ones you want to hear, but once you got past Angela's kooky clothes and her little eccentricities, she was a pleasure to be with. And really smart."

"Little eccentricities?"

"Well, yeah. She was, I think, obsessive/compulsive. She didn't like to be touched by strangers—she freaked out if anyone accidentally brushed past her. Oh, and she hated people seeing her face, so she brushed her hair forward over it whenever possible. She had just about everything on her body pierced, and she was a strict vegan. Woe betide anyone she bumped into wearing a fur coat. They'd get an earful of the famous Angela Matheson invective."

"And yet she was a good student?"

"Diligent. I think she was desperate to become as great an artist as her father. I got the sense that she believed learning about paper might help."

Charlie absentmindedly played with the button on her pen. "And did it? Help, I mean?"

"No, not really."

Sympathy for Angela flooded Charlie's heart. "Artistic talent isn't always something that can be inherited, you know, no matter how hard you try."

"Oh, Angela definitely had talent: it was just so very different from her father's and I don't think she ever came to terms with that. But her work was innovative. Bold. I thought she had a great future ahead of her. It came as such a shock when she, well, you know. It was the last thing anyone expected."

"Does anyone ever expect suicide?" Charlie replied, curtly. In the silence that followed, she rose and extended her hand. "You've been tremendously helpful. Thank you."

"Oh, have we finished already?" Lori asked. Then, "May I ask you something? Something personal?"

"Of course," Charlie replied, with a smile that didn't quite reach her eyes.

"Are you . . . Have you and Alan, I mean, well, are you in a relationship?"

"Good gracious, no. It's a strictly professional collaboration, that's all." There was a longer silence. "Why do you ask?"

Lori stepped closer to Charlie, and lowered her voice. "It's just that, I mean," she began, struggling to find the right words. "Be careful."

"Careful of what?"

"I know it sounds stupid, but be careful of yourself."

Making a hasty exit, Charlie reflected on the powerful hold Alan seemed to have held over Lori Hunter.

So, it wasn't just Angela who had been desperate to impress him.

10

RAJAK FLOODS THE compartments of her sleeping brain as she lies in a tangle of sheets. So close she can almost smell it.

Ridiculous, to remember everything so vividly.

A red-roofed village tucked away on rolling hills at the bottom of a mountain. Several hours' drive southwest of Kosovo's capital, Pristina. Its population overwhelmingly Albanian and Muslim.

Slobodan Milosevic's forces have done a superb job here. The Yugoslavian dictator's "scorched earth" policy of ethnic cleansing has been stunningly effective. Only a hundred or so unarmed civilians remain, most of them elderly. The only young people are a handful of children, or women, pregnant from rape.

Charlie is working alone and dressed in peasant garb to avoid attention. She reaches Rajak by Jeep that cold January afternoon. Breaking away from the rest of the journalistic pack. Hungry for a feature on what it is like to live under constant threat in a ravaged town. Hoping that she might happen upon something that will become exclusively hers.

"I think it'll be worth the trip," she tells her foreign editor. "It's the fear as much as the danger itself these people have to face. I want to report on what that fear must feel like, day to day."

"Okay," he replies, his scepticism echoing hollowly down the telephone line. "But as soon as you've finished, I want you to head back to where the real action is."

Less than an hour after Charlie arrives in Rajak, however, the Serbs return.

Happenstance.

She hears the distant gunfire; sees the unexpected tanks crest the hills. Sniffing the air like a dog, she senses what is about to unfold. With only a notebook and camera and no written authority to be in this sector, she knows she'll have to stay hidden until she can file her report. She can taste a heady mix of excitement and fear. Something big is about to happen. As so often before, she's caught in the thick of it, helpless to prevent disaster and oblivious to her own fate. Her heart pounding hard against her rib cage, she also knows that—as the only reporter here—this is her very own scoop. She can't deny the thrill that gives her.

Hurriedly, she finds a hiding place. The ravaged cellar of a bombed-out house. Fumbling in the dark, groping for a handhold, she pulls the wooden floor-hatch tightly shut behind her. Making her way down the steep stone steps, she fights her way through cobwebs and pungent barrels of salted meats and pickles to a corner. Here she will be safe. Here, through a crack in the stonework, she can watch what is happening.

She feels the tanks rumble into the village, listens to the screams and cries of those caught in their path. She holds her breath as she sees, through her spy-hole, a cluster of men being led away towards the woods. All are elderly or sick. They stumble in front of the guns, their hands bound tightly behind their backs. One man stops to vomit and is beaten brutally about the head with the butt of a rifle. Minutes later, a volley of shots ring out in the distance. It comes from the woods.

Charlie hears them before she sees them. A whimpering somewhere behind her in the darkness. Turning, astonished, she clicks on the slender flashlight she wears looped on a cord around her neck. Its narrow beam carves the gaunt faces of nine women and girls, huddled together in the corner opposite. A young dog, her squirming puppies suckling, thumps her tail in greeting. Her eyes never leaving Charlie's face, the bitch licks each pup carefully with a long, pink tongue.

Charlie is not alone. Worse, she is somewhere she might easily be compromised. Fear crowds her throat. There is no time to escape. No chance to find a new hiding place—somewhere she can maintain her physical and mental distance. Pressing a finger to her lips, her eyes flash a warning to her terrified companions. Peering out again, she watches and waits.

There is only a short lull before smoke fills the air. In the failing evening light, Charlie can just make out the black leather boots of the Serbian soldiers. They are searching, looting, and systematically burning every house, carrying flaming torches made of rolled-up cardboard and sticks of wood doused with petrol. This is what they came back for. To wipe Rajak off the map. Grind its ethnic ashes into the dirt.

Smoke begins curling its way through the floorboards above. One old woman begins to cough. Her mouth is hastily muffled with a headscarf by those around her.

Heavy footsteps above them reverberate through the hollow space the ten women occupy below.

Charlie turns her green eyes to the ceiling and howls silently into the abyss of her soul.

11

*C*HARLIE COULD STILL remember when her grandfather took her to see his favourite Turner. She could still feel his hand clasped tightly around hers, a loose bag of bones held together by ageing sinew.

She'd sat with him on a featureless bench in front of his favourite watercolour, *Loss of an East Indiaman,* and waited for him to speak. Air had rasped through what remained of his ravaged vocal cords, hissing its protest, before he managed the most words he'd spoken all day.

"The sinking of the *Halsewell,*" the alien voice had wheezed as he pointed a crooked finger at the painting before them. "Hundreds died. This is the true horror of a shipwreck." He was speaking, Charlie knew, from the bitter experience of a war spent at sea, watching the ships around him torpedoed and sunk, seeing his comrades die.

Intensely atmospheric, Turner's painting depicted the *Halsewell* lying half on its side, mast broken, in the violent waters off the Isle of Purbeck. Passengers clung to what was left of the shattered wreckage as the heaving waves engulfed them.

If Granddad could have said more, he'd have told her to note the simple use of colour and how, in the background, the brightest focal point came from the bluey-white sea spray, splashing up majestically over the ship's bow. Charlie could see it was created by the repeated scratching at the paper beneath, giving the effect of a brilliant white tunnel, leading perhaps to Heaven, into which it seemed the wreckage was being inexorably drawn. The rest of the horrific scene—the sinking vessel in the fermenting sea—was painted in two predominant colours, blue-grey and yellow-ochre. The latter was used to colour a block of abject terror at the core of the picture, as the hapless souls caught up in this terrible catastrophe awaited the inevitable.

By bringing her to see this most striking image, Charlie knew her grandfather was trying to prepare her for the inevitability of his death.

All these years later, she found herself standing in front of the same painting. For a moment, she felt just like the gawky teenager she'd been back then, awkward, afraid to voice her fears. Terrified of saying goodbye. She could almost smell the musty scent her grandfather's skin exuded in those final years of his life, as if it were concealing something unpalatable in its papery folds. She now knew it was the sweet stench of death.

CHARLIE DRIFTED ON the tide of her memory for a moment, before feeling a hand in the small of her back leading her gently away from *Loss of an East Indiaman* and on through the echoing rooms that housed Turner's other fine watercolours.

"These rooms are my favourites," Alan said softly. "They have the kindest light."

Now that she understood so much more about painting and the process of papermaking, Charlie was able to study this constantly changing selection of Turner's thirty thousand watercolours with a far greater appreciation of what the artist had been trying to achieve. She could almost make out the faint grid lines of the wire mould used to make each sheet—even, in some instances, the watermark. She could certainly spot the rare blemish, an air bubble or a stray hair, and see the way the paper sometimes cockled at the edges under Turner's brutal hand.

"Paper, especially artist's paper, lives only to be obscured," Alan reminded her. "It is painted and overpainted, soaked, spattered, and abused. Its purity shines through in only a few places, illuminating, contrasting, and highlighting the artist's work. Its quality and absorbency is an integral part of the work, juxtaposing the background and the foreground. Good paper can make or break a painting. It's that crucial."

They wandered amiably through the gallery, stopping and studying, discussing techniques, occasionally brushing against each other as they walked and talked. Charlie liked the way Alan enjoyed listening as much as speaking and how he seemed genuinely interested in what she had to say. She envied his physical carelessness, the natural way he moulded his gait to her own, less elegant walk.

She wondered, too, what others might have made of them, the smiling couple, conspiratorially discussing each work, oblivious to those around them, treating the gallery as if it were their own. A small bubble of happiness rose unexpectedly in the back of her throat.

Then something in a picture of a woman's face reminded her of Angela, and the bubble burst, flooding her mouth with a bitter taste. How could Alan be so carefree? What falsehoods drove him to appear so calm when his only child's body lay, riddled with worms, in a cold grave? Staring at him hard, she wondered, not for the first time, what drove him.

Catching her eye, Alan frowned and, just for an instant, she thought she had a fleeting glimpse of his pain. Surely she was wrong. Surely, like her, he felt the weight of gravity pressing on him each morning, surely he knew the supreme effort it took to force himself to get out of bed and rebel against it. Maybe he, too, feared the creatures that rose from the depths of the night. What an odd pair they were, she and he. Both touched with tragedy, both with much to hide, each one valiantly putting on an Oscar-winning performance of normality. Pushing Angela to the recesses of her mind, Charlie gave Alan a small smile of encouragement.

Escorting her across the parquet flooring to the end of a long, ingeniously illuminated display, he positioned her before the one painting he'd specifically brought her to see, the oil he was re-creating in watercolour, stepping back a pace to allow her to take it in.

Crossing the Brook was, indeed, magnificent. The gilt-framed canvas, first exhibited in Turner's fortieth year, was over six feet square and luminous with the hues of the Devonshire valley. The thick forest, the silvery blue light of the distant hollow, a multiarched bridge spanning the river. Charlie moved closer, her eyes settling on the painted figures. Apart from the young woman in the water, hitching up her skirt and leaning against some fallen rocks, followed by a dog, she was surprised to see another person in the picture.

A young girl sat at the water's edge, gazing pensively at her own reflection in the shallow water. Deep shadows surrounded her. Behind her, a little lane led to a dark brick tunnel framed by tall, overhanging trees.

The woods.

Charlie shivered involuntarily.

"Don't you like it?" Alan asked at her shoulder. She turned to see his grey eyes stray from the painting to the curve of her collarbone and the soft indentation at the base of her throat.

"Of course. It's stunning." Charlie swallowed. "It's just the...I suddenly felt cold, that's all. It must be the air-conditioning."

"Is that all?"

Charlie turned and stared up at Alan. "Why?"

Alan was so close that she could feel his breath on her cheek. "Don't you think there's something about his work, his layering of paints and pigments, that is sensual? Doesn't it make you long to reach out and touch it, Charlie? To feel the ridges of paint beneath your fingers?"

Charlie's heart was a trapped butterfly in her chest. Glancing over her shoulder, she saw that only a few other people lingered in the gallery; the realisation made her suddenly ill at ease.

Laughing and taking a few paces back, she replied, "I'm sure you find a lot of things sensual, Alan." Without thinking, she blurted, "Lori Hunter certainly seems to think so."

Alan was not to be deflected. "Never mind her. What about you? What does this painting make *you* feel, Charlie?" Motionless in a shaft of light, still staring at the masterpiece, there was something compelling, almost erotic, in his intensity.

"I, er, don't know," Charlie faltered, pinching the flesh of her arm hard between her thumb and forefinger. The muscle beneath her left eye threatened to twitch. Her head felt thick with the wine they'd shared over lunch.

Alan was still close, close enough to reach up and kiss, and, to her surprise, part of her wanted to. But the fear of such intimacy terrified her. No matter how much she told herself that it was probably time to rediscover the faltering steps of the dance that didn't always have to be brutal, she was afraid. Like the savage despoliation of her crude attempts at painting, she dreaded the power of her memories ruining something that should only be beautiful. And somehow, she felt instinctively that she was in the presence of danger.

"I'm not sure what you mean," she mumbled, feeling her neck colouring and trying to diffuse the intensity of the stare that had now transferred to her, "but if it's all the same to you, Alan, I'd really like to keep this relationship on a professional basis . . . at least until I've finished my research."

Her companion folded his arms across his chest and gave her a quizzical look. "Of course," he replied, smiling easily, the crevasses deep around his eyes. "Forgive me, Charlie. I've misled you. I wasn't for a minute suggesting anything else."

CHARLIE PULLED THE car to a halt outside her parents' home and gathered up her few belongings. It had been a long drive; she was lucky to have arrived before nightfall. An overturned lorry had blocked the South Circular, spilling industrial rolls of toilet paper across the road like snarled ticker tape. White streamers had flapped on the verges in the wind, or wrapped themselves tenaciously around road signs and trees. In the pink dusk, men in yellow coats scurried after the fugitive pieces as if chasing the tails of kites.

Granddad had made her a kite once. He'd stretched waxed orange paper over a flimsy wooden frame and allowed her to glue dozens of tiny paper squares to it, each one a different hue. They'd launched it at Bracklesham Bay, the taut strings lifting her, pulling at her small fingers, as the wintry wind whipped and dipped the gaily coloured triangle high and the seagulls wheeled noisily around it. Her feet crunching on the shingle, she'd had to dig in her heels and lean back against the wind to control the frenzied paper bird tugging at her hands. Her grandfather had stood a few feet away, hurriedly sketching the angle of her tug-of-war with the elements. Charlie and her handmade kite forming a perfect tick.

Scooping up the garish orange-and-black tiger lilies she'd bought for her mother and the bottles of wine for her father, she locked her ageing Volkswagen Golf and headed up the narrow brick path to their front door. Ringing the bell, she heard Henry, her parents' Norwich terrier, bark to alert his owners that an intruder was applying for entry.

Charlie braced herself for what was to come. That first glimpse of her father after a few weeks apart always came as a shock. In her mind's eye, he was still the robust young man of her youth, smelling of new leather and pipe tobacco, heading off on the 7.48 commuter train to the Ministry of Defence, briefcase in hand, *Daily Tribune* in a tight roll under his arm. But since his retirement five years before, Ed Hudson had diminished visibly. No longer fully erect, his body was hunched over and his skin was almost transparent as it stretched over his cheekbones; his eyes were sunken into their hollows. Each day saw him shrinking, sweeping him, she felt, irrevocably closer and closer to her grandfather.

"Hi, rabbit, come in." He stood before her, doubled over in what he would call mufti—beige slacks, shirt, buttoned-up cardigan, and tie (always a tie)—smiling wanly. She hugged him, pleased by his affectionate use of her childhood nickname, and trying not to notice how much bone she could feel through his clothing.

"Hi, Dad. How are you?"

"Oh, not bad, considering my great age and increasing infirmity," he replied. Removing his reading glasses, he revealed deeply scored indentations on the bridge of his nose. There was a glint in his pale blue eyes, and his clothes still smelled vaguely of the bonfire he must have lit earlier that afternoon. There was also a faint tang of gin.

Henry, up on his back paws, thrust a questing wet nose into Charlie's hands and wagged his tail wildly. Reaching into her coat pocket, her fingers found the dog biscuit she'd bought specially. It was only halfway out when he snapped it from her grasp and raced off down the hallway with it proudly between his teeth.

Her mother sailed out of the living room towards her, arms outstretched like oars as Charlie stood stiffly in her path.

"Charlotte," Marjorie Hudson cried regally. "How good to see you. You look tired, dear. Come, you're late for supper."

After a creamy fish pie, which Charlie hardly touched, the three of them sat companionably at the dining table, drinking the wine she'd brought. They chatted about the weather, the dog, the shocking cost of house prices in the area, and whether or not to hard-prune the standard roses Granddad had planted. Charlie's father looked as if he wanted nothing more than to slump into his favourite armchair in front of the television, but he resisted her attempts to escort him there, protesting that he didn't see her often enough.

"How's the writing going?" he asked, sipping the half-decent Mâcon she'd been surprised to discover at a garage shop. "Are you making headway?"

"I'm getting there," Charlie replied protectively, unwilling as ever to discuss a work in progress. She carefully folded her mother's expensive paper napkin into a neat square and laid her hand across it. "Although this one seems to be taking so much concentration. I think I must be getting old!"

Her parents laughed at the thought. Although she was forty-two, they still considered Charlie the baby of the family. With her elder sister Fiona married off and living in Derbyshire, dividing her time between the primary school where she taught three days a week and the printing business she ran with her husband, it was Charlie they'd come to regard as the more exotic child.

"Charlotte's always on the go," her mother used to regale her friends in front of her. "I don't know where she gets her energy. It exhausts me just to watch her. She's been to more countries than most people can name and yet she never forgets birthdays, and pops down to see us whenever she can. Takes after my side of the family, of course. The Mackays were always so thoughtful."

Truth was, Marjorie and Fiona were much more alike, fiercely united in a jealousy of Charlie that stemmed back to the days when her grandfather was alive.

Now the mother and younger daughter sat side by side, mentally circling each other.

"How's Nick?" Her mother pulled the pin and lobbed the grenade before sitting back, innocently, as if someone else was responsible.

"He's fine," Charlie replied, instantly wary. "I saw him last week for the first time in over a month. He sends his love. He's hoping to come and see you himself as soon as he gets a chance. Now that he's reached such stratospheric heights on the paper he only gets Saturdays off, and that's usually spent catching up on his sleep or reading the competition."

"He's a good lad, that Nick." Her father picked an imaginary speck off the white damask tablecloth. "The son we never had." He looked up at his daughter, his eyes flickering his gratitude.

"I know, Dad," Charlie responded. "He was a good husband, too."

Her mother hitched up her bosom before her next salvo. "Well, if you hadn't gone gallivanting off round the world chasing wars, young lady, things might have been very different."

"What, and deprive you of the chance to play the beleaguered martyr with your friends at the WI?" Charlie hissed without thinking, screwing her carefully folded napkin into a tight ball.

Marjorie Hudson opened her mouth to reply, but her husband's glare snapped it shut.

"Leave it, Marjorie," he barked protectively. "There's no use going over all that again. They've made their decision and it's got bugger all to do with us."

A visit to her parents always left Charlie exhausted and slightly breathless. It wasn't just the thickening silence and the centrally heated air without a single open window that stifled her. Things just didn't seem the same since her grandfather had died.

She still found it impossible to walk past his old room without peering in. Inhaling deeply, eyes closed, she longed for a faint trace of his hair oil, or the distinctive scent of his leather shoes. She could almost see his Decca gramophone in the corner, his treasured LPs stacked beside it. Or his collection of shells, pebbles, and driftwood, all jumbled together in an old artist's box. His clothes—tweeds, corduroys, and collarless linen shirts, complemented with vibrantly coloured cravats—would be draped over the clothes horse. On the now bare walls had once hung hauntingly beautiful prints by the great masters—Turner, of course, but Constable, Titian, and John Singer Sargent, too.

But the space he'd inhabited no longer bore any trace of him. Why would it, after all these years? Marjorie Hudson had long ago turned it into a crafts room for her numerous hobbies. There stood the freestanding mahogany embroidery frame—a gift from Charlie last Christmas—a basket full of coloured wool, and a tatty tailor's dummy studded with pins like some giant voodoo doll. All that remained of Granddad was a small, framed black-and-white photograph on a shelf. In it, he sat at his easel on the beach at Selsey Bill, a panama hat cocked jauntily over one eye. Knock-kneed at his side was a twelve-year-old Charlie, her chin resting on his shoulder, a starfish hand on his arm.

"It's the best photo I have of him," her mother would say, especially in Fiona's hearing. "It's really not important who else is in the shot."

Charlie picked up the photograph and ran her fingertip over the familiar silhouette, trapped now on a fading square of paper. With the knowledge she'd recently acquired, she couldn't help but consider the process by which it had been created. Cotton pulp would have been beaten in a special tile-lined machine so that no metallic particles came into contact with it, for fear of their reaction with the chemicals used later. Coated in light-sensitive solutions, the paper would have been carefully sized to allow the print to develop quickly. Then it would have been given a gloss or matte finish, before being machine-dried and guillotined into precisely measured oblongs. Each one a perfect miniature creation. Virginal. Just waiting for its chance to be placed under a photographic negative in an enlarger and blasted with a beam of light to imprint an image onto its pristine surface. Immersed in a solution of silver nitrate, the chemicals would magically release the contours and the colours, the shadows, and the light. All that, just to capture an infinitesimal fraction of a second on a Sussex beach, and freeze it for all time.

Holding the frame like a prize, Charlie stood in the middle of the room and allowed the memories to come. In her mind, she could still sense her grandfather, bent over his desk, or reading in a pool of light in his armchair. His presence in this house had been the glue that bound them all together. Without him, they'd come unstuck.

WITH HENRY ZIGZAGGING after a scent before her, Charlie escaped the house and plodded on up the hill towards the cemetery and remembrance gardens first planted when Queen Victoria was on the throne. Glad of the sweet, cool air, she sought her spot beneath the branches of an old cedar tree, and sat on a bench dedicated to a man she'd never met— *"Harry Bailey, died 1978, who loved this place."* Directly opposite lay a solid granite tombstone bearing her grandfather's name. *John "Jock" Mackay, Victoria Cross. 1909–1982.*

The day they'd laid him in that open wound in the ground, she'd just turned eighteen. It had been a perfect day for a funeral—windy and chill, with a bleak northeaster blowing hats off heads and rustling the leaves on the sodden trees. A few of her grandfather's old comrades had shown up, some in uniform, brightly coloured ribbons fluttering at their breasts, but her mother hardly noticed them, shrunken inside her overcoat, childlike tears dripping down her face.

Charlie had watched as his coffin was carefully lowered into position. She felt each clod of earth thud down onto its lid. All she could wonder in that instant was if her grandfather was silently cross with her. Angry at being there instead of committed to the waves. *"The sea,"* he'd rasped. *"I want to be buried at sea."* It was a wish her mother had rejected as "whimsical."

From her grandfather's grave, Charlie could see the sprawling suburb spreading across the valley, glistening with the warm lamplight of dusk. She could just make out her parents' home, its immaculate, white-painted gables visible within the neat row of near-identical Edwardian houses. Soon, everything around her would be cloaked in darkness.

"Well, here I am again, Granddad," she sighed, rubbing Henry's silky upturned ears. "Back with the Aged Ps. Nothing changes." Thinking for a moment, she added, "Well, actually something has changed. I've—I've met someone. Someone special. Or at least, I think he could be. I just don't know what to do about him yet."

Her grandfather knew all her secrets. Always had. So did Harry Bailey's bench. And the dog, too—when he wasn't burying his nose in the soft earth, sniffing for possibilities. The three of them had listened to outpourings she had never been able to share with another living soul. Their one great advantage was that none of them could answer back. Nor could they judge, criticise, or offer meaningless advice. They certainly couldn't give her that dreaded look of her mother's which meant one thing—that Marjorie was filing her comments away in some mental black book.

Only once did Charlie see her father stealing up the hill after her, curious to see where she went. He did it, she knew, to counter Marjorie's conviction that their daughter was sneaking into one of the town's pubs.

Charlie had overheard them talking about her. "You mark my words, she's developing a problem, that girl," her mother had insisted, hissing at him in the kitchen while she briskly stirred the lumps from her custard over a flickering blue flame. "Did you see how many she sank before lunch?"

Charlie's father openly rebuked his wife for such uncharitable thoughts, but Charlie knew he secretly had them, too. He knew, more than Marjorie, how much of a beating life had given her, and wouldn't have been at all surprised if she'd chosen to seek solace in the bottom of a bottle. After all, he was only too familiar with how effective alcohol could be in drowning the screams of frustration inside one's head.

But when he watched her sit wearily on the bench, and the dog fall in at her side, it must have become clear to him that hers was a well-worn routine. The wind would have been too high for him to hear what she was saying that particular afternoon; he would only have caught snatches of words from his hiding place behind a Gothic family crypt. Even from the corner of her eye when one of her sobs was carried to him like a fallen leaf, he, thankfully, let her be. She saw him pull up his collar, and turn his back to the wind and her misery.

Whenever she returned from her nightly "walk with the dog," Charlie was calmer somehow, more settled, although always a little dazed.

"That'll be the vodka," Marjorie said in a stage whisper to her husband as they bade her good night and watched her climb the stairs. "Maureen's son-in-law took to the bottle. They always drink vodka because it has no smell."

Charlie was grateful that her father's sharp flick across her mother's hand with the corner of the tea towel prevented her from saying more. He clearly knew it was the deep-felt need to be with her beloved grandfather that was Charlie's salve, but it was not something he or Charlie was about to share with Marjorie Mackay Hudson. She'd refused to understand that when Jock was alive. She'd never understand now.

12

*H*ow's the book coming?" Charlie's agent, Nigel Armstrong, demanded during one of their rare lunches together. He'd chosen a French bistro not far from his Fulham office rather than anywhere swanky.

That's what she liked about Nigel. He always played it straight and never tried to dazzle her with his expense account. There were people she knew, fellow authors, with agents who sent them gifts on their birthdays, champagne at Christmas, and bouquets of flowers to mark their latest publication. Nigel didn't even know when her birthday was, but he was one of the best critics of her work and when it came to the crunch and he was needed at her side at some high-powered publishing meeting, he never failed to impress. The very fact of his being there, she knew, pushed up the advance.

"Very close," she told him happily, spearing a piece of oak leaf lettuce with her fork.

"Great," said Nigel, slurping on his wine. "And is Sir What's-His-Name being helpful?" He prodded at his *confit de canard*, his heavily lined features frowning under his shock of grey hair. He looked tired.

"Extremely," Charlie admitted. "Sir Alan couldn't have been more accommodating. He's lent me loads of research data, introduced me to some first-class experts, and he's even painting a watercolour in homage to Turner especially for me. If it comes out well, we're going to use it for the jacket."

"And what about the marketing side of things? Do you think you have enough commercial material to make it work? I mean, what do you think is its USP?"

Charlie sipped her mineral water and tilted her head, forgetting for a moment what he meant. Then she remembered. Unique Selling Point. Publishing-speak. "Well, Alan's painting should help enormously on that front, but there are lots of other plusses. It's not all dry history. Turner led a fascinating and complex life, you know, with a tragic childhood, two mistresses..."

Nigel's eyes lit up. "Oh, yeah?"

"And the paper he worked on was used by everyone from Hitler and Chamberlain to Kitchener."

Nigel discarded his cutlery, took a tiny pen and notepad from his breast pocket, and scribbled that down. "Hitler," he wrote. "Mistresses. Kitchener." Looking hopeful, he asked: "And is there any love child involved?"

"Two, actually," Charlie informed him, giving him the names of Turner's illegitimate daughters. She thought of their namesakes, the pair of elegant cats adorning Alan's Suffolk studio, and repressed a wistful sigh.

"Better and better," Nigel enthused, scrawling their names down, too. "Will this Sir Alan fellow agree to his painting being used to promote the book as well as for the jacket?"

"Almost certainly," Charlie replied. She took another sip of water and carefully placed the glass back on the table. "But just to make sure, I'll probably go to bed with him."

Nigel looked genuinely shocked for a moment. Then he laughed aloud. "Good one! You nearly had me for a minute there. I mean, I know he's loaded, but he's not exactly your type, is he?"

Charlie could feel her face fall ever so slightly. "Oh?" she said. "Really? You don't see me with Sir Alan Matheson?"

"Never in a million years!" Nigel chortled, summoning the waiter over to order more wine. "He's not your type." Scanning the menu, he pointed to what he wanted and waved the waiter away. "Funny bloke. Met him once. Couple of years ago. Came to see me. Wanted to put a book together. Something to do with a collection of unpublished drawings by his dead daughter. They were bloody awful, to be honest. All about incest and abortion and blood. Surrealism, he called it, but hardly marketable material. I turned him down flat."

Charlie pushed away her plate of Niçoise salad, her appetite gone. No matter how hard she tried to keep her at bay, it seemed, Angela Matheson kept returning to haunt her.

CHARLIE HAD LEARNED long ago that the way to keep her mind from endlessly replaying images that seared into her brain was to immerse herself in her work. Intense concentration on the minutiae had often freed her from the complexities of her past.

Back at her east London flat, silhouetted in a pool of light at her desk late into the night, surrounded by books and clippings, articles and papers stacked neatly on every surface, she knew she was closing in on her quarry. The ground was prepared and the bait laid; all she needed was to wait for that elusive spark that would illuminate for her how it would all come together.

The voices of Turner, Whatman, and Ruskin were jostling for supremacy in her head, and now that she had done her duty in visiting her parents, she was yearning to escape to her Suffolk hideaway and really start listening. Work would, if nothing else, put some physical distance between her and Alan, pushing her next encounter with him still further away. This was a good thing, she told herself. His openly sexual approach at the gallery had unnerved her more than she'd realised. She couldn't stop thinking about what would have happened if she'd just kissed him there and then. Would he have kissed her back? Might they have ended up doing something more? No. She needed time to think.

Staring up at the formidable Inca warrior mask of papier-mâché that she once made, which stood sentinel over her desk, she tried to clear her mind of everything else that was troubling her. Not just the lingering unease she felt about Alan's tragic daughter, but more recently Lori Hunter's unexpectedly urgent warning to be wary of her feelings for Alan, and Nick's interference, too. The question was, which of these many distractions were causing her nightmares to recur?

Paper. Come on, Charlie, she chastised herself. This book isn't going to write itself. In the profound resonance of paper, she could surely find spiritual as well as intellectual release. She always had before. What was it Alan had said? That paper's strength and its fragility embodied the human spirit? Surely it could embody her own.

Picking up the notes she'd made on the Whatman paper mill, her eyes flicked from her notepad to the screen of her laptop computer and back again.

Reading aloud as she typed, she spoke each word as she wrote it, a trick she'd learned long ago from an article about one of her favourite novelists. Somehow doing so gave her a taste for the structure and rhythm of a sentence in a way that reading silently never did.

"It was in 1740, thirty-five years before Turner's birth, that James Whatman the Elder took over Turkey Mill on a deep and narrow gorge on the River Len, a mile above its confluence with the River Medway," she began. "Within two decades, he had turned it into the largest paper company in England. A severe man in the ubiquitous white wig and white ruff collar of the time, James Whatman had a stern face and a dark, penetrating gaze." Charlie peered at the portrait she'd discovered of him in an archive and couldn't quite decide if she liked the look of the paper pioneer or not.

Studying her notes, she recalled the beautiful Whatman product. In the hours Charlie had spent in the Kentish museum's library, she had marveled at the quality of the paper she was handling—James Whatman's paper—the ink marks pure and bright, its colour and form so well preserved after more than two hundred years. There were letters and numerous papers, mainly personal correspondence between James Whatman the

Younger and his staff. One document referred to the Rag Workers' Sick Club, a society to care for those women made ill from the many diseases carried in the rags.

"There is a clear onus of responsibility, " James Whatman wrote prophetically, *"which falls on me and my fellow mill workers, to provide some basic levels of health care for our menial workers."*

The details of the running of the mills in the country's most important papermaking centre were fascinating, not least the owners' constant preoccupation with the acquisition of fine linen rags, many of which had to be imported after the Napoleonic War, when Britain's own supplies had been plundered. She came across ledgers that showed that James Whatman bought one hundred and fifty tons of rags a year from rag merchants as far away as Italy, which constituted, at £5,500 per year, his greatest annual expense.

"The Romans, it seems, have done it again, " Charlie had him admit reluctantly to his wife. *"Not content with giving us viaducts and roads, sewage systems and wine, they are now providing the best materials for the world's finest paper!"*

Anyone who needed fine paper bought Whatman's. William Blake used it for his illuminated manuscripts such as "The Book of Job" and "Jerusalem." Staff at the Public Records Office and British colonials in India purchased it for letters and ledgers. George Washington kept his private accounts on it. Lord Kitchener's appeal for volunteers during the First World War was printed on it.

A surprise find deep in the archives was a sheet of Adolf Hitler's personal writing paper. Retrieved from his Berlin bunker, it bore a Whatman watermark. Charlie was thrilled at the prospect of including a photograph of it in the book. She resolved to discover if the paper British Prime Minister Neville Chamberlain so notoriously waved on his return from meeting with Hitler was indeed manufactured by the Kentish mill.

"I have in my hand a piece of paper, " Chamberlain had famously said, returning to Britain from Munich in 1938. *"This is peace in our time."* A journalist at heart, Charlie knew a unique selling point when she saw one.

That link with Whatman would impress even Nigel; she congratulated herself.

Whatman paper remained in production until the mid-twentieth century, but, after two world wars and the advance of machine-made papers, its sun had set. The name would lie dormant until it was taken up again two decades later and given to a new line of mould-made cotton art papers. The last stocks of handmade vintage paper had long been dispersed to stationers and art suppliers around the country. It was from just one such dealer, in the back streets of Ipswich, that Alan had purchased his precious cache, taking out a hefty bank loan to do so.

Alan. There he was again. Uninvited, he kept stealing across her thoughts. Setting down her pencil, Charlie closed her eyes. This is ridiculous, she chastised herself. She was meant to be working, leaving all thoughts of Sir Alan Matheson and his fractured family behind. Had he stored his last-known supply of paper in a sterile bank vault to prevent his crazy daughter from setting it alight in an act of unforgivable hatred? Why had Angela hated him so much? What could that urbane Englishman have possibly done to arouse such venom in his only child? And what was it about Angela that kept tugging at Charlie, like the relentless torque on the string of a kite? Angela's descent into madness, perhaps? Her incarceration in a psychiatric hospital? Her suicide? Madness and suicide were no strangers to Charlie and now, just as she was making real progress, she felt as if she was being pulled back to memories she'd hoped to one day forget.

THE NEXT TIME Charlie looked up, four hours had passed. She blinked at the hands of the clock and wondered if she was reading it correctly. Reluctantly leaving James Whatman and his increasingly strident voice behind, she dragged herself back to the present. Rotating her aching neck and shoulders, she closed her notebook and yawned. Her eyes felt gritty and her brain scrambled. What she needed was a brisk walk.

Swigging mineral water from a bottle, she strolled through her local park, wrapped up in her secret thoughts. Only the ringing of her mobile phone jolted her out of them.

"Yes, everything's fine," she assured Alan as she kicked her way through some early fallen leaves like a child. "The Kentish archives held some wonderful material; thanks for suggesting them. And weaving Whatman's life and work into Turner's own story is working pretty well. Now I just have to focus more on Ruskin to find his voice, too."

"Well, it sounds like you had a very productive day," he told her, "I look forward to hearing more about it. . . . Why don't we discuss it over dinner?"

"No, thanks," she replied flatly. "Tonight my only date is with a hot bath."

The call over, she placed the butt of her hand against her temple to stop the alarm bells ringing in her head.

A curse sliced through the evening's stillness. A brawl was spilling out of the launderette she was passing. A young woman holding a tiny baby loudly berated two men fighting on the pavement right in front of her, the air blue with her language. Charlie stopped in her tracks, hackles up.

"Stop it! Stop it, you two!" the woman screamed, so close Charlie could smell the alcohol on her breath. "It doesn't fucking matter, Terry! Let it go, will you? Terry!"

Bumping into Charlie as she staggered backwards, the woman thrust the baby into her arms without a moment's hesitation. "Take her for me, would yer?" she said.

Charlie tried to draw back but was given no choice. The infant she now held gazed up at her, eyes wide, smelling of talcum powder and warm milk, as its mother leapt onto the back of one of the men and, screeching, began pummeling him about the head and ears with her fists.

"Oi, get off me!" the man protested, as his opponent, spotting the advantage, punched him in the stomach and all three tumbled back onto the pavement, yelling.

Instinctively, Charlie protected the baby's head with her hand and swung away from the noise and the gathering crowd. Retreating into the launderette to wait for the scuffle to end, she pushed a pile of tabloid newspapers to one side, sat on a bench, and stared hard into the infant's face.

"Well," she soothed uneasily. "I suppose we'd better stay here for a bit, you and I."

The baby gurgled, its eyes bright, and then smiled, its open mouth revealing two rows of bubble-gum-pink gums. Charlie swallowed dryly and made herself smile back.

"That's better," she said, and turned away, concentrating on the rhythmic sloshing of water and clothes in the glass-fronted machines. Someone had left a tissue in a pocket of the load directly in front of her. Scraps of soggy pink paper flecked the garments spinning demonically inside.

Tiny fingers yanked at her hair.

"I expect you want my undivided attention," Charlie said, smiling properly this time, and sitting the infant on her legs to bounce up and down. Her earliest childhood memory was of being lifted and bumped like this, gurgling with delight as Granddad cooed back at her dotingly. Not a day had gone by when she hadn't been certain of his love.

"It's not fair!" her sister Fiona would complain to their mother bitterly, her pouting bottom lip doing nothing for her looks. "Why won't Granddad spend that much time with me?"

"I know," her mother would murmur wistfully. It wasn't until years later that Charlie realised Fiona wasn't the only one who was resentful.

She was vaguely aware of a police siren and more scuffling and cursing outside the glass. But when a hand was laid lightly on her shoulder, she shook herself back to the present day and looked up.

"Sorry about all that." The red-faced young mother shrugged her thin shoulders. There was a ragged new scratch across her right cheek. "I've got to go down the nick and pay Terry's bail, although why I fucking bother, I'll never know."

"Yes, of course," Charlie said, rising to hand her the baby. "Here."

As the woman reached for her daughter, she brought up fingers that held a freshly lit cigarette. Charlie flinched and pulled back, almost dropping the child. She felt the colour leech from her face.

"Sorry," the young mother said, grimacing. "Filthy habit." She took a greedy drag before dropping the cigarette and grinding it beneath her heel into the grubby linoleum floor. Blowing a stream of blue smoke, she pried the child from Charlie's arms.

"Say good-bye, Angie," the woman commanded, waving the child's cupped pink hand.

"Sorry?" Charlie said, shaking her head as if to rouse herself.

"Kid's called Angela," the mother explained cheerfully, and stood staring as Charlie pushed away, out into the welcome chill of the blustery September evening.

BACK HOME AFTER a solitary salad not much enhanced by three-quarters of a bottle of mediocre claret, Charlie turned on the bath tap. Water gushed out, spitting and hissing as the old pipes rattled under the pressure. Retrieving a small bottle of essential oils from the cabinet, she allowed a few drops to fall into the steaming water, before stepping out of her clothes and sliding beneath its slippery lavender and lemon meniscus.

With just the light from a few candles casting soft shadows across the room, she immersed herself up to her nose and stared at the ceiling. A crack in the plaster extended from one corner almost to the ornate rose in the middle. A spider had spun a web across the chasm and was bravely making its way across, like some miniature high-wire walker.

How many times had she lain in a bath like this one staring at the ceiling in hotel rooms around the world? How many nights spent away from Nick? When was it that she'd first begun to realise she no longer needed him?

"I can't imagine why I'm here and you're there," she'd write at first. *"It seems insane now that I even came. You're the best thing that ever happened to me, and here I am, risking everything. Please wait for me, all my everythings, C. xx"*

The letters never stopped. Even in the worst hellholes, she'd managed to find a scrap of paper, a pen, and a solitary stub of sputtering candle. She'd write into the vacuum, stockpiling her letters until she came across someone who was heading out, who could post them for her when he reached civilisation. Nick told her later that he wouldn't hear from her for weeks and then seven or eight letters would arrive all at once, crumpled and torn, but still full of her passion for him. He would read and reread them, he'd confessed, turning their fragile surfaces over and over in his hands before storing them in the beautiful silver box she'd bought him in Damascus.

When had she begun to run out of words? Her long stint in the Middle East was swiftly followed by longer tours of duty in Croatia and Bosnia, in between dangerous return trips to the Lebanon. Every time she was in a new place of risk, he told her he could somehow sense her vulnerability all those miles away. The hairs would rise on the back of his neck and he wouldn't be able to settle until he knew she was safe. When had she forgotten what to say to the man she'd married in a blizzard of confetti in a Kentish country church a decade earlier, her father standing rigidly at her side? It wasn't that she didn't still love Nick; it was just that she was different now. He was part of an older, saner life.

As her experiences became increasingly difficult to relate, her letters began to take on the tone of a telegram.

"Shelling bad today," she'd tell him, her handwriting increasingly spidery. "Rescued a stray dog from a burning building. Reuters man killed. Will call from the capital.
All my everythings.
C. xx"

She couldn't bring herself to tell him that the scrawny mongrel she'd adopted and given the name "Cinders" was blown up by a land mine a week later, or that Danny from Reuters had been one of her dearest friends, with his Tennessee drawl and zany sense of humour. How could Nick ever understand how desperately she missed them?

And once she'd started to keep things from Nick, to hoard her untellable secrets, she found she could no longer communicate to him when they were actually together. Life on the front line left her tense and uneasy, and she struggled to relax during their reunions, to find the familiar comforts in his steadying physical presence. But no matter how hard she tried, she always felt as if her private space—so carefully built up around her—was being invaded by a man to whom she owed so much but for whom she no longer knew how to give of herself.

Nick was patient at first. He'd woo her back into his arms and into their bed, a place where there'd previously been nothing but pleasure and release. But his frustration became increasingly evident. She could tell he was hurting, and that he needed to hurt her in return. What started as a sort of spirited sexual game, to try to tease her back to the way she used to be, became increasingly dark. After a while, the pain came almost as a relief. She never once cried out, and the more she remained silent, the more he seemed to misconstrue her response. Now when he hurt her, she'd arch back and take it all, glad, at last, to be feeling something.

Passion. It had been so long since she'd experienced it, she'd almost forgotten the sensation. Using her big toe to top up the hot water in the bath, she stared down at her body, its peaks and curves glistening above the slick sheen of oil, and forced herself to imagine what it might feel like to allow a man's hands to touch her again. Someone gentle, someone kind, someone who didn't want to hurt her.

Cupping her breasts in the curls of fragrant steam, she ran her thumbs gently over each nipple and watched them harden in response. Sliding her hands under the water, she found her stomach and spread her fingers quickly towards the sharp curve of her hips. Lowering her head so that the steaming water almost completely covered it, her heartbeat pounded in her ears as her fingertips probed further. Pressing her eyes shut, she slid deeper into the water, immersing herself completely under its oily surface.

13

SHE SMELLED HIM before she saw him. She'd no idea how long Alan had been standing in the half-open doorway of her cottage, watching her chop coriander; but above the delicate scents curling up to her, the breeze suddenly brought her the scent of linseed oil that seemed to cling to him.

"Good evening," he said. He was smiling broadly, a bunch of yellow sunflowers held carelessly in one hand, a bottle of champagne in the other.

Charlie turned hastily and felt the blood rush to her face. "Hello. Please, Alan, come in."

"These are for you," he said, handing her the sunflowers.

"Thank you," she replied. "How lovely."

"They remind me of my house in Italy, which you must come and visit sometime. The Italians call them girasole, which means 'that which turns to the sun.' I think we can all relate to that."

Unwrapping the heavy blossoms from their blue crêpe paper, Charlie reached for a fat green vase and filled it with water. Standing it on the edge of the table, she began to arrange the blooms haphazardly, aware that her every movement was being watched. Accidentally dropping one onto the terra-cotta floor, she bent to pick it up at the same time as Alan did. Their heads bumped.

"Sorry," she mumbled, reaching for the flower. His hand brushed hers, making her flinch involuntarily.

"So, how's everything?" he asked, straightening and stepping away.

Breathlessly, Charlie answered, blurting out news of her latest research. "I've been making all sorts of fabulous discoveries. You were so right to set me on this journey."

"What discoveries?" he demanded, leaning against her old pine linen press.

"Did you know that it was Whatman's who introduced wove paper to Western papermaking? They made it by weaving the mould tighter, making the paper almost like a cloth and much smoother without the telltale wire marks."

As she chatted away, happy to be on safer ground, Alan listened with the fascination of a keen student. Pouring them both a glass of champagne, he watched her ladling stock into a pan on her chipped enamel Aga and seemed childishly comforted. Charlie suspected that neither of his wives had much culinary skill.

It had been a long time since she'd cooked a meal for someone and she was surprised how nervous she had felt earlier in the day. After carefully selecting the menu, she'd arrived from London, her car laden. Stopping to inhale the freshening breeze that whipped strands of hair wildly around her face, she'd seen the light slanting across the sea in the distance and resisted the urge to run to the beach. Pushing open her green picket gate, she'd stared with a smile at the place that had become her haven.

Turning the key in the lock of the stable door with its satisfyingly solid bolts and hinges, she'd swung it open and, awkward with her purchases, backed her way inside. She hadn't been up for a few weeks, but the cottage smelt dry and she noticed with relief that the little dish of mouse poison she'd left out hadn't been disturbed. Much as she cursed her uninvited guests for nibbling their way through packets of dried foods and leaving tiny black droppings all over the shelves, she didn't relish dealing with a dead mouse. She was no longer so good with bodies.

Resting her heavy bags on the kitchen table, she'd rummaged through them to find a bottle of wine, discarding its green tissue paper and opening it with some urgency. The first glass had given her the courage to get started. With deftness she thought she'd forgotten, she washed and cracked open a crab, poached a salmon, and gently steamed some mussels. By the second glass, she was straining herby fish stock through a sieve and really getting into her stride. When the bottle was half-empty, she laid the table, prepared a salad, and began tidying up.

Tipping a brown paper bag of oranges into a blue china bowl, she arranged some roses in a large white china pitcher and swept the old ashes from the wood-burning stove. Screwing up pages of a newspaper into long twists, and layering them with thin chips of kindling just as her grandfather had taught her, she laid a new fire. Now that September was here, the evenings were growing chilly.

Upstairs in her cream bedroom with its old pine furniture and clean, fresh look, she dusted away the cobwebs that traced a ghostly line from the table lamp to the window, puffed up the plain cotton pillows on her bed, tidied away any personal belongings, and cleaned the roll-top bath. By the time Alan was due to arrive, both she and her home had been scrubbed to within an inch of their lives.

Now that he was here, she was glad she'd gone to all that trouble. She had deliberately chosen her Suffolk cottage as the venue for this latest encounter. She needed to be somewhere she felt safe from any sense of danger or intimacy. He was working in the studio of Pear Tree Farm this week and she reminded herself that, after their early supper and a few hours' work together, he could easily head home.

"Good health," she said, raising her glass flute in salute. For a moment they stared at each other in silence until she turned away and broke the spell.

"I see you have a full set of the Adrian Bell Suffolk trilogy," he said, reaching for one of the volumes on her bookshelf and opening the pages. "Gosh, these are the 1929 Bodley Head limited editions, illustrated by Harry Becker. Quite a prize!"

"Harry Becker is my favourite Suffolk artist," Charlie declared from the range.

"Mine, too." Alan smiled.

"Going back to wove paper," Charlie deflected, "I believe it changed the face of watercolour painting. Watercolour had been used for centuries, but until the early nineteenth century the paints merely added colour to something already drawn in ink, all with a very linear structure. The wove paper, which was smoother, seemed to bring watercolour paintings to life. Artists started to use the paint much more freely, just as they had been doing for years when painting with oils. For the first time, the colours themselves were allowed to create form and image. Correct me if I'm wrong but it was like the paper set the painters—and the paintings—free."

Charlie removed the pan from the heat and spooned the contents onto a blue-and-white willow-pattern platter. The prawns and mussels, crabmeat and salmon lay invitingly atop the glossy Arborio rice. The air was rich with mouthwatering aromas. Angrily, she swatted at a bluebottle that dive-bombed the stove, trapping the insect fatally between her hands.

"I *hate* flies," she spat without thinking, brushing the dead fly into the bin. A foul memory pushed its way roughly to the surface but she crushed it as ruthlessly as she had the insect.

Forcing herself to breathe, she carried the platter to the table, pushed the bowl of crisp green salad to one side, and laid it down. Wiping the perspiration from her forehead with the back of her hand, she inadvertently loosened a tendril of her hair, which tumbled in front of her eyes. Ignoring it, she picked up a knife. She cut two slices of thick wholemeal bread, fresh from the bakery that morning, refusing to meet Alan's probing gaze.

"What I've been wondering is, would you say it was actually the *paper* that made those artists paint in a new way?" she persisted. "Wouldn't they have come to work like that in the end anyway?"

Alan smiled, his eyes on hers, and sipped from his glass. "Probably. People were tired of the old-school methods. They wanted something fresh and new and exciting. Watercolours suddenly became astonishingly trendy—they even superseded needlework in popularity among ladies of the time. Artists' shops opened across London with names like The Temple of the Muses and The Repository of Arts. People were invited to spend the day in them, browsing, socialising, and speaking of everything to do with watercolours. They were, I suppose, the Internet cafés of their day."

"I like that." Charlie grinned. "Remind me to write that down later."

She spooned risotto onto a pale green plate and handed it to him, garlic and herbs wafting in a trail of steam.

"You could have Ruskin explaining how watercolour societies sprang up across the country," Alan suggested. "He'd be the first to criticise the old guard, who feared that the growing popularity of watercolours could adversely affect the production of fine oil paintings. They needn't have worried; oil paint would always be the serious older brother. Charlie, this is *delicious*!"

"Don't sound so surprised. I do know how to cook, you know. I just don't do it very often."

"Really? And what other talents are you hiding from me?"

"Well, at the risk of sounding like a contestant on *Blind Date,* I'd like world peace and I enjoy gardening, music, poetry, and watercolour painting." Charlie found herself laughing.

Alan halted his fork midway between his plate and his mouth and examined her. "My, my. I don't suppose you'd ever allow me to see any of your paintings?"

"Never in a million years!" She forced a careless laugh. "And it's not out of a false sense of self-effacement, I can assure you. They're dreadful—worse than those of an incompetent child. My grandfather was exasperated by my lack of talent, as I'm sure you would be. I desperately wanted to be better, but when I realised I never would be, I stopped painting seriously. Instead, I've been using words to create portraits on the paper Granddad taught me to revere. Now I don't paint for any other reason than that I enjoy it. It's a kind of therapy."

"Therapy for what? What on earth would someone as well balanced as you need therapy for?" His face grew serious.

Charlie felt the earth tilt momentarily. How easy it should be to tell him everything now, as he gave her that all-consuming stare. How tempting. What a relief it might be to bare her soul at last to someone who seemed so intuitive, so forgiving. To release the secrets from her mental Pandora's box. But instead, she shook her head crossly and asked herself how much she really knew about this man who, according to the newspaper headlines, had terrible secrets of his own. Taking a gulp of her champagne, she almost choked on the bubbles.

"Well balanced?" She giggled. "If only you knew."

But Alan wouldn't let her off that easily. "Tell me," he urged, putting down his fork and gently covering her hand with his.

Charlie felt every sinew in her body tighten as alarm bells clamoured in her head. Looking into those pale eyes that seemed to change colour with the shifting light, she said firmly, "Trust me. You really wouldn't want to know."

Before she could stop him, Alan lifted her chin with his hand. "On the contrary, Charlie. I want to know *everything* about you." Then he leaned across the table and planted his mouth firmly on hers.

Jumping back, overturning her chair in the process, Charlie crashed against the Aga, almost upsetting the risotto pan.

From his seat, Alan looked up at her in confusion. "I'm sorry, Charlie. I didn't mean to startle you."

Charlie stared down at him, taking in every word, reasoning furiously with herself. She felt acutely aware of every sight, sound, and scent in the room around her. This was her home, she had to remind herself. Her safe haven. Alan was an invited friend. No—more than a friend. A kindred spirit. Someone who knew what it was to suffer. He'd been nothing, would be nothing but kind.

Unable to speak, she watched and waited, every inch of her body coiled for flight, yet unable to move an inch.

"Perhaps I should go," Alan said, standing cautiously and moving back a few steps as if he was afraid to turn his back on her until he was out of the door.

Charlie's fingers slowly relaxed their grip on the cooker. "I—I'm sorry," she finally murmured, forcing her arms to her side in a conciliatory gesture. She heard herself saying, "Please. Don't go. I don't want you to."

Alan frowned, looked torn between staying and leaving. "Well, what exactly do you want, Charlie?"

She studied his face, her eyes lingering on the angular curve of his jawbone and the way the evening light caught his hair. His eyes bored into hers, unable to hide either their curiosity or their desire.

Embarrassed by her behaviour, unwilling to ruin this, too, she began to speak. "I—I want to tell you something. To explain." Her voice was stripped of all feeling. "I had an accident. In Kosovo. I—was—running—from—something—and I was hit by a vehicle. They patched me up but, well, I haven't really been able to, you know, be with anyone, ever since." Explanations began to form in her mind, but she pressed her lips tightly shut to prevent them from saying more.

"I'm sorry," Alan told her, inadequately. "I didn't know."

"I—I don't want this to change anything, Alan. Please. I just want us to carry on as we are. Good friends."

He looked away.

"I mean it, Alan," Charlie insisted. "Your friendship means more to me than you will ever know. I—I don't make friends very easily anymore. Please, can't we just sit down and finish our supper and pretend that nothing happened?"

He sighed, then shook his head. "Maybe I should just go. I think I've lost my appetite. I'll see you soon, okay?"

Charlie stood stock-still, staring at the space he'd just inhabited in her kitchen, waiting for the sense of him to pass. The second she heard the latch on the garden gate click back into its well-oiled haven, her knees buckled from under her and she folded into a chair, blood seeping back into her face at last.

14

OVERWHELMED BY TIREDNESS, Charlie locked and bolted the front door, abandoned the disordered kitchen, climbed the stairs to her bedroom, and flung herself across the bed.

Safe.

Just her. Alone.

Or so she thought.

The creak of the cellar door opening inside her brain fires searing electrical impulses along every nerve ending in her body. Her eyes roll from left to right in their sockets, restless under their lids.

There they are, the murderous brutes, peering into the Rajak cellar, laughing as their flashlights arc wildly around the space her mind refuses to abandon. A chill grips her heart as she bears reluctant witness yet again to her worst nightmare.

She hears the first dusty boot lower itself onto the top step. She shrinks into her corner, cowering into the cobwebs and sacking, hoping beyond hope that she hasn't been seen.

The dog across the room growls a warning at the intruders. There is a sharp yap from one of her pups. A burst of automatic gunfire silences the poor animal. Orange-white flashes filling the room with noise and light and the pungent stink of cordite. Whimpering cries ring out from the surviving pups. One of the women loses control of her bowels.

The first boot is swiftly followed by another, and still more step menacingly down into the darkness, bringing terror and evil and madness. As Charlie's cellar-mates—even the children—are dragged one by one, wailing, into the dusk towards the woods, she knows, with an astonishing clarity of mind, what is to come.

Rigid with fear, a helpless witness to this heinous atrocity, she knows that when the screaming stops and the torch beams return, it will be her turn.

An image of Nick storms her paralysed brain—their final, doomed attempts to make love after her return from Rajak and the terrors it held. His wish to soothe her with his kisses and bring her pleasure without fear or pain. But Nick's anger was still there, stronger still, and after Rajak, it petrified her.

SEEKING COMFORT THE only way she knew how, the taste of Alan still on her lips, Charlie stood under the shower, inhaling aromatic oils and watching the soapy water cascade down her body.

Spreading the fingers of her right hand into a fan, she clenched her jaw and forced them to seek the angry V-shaped scar that ravaged her lower stomach. Her fingertips traced a familiar path along other, equally vivid scars, cross-hatched with stitch marks like narrow-gauge railway tracks which led to branch lines of hidden rods and pinions. This was all she had left to show for her time in Rajak, this violation of her pelvis and lower torso, a complex map of injury to flesh and bone. But what of the deeper scars? The ones that still ravaged her brain? When would they start to heal?

Emerging from the shower, she pulled on an oversized T-shirt and wandered in bewilderment around her cottage, her fingers searching for traces of where Alan had been. He was probably halfway to London by now, fleeing the madness he'd seen in her eyes, but his essence remained. There, on the cushions of the sofa, she could still make out the soft indentation of his body. Across the creased tablecloth, she could see where he'd flung his linen napkin. The smell of him still clung to it.

At the kitchen table and on the work surface were the remnants of the food they'd begun to share. Parmesan cheese slumped sweatily in its greaseproof paper. A half-sliced granary loaf. An open bottle of wine and their champagne glasses. She reached for his and pressed her lips to where his had been.

What was it Lori Hunter had said? Beware. Of yourself. For the first time, she felt she truly understood the power Alan could hold over women. And it terrified her.

Pulling on jeans and piling her hair on top of her head, she set about restoring order to her life, stuffing bottles and rubbish into bin liners, scrubbing the kitchen floor, tackling the washing-up, and sweeping the grate. Only when every window was transparently clean, each work surface spotless, and everything hard and gleaming again, did she pause. Taking the twisting oak staircase two steps at a time, she grabbed a chunky knit sweater, released her hair from its clasp, and rushed from Rhubarb Cottage, slamming the front door behind her.

Within minutes, she was striding purposefully towards the sand and shingle, the wind catching her hair, the evening sun painting everything golden. Blythcove. She remembered the first time she'd found it on the Ordnance Survey map, her finger traversing the swirling contours that marched across the folded creases of paper. A dead-end between such ancient-sounding places as Benacre and Easton Bavents, with roads called Cut Throat Lane and Black Walk, it had once been an important medieval fishing village, with one of Suffolk's finest churches. All that was left after centuries of being swallowed by the ravenous sea were a handful of cottages like hers, a sixteenth-century farm, a Georgian rectory, and the ruins of the church itself. When Charlie moved into Rhubarb Cottage, she became the twelfth person living in the parish, described in one local guidebook as "*a lonely place, on the way to and from nowhere.*" Perfect.

The village itself had been claimed by the North Sea in the seventeenth century, and the original church—one of three in a triangle of impressive coastal churches, the others being at Blythburgh and Southwold—was dismantled. But the church's massive tower had been preserved as an important landmark for ships at sea. It was in the reign of Charles II that the present thatched church of St Andrew's was built within the melancholy shell of its predecessor, its high stone arches a home for all manner of seabirds. Within its flinty outer walls, ancient tombstones bore testament to such resonant old Suffolk names as Tink, Spoor, Pepper, Hilleary, Muttit, and Blowers. At all times of the day St Andrew's looked magnificent, but it was at sunset, with the light low on the stone walls and the shadows slanting long behind it, that Charlie never tired of looking at it.

Just a few hundred yards beyond the church and her cottage, the narrow tarmac lane known as Long Row came to an abrupt end, eighty feet above the beach on a crumbling yellow cliff. Standing on the cliff edge, imagining the ancient fishing village the road once led to, Charlie breathed in the sea air. Gnawed incessantly by the encroaching waters, the remaining cliffs were peppered with rabbit burrows now used by sand martins and topped with gnarled ash trees, their twisted roots naked and exposed. More venerable examples lay bleached on the sand, like the polished white bones of dinosaurs. Charlie liked to sit astride them, watercolour pad in hand, sketching their contorted limbs as the seabirds wheeled and circled overhead. Contorted limbs. She shook her head to erase the image that unfurled like a screen in her memory. Gassed Kurds in Iraq, their arms outstretched, fingers stabbing accusingly at the sky.

"Stop!" she shouted in a cry that died somewhere up with the seagulls, and the image faded.

Pebbles. She'd look for pebbles. The distinctive ones with a hole through them. A weak spot weakened further by the power of the sea, hollowed out until it was big enough to see daylight through. Hag stones, the locals called them. They were few and far between, but more common on this coast than almost anywhere else in Britain. Collect enough and string them up on a piece of twine. Hang them above your bed, or in your windows and doorways, and they'll keep away evil spirits. Charlie had one hanging at every aperture of her cottage.

When she'd first started searching for them, they had been physical therapy. Her limbs stiff, her face grey, her body complained bitterly each time she bent to pick one up. With each pebble, the bending became easier and she was eventually able to discard her stick. Each hag stone she collected represented a stage in her recovery, and those she hadn't strung up at the windows lay like old friends in crude earthenware bowls around her cottage.

Picking her way down a footpath through the ferns to the beach, she followed the straggling line of sea wrack and driftwood that last night's tide had hurled to the shore, and found a pebble at last. Reaching for it, she turned it over in her palm, loving the way the tiny hole at its core had been smoothed by time and the passage of waves. She breathed in the traces of seaweed and salt that still clung to it, smells that made her long for fresh oysters and chilled white wine.

Out at sea, the muddy grey water heaved and swelled, its spent waves hissing into the shingle. A curlew threw out its warbling call on the nearby reed marshes; an oystercatcher dabbed and pecked at the worm casts on the sand. It was sunset before she turned back to the cottage, the late amber light etching shadows across the earth. The autumn colours of the trees in her cottage garden glowed in the sun's measured track.

A glass of something cold and fizzy, she decided. Prosecco, from Italy. Then she'd sit at her computer and write. Write for all she was worth. Turner. His papers. Whatman. Ruskin. She mustn't lose sight of her project. Mustn't let this temporary glitch blind her. Her work had always saved her in the past—from her parents' inadequacies, from her grandfather's death, and from all she had experienced as a journalist. It would do so again.

Slipping the hag stone into her pocket, she headed back, leaving footprints in the wet sand.

SHE OPENED HER notebook and started to read as the bubbles in her glass popped. The disturbing story of Turner's mother, Mary Marshall, pulled at the core of her.

Charlie tried to imagine what it must have been like for Mary, married late, a mother of two small children in her mid-forties, to lose her beloved youngest, Mary Ann, when the girl was four. Childhood mortality had been far more common in Britain, as it was in so many of the third-world countries Charlie had more recently had the misfortune of visiting. Poverty and death were comfortable bedfellows. But grief at the loss of a child was surely universal. Poor Mary Turner never recovered.

Like Sarah Matheson, Charlie remembered ruefully, her thoughts tugging her back to Angela. Sarah's loss was even more complete. First her daughter and then her husband. A cruel double blow.

Instead of finding solace in the life of her surviving child, Mary so frightened her young son with her grief-stricken rages that he was sent away from her, first to relatives in west London and then to the seaside town of Margate.

"I believed I must have been somehow to blame for my mother's illness," Charlie had a melancholy young Turner write in his diary. *"Why else would I have been so cruelly banished?"* Although, the artist would later admit, the banishment became a blessing, as the keen student of light and shadow reveled in the watery landscapes of the quintessential English resort.

By the time he returned home to London, however, his mother had completely vanished from his life. Diagnosed as an incurable schizophrenic, Mary Turner had been sent to the Bethlem Hospital for Lunaticks in Moorfields, better known to all as Bedlam.

Entry to Bedlam was usually irreversible, and from the day she was admitted, Mary never saw her family again. A year after her admission, she'd been transferred to the Incurable Department, where primitive treatment included chains, cages, beatings, bloodlettings, and straitjackets. The temperatures inside the asylum plummeted so low in the winter that many inmates lost fingers and toes to frostbite.

Mary Turner died in Bedlam in April 1804, just as her celebrated son was preparing to open his first gallery. There is no record that he ever visited her, or even mentioned her in conversation to friends and associates. Turner, Charlie felt, seemed to have been both ashamed and afraid of his mother. His greatest fear, common at that time of medical ignorance, was that her madness would be infectious or hereditary.

"Oh, what is this lunacy that resides deep within us all," she had him rage one sleepless dawn, *"waiting to be spawned by some unhappy vagary of fate?"*

Throwing himself into his work, Turner vented his deep emotional turmoil in the swirling vortices of colours and textures in his paintings. The paper he so carefully selected and then brutalised, the speed and ferocity with which he worked, all indicated, Charlie felt certain, terrible inner torment. His pain helped make him the phenomenal artistic force that he became.

Turner's relationship with women throughout the rest of his life seemed shaped and stunted by his sense of loss. He never married. He had relationships only with widows, who acted as mother-substitutes. He'd lost his sister when he was eight years old, and then he'd lost his mother.

In many respects, it seemed to Charlie, he never got over either loss.

15

*P*AIN. LOSS. BEDLAM. She thought she'd been there two years ago, but how little she knew. She could only begin to imagine what life must have been like for Mary Turner, confined within the grim stone walls of that hideous madhouse. Charlie's own "madness" had been treated with a comfortable private room in a sumptuous clinic, fresh flowers, everything she could possibly need. The demons that had haunted both her and the tortured Mary Turner may have been similar, but her care couldn't have been more different.

Even when she'd awoken angry and disappointed from what she'd believed to her last, desperate act, her head thumping from the cocktail of pills she'd forced down her throat, she'd been surrounded by those determined to see her healed and well again.

Poor Angela Matheson had also known the intoxicating allure of madness and the pure absolution of responsibility that accompanies it.

Long before she stepped to her own personal brink, Charlie knew how it felt to look death in the face and defy her fear. She'd done that a dozen times in war zones, as shells fell around her and the earth erupted in screaming pillars of sand and rock. Most of all, she'd known it in Rajak.

Even as a young reporter covering inquests, she'd wondered at the twists of fate that saved one life while remorselessly taking another. The commuter who overslept and missed his doomed train; the mother who did the school run as a favour to a friend only to be struck by a bus; the murdered teenager whose only mistake was to turn back to use the lavatory at the nightclub.

In her own strange way, Charlie grew quite accustomed to death. There was something alluring about its finality. Children murdered in their beds by flying shrapnel remained forever young. Colleagues killed in the line of duty were preserved in time, at the pinnacle of their careers. Slaughtered on the fields of war, such reporters would never face decline and decay; not for them the humiliating erosion of stardom, as younger rivals clawed their way up the ranks.

Given her almost daily diet, Charlie came to accept that death was something to be expected. On each breath, it could come anytime. When others railed bitterly, she kept her counsel. She knew that it was simply the victims' turn. They hadn't been in the wrong place at the wrong time, but in exactly the *right* place. The answer to the question "Why me?" is "Why not me?" All one could hope for was not to die alone.

Many thought her cynical, even her friend Carrie, who simply couldn't bring herself to share Charlie's morbid fascination with the final seconds of life. Increasingly, as Carrie recorded through her lens what man was capable of doing to his fellow man, the photographer was overcome by the power of her witnessing and unable to function under its weight. Charlie knew Carrie wondered why she didn't feel the same.

The sharp contrasts of their extraordinary lives only made matters worse. One minute they'd be on the road, living in desperate conditions, where nothing made sense. The next they'd be back home, making fumbling attempts at normality while still raw from exposure to the insanity of the rest of the world.

Carrie returned to a house empty by choice, where she could wade through such days of transition alone. For Charlie, however, it was different. Within a short time of unpacking her rucksack, she'd have to co-host some dinner party Nick had unwisely arranged in her honour. The guests were people of influence, who Nick hoped would support his ambition to be editor. Charlie, fresh from a war zone, was his secret weapon.

Her air of danger and relevance impressed even the most recalcitrant backer.

What he failed to notice was that she felt increasingly unable to breathe the air of those Nick courted. Unable to register the alterations in her surroundings, she'd only half listen to the conversations swirling around her of nannies or tuition fees or the problems of parking in London.

Inevitably, some bright spark would turn to her and ask: "So, Charlie, what was it like out there?" Her mind would bulge with the memories and, under the table, she'd secretly press the prongs of her fork into her thigh to anchor herself to reality. Only once did she crack.

"Well, Jill," she'd begun drunkenly, laughing, as their guests turned to listen. "I contracted dysentery, was shot at daily, and watched the severed leg of one of my interpreters fly past me when he stepped on a land mine. Could you pass the cheese?"

The laughter had died on her lips.

After that unfortunate evening, she resolved to hold her tongue, for Nick's sake if not her own. Instead, when the question next came, yanking on the chain of her self-control, she poured herself a glass of wine with an impressively steady hand, reeled off manageable sound bites about how fascinating it had all been, glossed over the gory bits, and changed the subject as swiftly as possible. She soon became uncannily good at deflection.

It was only when the guests had gone and the candles were sputtering that Nick would sit her down in front of the dying embers of the fire. "Sorry," he'd say, miserably. "I thought it'd do you good to see ordinary people. But I was wrong, wasn't I?"

Drunk and impossibly tired, she'd stare into the flames, feeling a tic pulse beneath her eye. "Ordinary," she'd repeat, wondering if she even knew what that meant anymore. Her tongue felt swollen and heavy in her mouth.

Looking into Nick's eyes, she knew exactly what he wanted. To fuck her there and then, like they used to. Her months away had always made the sex more interesting. Now things were different. Whereas previously she didn't seem to mind what he did to her, now she was slowly withdrawing into the secret world only she inhabited.

Trouble was, although he had some idea what she'd been up against—what sent her to that private refuge—he didn't know the full story. Few did. Sitting at his desk in his office, watching report after report scroll up on his computer screen, or enduring countless news bulletins blaring out from the newsroom television set about how "hell was breaking out," simply wasn't the same as being there.

Once when Charlie returned to him, her eyes bleak, she showed him the crumpled piece of paper she'd folded into the bottom of her shoe when she believed she'd never see him again. *"Nick, I love you and I'm so terribly sorry,"* it said. *"All my everythings, Charlie xx"*

She told him what had happened only reluctantly. The helicopter she'd been traveling in had been forced down into an area controlled by rebel forces. She and a cameraman found themselves sharing a ditch as the gunfire drew closer. Remembering with a shudder what she'd seen the rebels do to those they believed to be allied to government forces, she had turned to her companion and begged, "Kill me before they reach me, if it comes to that, okay?"

The craggy-faced veteran of a dozen wars considered her request for a moment, a hand-rolled cigarette stuck to his bottom lip, one eye narrowed against the smoke. Then, mutely, he nodded his agreement. Charlie slumped back, trying hard to banish the thought of his nicotine-stained fingers sawing a knife through her windpipe, her essence pumping into the sand. Slipping in a note to Nick before tying up her bootlaces so tight that the leather pinched her skin, she waited.

"I'm so glad I've got you back," Nick told her, when a miracle had plucked her from the jaws of death once more. He kissed her on the lips and buried his face in her hair. Every muscle in her body tensed until he released her and allowed her to slip quietly up to bed. By the time he joined her, she pretended to be asleep. She felt him, silent, angry, as he slid in behind her, his fist curled against the warmth of her back.

On dutiful visits to her parents, she'd flee both them and Nick, hurrying to the cemetery with the dog at her side. Her grandfather had known the sweet stench of death that clings to the mucous membranes and sticks in the back of the throat. Granddad had been to war; at least he understood.

She and Nick both knew it wouldn't be long before the call would come, usually in the early hours of the morning, from some hapless night reporter on the foreign desk, interrupting her hard-earned leave.

"Hi, Charlie. It's the Foreign Desk. Sorry to wake you, but the editor asked me to call. There's been another wave of ethnic cleansing in the Balkans. He wants you to catch the first available flight out."

Kosovo looked much like Bosnia, which looked the same as Croatia, which bore uncanny similarities to Iraq. Open graves and bloated bodies mirrored those Charlie had seen in places she could no longer even recall. Her work became sloppy and she began missing deadlines and confusing names. One grisly adjective after another rioted in her head.

Nick became increasingly impatient for her to fly home. She could hear it in his voice. Journalists and photographers were being shot at almost daily; he and Charlie both knew she was running out of lives. At Carrie's suggestion, he'd booked a couple of weeks in a remote cottage on a Hebridean island, off the northwest coast of Scotland. No fax, no phone, just him and Charlie. He told her he'd planned everything from the first walk on the white sand beaches to the last bottle of wine by a fragrant peat fire. Nobody would bother them there, he vowed. She knew what that meant, that no one would be able to interfere, to distract him from the sort of reunion he had in mind. His anger and resentment blistering beneath the surface, he was probably aroused just by the thought of what he'd like to do to Charlie once he had her completely to himself.

"This'll be just what we need," he told her when she rang on the satellite phone from Banja Luka. "Some time on our own, away from everything."

"Yes," she replied, brittlely. "Away from everything."

Later, she found out that when he'd turned on the breakfast news the following morning and heard of the latest push against the Muslims, he'd hurled his bowl of cereal so viciously across the room that it smashed against the wall. He knew then he'd lost her.

"Fuck Slobodan Milosevic!" he shouted, before slumping to the table in a crumpled heap of misery. "And fuck Charlie!"

SHE WAS ALREADY damaged goods, but it was the events in that little red-roofed town called Rajak a few weeks later that finally broke Charlie. And not just physically. Her mind, already on overload, imploded. Death, her most familiar companion, never seemed more alluring.

"Genuine cases of suicide always take their shoes off," a coroner's officer once told Charlie, in her earlier, simpler life. "It's one of the ways we can tell if someone's topped themselves or not. Those who've been murdered or accidentally killed never do."

In the bedroom of that opulent clinic they sent her to after Rajak, she weighed everything up evenly in her mind, and came to a careful conclusion. Removing her shoes, Charlie placed them neatly by the side of the bed. She'd never felt calmer. There was an unexpected, blissful elation to wrenching back power.

"Take control," the doctors had been telling her for weeks. "Harness your experiences, learn from them." They were right. Her life had been hurtling headlong off its axis for years. Now she was simply putting an end to its anarchical course.

She left no note. Although she'd fingered a piece of beautiful Fabriano notepaper for almost an hour, her fountain pen poised above it searching for the right words, in the end she'd left the page untouched on the table by her bed. The shoes would tell the coroner what he needed to know. Nick would understand. And anyway, he already had the only note he needed, in his silver box at home. It was written in a parallel universe maybe, but it carried the same intent:

"Nick, I love you and I'm so terribly sorry. All my everythings, Charlie xx"

Half smiling, she'd lain down on the bed and waited for the darkness she knew would come.

16

"A POT OF EARL Grey, please," Charlie asked the waitress as she sank gratefully into a wooden chair with her carrier bags. Strong, hot tea was what was needed to distract her, she'd decided, and, after a day traipsing through Norwich doing some early Christmas shopping to avoid the crowds, she'd slipped into a corner teashop along a cobbled back-street. Spotting plates of buttered scones on the adjacent table, she remembered that she hadn't eaten all day and allowed herself the possibility of a piece of toast.

Granddad loved his afternoon teas. He'd loved to take her to Tunbridge Wells for what he described as the best fruitcake in the country. Served in an elegant Victorian hotel while a string quartet played in the corner and silver-haired couples glided expertly around the floor, the thick slices of cake tasted to Charlie like manna from Heaven.

She loved watching the old people dance. Years fell from them as they whirled their partners against a backdrop of date palms planted into Edwardian china pots. Hunched torsos were miraculously straightened, clumsy feet in ugly shoes became elegant in motion, and gnarled hands clasped each other with true grace.

When he'd eaten his cake, Granddad would stand and bow and hold out his hand, before leading a delighted young Charlie onto the polished dance floor. Placing each foot lightly on his shiny size ten shoes, she'd cling to the back of his thighs, feeling the strong muscles through the twill, and laugh, head thrown back in delight, as he whirled her around and around.

Their secret tea dances spanned her childhood and she cherished them long beyond the days when she was small enough to stand on his feet. The hotel in Tunbridge Wells became one of their special places, somewhere they could escape from the increasingly stifling atmosphere at home. Sitting on the terrace of that same hotel with him only a few months before he died, she'd watched him wield the teapot and offer up a platter of some indulgence or other, annoyed to notice some of her mother's mannerisms in his careful ritual.

Sipping from her cup of fragrant Earl Grey, she'd listened to the silence that the throat cancer had forced upon him. His clothes bunched around him, cruelly accentuating his shrinkage. But his eyes—the green eyes that had bypassed her mother's generation and come straight to her—hadn't changed. One glance spoke volumes and she knew that, on this occasion, he'd brought her here to reprimand her.

"But Mum's driving me crazy with all her rules and regulations," Charlie had complained, hating the whine in her voice. "I'm almost eighteen. I should be allowed to stay out till midnight if my friends can!"

Granddad nodded to show he understood her frustration.

"I can't wait to get away," she continued, cramming half a doughnut into her mouth. Sugar cascaded down her black T-shirt and she brushed it off angrily. "Fiona didn't hang around after she finished college and I certainly don't intend to."

She looked up, suddenly smitten with guilt.

"Will you be all right when I'm gone?" she asked, reaching out to squeeze his skeletal hand. The assumption that he'd be alone, despite the presence of her parents under the same roof, was completely understood.

He smiled that smile that lit his eyes and lifted his craggy face.

"But I guess it might make it a bit easier on you if I tried a bit harder with Mum until I go?" Charlie asked, still holding his hand.

Her grandfather's left eyebrow arched.

"All right, Granddad," she acceded. "I promise I'll try. But don't blame me if it doesn't work."

He smiled his relief but, just for an instant, she caught a glimpse of a sorrow so intense it stunned her.

"I wish you could escape, too," Charlie sighed. She wasn't sure, but she thought she saw a glint of something misty in his eyes.

AFTER HER SOLITARY tea in Norwich, Charlie left the buttered toast she'd scarcely touched on her plate and stepped out into the cool autumnal air. Guilty at her memories, she finished her shopping quickly, settling on some gardenia perfume and a beautiful grey silk scarf speckled with brightly coloured butterflies for her mother. For her father, she bought the new encyclopaedia from the Royal Horticultural Society.

Treating herself to a large glass vase for the latest bouquet of sunflowers Alan had sent, which lay waiting in the sink at Rhubarb Cottage, she felt childishly happy at the thought of arranging them once she got home. It had been over a week since she'd seen Alan, ten whole days since he'd tried to kiss her. He'd left for Italy shortly afterwards, claiming a need to work, and—ashamed of her reaction—she was grateful to him for putting some distance between them.

"You're welcome to visit me here anytime, Charlie," the short note that arrived with the flowers had said. *"You'll have your own room, and the weather is idyllic at this time of year. We could work together on the book while I paint. No strings. Think about it. A."*

She was flattered by his offer and relieved that he wasn't closing the door on their collaboration, but she couldn't yet force herself to think about their next encounter. Hastily penning a reply, she wrote: *"Thank you for the sunflowers and the kind invitation. Thanks, too, for your understanding. Like the flowers, I may, too, turn to the sun one day. Charlie."*

Her mind now with him in Italy, she wandered in and out of a few more shops, humming softly to herself. It was some tune of Alan's that was always playing when he painted. Purcell, she realised, and stopped humming. She fingered ridiculously expensive shoes, tried on some thick winter coats with deep fake-fur collars, and bought some gilded Christmas cards with camels on them that reminded her of the Middle East.

Chancing upon an old-fashioned art shop down a narrow side street, she impulsively stepped in through its low doorway and breathed in its distinctive smell. Alan again. Lingering in her nostrils and her imagination. She squeezed her way past an unsteady pile of cardboard boxes, a recent delivery, and began searching through the paper selection. Picking up a book of modern watercolour paper with the name Whatman emblazoned across it, she flinched and held a piece up to the window, to better examine the mottled effect of the dried cotton pulp within it.

Studying a corner, Charlie could see the tiny fibres beneath the chemically sized surface, their hairlike fragments causing the distinctive roughness of a frayed edge. But there was no comparison to the Whatman's paper Alan had shown her. This was a shabby cousin, barely worthy of the mill's illustrious name. Like Alan, she found herself mourning the romance of a bygone age and the disappearance of the ancient skills, along with its magical names. No longer did one speak of demy, atlas, crown, elephant, emperor, folio, foolscap, and post. No more reams or quires either, only numbers of sheets or metric weights per ream.

Paper. How widely it was taken for granted. She'd spent most of her life writing articles published on flimsy newsprint for others to read or to ignore. How terribly important those reports had seemed to her at the time; how much she'd risked for the chance to chronicle an event for all posterity. Now those articles were yellowing deep in the bowels of a cuttings library, tomorrow's recycled pulp, nothing more. The writing she did now must be different. Bound in a book. Meaningful. Enduring. Her legacy.

Looking out of the window, her mind elsewhere, her eyes slowly focused on a discreet brass plaque on the opposite side of the street. *The Waller Clinic*. Where had she heard that name before? Her mind jolted so suddenly, she dropped the paper in her hand.

The Waller Clinic. The place where Angela Matheson had taken her own life. Alan's daughter. Of course.

Staring up at the five-storey Georgian townhouse behind whose elegant façade lived all manner of sad souls, Charlie conjured up the image of the striking young blonde whose photograph she had pinned to the corkboard on her wall.

"Royal artist's daughter kills herself," the headlines had screamed.

Somewhere deep inside her head, Angela was still calling. Before Charlie knew it, she found herself opening the art shop door, its bell tinkling, and walking straight across the street towards the place where Alan's daughter had died.

Crêpe

A fine, often gauzelike fabric

with a wrinkled surface; thin crinkled paper

17

When Carrie rang to invite herself to stay for a few days, Charlie eagerly embraced the chance to spend some time with her closest friend. They arranged to meet at Norwich Station as soon as Carrie's train arrived from Manchester.

"Hiya!" Charlie said, hugging her friend. "Great to see you."

"And you." Carrie kissed her cold cheek. "You look fantastic."

"Thanks."

"No, really! Let me look at you. Something must have happened, Charlie. You look like the girl I used to know."

Charlie bowed her head, feeling the glow from the pink T-shirt under her jacket adding to the colour in her cheeks. "Come on, you must be starving. Let's find some lunch. I know a great tapas bar just around the corner."

Taking a seat at one of the empty tables outside, Charlie signaled the waiter and asked for a bottle of Rioja and two menus.

"Don't you want to go in?" Carrie asked, peering longingly at the cosy interior. "It is almost winter, you know." They were the only ones braving the elements.

"No," Charlie said, too quickly. Looking up, she added softly: "It's smoky inside."

"Oh, okay."

"So, how are you?"

"Terrific," Carrie replied, drawing her coat around her. "Work's keeping me out of mischief, sadly. There never seems to be any shortage of drug addicts, broken families, orphans, and delinquents to while away the time I should really be spending looking for a new boyfriend."

"Still haven't found Mr Right, then?"

"Not yet, but there's always hope. In the meantime, it's nose to the grindstone."

"I still find it a bit weird to think of you doing social work. You'll always be a photographer, to my mind, and a bloody good one, at that. But I'm glad if you've found your niche. Lord knows, I couldn't do it. I'm far too selfish."

Carrie laughed. "I'll take that as a compliment. Seriously, though, despite all the red tape and the abuse and the crap I put up with on a daily basis, there are moments when I really feel like I'm making a difference— the abused teenager who finally opens up to me, the mother who agrees to get counseling for her troubled son. Such moments, which may be pivotal in these people's lives, are what keep me going."

Their wine arrived and she sipped at her glass, before placing it carefully on the table and taking a deep breath. Reaching into her bag, she pulled out a card in a sealed blue envelope. "Before I forget..."

"What's this?" Charlie asked, taking it from her.

"It's from Nick. It arrived in the mail a few days ago. He called and asked me to pass it on when I saw you."

Charlie stared at her friend for a moment before sliding her finger under the edge of the flap and pulling out a card. The picture on the front was of a Labrador puppy, looking reproachfully over his left shoulder, his tail between his legs. Inside, Nick had written just one word. *Sorry.*

Charlie bowed her head and gulped back the unpalatable memory of the note of apology she had once written to him. "What's this for?"

"Upsetting you on the phone a few weeks ago, apparently. He says you've been avoiding him ever since. He also said to tell you that you were right and it's none of his business, whatever that means."

Charlie smiled wanly. "Don't look so worried. I won't shoot the messenger. I guess he thought I wouldn't open anything if he sent it directly to me." She paused. "What Nick doesn't understand is that I'm big enough to make my own mistakes."

"Have you made a mistake, then?"

"No. Not yet."

She fell silent as the waiter returned to take their orders. Carrie leaned forward. "Is everything okay?" she asked.

"Yes, fine."

"How's the book?"

"Different. Challenging." Charlie couldn't hide her enthusiasm. "There's so much to be discovered about paper and Turner and this extraordinary relationship between the two. I'm learning something new every day. If history had been like this in school, I'd have paid much more attention."

"Sounds intriguing."

"It's fascinating. Do you remember that amazing souk we found in Baghdad? Where those Arab craftsmen made each sheet of paper before binding them with vellum and embossing the covers with gold leaf? And how you had to leave me there in the end because two hours just wasn't long enough for me? Well, that's what I feel like about this project. The time I have simply isn't enough."

"I'm really pleased it's working out. It must be so satisfying writing about something that's always interested you."

"It is."

The waiter arrived with their food and they unfurled their cutlery from their napkins. "How's everything else?" Carrie asked.

"Great."

"Great is good. Great is better than good. Is there anything I should know?"

Charlie almost laughed. "You've already admitted you've spoken to Nick, Carrie," she scolded. "You don't have to pretend he hasn't filled you in on my professional relationship with Sir Alan Matheson."

"Well, Nick has rung a few times, but only because he's worried about you. And, by the way, he seems to think there's a lot more than 'a professional relationship' going on!"

Ignoring her salad, Charlie pulled out a pen and began a small circular doodle in the corner of the crossword she'd half finished at the station before Carrie arrived. "Well, that's all it is, so there's no need for Nick, or you, to worry. I'm not about to do anything stupid."

"Why would having a relationship be stupid?"

"Because—well, it's complicated, but it just would be," Charlie replied, drawing ever increasing circles. "As I'm sure Nick probably mentioned, Alan's a lot older than me and to his mind probably totally unsuitable. You need hardly have bothered to ask, really."

"Okay," Carrie began warily, "what's the real problem, Charlie? Nick and I often chat, you know that. Why are you so upset? Listen—I've known you both a very long time, so don't think I believe everything he says. Now, please—tell me more about Alan. What's he really like?"

As Charlie picked at her plate of food, she gave Carrie a brief history of the artist, touching only lightly on the tragedy of Angela's life and his two ex-wives. Carrie listened in silence.

"And do you like him?" she asked bluntly, when Charlie had finished.

"Yes," Charlie replied, meeting her friend's steady gaze. "I like him a lot. He's fantastically talented and incredibly bright. He's kind and supportive and I couldn't possibly have got this far on my book without him. But that's all there is to it. Sorry to disappoint you and Nick, but there's nothing more to it than that."

Carrie spoke carefully. "Well, Alan sounds interesting, to say the least. And so what if he has some history? Other people's suffering has always been a bit of an attraction for you."

"Has it?"

"You know it has, Charlie."

"Oh God, am I really that screwed up?"

"You can be. And as for Nick, let's face it, he'd find it hard to accept you spending time with anyone else but him."

"Nick forgets he's not my husband anymore."

"Well, strictly speaking, he is," Carrie reminded her friend gently.

"You never did get that divorce, remember? So you can't really blame him for being confused."

"Poor Nick," Charlie replied, fidgeting in her seat.

"Nick will be all right; I'll make sure of that. And anyway, he's got Miranda now." She picked up her fork, then said, "I think his main concern is that this connection with Angela might bring on some sort of relapse in you."

"Why would it?"

"Think about it, Charlie. The first man in years you've chosen to spend time with turns out to be carrying some pretty heavy emotional baggage, which happens to include a daughter who killed herself. The question is, was that what drew you to him in the first place?"

"No! We met purely by chance and started talking about the book. It was only later that I found out about Angela. I was as shocked as Nick, but then I was sort of intrigued. . . ." She stopped abruptly.

"I'm sorry, Charlie. Listen, forget I said anything. It's none of my business."

"It *is* your business, Carrie. Everything that happens in my life is your business. Without the love and support of you and Nick over the last few years I wouldn't even be here right now. And, if you must know, I do sometimes wonder what I'm doing."

"What do you mean?"

"Well, look at me. You're right. I'm writing a book, essentially for my dead grandfather, about a man who died a hundred and fifty years ago after spending much of his life in torment. I'm working alongside a man whose life has surely been shaped by madness and suicide. I'm on the run from my past and yet I'm somehow still locked into it. None of this was anything I planned; it just happened, but now I feel like I'm being sucked into some sort of vortex."

"It doesn't have to be like that, honey. You can walk away from all of it. Start again."

"No," Charlie said, sharply. "I know this might sound crazy, but this feels like a test I have to pass. Life will always throw up links to my past if I look for them. If it wasn't Alan and Turner, it would have been something else. Trust me. I feel like I need to stop running away. I like Alan, I really do. God knows I might even take a gamble with him one day. So I have to face this or I'll never do that, or come to terms with everything that's happened—my failed marriage, even my own spell of madness. Am I making any sense?"

"I think so."

"I have to take control again, Carrie. In fact, I've already begun. I'm going to find out the hard facts so that I can prove to myself and everyone else that there is nothing sinister lurking around the corner, waiting for me."

"What do you mean you've already started?"

"Since the day I found out about Angela, I've never stopped thinking about her. Then, two days ago I found myself in Norwich standing outside the clinic where she committed suicide."

"Wait. What? How? My God, what did you do?"

"I went in."

"Charlie!"

"It was okay. I mean—oh, I don't know what I mean. Those places are all pretty much the same, aren't they? You've seen one loony bin, you've seen them all."

"Did you find anything out?"

"Yes and no. The receptionist was wary of me at first and I don't blame her. I just made some general enquiries about the clinic and the facilities it offered and asked if I could see one of the rooms."

"What reason did you give?"

Charlie smiled mischievously. "I told her my best friend was an alcoholic."

"Cheers." Carrie raised her glass to her lips and took a large gulp.

"One of the nurses gave me a guided tour. We got chatting. I asked her if she remembered a patient called Angela Matheson."

"Did she?"

"Yes."

"What did she say?" Carrie urged.

"That's just it," Charlie said, shaking her head at the memory. "She said something I still can't quite understand. I told her I was a friend of the Matheson family and that they had recommended the clinic, despite what happened to Angela."

"Well?"

"This woman stopped dead in her tracks and laughed in my face. '*Despite* what happened to Angela?' she said. 'I would have thought they'd have recommended us *because* of it.'"

"What do you think she meant?"

"I have absolutely no idea."

"So what did you do then?"

"Nothing, I just left. What else could I do?"

The two women sat in thoughtful silence for a few moments. Finally, Carrie said, "None of this is important, Charlie, not any of it, unless you think you and Alan might have some sort of future together. And from what you've said, you could."

"At the moment we only seem to have a past," Charlie replied, "my crazy past mostly, with a bit of his thrown in for good measure." Avoiding her friend's eyes, she added, "Right now, it's the present that matters, isn't it? I don't want to think beyond that."

"Well, then, what do you want from the present?"

"I'm not really sure I know," Charlie replied, but deep in her heart the more she thought about Alan, the more she spoke of him, she suddenly knew—more clearly than ever before—precisely what she wanted. And she knew exactly where to get it.

18

TRAVELING DOWN THROUGH Tuscany on the train from Florence, Charlie pressed her face to the window and marveled. Vast fields of browning sunflowers, their golden glory just a memory, filled the foreground. Cool, dark cypress trees punctuated the horizon like exclamation marks, each shadow the gnomon of a sundial on the undulating hills. Lush olive groves and vineyards provided the scorched earth with welcome splashes of green. It was a powerful, magical landscape. Hadn't Byron once written that he was "drunk and dazzled" by its beauty? How Charlie wished she'd brought her watercolours.

Turner had loved Italy. He'd painted it many times before he traveled there, his images of classical ruins inspired by Byron's poetry and his lifelong passion for Aeneas's heroic adventures. Perhaps because of the unusually close relationship he developed with his father in later life—the two men thrown together in the face of his mother's madness—he empathised greatly with the *Aeneid*'s themes of filial piety and longed for such grand adventures abroad. His first historical painting had been of Aeneas and the Sibyl at Lake Avernus. He'd gone on to paint Dido and Aeneas in a number of poses and settings.

The artist's first journey to what he called the "classic ground" of Rome, Naples, Florence, and Venice in 1819 was the start of a love affair that was to endure for the rest of his life. The sweeping landscapes entranced him, as did the southern light. Powerfully moved by its brightness, his work began to take on a new luminescence and become even more atmospheric; he layered pearly films of colour onto paper and canvas; many of his paintings were based entirely on the effects of light. Even his oils began to take on a more iridescent look, resembling the pure transparency of watercolour.

This wasn't Charlie's first visit to Italy—she and Nick had come here years before—but it was her first since she'd attempted to see life through Turner's eyes. No wonder the master and so many of his contemporaries had fallen under the spell of this place. No wonder Alan had a home here.

She had deliberately chosen to travel by train rather than plane to give herself time to compose her thoughts. It was while talking to Carrie about Alan that she'd finally realised how intensely she missed him. How she longed to talk to him about what she had written or learned that day, or to simply sit in silence watching him paint. Only when she was with Alan did her life seem to make any sense. This project of theirs had brought her the first joy she'd felt in years. She had fallen in love with the notion of watching it burgeon from a fledgling idea to a fully grown creature. This would be something permanent, something positive; a contribution she could make that would be enduring, unlike the transient despatches she'd filed from battlefields and war zones.

There was still much she needed to deal with about her feelings for Alan, and she knew that all too well, but for now she just wanted to be in his presence, to hear his voice and continue to blossom under his gentle care.

Alighting at Chiusi station, a few miles from the reedy shores of Lake Trasimeno, and resisting a porter's attempts to carry her case, Charlie showed a taxi driver a folded piece of paper with Alan's address scrawled across it. In her limited Italian, carefully rehearsed on the train, she asked him to take her there.

"Potrebbe mi portare a Porto, signore?"

The fare agreed, they set off in a rusty Fiat that showed remarkable agility for its age as it sped along the winding Umbrian lanes towards the little village of Porto. The picturesque hill towns and churches along the way were enchanting, as were the devotional shrines with their candle-lit Madonnas, and the peaceful *"città di morti"*—cities of the dead—their stacked stone tombs enclosed within high walls. But sitting in the back of the taxi, the sound of her heart beating in her ears as she drew closer and closer to Alan, Charlie barely noticed them.

She recognised his house instantly from the many paintings of it Alan had around his Suffolk home. Villa Girasole. House of Sunflowers. With its peeling ochre paintwork and green-shuttered windows, it was exactly as his canvasses had depicted it. She braced herself as the Fiat shot through the open wrought-iron gates and headed up the gravel drive, its tyres sending up clouds of white dust. Coming to a halt at the steps, which led to an ornately carved oak door, the driver got out and helped Charlie from the car.

"Grazie tante," she said, pressing a folded wad of Euros into his hand. As his car trundled back down the drive into the settling dust clouds, Charlie found herself trembling.

He was in his studio, a beautiful airy room with marble floors and a high ceiling adorned with faded eighteenth-century frescoes. Gilt ormolu furniture stood elegantly near the carved fireplace, and bolts of delicately embossed fabrics were stacked in a corner. Although Alan was surrounded by his paints and the familiar tools of his trade, there was a much more ordered, genteel feel to the room compared with his Suffolk studio.

He stood concentrating intently on the finishing touches to a small oil of an Italian peasant woman bent double, picking grapes. His hair glinted metallically against his skin, lightly tanned. Charlie felt a stirring deep within her.

Alan looked up. The sun shining through the generous windows seemed to leave him backlit, as if he were deliberately posing for a photograph of the great master at work in his Umbrian studio. When he saw her, his face changed instantly.

"Charlie!" he cried, hastily laying down his brush and wiping his hands on an old rag.

Charlie stood motionless in the doorway, unsure of what would follow. Part of her wanted to run away, to protect herself—and him?—from what now felt inevitable.

"What a surprise!" Taking her hand as if to kiss it, they were the last words he was able to speak before he found her mouth planted firmly on his.

Her action surprised her almost as much as it did him. But his lips felt so soft, and the scent of his skin was so heady that a long-forgotten wave of heat rippled through Charlie. When she was done, he drew away and placed his hands on either side of her face, to study her eyes.

Tentatively, she opened her mouth and allowed his thumb to slide along her bottom lip. Reaching up, she kissed him once more, tasting him, relishing the sensation and the intimacy.

"Alan, I—I ..."

His eyes were luminous. The grey had almost completely disappeared into the black. Smiling, he pulled away again and looked down at her, his hands still cradling her face. "My Charlie," he said, before reaching for her once more.

Something inside her urged him to continue, to allow herself to be loved again. She didn't want him to stop this time, she wanted him to cover her skin with kisses; she wanted what she'd really come for.

"Is this okay?" Alan asked, bending down to brush the nape of her neck with a tenderness she had almost forgotten.

"Yes," she murmured.

"And this?" His lips found hers.

She shivered as one of his hands slid from her neck to her breast. The other slipped up under her shirt and pressed itself into the soft indentation in the small of her back. Her heart fluttering in her chest like that of a tiny bird, she watched dispassionately as he opened the front of her shirt and unclipped her bra. She flinched only slightly as his hands cupped each breast, taking the weight of them, gently stimulating them with his fingertips. Paralysed, powerless, she didn't, couldn't pull away.

Pressing her eyes shut as he nuzzled softly at her neck, Charlie held herself quite rigid, waiting for the flashback to flood her brain, to ruin everything as it always did, but it didn't come. Something about the way

Alan held her so close to him allowed no room between them for the horrors of Rajak that had always previously intruded between her and Nick. That was then, she reminded herself. Long ago. This was now. Now things could be different.

Reaching for his mouth, she felt him respond. Her breathing ragged, she could sense desire she believed she'd lost long ago snaking insidiously through her. Her skin felt softer, looser somehow; warm from the inside out, as if soothing water were flowing all over her body. Staring intently into Alan's eyes, keeping him and the now focused in her mind, she didn't resist as he led her to a nearby sofa. Nor did she stop him when he lowered her gently onto it.

She wanted to say something, to cry out a warning as Alan slipped off her shirt and slid her trousers down over the sharp bones of her hips. But she seemed to have lost all power of speech. No words of warning came, no cry was emitted, and not even above the sound of waves crashing in her ears did she hear his small gasp when he came across her scar, and—with an almost morbid fascination—gradually exposed the rest.

Acutely aware of every blemish across her ravaged lower torso, mortified by their ugliness, Charlie held herself taut as Alan ran his fingers across their peculiar ridges and contours, each as familiar to her as her own face. Her mind was far away, lost, as she braced herself to go through something she never thought she'd be able to contemplate again. Surely now the flashback would come, to rescue her from this? Crying out with sorrow and relief as Alan's lips traced a line along the scar that ploughed the deepest furrow across her belly, she knew then that she couldn't be saved. Relenting at last, she raised her hips to him hungrily.

They made love for over an hour, neither one speaking. Both knew instinctively somehow that the sound of a human voice would have broken the spell that had allowed Charlie to finally surrender. The warm afternoon breeze smelling of fresh lavender billowed the muslin curtains at the window and caressed their flesh. Each time Charlie thought Alan was spent, he'd begin again, his appetite for her unsated.

It felt like coming home.

Afterwards, they lay still, his hands pinning hers, his breath hot against her throat. Squeezing her eyes shut against what she knew would come, Charlie bit her lip and tried to contain her tears. But they burst defiantly from the corners of her eyes, dripping silently down the side of her face.

Lifting his head, Alan stared hard at her, frowning.

"I'm okay," she assured him, the sound of her voice suddenly strange in that room. "I'll be okay."

Stroking her hair with his hand, he leaned forward and kissed her on the forehead. It was a touching gesture. Like that of a father to his child.

THEY REMAINED HIDDEN away in the villa for three days, venturing out only for fresh supplies or to stroll his beautiful vineyards. All thoughts of work were forgotten, all other demands ignored. Mostly, they just lay side by side, touching each other's body, relishing their sudden happiness. They scarcely spoke. Neither wanted to do anything to shatter this fragile thing they'd discovered.

Charlie hardly recognised the feelings that swept through her. She'd forgotten what it was like to feel emotions she thought she'd banished. Safe in the harbour of Alan's company, sheltered for a while at least from the tempestuous storms of her past, she allowed herself to rediscover hidden aspects of herself and to map out new, uncharted waters.

Alan was a master at his craft. When he made love to her, it was almost as if he was painting her—never had she felt more acutely aware of her skin, its contours and curves, of the physical sensations he could summon at will. Studying her, making her wait, he seemed to savour both the power he held over her and the emancipation he brought to her mind. Part of her felt like she'd been waiting her whole life for him to set her free. Although, of course, she would never be completely free of the past. And neither, it seemed, would he.

One morning, coming down to breakfast, Charlie accidentally overheard a telephone conversation Alan was having in the hallway. It soon became clear to her, as she froze on the stairs, out of sight, that he was talking to his ex-wife.

"No, I don't know when I'm coming back to London, Sarah." His voice was icy. "It's not something I've given very much thought to and I'd be grateful if you'd stop calling and interrupting me when I'm working. You know how I hate that."

Charlie flattened herself further against the wall above the twisting staircase, anxious not to be seen.

Alan sighed. "I'm not alone. There's a writer with me. We're collaborating on a book...."

"Not that it's any of your concern, but yes, she's a woman. And, if you must know, she's young and attractive and I'm sleeping with her. Now, would you like her full name and telephone number so you can get your spies to make their usual enquiries, or have you already done that?

"Well, that's entirely a matter for you. But don't expect me to have anything to do with it. Now I really must get back to my studio. In case you've forgotten, some of us have to work for a living. Good-bye, Sarah."

Cursing under his breath, he stalked off into his studio, slamming the door behind him. He skipped breakfast and didn't emerge for hours.

Maria, Alan's housekeeper, confided to Charlie that Alan's ex-wife telephoned frequently. "He no like when she call." Maria clucked softly and shook her head. "He say to tell her he is out."

She had more surprises for Charlie. "Signor Alan spend many millions of lire me," she said, her English almost impenetrable, "for my heart." She patted her chest. "I have surgery. He no let me pay him back and he make sure my family okay." Making the sign of the cross with fingers gnarled with arthritis, she added, "Signor Alan, he very good man."

When Charlie confronted Alan about this secret generosity, he brushed it aside. "It was merely a business arrangement," he said, dismissively. "Where else could I find such a cheap cook?"

"And the bouquet you sent her every week until she recovered, I suppose that was just business, too?" Charlie asked, suppressing a smile.

"Sunflowers are ten a penny round here," Alan replied.

Away from the constraints and responsibilities of London and Suffolk, away perhaps from the bitter memories of England, he showed her the real Alan Matheson at last. Relaxed in the surroundings he clearly adored, he proved himself to be a kind, considerate, and urbane companion. He escorted her to all his favourite haunts, buying her meals and gifts, flowers and trinkets. Shopkeepers and restaurant owners alike treated him with respect and genuine affection. He was a generous host and a gracious customer. She felt happy to be at his side and, relieved that nothing had yet spoiled what she had found, she allowed her own guard to slip a little, too.

"Where would you like to go tomorrow?" he asked her one night as they peeled pears by candlelight, lying together in a tangle of sheets. "How about Gubbio? It has a wonderful restaurant where they serve some of the finest truffles in Umbria. Or Urbino, perhaps? I could show you the paintings by Piero della Francesca, or the remarkable Marquetry Room at the Palazzo Ducale."

"Fabriano," Charlie replied determinedly, her mouth full of juicy pear flesh. "The paper museum."

Alan's nose wrinkled. "Really? Doesn't that qualify as work? I thought this was meant to be a holiday for you."

"Well, you're working, and besides, I really want to see it," she insisted. "And so should you. Fabriano is the cradle of papermaking in the Western world. I looked on the map and it's only two hours' drive away. Please?"

Shrugging his shoulders, Alan acquiesced.

STRUNG OUT ALONG the banks of the River Giano at the far end of the dramatic gorges of the Esino Valley, the Fabriano paper mills lay at the westernmost part of the area known as the Marches, close to the border with Umbria. Alan had become more enthusiastic about their trip once Charlie told him that Dürer and Michelangelo, Raphael, Goya, and Bodoni had used paper from Fabriano. His interest had been further fired when she added that some of Turner's Venetian watercolours, in particular *The lovers, a scene from Romeo and Juliet,* had been painted on paper made by the town's largest mill, Cartieri Miliani.

The town was also famous as the birthplace of Gentile de Fabriano, the renowned fourteenth-century artist whose finest religious frescoes once adorned the Doges' Palace in Venice. But when they arrived in Fabriano, there was little or no sign of recognition for its most famous son, a fact that irritated Alan intensely.

"They'll honour some footballer who plays for AC Milan," he said crossly, "but they won't bother to remember someone whose name and talent has survived more than six hundred years."

"Never mind," Charlie soothed, "I think you'll enjoy the Museo della Carta. According to the guidebook, it's housed down a little side street in the former monastery of San Domenico."

The museum not only proved difficult to find, but it was closed to the public. Charlie and Alan could find no one around who might let them in. While Alan stalked off to seek help, Charlie buried her nose in the guide-book. In the time that it took him to return, she learned that the main working mill they had passed on their way into the town produced a staggering 900 km of paper each day, including watermarked paper for bank-notes of various currencies all over the world. She was astonished to discover that as far back as the fourteenth century, Fabriano's paper mills were producing a million sheets of paper a year.

After a wait of some thirty minutes, during which time Alan nearly gave up and went home, a young Italian named Marco finally arrived on his Piaggio, his shoulder-length hair damp from a sudden rain shower. "We're not normally open today," he explained. "But for Sir Alan Matheson, we are open twenty-four hours a day."

Charlie reddened. Alan had clearly pulled rank.

Marco led them through some double doors and into an open court-yard, in the centre of which stood a huge glass cabinet. It housed a print-ing press made of ancient olive wood.

"We are one of the few manufacturers who still employ the traditional ways," Marco explained amiably in excellent English as he walked them across the courtyard and towards a vaulted room which housed the small production line the museum maintained for practical demonstrations. "The pulp we use today is made from raw cotton in its natural state."

"Not linen?" Alan interjected stiffly.

"No, signore. These days it is impossible to acquire linen of the right quality or in sufficient quantity. There are too many synthetics in the production. The men who work the vats use the same techniques as they did in the thirteenth century, and the papers we produce are sized in the bone glue or *gelatino* of dead animals."

Charlie closed her eyes and inhaled. The museum smelled of wet pulp, of toil, gelatine, and paper. Not quite the crisp, clean smell of Alan's art paper, but not dissimilar, and strangely comforting.

Opening her eyes, she watched with fascination as three burly men, their sleeves rolled up, hauled the metal moulds out of the dripping vats, the grey-white pulp clearly visible on the surface. Dipping them and turning them again, the vatmen deftly applied another layer of pulp to the mould, at a slightly different angle to before, to provide a cross-weave in the fibres which, when dried, would add strength to the paper. On the mould itself, Charlie could just make out the intricate pattern of wires stitched to its frame, which would make changes in the thickness of the pulp to form a watermark.

"How many times will they dip the mould?" Alan asked Marco.

"As many as twenty," the young Italian explained. "Depending on the type of paper they're making and the requirements for its strength. It is very hard work. Our Esportazione paper requires three craftsmen for a single sheet."

"Are they given free beer?" Charlie asked, recalling the black-and-white photograph Lori Hunter showed her of the vat men in their paper hats drinking their fill from the keg of local ale brought each day to the factory floor.

Marco laughed, his dark eyes beaming at Charlie with undisguised flirtatiousness. "This is Italy, signorina. We drink only wine. And, yes, the men may have as much as they like. Perhaps I could offer you a glass later?"

At the rear of the room stood the huge drying machine, again made of olive wood, on which the individual sheets of paper were clipped into place on a large wheel by a simple device that used gravity to grip it between two fingers of wood. Alan was losing interest in the process by this time and seemed far more concerned with the frisson between Charlie and the impossibly handsome Marco.

From the moment their guide rode up on his little scooter, his long black hair dripping, his jeans tight around well-formed legs, Charlie had been slightly on her guard. Marco exuded sexual energy. His hand at her elbow as he led her through the museum's impressive exhibition of watermarks, he virtually ignored Alan as the older man followed behind them.

"And now, as a gift to the *bella Inglese*," Marco announced, presenting Charlie with a small package, "here is some of our finest-quality paper to take home. I hope you enjoy it." Leaning forward, he kissed her gently on each cheek, before pulling her to him in a long embrace.

Her face half-buried in his hair, Charlie caught the expression on Alan's face and pulled away hastily. "Thank you, Marco. *Ti ringrazio tantissimo*." Turning to Alan, she held out the package and said: "Here, tell me what you think."

But before he could volunteer his assessment, Marco had stepped between them and handed Alan a similar, notably smaller, package. "For Sir Alan, father of the *bellissima*," he said.

ALAN SULKED ALMOST all the way back to the villa, driving like a lunatic along the winding Italian roads still damp with the morning's rain. Charlie watched him out of the corner of her eye while trying not to laugh. Even though she'd explained the situation to Marco and their guide had apologised profusely, Alan was not to be appeased.

"You were flirting openly," he proclaimed petulantly.

"What if I was? Marco was extremely attentive."

"He is too young for you."

"No, he isn't," Charlie bristled. "We are about the same age."

"Better than being thirteen years older, I suppose."

"Fourteen," Charlie corrected him with a grin. Seeing that he didn't return it, she gasped, "Alan Matheson, I do believe you're jealous!"

"Nonsense! I simply take offence at being mistaken for your father." Then, more softly, he asked: "Is that what other people think, too?"

Charlie squeezed his thigh. "I don't care what other people think." Moving her hand slowly up his leg, she felt him shift slightly in his seat. Keeping her hand where it was she whispered: "And that's hardly the response of an old man, now is it?"

They stopped near an abandoned olive grove, a place where nature had encroached with long, tenacious fingers. The twisted trees were almost hidden by the wild grasses and flowers that choked their roots. Alan retrieved a blue wool blanket from the boot and spread it on the sweet-smelling grass. Without a word, he lifted Charlie into his arms and placed her gently down upon it, her long hair fanned out behind her. The air was cool and damp and her flesh shrank as he deftly slid off her clothes. Somewhere in the far distance, she could hear a tractor ploughing its methodical way through a meadow.

Within minutes, she was warm again, lost to the sensation of skin against skin. Her eyelids flickering at the light filtering through the branches of the trees and the blue sky beyond, she could hear the pulse in her ears. Pulling on the grass between her clenched fingers, she gasped as Alan's hands pushed her thighs apart.

They fell together afterwards, rolling off the blanket and onto the grass, both breathless. Alan clutched his chest as if in pain, but the grin on his face told her he was fine. Charlie's eyes filled involuntarily with tears and Alan kissed each one as it rolled silently down the side of her face. Still locked together, her head resting on his shoulder, they lay like that until his breathing quietened and the autumnal breeze made her shiver.

"I'd like to spend the rest of my life here, with you," Alan said quietly, his lips pressed to her ear.

Charlie turned to him and smiled, admiring the musculature of his chest and shoulders. Gently, she brushed a lock of hair back from his face.

"I'm serious." Alan stared at her with an intensity that made her shiver once more. "You bring out the best in me, you know."

"Is there a worst?"

He closed his eyes without giving her an answer.

Suddenly cold, Charlie sat up abruptly and threw off the blanket, reaching for her clothes. Slipping on her jeans, she sat back and looked down into Alan's face. "Let's get out of here and find something to eat. I'm starving." Her mind full of unquiet thoughts, she added softly, "Don't rush me, Alan, please."

19

CHARLIE WOKE SUDDENLY, convinced she must be having a bad dream. But when she opened her eyes and listened for her screams in the silence, she realised it was Alan, not she, who was crying. Leaning up on one elbow, she watched in the half-light, as he tossed and turned, whimpered and cried out against the images that were clearly raging inside his head.

Unable to bear it anymore, she was just about to reach out for him and shake him awake, when Alan sat up with a sudden gasp and cried out.

"Angela!"

Turning to face Charlie, his expression tortured, he clung to her suddenly and sobbed and sobbed against her bare breast until he was completely spent. Falling asleep in her arms finally, he slept soundly and deeply until first light, when he rose from their bed before she was fully awake to take a long swim.

"Tell me about Angela," Charlie asked when he returned, still wet from his dip. "You cried out for her in your sleep last night."

She studied him carefully as he considered his answer, and steadied herself for his reply and the conversation she fully expected to follow. This was it, then, the moment she'd been waiting for but also dreading.

The moment when he'd tell her of his dead daughter at last. But nothing in Alan's demeanour changed, and not a glimmer of his nighttime pain showed in his eyes.

"Oh, she's not important now," he said, rubbing his bare skin brusquely with a towel. Turning to Charlie with a mischievous wink, he added, "What is important is just how exactly, Ms Hudson, do you plan on earning your breakfast?"

Charlie's appetite had returned with a vengeance and she looked forward to every mouthwatering meal prepared by Alan's housekeeper, Maria. She worked off any extra pounds in his bed, or in the pool, where she, like him, swam fifty lengths every morning, her body slicing through the aquamarine water like a fin.

"Why would you ever want to leave this place?" she asked with a smile one morning, wrapping herself in a white toweling robe and joining Alan, who sat drinking coffee on the terrace above the pool. Buttering herself a slice of walnut bread toast and spreading it with homemade marmalade, she ate hungrily.

"I wouldn't if you were here." Alan grinned up at her. He'd just emerged from his studio after three hours painting, eager to catch the early morning light. The scent of linseed curled up from his skin as she stood behind him.

"It's so beautiful," she said, staring at the scorched hills that flowed from the villa like a giant bolt of linen. "If it were..."

Words failed her suddenly as her attention was distracted. A wasp that had been feeding on the marmalade spoon on the table launched itself unsteadily into the air and flew straight towards her. Frozen to the spot, she followed its path, resisting the urge to wave her hands and bat it away as it buzzed annoyingly around her head.

"Hang on, I'll swat it off," Alan said, leaping up with a folded napkin.

"No!" Charlie snarled. "Keep absolutely still!"

Taken aback by her insistence, Alan did as he was told. They both watched as the striped insect hovered for a few seconds near her face and head until, curiosity apparently sated, it flew off.

Charlie sighed heavily and sank into a chair.

"It wouldn't have stung you," Alan reassured her. "I'd have killed it first."

"Maybe you would have, maybe you wouldn't. But if you'd angered it and it had stung me I could be dead right now and you'd be breakfasting alone."

"My God! What do you mean?"

"A wasp stung me once when I was six. My arm blew up three times its size and I had to go to hospital. Three years later I trod on a bee in my parents' garden and nearly died. I have something called anaphylaxis. I carry a syringe of Adrenalin everywhere I go in case I'm stung. Without a shot my airways close up and I could choke to death."

"Oh, my God, Charlie! Why didn't you tell me?"

Charlie gave him a smile of reassurance. "Thanks, Alan, but you mustn't worry. The reaction can be immediate, or it can take several hours. Either way, there's usually plenty of time for me to tell someone where the syringe is." Seeing his mind racing through the possibilities, she added, "Come on now, forget about it. Didn't you say last night that you had something you wanted to show me?"

Leading her barefoot into the cool of his studio, he allowed her eyes a moment to adjust to the light. On his easel was the large piece of Whatman's paper he'd removed from the bank vault what seemed like an age before. Standing so close she could touch it, Charlie stared long and hard at the work in progress. *Crossing the Brook.* Alan's homage to the great Turner. He had covered the entire sheet in a series of blue and yellow washes that, layer upon layer, gave it misty depth and fragile beauty. She had seen completed watercolours of Turner's not dissimilar to this— where the artist had begun with something formal in mind, but decided to stop and leave it unfinished and imprecise.

To the left of the picture, Alan had roughly sketched in the tall trees that Turner had used to give framework, and the foreground had been overlaid with more browns and blues to signify where the water would go. There was an extraordinary quality of light about the painting. It was indeed Italian in its iridescence, as the whiteness of the paper breathed a new, vibrant intensity into the colours.

But, for her, the most strident feature emerging from the chrysalis of paint, the one which had made her shiver in the Tate all those months before, was still the group of dark trees to the right, forming a sinister canopy where their leaves touched and intertwined, a tight mesh where no light could penetrate.

Charlie peered into its shadows and found herself trembling once again.

IN HER DREAM she is in southern Iraq. A place called Karbala. A holy city sacred to Muslims, not far from Babylon. After hours crossing shell-pitted roads and temporary bridges erected to replace those bombed by the Allies, they find the city in ruins. The delicate turquoise dome of the mosque to which thousands of pilgrims once journeyed lies shattered into a million pieces. As Charlie and her fellow journalists are driven in through its machine-gunned gates, the city's buildings bear testament to the devastation of war. Each structure is decimated, a blackened skeleton.

Rigid with dread, Charlie walks again through the silent streets. The stink of death fouls the air. It was here that the hopeful Shiite rebels had risen up against Saddam Hussein's ruling Ba'ath Party immediately following the first Gulf War. Here, too, that they were so brutally crushed. By the time Charlie arrives, it is impossible to tell which of the rotting corpses are those of the Ba'ath party followers and which are those of the rebels.

The Iraqi authorities seem to take great pride in parading her around this Hell on earth. They lead her to the edge of a deep pit: a place of such horror that no imagination could invent it. The stench and the flies are overwhelming. Sensing fresh prey, the insects swarm around her eyes and mouth. Uttering a small cry of revulsion and batting them away with her hands, she startles a dog in the pit below. It scurries off, its tail between its legs, a half-eaten human hand in its jaws.

Recoiling, curling instinctively into a fetal position in Alan's bed, her mind leads her on, to a gleaming white marble house. Wearing thin-soled leather sandals bought in a souk in Basra, she carefully picks her way through the broken glass along the cool, dark corridors leading to the inner chambers. No sunlight penetrates here, either. Her breath quickens.

Unsuspectingly, she follows the corridor to its natural conclusion. A small room. Windowless. Lined from floor to ceiling with marble. A place she's revisited in her mind a thousand times. Her eyes dart right and left, taking in every detail, every inch of the scene before her.

A simple wooden chair, skewed slightly to the left. The hanging ropes, their fibres hewn roughly with a knife. The ground cluttered with the detritus of torture. Sweaty bandanas torn from necks. Crimson handprints beside great arcs of blood splattered up the walls. The air buzzing with flies. Thick with the sickly smell Charlie has come to detest.

Three steps into the room, Charlie's sandals sink deep into blood. It forces its way up and between her toes. All around her lie festering body parts. Ears. Noses. Fingers. Toes. To the left of her foot, a young boy's face grins up at her from his grubby paper identity card. A penis, roughly sawn from its owner, lies shriveled at its side. Charlie opens her mouth in a silent scream.

ALAN HAD NEVER heard anything like it. Waking with a start, for a moment he didn't know where he was and blinked blindly in the semidarkness. Jumping up, he switched on the lamp at his bedside and glanced at the clock. It was just after four o'clock in the morning and Charlie was nowhere to be seen. Her place by his side was crumpled and hollow. All around him, the ancient house breathed quietly. The balcony windows were open, the curtains softly billowing, the moon's flat white radiance flooding his garden. He stepped forward and peered down onto the terrace, half expecting to see her body broken on the paving below. Turning back to the room with relief, he spotted something sticking out from beneath the four-poster bed.

"Charlie? Charlie?"

Going down onto all fours, he could hardly believe his eyes. In the blind, black space beneath the bed, she was crouched like some wild animal, snatching for breath, shaking spasmodically. Her skin like wax, her mouth was round with terror, her hands clawing at invisible demons in the air.

"*NON BUONO,* " was all the *dottore* from Porto would observe. "*Grave.*"

"I know it's not good," Alan remonstrated impatiently, "but what can you do to help her?"

"*Bisogna la tranquillità e il sonno.*" In broken English, to Charlie, he added: "You must be sleeping."

Charlie smiled weakly and closed her eyes. She wished everyone would leave her alone. She'd simply overdone it. She'd be fine.

Clearly stung by her silence, Alan retreated to his studio, but he seemed too distracted to paint. She watched as, irritably, he put away *Crossing the Brook.* Instead, he stretched canvasses and cut up the precious few sheets of paper he'd brought with him, preparing various backgrounds for future use.

It was mindless, gentle work that distracted him from the perplexing subject of Charlie. She lay on the terrace outside, a few yards from his studio door, equally perplexed by him. Had her nightmares returned because she was allowing herself to feel again? Was that also true for him? Since splitting up with his second wife, Diane, Alan had, Charlie knew, deliberately spent his time doing exactly as he pleased, away from the crazy women in his life. Now here he was, calling Angela's name in the night. Was it a coincidence that he now seemed to feel responsible again for someone whose life was not as straightforward as might first have seemed?

By the time Alan had completed seven backgrounds, he seemed in urgent need of Charlie's company. After searching for her on the veranda, she could hear him wandering through the house, calling her name. He found her in her cool, shuttered room, fresh from the shower, tanned and wet. She was packing her suitcase.

"What are you doing?" he asked, the smile wiped from his face.

Charlie stopped and turned. "I'm going home, Alan. It's time I went back to work."

Alan stepped forward and placed his hands on her bare shoulders.

"But you're not strong enough yet. You can't possibly travel back to England alone. Now, please, don't be silly. Stay. At least until you're fully recovered."

Charlie removed his hands and tilted her chin at him defiantly, her wet hair clinging to her shoulders like seaweed.

"I'm fine," she insisted, refusing to waver. She'd been thinking about it all day, and having made the decision, felt washed with relief. It was time for her to take back control. It wasn't that she was running again, she told herself; she just felt strangely vulnerable this far from home.

"I'm not an invalid, Alan. I had one bad night, that's all, and now I'm much better, thanks to you. But I've simply got to get home. I must visit my parents and I've a million other things to do, including finishing a book, remember? I'm not like you. I can't just go swanning off around the world on a whim. It's been wonderful here, really it has. You've given me so much. You've made me strong again. But now it's time for me to go ... before, before, I spoil everything." Staring into his dejected face, she added, "I'll see you when you get back."

Slumping onto the corner of her bed, Alan sat silently as she finished her packing, watching her neatly fold every garment and lay it gently into its allotted space. "But we haven't had enough time ...," he began lamely.

Charlie stopped what she was doing and stared down at his face with sudden seriousness. Sitting next to him, she spoke slowly. "There'll be time enough for us soon, Alan. All that matters is that we've had these wonderful few days together."

Alan nodded reluctantly. "Okay, darling, if you say so." He ran his forefinger slowly up her thigh, his pupils dark and eager. "But you will miss me, won't you? ..."

Sick with desire, Charlie pushed her case to one side and lay down on the bed beside him, her green eyes glimmering in the half-light.

20

$\mathcal{S}$HE EMERGED FROM the shower to the insistent ringing of the telephone. She'd first heard it above the noise of the running water as she soaped herself down, ignored it as she massaged yet more shampoo into her hair, and listened as the answering machine cut in. Two minutes later, the phone rang again. Somewhere deep in her handbag, her mobile went off and then died, and then the phone rang again.

Reluctantly relinquishing the cleansing heat of the stingingly hot jets, she draped herself in a bright red towel and padded into the lounge, leaving wet footprints across the wooden floor.

"Alan?" she said, laughing as she picked up the phone. She'd expected him to call to see if she'd arrived home safely, but, for goodness' sake, she'd only been back an hour.

"Where've you been?" Nick demanded tetchily. "I've been trying to reach you for ages. Your mobile's dead and I didn't want to leave a message."

"Oh, sorry, I only just got back from Italy. My battery's down and I was in the shower," she said, flicking her dripping hair back from her shoulders and rubbing it with the corner of the towel. "Why? What's up?"

"I'm afraid I've got some bad news. Fiona called me when she couldn't get hold of you."

Suddenly cold, Charlie reached for the back of the sofa and swallowed before speaking. "Is it Dad?"

"No," Nick replied gently. "It's your mum. She had a heart attack yesterday. She's in intensive care and, well, Charlie, they're not sure she's going to make it."

Charlie felt the room tilt as she dropped her towel. It lay before her on the hardwood floor like a spreading pool of blood.

NEGOTIATING THE BUSY south London traffic, her head was full of voices—her own, her mother's, Nick's, Alan's. Their words fluttered around inside her skull like confetti.

Nick had offered to drive her but she'd declined, needing the time alone. She'd be fine, she told him and, after stuffing a few warmer items into her suitcase, she folded herself into the driver's seat and headed south, the melancholy strains of Mozart's Adagio in E major filling the car.

The winter weather was closing in. Slanting silver needles of rain beat a tattoo on the windscreen. Her only jacket was the one she'd traveled home from Italy in and when she stopped for petrol, the wind sliced through the thin fabric. Clambering back into the car, cold and wet, her teeth chattered and her fingers fumbled with the keys. Turning on the ignition, she fired up the car and, rather shakily, rejoined the South Circular. On the seat next to her lay a bedraggled bunch of orange and yellow chrysanthemums, wrapped in purple crêpe paper—the only flowers the garage had for sale.

Her mother. Marjorie. Granddad's only child. A bastion of the local community, chairwoman of the WI, baker of award-winning cakes, indomitable, immortal somehow. Somehow Charlie had thought her mother would always be a distant figure of resentment.

Their relationship had never been comfortable. It wasn't Marjorie's natural imperiousness or her middle-class snobbery that irked Charlie so much as her insensitivity. Charlie sometimes couldn't believe she'd sprung from the womb of a woman who had so little understanding of the world outside her own.

Her mother had blocked what details she'd been told of Charlie's experiences in Kosovo from her mind, unable to process such difficult information. She'd never even read Charlie's first book. She'd commented on how depressing the photograph on the jacket was, and then handed it straight over to her husband, explaining: "I've never much been one for reading, dear." But at any one time, sitting next to her armchair and on a low table alongside the impounded TV remote, would be three hardback novels she'd borrowed from the library.

Part of Charlie's problem, it seemed, was that she could never live up to her older sister Fiona. Fiona had never been rebellious. Fiona had never been caught smoking in the greenhouse. Fiona had gone into the teaching profession young and married a thoroughly dependable sort. The impulsive Charlie had, on the other hand, wilfully chosen the ignoble profession of journalism and then traveled the world covering all sorts of events Marjorie had little or no interest in.

"Why can't you stay home and write about *nice* things?" she'd ask. "There are so many important women's issues that should be given a proper airing. You should come along to one of our WI meetings and listen to some of the topics we debate. It's not all jam and 'Jerusalem,' you know."

Nick, with his promising prospects and natural distaste for war zones or disasters, was seen as a blessing. "He is such a rock and his family are perfectly acceptable," Marjorie had informed Charlie. "Now hopefully you'll settle down and give us some grandchildren." But when Charlie's job only took her farther away and for longer, her mother all but disowned her.

"I simply can't see the attraction of risking your life for a few articles buried in the middle of the newspaper that no one ever bothers to read," Marjorie insisted. "I've never been a fan of the foreign pages." Her chief area of interest, after the features pages, was the "Hatch, Match, and Despatch," as she called the announcements page. She was forever cutting out notices of births and deaths and sending them off to faraway friends with enigmatic notes such as: *"Did you see this? Bunty Hawkins died. Poor Bob. Although it'll be interesting to see how much she left him when the will's published."*

When Charlie eventually returned from Kosovo—her mind and body broken—her mother simply refused to accept what had happened. Not that Nick and her father ever told her the full story. They daren't. "Well, what on earth did she expect, going off to places like that when there's a war on?" was her only remark. "You can tell Charlie from me, I must have warned her a hundred times."

Now, seven years later, Charlie was forced to face up to the shocking concept that her mother might die before her.

Entering through the automatic double doors of the Kent General Hospital, bracing against the rush of memories of another place, Charlie was assailed by the peculiarly sweet scent of sickness, the distinctive squeak of shoes on linoleum. Everything grated roughly against the raw areas of her mind.

As she stepped tentatively into the intensive-care unit, resisting the temptation to run, she spotted her dad by a bed. In it lay a figure under a white blanket and partially obscured from her view. The smell of disinfectant made Charlie want to retch, but she swallowed the bile, reached for her father, and squeezed his bony shoulders so tight that he whimpered. Busying herself by fetching him a Styrofoam cup of coffee, and sipping from her own, she deliberately scalded her tongue to anchor her to the moment, and ordered the voices in her head to be silent.

Staring at her mother wired up to all manner of bleeping machines for the first time, her overriding emotion was not of sorrow but of guilt. Guilt that she was secretly relieved it was her mother, not her father, who'd go first. Guilt that she hadn't been a better daughter. But there was also something else, something she couldn't identify at first. It was sheer, bloodless terror at the idea of losing this woman she'd known her whole life. Of not having the familiar scents of Elnet hairspray and Revlon powder, of fish pie and bowls of banana custard topped with hundreds and thousands, of mugs of hot chocolate, of being tucked into bed at night, her back rubbed when she was ill.

By the time Fiona arrived by train from Buxton and the sisters were reunited in the strange half-light of the ward, Charlie had steadied herself enough to be of some use. Fiona was done in. She'd spent the journey terrified that she'd be too late to say good-bye. When she arrived to find her mother's heart still resonating across the monitor, she all but collapsed with relief.

"It's okay," Charlie told her, patting her back as her older sister sank a soggy face into her shoulder. "This won't beat her."

Fiona seemed considerably older and not just from her palpable grief. The two sisters still looked remarkably alike, the echoes of their parents as young people in their shared DNA, but grey now peppered Fiona's tousled brown hair and her top lip was tightening and taking on the heavy lines of her mother's.

Their father looked like a ghost. Pinned to the wall near his wife's head, gripping the bed rail, he had a grey transparency about him in that white, white room that only added to the sense of the ethereal. If anything, he looked even worse than their mother, whose own skin had taken on a deathly pallor as she lay deflated on her starched cotton pillow, as if someone had let all the air out.

Charlie realised with a shock that, when her father looked at his wife, he still saw the woman she'd once been. To his mind, she would always be the young girl he'd fallen for fifty years earlier; the mother of his two children, and his chosen partner on the journey into old age. She'd waved him good-bye each morning as he left for the station, the corned beef sandwiches she'd made neatly wrapped in his briefcase; she'd welcomed him home each night with a large gin and tonic. They'd lain alongside each other in the same bed at night, whispering their secrets. Each one giving the other a reason to get up the next morning.

"Come on, Dad," Charlie cajoled, taking him by his elbow. "The doctor said she's stable and there's nothing more you can do tonight. Take Fiona home and settle her into her old room. I'll see you both first thing in the morning. Okay?"

Like a small child obeying a parent, her father shuffled from the room at Fiona's side, both of them too drained to resist or to be surprised by Charlie's apparent strength. "Take care of her for me, rabbit," her father whispered. "She's all I have left."

Charlie stopped herself from pointing out that he still had her and

Fiona. After all, he was probably right. His two daughters had abandoned him years ago.

Shutting the door against the persistent sounds of others in the corridor outside, Charlie sat in the plastic chair Fiona had just vacated. Taking her mother's hand, she began to stroke it. Charlie stared hard at her mother, and tried to see what she hadn't seen for years. She so desperately wanted to picture her through her father's eyes, to maybe even see a look of Granddad's in her mother's closed face. But she could see nothing.

Leaning forward, she whispered, "Why didn't you ever join us, Mum? Granddad and I didn't keep you out deliberately, you know. It wasn't an exclusive club. You could have joined in at any time."

21

CHARLIE'S GRANDFATHER HAD never felt closer in the days that followed, as she slept in her old bedroom at her parents' house between visits to a slowly recovering Marjorie.

It was as if he was constantly with her, inside her head, urging her to find a way through this current labyrinth and beyond. Overwhelmed with sudden sorrow, she often found tears streaming down her face as she mourned his death in anticipation of the next one.

"Why did you do it, Granddad?" she sobbed out loud in the darkness. "Why did you leave us like that?"

She was so tired of the question which had been hammering on the inside of her skull for years. She was weary of never knowing the answer. Most of all, she was sick of all the secrets and lies. "Don't you dare tell anyone about this!" her mother had spat at her, the day the ambulance had appeared outside their home. "Not a word!" Marjorie had repeated, as she'd slyly pocketed the empty bottle of pills and the note Granddad had left neatly folded on his bedside table. It was not an instruction she repeated to Fiona or their father. She knew they wouldn't let her down.

While a teenage Charlie was struggling to take in the enormity of her grandfather's death, even as his body was being shunted onto a stretcher to be transported to the hospital morgue, she had stood in the doorway whispering to herself the words he'd scribbled on his suicide note, so that she would never, ever forget them.

"Try to leave something beautiful behind," was all he wrote. It had been clear to her for some time that he could no longer face the colourless world his illness had cornered him into, so dulled by morphine that he could no longer paint. But she also feared that the imminence of her leaving for college may have forced his hand.

It wasn't so much her grandfather's death that upset her mother. It was, rather, the manner of it. Expecting him to die quietly in a hospice of the cancer that he'd stoically battled for so long was one thing, but to discover him like that was another. It was not what Marjorie Mackay Hudson had expected from her war hero of a father at all. No matter that he'd chosen to end his life in his own way, with dignity and triumph. Marjorie had never recovered from the humiliation and the shock. And neither, Charlie realised, had she.

Now her mother was battling with her own mortality—a fact that left Charlie breathless with fear. No matter how imperfect her relationship with Marjorie, she was her last link to Granddad. And all that was left behind that was beautiful was her grandfather's paintings, hidden away somewhere by Marjorie. Charlie wished she could study them now.

She wondered if Angela had felt the same as Granddad when she'd committed suicide. That she was wresting back control and making her own dignified exit? What beautiful thing had she left behind? Her paintings, perhaps? Charlie suddenly felt an intense need to see all she could of Angela's work, to examine every piece closely, to touch them, to try to learn something—anything—of the woman, from the way she had handled paint and daubed it onto the paper. Had Angela inherited any of her father's brilliance, or were her paintings like Charlie's, shabby imitations of the real thing? Did she ever work in Alan's studio, easel to easel with her father, painting in companionable silence? Or was it that very proximity to her father's genius which had driven her to desperation? Could it have been Angela's bitter realisation that she could never be as good as Alan that had finally driven her to take her own life?

Charlie had spent her life since her grandfather's suicide trying to block the desperation of his final act from her mind. Had he been happy or sad when he washed down the pills with a slug of whisky? Did he even think how Charlie would feel after he was found? His suicide was never spoken of again.

"If anyone asks, he slipped away quietly after a long struggle with cancer," her mother insisted. Just to make sure they understood, she paid for a lengthy announcement in the Hatch, Match, and Despatch columns, confirming the same.

And then when Charlie had attempted to take her own life in the clinic, the pattern had repeated itself. No one spoke of it. Not one member of her family, not Nick, or Carrie, ever once asked her why, or what she had been thinking. Of course her psychiatrist prodded and probed, but the rest of the world erased her ugly moment of madness as if it had never happened. It was a secret she would take to the grave. Just as Angela Matheson had.

Charlie came to realise, as she lay awake night after night in her old bedroom, waiting for Marjorie to get better, that she couldn't just lie back and float on the tide of life anymore, or allow others to shape her history for her. When the doctors told them that Marjorie would almost certainly make a good recovery, and Charlie realised that her mother would come home and expect everything to return to the way it was, she knew she couldn't allow that. Patterns needed to be broken. That would mean bat-tling hard against the tide of unresolved issues with her parents, and with Nick, too. It would also mean she must finally decide what she really wanted from her relationship with Alan.

If they were to have any sort of future together, if she were to allow herself to give herself totally to this enigmatic artist who had helped her to take the most courageous steps towards her future since Rajak, then she had to know exactly what she was getting herself into. To stop the pattern repeating itself yet again. No one was better qualified than Charlie to ask those difficult questions, to find out what had pushed Alan's talented, beautiful young daughter to the point when ending her own life seemed a better option than continuing it. No one had bothered to find out with Granddad, nor sought to ask Charlie, but surely Angela deserved better?

. . .

RETURNING TO HER London flat, she set to work immediately. Laying out the copies of all the newspaper cuttings she'd selected on her kitchen table, she made herself a cup of coffee and examined them closely. An open notebook at her side, she jotted down the names and details of the police officers who'd investigated Angela's death, those of the mourners at her funeral, the coroner's office, and the pathologist who conducted the postmortem.

She was pleased to come across the name of Dr Steve North, someone she knew from her time as an inquest reporter. Most of the London pathologists had become known to her as she'd traipsed around the coroner's courts, but Steve North was someone she'd particularly liked. Steve had been as much of a novice as she was back then, but had gone on to become one of the Home Office's brightest stars. Flicking through an old Filofax, she found the number of his private office and picked up the phone.

"Hello, is that Dr North's secretary?" she asked, pen poised above the pad. "Oh, I see. Then can you give me his new number?"

Four calls later, she tracked him down. He'd just finished giving a practical demonstration on forensic medicine to the rookies at Hendon Police College. She wondered how many would-be constables had fainted at their first sight of a body, as she very nearly had. Steve sounded surprised to hear from her. He suggested they meet for a lunchtime drink in the West End, as soon as he'd returned the cadaver he'd borrowed.

"What's up, Charlie?" he asked, suspicion in his voice. "Lovely as it will be to catch up, this can't be just for old time's sake."

"Not exactly," she admitted. "I need to pick your brains, Steve."

The fifteen years since they'd last seen each other had been crueller to Steve North than to Charlie. His once distinctive flop of blond hair had retracted dramatically. Deep lines formed a complicated facial map leading to a cluster of wrinkles round his mouth and eyes. His body sagged with a tiredness that was only to be expected after years of predawn phone calls to murder scenes. But his blue eyes lit up when Charlie walked into the Soho pub he'd suggested, and as he stood to shake her hand warmly, she recognised traces of his old, charming self.

"I must say, Charlie, you look wonderful. You've hardly changed at all."

"Thanks. Neither have you," she lied. As she kissed his cheek, she recalled in a flood of embarrassment that they'd once slept together, disastrously, long ago. Unless she was mistaken, he had something of a foot fetish. "Now, what can I get you to drink?"

Ensconced in a quiet corner of the bar, Charlie quickly glossed over what she'd been doing with her life and instead quizzed Steve about his. She'd seen his name in the paper a hundred times, in the coverage of some of the most famous murder trials, and told him, honestly, that she'd often meant to call and congratulate him. He had, she now discovered, been married and divorced, had two children, the eldest of whom had Down's syndrome, and lived in Surrey with his current partner, an ambitious criminal lawyer whose name Charlie recognised.

Sipping from his pint of bitter, Steve's impatience finally got the better of him.

"So, nice as it is to see you, Charlie, what exactly do you want?" he asked bluntly. "You may no longer be a journalist, but I know when I'm being schmoozed."

Charlie smiled and nodded. "Angela Matheson," she said, watching his face for any response.

There was none.

"Suicide," she pressed. "Six years ago. Daughter of Sir Alan Matheson, the artist. Ring any bells?"

"Ah, yes," he said, rubbing his chin in a way she'd forgotten annoyed her. "Some posh clinic outside London somewhere, wasn't it? Overdose?"

"That's right."

"What about her?"

"I just wanted to know if you could remember anything about the case, anything at all. I'm working with her father on something and I'm curious."

"Just curious?" Steve's eyes narrowed. "You could have looked the case up on the Internet." Waving his hands at the empty glasses and half-eaten sandwiches that littered their table, he added, "This is a lot of trouble to go to for idle curiosity."

Charlie knew she was cornered. "Well, yes. To be honest, there's been some talk, from some former colleagues of mine; rumours that there might have been something untoward about Angela's death. I don't honestly believe a word of it, but I wanted to know what you thought."

"From what little I can remember about the case, I shouldn't think there's anything particular to worry about. She was a pretty young thing, as I recall. Quite troubled, by all accounts, but pretty. She stockpiled a handful of the tranquilisers they gave her every night before she went to bed, sat in an armchair in her room, and then swallowed the lot. She was found early the next morning by a member of staff."

"Is that it?" Charlie asked. "Nothing else?"

"I'd have to look up the file. But I don't think so, no."

"Nothing at all? No suggestion of anyone else being involved?"

"Oh, no, I'm sure not. How could there have been? But you'll have to ask the relevant coroner's officer about that."

"Was that Richard Dutton from the Norfolk division?"

"You have been digging. Yeah, that rings a vague bell. Dutton would probably be more helpful. I do way too many of these things to remember the minutiae. There was something, though. The girl's mother. The poor woman insisted on identifying the body at the morgue although nobody thought it was a good idea at the time. But in the end it wasn't her that broke down, as was expected. It was the father. Sir Alan What's-His-Name. He collapsed. The mother just stood like a statue, staring at her daughter's body."

Charlie's sudden sympathy for Alan momentarily stalled her. "Thanks for your help," she said finally, closing her notebook. They finished their drinks simultaneously and stood to leave. Pulling on her jacket, Charlie bent forward to kiss him lightly on both cheeks.

"If I think of anything else, I'll call you," he said with a smile, slipping a cardboard beer mat with her number scrawled on it into his coat pocket.

"There was just one thing," Charlie said, as he yanked opened the heavy door of the pub to let her through.

"Yes?"

"Can you remember, Steve: Was Angela Matheson wearing shoes at the time of her death?"

"Oh, yes," he said, nodding. "I distinctly remember slipping her shoes off on the slab. I never forget the feet."

22

RICHARD "DICK" DUTTON had been retired early from the Norfolk Coroner's Office. He lived with his wife in a mobile home on the outskirts of Margate in Kent. It had taken two letters, several telephone calls, and, finally, the personal intervention of Dr Steve North for Charlie to track the ex–coroner's officer down. Only with the greatest reluctance had Dutton agreed to meet her, and then only in the anonymous setting of the seaside town's shabby Dreamland Fun Park.

As Charlie pulled her car into a parking space a few yards from the blustery seafront, her mind was humming with the sights, sounds, and smells of her childhood—candyfloss, toffee apples, and salty sea spray, her grandfather's hand protectively clasping hers as he walked her up and down the esplanade or stepped her cautiously through the intricate mosaics of the Shell Grotto, millions of tiny shells pressed into the chalk walls of a dank cavern.

Margate had been Turner's home for many years. It was a place he'd finally found some peace. More than a hundred of his works had been inspired by this coastline. Here he'd returned in later life and taken up with Sophia Booth, the widowed landlady of a seaside boardinghouse. With Sophia, he'd been able to hide from the world and pretend to be something he wasn't: ordinary. He even took to calling himself "Mr Booth," a fact which gave Charlie a chance to invent an entire correspondence between him and Ruskin.

"As Mr Booth, I can disappear into a whole new persona that bears little or no comparison to the complexities of my real life," he wrote. *"For the first time, I can see the great attraction of madness, of the ease it provides to escape from a world one is tired of, without ever leaving one's own home."*

Ruskin, in turn, reported that Turner spoke of the Thanet skies as being some of the best he had ever seen and that he was painting "like a demon" in the environment he so loved. Charlie made a note to speak to someone at Kent County Council about their eleven-million-pound Turner Centre for the visual arts, designed to rise from the end of Margate pier like a giant pebble upended in the sand.

Sitting on the shore, sketching and painting boats, sunsets, skies, fishermen, and sea squalls, rekindling his love affair with water, Turner had, as Mr Booth, sought to escape the ghosts of his dead mother and sister. Grief, loss, and guilt continued to assail him in equal measure. But escape wasn't to be had. Some of his darkest works, spawned perhaps by the nightmares which plagued him for much of his life, were created here on the Thanet coast.

A seasonal winter storm became a painted vortex of hurtling water and screaming air. Misshapen fish became hideous sea monsters lurking in the waves, or sharklike creatures tearing at the flesh of the dead and dying thrown overboard from slave ships. The ageing artist saw, in the sea, his own mortality. Charlie understood Turner's visions only too clearly.

SHE CLIMBED OUT of the car and quickly shielded her face against the wind that drove into her from the east. It was all she could do to stop the door from being ripped off its hinges. Shivering, she felt a long way from the balmy warmth of Italy. A fat seagull looked up at her from the windswept beach, its claw clamped around a dead fish. Deciding she was of no interest, the bird continued gorging on the rotting flesh. A rival gull, riding the wind, shrieked overhead, startling her.

Pushing open the heavy glass door to the Tower Café, her nostrils were immediately assailed by cigarette smoke. Scanning the room through the fog, she identified the only person who could possibly have been a policeman and hesitated, wondering for a moment if she could lure him out into the fragrant sanctuary of her car and away from the smell that seemed to congeal the blood in her veins.

But Richard Dutton was intently bent over a tabloid newspaper, a cigarette dangling between his fingers. Steeling herself, she stepped forward.

"Mr Dutton?" she asked, smiling and extending a hand.

"Yes." He looked up with a scowl. "How'd you know?"

"Just a hunch," she replied, registering the little details which betrayed him. The short-cropped hair, the comfortably flat brogues, the hands the size of dinner plates, and the posture of a man who'd sat brooding over a thousand cups of tea in police canteens. He might as well have been wearing a uniform.

"Can I get you another?" Charlie asked, pointing at the brown sludge that half filled his cup. Dutton nodded and she returned a few minutes later with two freshly filled mugs.

"I'd just like to start by saying that I don't really see the point of all this," he announced glumly, stirring an extraordinary amount of sugar into his. He reminded Charlie of a bloodhound, his jowls pronounced, his expression permanently bleak. Too much fried food with those teas, she surmised, seeing the wide expanse of flab pressing up against the edge of the table. A greasy paper napkin on a ketchup-stained plate pushed to one side told her he'd already succumbed to the cafeteria's all-day breakfast. She guessed immediately that he was one of life's complainers; he'd probably been retired early to silence his whingeing.

"The point of what?" she countered breezily.

"This," he replied, impatiently flicking his wet teaspoon at her. "Raking over old ashes. Dr North asked me to meet you as a favour to him. If he hadn't, I'd never have agreed."

"Well, I'm very grateful to you for sparing me a few minutes of your valuable time. I promise it won't take long. I just need some information and Steve—Dr North—told me you'd be just the person to ask. He said you were one of the best in the business."

Interest flickered in his eyes. "I tried, which is more than most." Dutton puffed his chest like a pigeon. "Not that it did me much good in the end."

"What do you mean?" Charlie asked, leaning forward with a notebook and resting her hands reluctantly on the grubby Formica tabletop.

"Oh, just that you can never really buck the system, no matter how hard you try. Those at the top always stick together. Like this Sir Alan Matheson you're so interested in, for example, and his stuck-up wife."

Charlie said nothing, knowing that the best way to interview someone was to say as little as possible. Let them fill the silences.

"All they had to do was to pull a few strings through their Establishment cronies and their dirty little secrets were brushed under the carpet as if they never existed."

"Really? How?"

"Well, North must have told you. About the note, I mean."

"Yes, he did mention something," Charlie lied, flicking through her notebook as if to search for the exact quote. "You mean Angela's suicide note?"

"That's right," Dutton responded, slurping from his mug.

"The one she left in her room? At the Waller Clinic?"

"Uh-huh." Dutton's lips pressed tightly around the thin stub of his cigarette. It had gone out; he flicked open a Zippo lighter and sucked hard as the paper caught light. Sitting back on her seat, Charlie fought to control the bile in her throat as the blue smoke curled towards her. Dutton saw her expression and attempted to waft the smoke away with one of his huge hands. "Sorry. Do you mind?"

"That's okay," she answered, too hastily. "So this note, what exactly did it say?"

"It spilled the beans, is what it did, it lifted the lid on their sordid goings-on. But because these people are so powerful, they made threats. They persuaded the coroner not to reveal the content of the note in open court. He ruled there'd been a note written at a time of great emotion and that the intention in the girl's mind was clear. I couldn't bloody believe it!"

"Why? Was there no clear intention in her mind?" Charlie asked, braving the smoke to lean forward and stare into Dutton's drooping eyes.

"Oh, yeah. There was no doubt she intended to do away with herself. But I couldn't believe they didn't allow the coroner to publicly state the reason why."

"The reason why?"

Dick Dutton took a deep drag. He rocked back in his chair, studying Charlie, his mouth twisting into an ugly smile as he enjoyed his few moments of power.

Then he leaned forward and looked around conspiratorially. "She'd been raped," he declared, triumphantly.

The information slammed into Charlie like a clenched fist. Drawing in a sharp breath, she fought to keep her features composed. "Raped?"

"Yup." Dutton nodded. "That's what she said in the note. She blamed it for everything. Wrote that's why she couldn't carry on."

"And who on earth raped her?" Charlie asked, willing Dutton to hurry up so she could rush out of this stinking place and run headlong into the cold, cold sea air.

A chill smile of self-satisfaction crept across his face.

"Her father. Sir Alan bloody Matheson. Fucking his own daughter, while his ice queen of a wife turned the other cheek. Those sick bastards should all be put down at birth."

23

NICK SLID THE high-security metal front door shut behind him and turned on the light. Dumping his briefcase and gym kit in the hallway of his Bermondsey loft apartment and throwing his suit jacket over a chair, he crossed the hardwood floor to a swan-neck lamp in the middle of the room. Turning it on, he surveyed the messy sofa and work surfaces with the indifference of an accomplished bachelor. Sniffing the stale air, he told himself he really must find a cleaning lady. Then at least she could empty the bins and disinfect the science project that was his kitchen. Heading for the giant American-style fridge, he pulled out a chilled can of lager.

"Honey, I'm home," he called out to no one in the empty space that was now his only sanctuary from the hectic lifestyle he'd chosen for himself. Not for the first time, he wondered how he'd allowed himself to become such a workaholic, addicted to at least six days a week at the newspaper, with hardly a moment for anything else. Had he been like that when he was with Charlie, too? Maybe that's why she'd sought adventure elsewhere in the first place. Worryingly, he couldn't now remember.

Clearing the clutter of newspapers, books, shoes, and empty pizza cartons from the sofa with a flamboyant sweep of his hand, he flopped down, feet up, and took his first draught of beer. Picking up the remote control, he stared blankly at the silent images on the giant flat-screen television. The choices were soccer from Brazil, figure skating from Paris, a wildlife programme on the Congo, another desperate Nicolas Cage movie, or umpteen mindless programmes about buying and selling houses abroad.

"Fifteen fucking channels and not a decent programme on one of them," he grumbled, tossing the remote to the floor. Perhaps he should have gone for a drink with the gang after all. Miranda was out with friends for the evening and he'd felt abandoned. His editor, the irrepressible Jake, was heading the usual crowd of hangers-on down to the wine bar but for some reason Nick couldn't face it. Watching Jake and his cronies slide into their usual alcohol-induced paroxysms of laughter and misogynist jokes held little appeal at the best of times, none tonight.

No, he'd promised himself a quiet night in, a chance to clear his mind and living space. He had a load of dirty washing piling up in the bedroom, sheets to change, floors to sweep, rubbish to bag up for the dustmen the following morning. Taking another swig of beer, he laid his head back on the edge of the sofa and closed his eyes.

Charlie.

Why did she always invade his thoughts whenever he was trying to relax? Truth was, he was worried about her. She'd not made any contact since her mother's recovery, and he really wanted to know how she was.

Crossly, he banished Charlie from his mind and hastily replaced her with an image of Miranda. Her apparent youth and inexperience had frightened him at first, but he needn't have worried; the new woman in his life was clearly well practised at the art of seduction. There were times when the hot-blooded redhead made him feel thoroughly corrupted.

Part of him—the deeply insecure inner core that only Charlie knew— couldn't help wondering if his position on the paper wasn't a factor in his budding relationship with Miranda. There'd certainly been unsavoury rumours flying around the office about her sleeping her way to the top. Whatever her motives, he had to admit that she satisfied his darkest desires. He couldn't remember the last time he'd felt so appreciated sexually. Why, then, did he feel that something was missing? That someone was always missing?

Charlie, of course.

Angry with himself, he jabbed the heels of his palms into his eyes. "When will it bloody end?" he yelled, sitting up.

The distinctive ring of his mobile phone made him jump to his feet. "The Self-Preservation Society": theme song for *The Italian Job*. It had seemed funny at the time, but he really must change that infernal ring tone. Plucking the phone from the outer pocket of his battered leather briefcase, he flicked it open crossly.

"Yes?"

"Nick?" the voice enquired gingerly, sensing his mood. "It's Charlie. I'm sorry, but I need to talk to someone and I can't get hold of Carrie. It's important. Are you alone?"

Nick sighed and looked around the empty flat. "Looks like it."

"I'll be over in fifteen minutes."

NICK COULD TELL it was something serious the moment he opened the door. Flushed, fidgety, her face furrowed, Charlie wrung her hands repeatedly and paced his floor in her overcoat.

"How about a drink?" he asked, knowing that a glass of wine usually worked wonders. He opened the fridge door and, for the second time that night, ignored the smell of half-eaten food well past its sell-by date. "Nothing fancy, I'm afraid. Just a bog-standard Chardonnay." Pouring her a glass, he manoeuvred her to the sofa. "Now, drink this and tell me what's up."

"I don't really know where to begin. . . ." Charlie murmured. "It's all a bit muddled. . . ."

Nick hadn't seen her this twitchy in ages.

"Does it have anything to do with Matheson?" he asked, instantly suspicious.

"Yes. Well, no. Maybe." She stared at her hands to stop the tremor.

Nick waited with mounting impatience.

"Carrie probably told you, I—I've been doing a little research into his background," Charlie confessed. "I've been to the Waller Clinic, where

Alan's daughter died, and have spoken to others about it, I've met with the pathologist who carried out the postmortem, and yesterday I interviewed the coroner's officer in the case."

"Whoa... Slow down," he said, holding up his hands in mock surrender. Charlie may have once been a top-flight journalist but he couldn't quite believe what he was hearing. Alan Matheson was her colleague, after all, not someone she was supposed to be investigating. That was his job. "Why are you doing all this?"

"I can't really explain, Nick, so please don't ask me to. I suppose I just felt like... like Angela was calling me, demanding that I find out everything I could about her death. That this was something I had to do in order to move forward, to work out what I should do next."

"And?"

Looking up, her eyes filling with tears, Charlie asked abruptly: "Nick, do you think it could be true? No, it can't possibly be... can it? I can't have been that wrong. Or was I always meant to find out?"

Nick was utterly lost. "Find out what?" he asked, placing his hand over hers to stop it from plucking at the soft folds of her trousers. "What is it, Charlie? What have you found out? Has Matheson done something to upset you? Because if he has, I'll fucking kill him."

"I'm sorry," she said suddenly, perhaps sensing his air of vindication. "I can't really talk about this right now. I made a mistake, Nick. I shouldn't have come here. I—I just didn't want to be on my own tonight."

Grabbing her bag, she headed for the door. Nick, dazed and worried, watched her go. Then he jumped to his feet.

HE FOUND HER sitting, staring at her steering wheel, trying to remember how to turn the ignition on. "Don't be stupid," he told her firmly. "You can't possibly drive, not like this. Come back inside." Seeing her hesitation, he added, "Charlie, I promise I won't ask you any more questions. You can just stay over and then see how you feel in the morning, okay?"

He lent her a T-shirt to sleep in, changed the sheets, and made up his bed, throwing a blanket on the sofa for himself. His mind was spinning with the little she'd told him, and he was appalled to find himself taking some sort of perverse comfort that his distrust about Sir Alan Matheson may have been justified.

He telephoned Carrie while Charlie took a long shower. "I haven't seen her this upset in years. Something's really spooked her."

"And you think it's something Alan may have done?"

"Haven't a clue," he replied, peeling open another beer. "Nothing she's said so far would even make it past the lawyers if it was presented to me as a story for the paper. God, Carrie, I've never even met the man and I've already marked him down as a bad guy. What does that say about me?"

"It says you care," Carrie replied. "So what do you think she found out?"

"Dunno."

"Should I come down for a few days? Try and talk to her, maybe?"

"Perhaps. I honestly don't know what to suggest. Listen, let's talk tomorrow. I'll see how she is then."

Carrie sighed. "Oh, Nick. I've been dreading something like this happening. Why, oh why, couldn't she just have met someone nice? Someone like you."

SOMETHING WOKE HIM a few hours later. His eyes opened and he sat bolt upright, confused for a moment not to be in his own bed. A second piercing scream fractured the night. Jumping up, he ran into his bedroom.

Charlie was crouched in a corner, her hands in the air, her face twisted and tearstained. "No! No! Get away! Get away!"

Running to her, ignoring the slaps and scratches she gave him as she flailed against him, he scooped her up in his arms, struggling, and carried her towards the bed. As he did so, one of her unpolished fingernails slashed at his right cheek, leaving a bright red weal.

"Charlie! Charlie!" he shouted as he shook her shoulders, willing her to return to him. "It's all right. It's me, Charlie. Nick."

It took much longer to calm her down than it used to. She huddled there, her hair snaked about her head, her eyes wild, shivering violently in his T-shirt. His arms around her, rubbing her back to calm her tremors, Nick buried his face in her hair and whispered, "It's okay, Charlie. Everything's okay. You've just had a bad dream. It's over now, Charlie. Sssh. Sssh."

As always, once the trembling stopped and the panic subsided, Charlie slumped against him like a small child, her body heavy with exhaustion. Lifting her gently, he laid her down on the bed and pulled the duvet over her. He knew, of old, that she'd fall straight off to sleep and would wake in the morning hollow-eyed but oblivious to the events of the night. Sitting by her side, he stroked her hair, smoothing the tangled strands from her face. "Sssh now. Go to sleep," he whispered. "I'll stay right here, Charlie. I promise."

A DISTANT SIREN roused him. Once again, he didn't know where he was. Studying the pale light filtering through the window blinds, he estimated it was shortly after dawn. Propped up against the wall, his neck stiff, he was still on the bed in which Charlie lay sleeping like a baby, her body curled in the fetal position, her left arm thrown across his bare legs.

For almost an hour, he watched the sun's measured track across the room, listening to Charlie's breathing, unwilling to wake her. But his bladder eventually got the better of him. Sliding out from under her, he slipped into the bathroom. He grimaced at his reflection in the mirror and examined the angry scratch across his cheek before splashing it with cold water.

Charlie didn't wake for another two hours. Nick had already texted his secretary to tell her he'd be late. He didn't want Charlie to wake alone. He heard her yawning before he saw her stumbling towards him, eyes ringed with dark circles, her hair disheveled.

Yawning again she stretched, her lithe legs flexing beneath his thigh-length T-shirt. "What time is it?" she groaned. She'd never been good at mornings.

Clicking on the kettle, he smiled. "After ten. Coffee?" Sniffing at a carton of milk and wrinkling his nose, he added: "Black okay?"

Charlie perched precariously on a bar stool, watching as he piled generous mounds of coffee into a glass *cafetière* and poured in boiling water. "What happened to your face?" she asked, peering at the ugly red gash on his cheek.

"Don't you remember? You weren't very gentle with me last night."

Charlie scoffed. "Seriously, Nick, you didn't have that when you went to bed, did you?"

Nick sat down opposite her. He handed her a mug of coffee as thick and black as crude oil. "Seriously? Well, then, I'm afraid you had another one of your bad dreams and lashed out a bit. It was my fault; I should have ducked."

The colour leeched from her face. "Oh, God, Nick. I'm so sorry—"

"At least there were no broken bones this time." Her nocturnal thrashings had cracked his ribs on more than one previous occasion. She'd also given him a black eye and so many bruises he'd lost count. He stopped smiling. "How long have these nightmares been back?"

Charlie cradled her mug in her hands and blew on the steam before replying. "A while," she said, her voice small. "A few months, maybe." She sipped at the strong black coffee.

"I don't suppose going to that clinic helped." Seeing the look in her eyes, Nick reached across the counter and covered her hand with his. When he and Charlie's father had escorted her to a similar clinic, staffed by those who'd promised to help her, Charlie had sat hunched in the front seat of his BMW like a terrified child as they'd pulled to a halt in the gravel drive of the imposing former rectory on the outskirts of Canterbury.

"Don't leave me here," she'd whispered through the waterfall in her head he knew she was still hearing.

"I have to, darling," he'd replied, his voice catching in his throat. "We've tried everything else, you know we have."

Ed Hudson leaned forward from the backseat and squeezed her shoulders. "Come on now, rabbit. We've been through this a dozen times and we've all agreed it's the best place for you. Let's not make it any more difficult than it is."

The two men had deposited the shell of Charlie in the marble-floored lobby, her suitcase at her feet, while they found a staff member to show her to her room. The *Tribune* hadn't skimped on the cost. The clinic was as plush as a five-star hotel. All that gave it away was the heavy security on the front door and the steel locks on the windows.

Three months. She'd spent three months in that gilded cage, much of the early days in the bathroom. Picking up a bar of soap she found on her sink on the first day, she spotted a single black hair stuck to it. She only just made it to the toilet bowl. The one thing that prevented her from screaming, she'd later confessed to Nick, was the fear that she'd never be able to stop.

For the initial weeks, she hadn't spoken at all. Closer to the brink of madness than at any other time in her life, he'd wondered if she'd ever be able to swim against the tide. But working with therapists and relishing the oblivion sedation brought her, she gradually caught up with her mind. Here, her new obsession with order was tolerated, her loathing of cigarettes accepted, as was her constant desire to wash and her wish for masking scents. She was allowed supplies of essential oils, and extra bars of soap for emergencies.

"It's just a phase," the doctors assured Nick. "This intense need for purging will eventually pass." Compared with the obsessions of some of her fellow inmates, hers were quite tame. With that knowledge came comfort; the reassurance that she was marginally less mad than the rest.

Solace was found from an unlikely source: papier-mâché therapy. Charlie wandered in through an open door of a sunny dayroom one afternoon and returned every day for a month.

"Papier-mâché literally means chewed paper," an instructor was telling the class. Papier-mâché. Charlie ran the words around in her mouth. Stopping in the doorway, she'd listened intently.

"In some households," the instructor continued, peering at his students through thick spectacles, "the servants of the rich were employed to chew the paper until it was pulp. Later they macerated it by hand. Some of the earliest examples of items made from this wet pulp, such as helmets and even coffins for highly prized falcons, date from China around A.D. 200. I promise I shan't ask you to chew the paper and we shan't attempt to be quite as ambitious, but it might be fun to see what we can make."

Joining in on the periphery, cutting out flimsy strips of newsprint, ignoring the fragmented words written across it that the reporters had taken so much trouble to write, Charlie moulded and pasted, snipped and glued until some recognisable shape emerged from her hands. Her enjoyment of one of the oldest art forms in history stemmed from her childhood, she admitted to her therapist.

"I can still remember the way the whole process smelled," she'd told Dr Rees. "Granddad would help me dollop wet newspaper onto the surface of balloons and flowerpots, and layer it with glue he made from flour and water. We even made animals."

Charlie now learned a different technique: how to turn the newsprint back to the pulp it once was, by soaking it in water overnight before mixing it with paste and using it as a kind of clay. While her fellow inmates modeled pretty floral bowls and vases, she harnessed the pulp's infinite versatility to craft angels and dogs, devils and masks. She was inspired by some of the fantastical papier-mâché masks she'd seen at the Carnivale in Venice, or the Mardi Gras in New Orleans. She thought of the gaily coloured piñatas filled with sweets that children in South America attack so joyously at celebrations; of her mother's heavily lacquered Japanese wall panel inlaid with mother-of-pearl; of the bleached white dolls' faces which had once gazed back at her in a toy museum in Paris.

The feel of the wet pulp in her fingers, the knowledge it imparted, seemed to soothe her. There was such simple pleasure in the process of creativity. Once dry, the pulp could be shaved or rasped, sanded or carved. It was durable and lightweight, decorative and utilitarian. What she could make from it was limited only by her imagination. She told Nick she longed to get her hands on every single news story she'd ever written, soak it in water to return it to its most basic form, then turn it into something lovely.

Something beautiful to leave behind.

When Nick arrived to take her from that place, Charlie had emerged looking the same but altered beyond recognition. In her hands she carried a large Inca-style warrior mask she'd made. "Someone to watch over me," she told him. Lighter than a feather, but heavy enough to anchor her to the car seat, she seemed glad of its weight in her lap during the long ride home.

The tragedy for Nick was that the purging Charlie had undergone behind those heavily locked doors included being rid of him. *The people we care for most are not good for us when we are ill,* Virginia Woolf had written, shortly before she'd filled her pockets with stones and walked into the River Ouse.

There had been plenty of glitches since: the nights Charlie could only half remember, the taste for the oblivion alcohol provided. Her mind had often strayed from its therapy-directed course but she'd always managed to pull herself up. Now, here she was, three years later, back to the nightmares, back to lashing out at Nick.

One pace forward, three paces back.

Was it the echoing corridors of the Waller Clinic and the terrible facts the coroner's officer had revealed about Angela Matheson's suicide which had brought back her demons? Or was she simply destined never to be free of them?

RETURNING TO HER flat later that day, Charlie came to an important conclusion. She had to stop behaving like the frightened creature she had once been. Even with her nightmares draining her reserves, she mustn't allow them to drag her back.

Adamantly refusing to believe what Dutton had told her about Alan, she forced herself to remember how kind and gentle he had always been to her; how he was with her in Italy. Dutton's ugly suspicions had come as a shock, that was all. A terrible shock. She was understandably shaken by them. But they were lies. She knew Alan. She'd made love to him. She knew him better than most. It couldn't possibly be true.

But she also knew, with an unshakeable certainty, that Angela Matheson wasn't going to go away. Nothing Charlie touched—her book, Turner,

Alan, or any aspect of the life she was trying to rebuild—was going to be free of Angela until Charlie untangled the mystery which had somehow opened up a road to her own past. The harder she tried to push Angela away, the more she was inexplicably drawn back to the dead girl's image, which now patrolled her days as well as her nights.

Her therapist had advocated that dreams were all part of her psyche. "As long as the pain's still coming out, being given vent somewhere, that is a healthy and natural response," Dr Rees had reassured her. He'd warned of her fragile emotional state and advised her not to put herself under any unnecessary strain.

How she wished she could confide in Carrie or even her parents, share her secrets with someone other than Nick. But she knew too well that if she articulated her concerns in any formal way, they might suddenly become real and take on a life of their own, whereas now they were merely flickering shadows, banished to the darkest recesses of her skull.

When had she become so secretive, she wondered. When she dishonestly told her friends that her grandfather had died of cancer? Or later, on those long lonely journeys to some catastrophic world event, bottling everything up so that no one would think less of her for her fear? Perhaps it was on her return from those desolate places, when she'd so wanted to lay down the burden of all she'd witnessed, but didn't feel able. If the scenes she had witnessed could damage her so badly, then who was she to harm someone else by sharing them?

And what good would spilling her secrets do anyway? Nothing could eradicate the grisly images from her brain or the foul stink from her nostrils. There was no erase button in her memory banks, not even stop. There was just rewind, pause, play, rewind, pause, play, as the images flickered back and forth across the invisible screen inside her head.

As sensitive to exposure as undeveloped film, Charlie hadn't dared let anyone close, until Alan. He alone had stripped off the carefully applied veneer of defence and laid her bare. Was it because he, too, was hemmed in by shadows?

Quelling her own misgivings, dispelling the damning lies Richard

Dutton had burned into her brain, Charlie persuaded herself that it was far better to ignore them. Angela's wild accusations were just the rantings of a damaged young woman at the most desperate point of her life.

The conversation she needed to have with Alan about Angela, and about the truth of her own past, hovered ominously between them, and she knew she couldn't avoid it forever. But she couldn't face it, not just yet. Her nightmares were sapping her, and Alan was still too far away to help. Long-distance confrontation was not her strong point. Better to pretend her conversation with Dutton had never happened, to push it from her mind and file it away for another day, a day when she and Alan were back together again. A day when she felt stronger.

No; for now, she needed their relationship to remain a blank page, a virgin sheet of paper, perfect in its sensuous formation, unblemished in all its raw beauty. There must be no imperfections. They would come, but she wasn't ready for them yet.

WHEN ALAN RANG from Italy and announced he'd be staying another ten days, Charlie's relief was palpable. If he sensed it down the telephone line, he didn't let on.

"The light's so good at this time of year," he explained. "I'm doing some good work and I don't want to break off just yet." Hearing her silence, he added, casually: "You're very welcome to join me again, Charlie, if you'd like to, although I'm not sure I'd be much company. I'm in the studio most of the day."

"No, no," Charlie responded as brightly as she could. "You stay out as long as you like. I'm busy here, too, remember? Cracking on with the book."

"Everything's all right, isn't it? I mean, you're still missing me madly?"

"Madly," she repeated. "But my friend Carrie's coming to stay with me for a few days. And I've got so much work to catch up on after the last couple of weeks that I'll be glad of the reprieve."

"Reprieve? You make me sound like a death sentence!"

An image of Angela lying naked on the mortuary slab, Dr North pris-ing her shoes from her stiffened feet, brought a flood of bile to Charlie's throat.

"I—I've got to go now, Alan," she blurted. "There's someone at the door."

"I'll call you in a day or two. And Charlie—"

"What?"

"Don't let anyone else touch you. That's my prerogative, remember?"

The line went dead before he could hear her retching into the sink.

Foolscap

A size of paper, about 330 by 200 mm;

foolscap paper, named from the former watermark

representing a fool's cap

24

*I*F CARRIE WANTED to see Charlie, it was an unspoken rule between them that she would always come south. It had been many years since the two friends had met in Carrie's hometown, and for good reason.

The last time they'd been together in Manchester was a warm June day ten years earlier. Charlie, seeking a respite after a particularly arduous month in Israel, had asked for a stint on the northern desk. Carrie had moved to the Midlands permanently by then, to decide her future. Charlie was looking forward to a quieter tour of duty and to working alongside her best friend again.

"It'll do her a world of good," Nick had told Carrie on the telephone, within earshot of Charlie. "She needs to relax a little and do some girlie stuff."

"I don't need to do girlie stuff, I just need to rest," Charlie snapped in the background. The pills had stopped working months ago. Sleep deprivation flayed her nerves.

"Let's find somewhere to have a drink," Carrie had suggested brightly when she'd met Charlie at the station that innocent summer's day. "You look like you could do with one."

They'd taken just a few steps into Corporation Street when Charlie stopped abruptly and grabbed Carrie's arm. Both of them could feel the rumbling reverberating within them, the unmistakable sound Charlie knew only too well. In an instant, she was transported to the streets of Ramallah and a suicide bombing she'd witnessed the previous year. Oh, God, the blood and dismembered limbs and the mutilated children in the back of that bombed-out bus. She'd never forget their screams. This was England, though, not the West Bank.

As the rumbling grew and everything rolled into slow motion, Charlie knew with horrific clarity that this was no flashback. Tackling Charlie to the ground and throwing herself across her, they looked up just in time to see an orange-and-white van parked outside Marks & Spencer erupt in a shower of metal.

The pressure waves that fanned out along the street and along all the streets for a quarter of a mile around shattered every ground-floor window and sucked the oxygen out of the air. In that eerie moment of stillness and quiet, the vacuum it created dragged upper windows out of their casings and popped complete frontages from shops. Only when the glass hit the ground did the furor begin. Of the two hundred people that were killed and the hundreds more injured in that obscene rending of space, most were hurt by flying debris and shards of glass.

Bowled along the street by the force of the explosion, still clinging to each other, Carrie and Charlie were rolled and tumbled and finally slammed bodily against a cast-iron wastepaper bin. Cowering together, shielding their faces and eyes, they crouched, waiting for that next uncanny moment of silence and calm they both knew would follow, the one before the sirens and the screaming, the shock and the agony set in.

Charlie was the first on her feet. "I'll phone the news desk while you fetch your cameras from the car," she'd yelled at her friend, as soon as the noise began. "Meet me at the top of the street in three minutes."

Carrie, who seemed unsure if she could even stand, gaped up at Charlie in bewilderment. Charlie rushed to a nearby telephone kiosk and dialed the number for her newsdesk. In the reflection of the shiny chrome she noticed that her cheek was bleeding and her clothes torn. "Hello?" she yelled into the receiver, pulling what was left of her blouse across her partially exposed chest. "It's Charlie Hudson. I'm in Manchester City Centre. There's just been a massive car bomb. IRA probably. It's serious. Tell the backbench I'm on the scene and I'll file as soon as I can. Carrie Kidd's with me so we have pictures covered but we'll need people at the hospitals and someone down at Scotland Yard. Clear the front page, Bill, this is a big one."

With that, she slammed down the phone and ran towards the worst of the carnage, just as everyone else was fleeing the other way.

Carrie confessed later that Charlie's composure had frightened her. As she staggered back to her car for her camera bag, tears streaming down her dirt-stained face, she wondered how many times her friend must have lived through such experiences to remain so controlled. The news instinct was so strong within Charlie. She seemed to have no choice but to act on it. For her, there was no time for personal feelings in a war zone.

Until that moment, Carrie had never quite realised what a pitiless automaton the endless treadmill of news reporting was turning Charlie into. As she pulled her cameras from the boot of her car, dreading the ghastly sights she knew she was about to capture forever through her lens, she made a private resolution to herself: she'd get out of a business that could harden hearts as big and tender as Charlie's.

BUT MANCHESTER WAS light-years away and the madness of that other life was firmly behind them now.

"Hello, stranger," Carrie said by way of greeting, when Charlie unlocked and opened the door of her flat.

"Hello, you," Charlie responded evenly, picking up her friend's rucksack. "Welcome to the nuthouse. Come on in. Hey, love the embroidery on those jeans! You look great."

Carrie laughed. "You wouldn't say that if you'd seen me at two o'clock this morning, trying to write up a care order. I should have done it sooner, but, as usual, I didn't leave myself enough time."

Charlie linked her arm through Carrie's and smiled. "Well, never mind all that. You can relax now. So, what would you like to do?"

"Oh, I don't know," Carrie said, her freckled expression impish. "How about the usual and a movie?"

Charlie's heart lifted. "My thoughts exactly. I've got everything ready."

When Carrie saw what was on the coffee table, she laughed aloud. Picking up a DVD, she turned it over in her hand and chortled. "*Ghost*! Didn't we watch that one in Basra?"

"Yup," Charlie replied, popping the cork on the champagne. "Four times, as I recall, the last during an air raid. The rest of the press corps, hiding down in the basement, thought we were crazy." They flopped onto the sofa together, shoes off, feet up on the table, to examine the contents of a box of decadently expensive chocolates.

"Now look at us," Carrie remarked. "That seems like three lifetimes ago."

"It was," Charlie replied, darkly.

The next few days the two friends spent together were some of their best in a while. They drank their way through just about everything in Charlie's flat. They slept until noon, went shopping, to the hairdressers, and for manicures, took indulgently long lunches, and did all the girlie stuff Charlie never did except with Carrie.

Carrie asked about Alan and received a carefully rehearsed series of bulletins. She heard all about Alan's fabulous house in Italy and the fascinating visit to the Fabriano mill; she was read whole chunks of the book Charlie and Alan were working on together, but Charlie told her nothing meaningful about her new relationship or what she had been so upset about when she'd gone to see Nick a few days earlier.

Both accepted that there was much more to tell, but both half-expected the secrecy. It wasn't that Charlie didn't want to confide in her best friend, it was just that she could only manage such confidences in short bursts, for fear the emotion of them would destroy her. She knew Carrie suspected something. Nick would undoubtedly have told her he was convinced that it was something about the suicide of Angela, but for now Charlie hoped that Carrie would sense that she needed to sort things out in her own mind first. In time, Charlie would tell her all that she wanted her to know.

· · ·

ON CARRIE'S FINAL day in London, Charlie agreed to go with her to a retrospective exhibition at the Barbican of news photographs by a mutual friend. Carrie had been perfectly prepared to go alone, but, to her surprise, Charlie insisted on accompanying her.

They rushed into the gallery straight from a boozy lunch, only to be faced with a series of stern-faced pseudo-intellectuals viewing the illuminated exhibits in hushed reverence. Stifling giggles, they abandoned their coats at the door and took their place in the orderly line that weaved its way around the numbered pictures. Carrie bought a catalogue, but Charlie said she didn't need one. She knew each pictured hellhole intimately.

Suddenly sombre, the two friends wandered through the gallery together, staring at the moody black-and-white pictures, each one silently absorbed in her own thoughts. Charlie felt Carrie watching her closely, noticing the tears in her eyes, almost certainly imagining she knew the reason. But she was a good enough friend not to say anything. She knew that the very fact that Charlie had even agreed to step foot inside this gallery was a mark of how much she had grown since the bad days. There'd been times when she couldn't even cope with a car backfiring, and if a helicopter flew low overhead she'd automatically fling herself to the pavement. There was also a time when she would have crumpled under the weight of memories these pictures would spark.

Charlie peered studiously into each glazed window of paper. "Bluey's all right, but he isn't you," she told her friend softly. "He doesn't have your eye for detail."

"Oh, I don't know about that. These look pretty terrific to me."

Suddenly, Charlie turned to Carrie. "Don't you ever miss it? You had such talent. It sometimes seems odd to me that all that vision and energy is now confined to saving lost souls."

"Isn't that exactly what we were trying to do back then?" Carrie asked quietly. "Save lost souls? Or at least report on their plight in such a way so that someone else could save them after we'd gone on to the next atrocity? What I'm doing now isn't so very different, you know. I'm still dealing with the suffering, with people who need me to try to make sense of what's happened to them. Only this time I don't walk away."

Charlie nodded. Once a story was in print, its victims were largely forgotten. Although after Rajak, of course, Charlie could never walk away again. As the sole survivor, and the author of the definitive account of those who didn't survive that day, she became a key witness in the international campaign against Slobodan Milosevic for war crimes. Her unexpected turn in the spotlight was as unwelcome as the events which led to it. To have written her account in her own way, privately, was one thing. To stand in a courtroom in The Hague and face brutal cross-examination by Milosevic and his lawyers had been quite another. The experience had nearly broken her all over again.

"How about you? Don't *you* miss it, my favourite lost soul?" Carrie asked.

"Occasionally," Charlie replied, honestly. "I'd be lying if I said there weren't times when I hear some big story breaking and wish nothing more than that I was on the next plane out. Then I remember what it was really like. How lonely it could be, and how bloody awful. I see that part of my life as if through frosted glass, it seems so distant. I think of all those colleagues of ours who are still alive, still out there doing it—at the expense of their marriages, their sanity, and their livers. They're either much, much stronger mentally than I ever was, or they are so badly damaged that they no longer know the meaning of reality. And then, of course, there's the guilt."

"Guilt?" Then Carrie nodded, knowing the answer to her own question.

"You know—for surviving when so many didn't. For living the life I lead now, doing pretty much what I want, when I want, when so many can't. It's crazy, but sometimes I actually curse my own good fortune."

Carrie squeezed her arm. "Charlie, I think you're forgetting something. Nobody who knows what you've been through would consider it good fortune. This is payback time. You're allowed to enjoy the rest of your life, you know. You've earned the right."

She stared at another photograph. "I'm not sure you're right about

Bluey, by the way." She gazed upon the shot of a baby boy, crying as he stood in a rusty cot in a Romanian orphanage, his skin caked in excrement, his nose full of snot. "I'd have been pretty proud of that one. How much more detail do you need?" Scanning the caption underneath, she exclaimed: "Hey, that was taken near Bacau. Weren't you there in 1990 after the fall of Ceausescu? When you went to do that piece on the orphanages?"

Charlie nodded. She felt her fists clench into balls as she waited for the first hot flush of memory to pass.

"What was it like?" Carrie asked.

"Dark, so dark inside. Oh, and the smell!" Charlie murmured, her mind exploring rooms long since closed. "I remember the children were dazzled by the light. They'd lived in the dark behind shutters for years. It took them ages to grow accustomed to the brightness. . . ."

"Go on."

"The people in the town believed the orphanages were full of monsters. The authorities had told them that those they could hear screaming were horribly disfigured, chronically disabled, or insane. But when the aid workers threw open the doors and carried these perfectly normal, horribly emaciated children down into the town, the locals fell weeping to their knees at the side of the road. None of them could believe how terribly wrong they'd been."

"What did they do?"

"They welcomed the children into their homes. They bathed, fed, and clothed them; they made them wooden toys and knitted blankets. The charity I was writing about harnessed all that guilt and shame and put it to use."

Carrie nodded. "And the article you wrote helped raise thousands in donations, as I recall. So that's a good memory, isn't it?"

"Yes," Charlie said softly, looking at Carrie with surprise. "Yes, I guess it is."

INHALING THE PUNGENT smell of the bright orange marigolds before she laid them on her grandfather's grave a few days later, Charlie thrust her hands deep into her jacket pockets and smiled, before taking her customary seat.

"Hi, Granddad. Here I am again. Thought I'd better make a duty call to see how Mum's getting along. Although I'm honestly not sure why I bothered."

Henry's nose buried itself in a pile of last year's leaves, his snorts blowing them upwards in little puffs. The terrier's activity dislodged a piece of pink tissue paper that lifted on the breeze and danced before them like a ballerina, pirouetting with each gust. It reminded Charlie of a music box she'd had as a child, the pink-tulled dancer reflected in a tiny mirror as it twirled in time to the tune. As quickly as it began, the dance of the tissue paper stopped. The breeze dropped and it fell, deflated, to the ground. No longer a ballerina. Just an unwanted scrap of paper.

"What I wouldn't give to be able to speak with you now," Charlie told her grandfather, staring at the granite headstone.

She paused to scratch Henry's upturned ears.

"I know I'm not wrong, Granddad. I do. I know Alan isn't what Angela claimed he is. I'm not so badly damaged that I can't tell a child-abusing rapist when I meet one.

"Alan Matheson is a kind and good man. That, I'm convinced of. And all the reports about Angela agreed she often went out of her way to deliberately antagonise her father. She tried to burn down his studio. Even in her final moments it seemed, she was still seeking to destroy him with a lie."

A shaft of sunlight broke through the clouds, but it was surprisingly chilly. The wind rustled the remaining leaves on the trees, sounding like the crumpling of paper. Henry, his face foolish, hunched against Charlie, trying to seek shelter in the lee of her coat.

"But what I can't figure out is why she would be so cruel. What crime could he have possibly committed for her to make such a terrible claim, knowing that it would destroy his career, her parents' marriage, Alan's whole life? Was it that she was jealous of him? Of his phenomenal success as an artist? Success she couldn't possibly match?"

As if on cue, a funeral cortege made its way up the hill, the gleaming black cars keeping pace with each other as their occupants sat bleakly inside. A little boy, no more than five, sat on his father's lap, his starfish hands pressed against the window. He saw Henry and grinned, banging his hand on the glass to get the dog's attention until his father seized it and crushed it within his own.

Ahead of them crawled the hearse, wreaths of flowers adorning a simple mahogany coffin, elegant white lilies cascading down the sides. A woman, Charlie felt instinctively. A young mother.

"I know how lucky I am to be alive," she told her grandfather wistfully, when the cars had passed. "And I know I should be making much more of this second chance. But before I do that, I need to find the strength to somehow face this final truth, whatever the consequences."

Henry, utterly miserable, looked up at her with pleading brown eyes.

"If I don't, Granddad, if all these questions remain unanswered in my mind, how will I ever be able to trust anyone again?"

25

THERE WERE TIMES in Charlie's life when, as a career woman with a firm idea of what she wanted from life, she'd been supremely sure of herself. To anyone looking in from the outside, she appeared to have it all—a successful marriage, a great job. She brooked no nonsense and was never one to let something, or someone, stand in her way. On the journey home from her parents' house that day she reminded herself that, in time, she could be like that again.

Within an hour of unlocking her front door and throwing her keys on the kitchen table, she'd taken the first decisive step. After contacting some former colleagues for an address, and receiving some fresh newspaper cuttings by fax, she prepared to take matters into her own hands. Short of confronting Alan, which she was still reluctant to do, there was only one other way to find out what lay behind these ridiculous allegations of Angela's.

Making her way to a smart mansion block overlooking a garden square in Knightsbridge, Charlie planted her feet on the doorstep and ordered her thoughts to be quiet. A laminated paper strip sandwiched between two others to the right of the front door spelled out the name of the person she had come to see. She recognised Alan's handwriting instantly.

Taking a deep breath, she pressed the buzzer. There was silence from the intercom. She pressed the buzzer once more, hearing her own heart beating.

"Hello?" a muffled voice reverberated through the mesh. "May I help you?"

"Mrs Matheson? Mrs Matheson, my name's Charlotte Hudson. You don't know me, but I'm a friend of your ex-husband's and I wondered if I could come up for a chat?"

Silence.

"Mrs Matheson?"

"This isn't she," the voice replied imperiously.

"Oh, well, is she there?"

"Not today," said the distant voice.

"Well, will she be there tomorrow?"

"I shouldn't think so."

"Okay, then, I'll call again in a day or two. Thank you." About to step away from the intercom, Charlie returned impulsively and pressed the buzzer. "May I ask to whom I'm speaking?"

After a brief silence, she heard: "A friend."

Charlie tried twice more to make contact with Sarah Matheson, with similarly unsatisfactory results. On the next occasion, the same voice answered and claimed to be alone. On a second attempt, later the same day, there was no reply at all. But when Charlie looked up, there was a sudden movement at the window, as if someone had just stepped away from the curtain.

Charlie persuaded herself that it was the challenge of actually meeting Sarah Matheson that drove her on. Her initial nervousness at the course she was attempting to take was soon outweighed by the frustration she felt at being blocked. It had been easier getting past the Republican Guard in Baghdad than penetrating Mrs Matheson's inner sanctum.

She filled the intervening days reading up on her chosen target. Sarah Matheson, née Sarah Hildon, had been *Tatler*'s Debutante of the Year when she first came onto the social scene in the early 1970s. Part of the dynastic Hildon clan whose very name spoke of old money and impeccable social pedigree, Sarah had grown up in Hildon Hall in North Yorkshire.

Her marriage to the young artist Alan Matheson had shocked her family, who'd consequently cut her off without a penny. By all accounts, it was to her credit that she'd remained with Alan in the face of such opposition. Eventually, however, she won her father over and, when he died, she inherited the bulk of his estate.

But according to several of the gossip column clippings, Sarah Matheson was emotionally brittle, and her unhappiness over the long rift with her family that her marriage had sparked made her even more vulnerable. She and Alan had lost two children in miscarriages, and she'd apparently never fully recovered from the suicide of her only surviving child.

Exasperated by her lack of success in meeting Sarah and painfully aware of Alan's intention to fly home from Italy in a day or two, Charlie tried once more, this time early in the morning. But, when she rang the bell, the same voice greeted her.

"Oh, hello there, it's Ms Hudson again. I'm so sorry to trouble you again but I was very much hoping to find Mrs Matheson at home this time."

There was an empty pause.

"Did Alan send you?" the disembodied voice asked suspiciously.

"No, oh no. He doesn't even know I'm here."

"What exactly do you want?"

Charlie hesitated. "I want, I need, to talk to Mrs Matheson. It's about Angela."

More silence.

Charlie could hear a low sigh. On impulse, she leaned closer to the intercom and softly said: "Mrs Matheson?"

With a brusque buzzing noise, the lock was released and the front door clicked open. Charlie pulled it towards her and stepped inside.

IF CHARLIE HAD expected Sarah Matheson to be a broken woman, still shattered by the death of her marriage and the suicide of her daughter, she was wrong. Instead, she was presented with an impeccably attired ash blonde in a grey jersey dress topped with a double row of pearls and matching earrings. Sarah Matheson's eyes were a rare blue, and her face was framed by high cheekbones, an aquiline nose, and unusually full lips. Looking closer, Charlie realised that the older woman was no stranger to cosmetic surgery. In fact, there could be little doubt she had been completely remodeled.

So this was the woman Alan had been so cold to on the telephone. This was the ice queen Richard Dutton had spoken of. The mother who stood like a marble statue over her daughter's body, eyes dry, while her grieving husband buckled beside her.

Sarah Matheson ushered Charlie in through a cloud of Chanel No. 5 and took her place neatly on the edge of a gilded ormolu chair to the left of an impressive white marble fireplace. Hanging in pride of place above the mantelpiece was a delicate watercolour of Alan's symmetrical knot garden in Italy. A gift from Alan, perhaps? Or a hard-won item in a bitter divorce settlement?

Hands clasped together, her feet crossed at the ankles, Sarah Matheson gave Charlie a doubtful glare and waited for her to settle onto the opposite sofa. Charlie found herself wishing she'd worn something more elegant than jeans, boots, and a plain ribbed sweater.

"Well, now that you're here, what do you want to know?" her hostess asked coolly.

In all her years as a journalist, Charlie had never been completely at ease with intruding on a stranger's grief. She'd rehearsed what she was going to say in her mind, but now that she was facing this extraordinarily composed woman, her words seemed wholly inappropriate.

"I—er—I'm so sorry if I seem to have been badgering you," she began, her fingers tightly interlocked. "I'd never have called so often if I'd realised it was you on the intercom all along."

Sarah Matheson examined Charlie distantly before studying her perfect fingernails. "I don't know what you mean. I had a friend here and she left as you came up in the lift. You must have just missed her. She did mention something about a woman calling before, but she never gave me any details. She's somewhat, how should I say it? Overprotective."

Charlie let it go.

"I'm sorry to say that I never met your daughter Angela, and I know very little about her, but I'm working with Alan on a book and I thought it might be helpful to me, I mean to our collaboration, if I knew a bit more."

Sarah Matheson fixed her with an icy stare. "Ah, yes, you're the one who's sleeping with him." Her tone was as measured as if she were remarking on the weather.

"Sorry?"

"You are sleeping with my husband, aren't you, Ms Hudson?"

"Ex-husband," Charlie couldn't help saying, but Sarah Matheson didn't flinch at the correction. "Yes, yes, I am."

"Marvelous in bed, isn't he? A truly accomplished lover," her hostess remarked with a twisted smile, rising swiftly and reaching for a cigarette from an inlaid wooden box on the mantelpiece. "Mind if I smoke? It's the last of my addictions."

Charlie was, by now, so nonplussed she could only shake her head speechlessly.

Sarah placed her cigarette in a long ivory holder which she slid between pouting lips, lit it, and blew smoke languorously across the room. Examining the young woman seated uncomfortably before her, she folded her arms across breasts too pert to be natural and looked down at her sympathetically.

"How long have you known Alan?" she asked, drawing deeply on her cigarette.

"Quite a few months," Charlie replied, her nostrils flaring, wondering how she could win back the balance of power. Wasn't it she who was meant to be asking the questions?

"And you believe you love him?"

Charlie stared up into those glacial eyes. "I—I don't honestly know how to answer that. Or even if I should."

"Come, come, it's a very straightforward question. I should think someone of your background should be able to give me a direct answer."

Charlie wondered what Sarah Matheson meant by "your background." Was she referring to the fact that she was a writer, or from an inferior class? Before she could answer, however, Sarah spoke again.

"Let me give you some advice," she said, stepping towards her. "Never mistake love for lust. Alan may be good in bed, but don't let that fool you for a moment. You'll think you're still in control, but—with Alan—you're not. And you never will be. Sex is an extremely powerful weapon in the wrong hands."

She turned and wandered towards the fireplace, staring up at the watercolour undoubtedly laid onto Alan's precious Whatman paper.

"I have only my memories now, but I've never forgotten what it felt like to be seduced by him. Although I'll always be grateful, I'm also painfully aware that I probably had a lucky escape."

"Lucky escape? What do you mean? Escape from what?"

"Maybe from him. Maybe from myself and what he brought out in me," the older woman replied, her gaze still fixed on Alan's watercolour. "Who knows?"

"Are you honestly suggesting I'm in some sort of danger?" Charlie asked.

Sarah Matheson raised a sardonic eyebrow. "Perhaps. It all depends what you're capable of." Grinding her cigarette into a silver ashtray, she added curtly: "Now, you'll have to excuse me, Ms Hudson. I'm having lunch with a count at San Lorenzo's. Come, I'll walk you down."

Charlie stared at the lipstick-stained stub for a moment before rising to follow her hostess from the room.

"This obviously isn't a good time," she said, trying to catch up while scribbling hastily on a scrap of paper from the notebook in her pocket. "Perhaps I could come and see you again? Here's my number. I really do need to talk to you about your daughter, Mrs Matheson. It's quite impor-tant."

They reached the hallway and Charlie handed Sarah the piece of paper. Slipping it in her pocket without troubling to look at it, and pulling on a pair of blue kid gloves, Sarah Matheson opened the door and stepped briskly down the stone steps to the street. Charlie followed plaintively.

"I just want to know what Angela was like," she panted. "Alan never speaks of her."

Turning to face Charlie as they both reached the pavement, Sarah said tightly, "Is it a wonder? Angela was a little bitch. She caused nothing but pain from the day she forced her way bloodily into this world till the day she did us both a favour and departed it." Steadying herself on the railings and extending a gloved right hand, she added evenly: "You may call me next week. I'm sure you have my number."

Charlie, too shocked to speak, took her hand.

"And by the way, my dear," Sarah added, almost as an afterthought. "It's *Lady* Matheson. Lady Sarah Matheson. My husband is a knight of the realm, remember it. Good-bye."

And she walked purposefully towards Beauchamp Place, leaving Charlie feeling like she'd just been mugged.

26

The timing couldn't have been worse: Charlie had to hurry straight from her encounter with Sarah Matheson to the comparative calm of a major London museum. She had an appointment with a respected conservator who'd promised to talk her through the finer points of paper care. There would be no time to dwell on the extraordinary exchange she'd just had in Knightsbridge.

Professor Andrew Walmsley was every bit the jolly eccentric he'd sounded on the telephone, fitting her mental image of James Whatman. Greying, bearded, and bespectacled, with a comic smile and an engaging manner, he shook her hand warmly, then led her through a maze of corridors and rooms to his specialist workroom.

"This is where we hold and restore all the works of art on paper, as well as many of the older books and manuscripts and our collection of hand-painted wallpaper," the professor explained, walking her through specially sealed double doors into a hermetically controlled storage space. "We can have no natural light, and our temperature and humidity are kept at a constant level to avoid corruption."

Charlie inhaled the cool, clear air and found comfort in the familiar scents. This is what she needed—silence, work, the methodical process of researching and writing. This would keep her safe from harm. But what harm? What possible danger had Sarah been referring to?

It took a moment for her eyes to acclimatise to the lower-voltage bulbs that created an ambient glow quite different from the bright glare of the previous rooms. "Our air here is constantly washed and filtered," her guide continued. "We have humidifiers and dehumidifiers on standby in the unlikely event that the air-conditioning should fail."

He donned a pair of white cotton gloves to prevent the natural oils from his hands coming into contact with any of the artefacts, and led her behind a black curtain. There he showed her rack after rack of padded vertical stalls placed one against the other. Each contained no more than two works of art, each separated by a foam spacer.

"Why the curtain?" Charlie asked.

"To block out what light there is," Professor Walmsley answered. "Works of art on paper, especially watercolours, are particularly affected by light."

"And the padding is presumably to protect them from touching each other?"

"Yes, and from being damaged during removal, of course. Some of our art works are many hundreds of years old. The slightest contact can cause them to disintegrate." He added with a smile, "As you can see, Ms Hudson, we take ourselves rather seriously."

Slipping off his gloves, he manoeuvred her back to a large table littered with microscopes and cameras, lighting systems and brushes, where he poured some coffee from a tartan-patterned flask he unearthed from the chaos. She cupped her hands around the mug he gave her, noticing in passing that it bore the logo of a well-known dangerous-sports club.

"Are these the ideal conditions for works of art on paper to be kept in?" she asked.

"Pretty much." Professor Walmsley grinned. "A place where the temperature is just so and the humidity kept between forty and fifty-five per cent to prevent the cellulose fibres in the pulp from deteriorating. The paper must be kept in a place deep within a building, away from any windows, as we are. Carpets and furnishings which can hold and emit moisture should be kept to a minimum. And then you have to be terribly careful about wood."

"Wood?"

"Yes. Anything like cedar which emits resins or strong odours is definitely banned. All other woods must be coated with a synthetic varnish to seal them. Other harmful substances include rubber, wool, some types of cloth, and decorative papers—they leech colour. Only linen or cotton tapes are used to bind any openings."

"Do you use silica gel to soak up excess moisture?"

"Oh, yes. It's vital for art works such as these. But you have to choose your gel very carefully and then keep it separately in the storeroom for at least two weeks before introduction, so that it has just the right temperature and humidity."

"This sounds like a logistical nightmare. Surely it can't be feasible for every library and university, museum and art gallery to take this sort of care?"

Professor Walmsley smiled as his hands rose and collected his spectacles from his face. "That's only the half of it, Ms Hudson. A true conservator should know and understand everything from the local weather and atmospheric conditions to what paper-eating insects and moulds might be indigenous to the region. Constant vigilance is required on cleanliness and use of appropriate fumigation, quite apart from monitoring the amount of light, the heat, the damp, and whether any other harmful substances might be affecting precious and irreplaceable works."

Charlie nodded, impressed. As she took a sip from her mug, the professor commented with a wry smile, "Strictly speaking, I shouldn't even have coffee in here. It qualifies as a foodstuff which might attract pests. But, sometimes, rules are meant to be broken."

"Besides which, I should think you need something hot to drink in here," Charlie replied, drawing her coat around her. "It's freezing."

"Not freezing, my dear," the professor corrected, pointing to a complicated gauge thermometer on the wall. "Precisely forty-two degrees Fahrenheit. I am one of the few people who can stand it. Many of my interns can only stay for short bursts at a time."

"What kind of pests would you have in here?"

"Anything from bookworms, wood lice, silverfish, and the common fly to mice."

"Mice?" Charlie asked, her eyes scanning the corners of the room for the telltale droppings she knew only too well from Rhubarb Cottage.

The professor laughed. "We don't have them here, but other establishments have suffered. Mould, mildew, and fungus are much more of a problem, though, especially when new works arrive that haven't been well cared for. There's always a risk that they'll contaminate the rest. That's where the disinfecting chamber comes in." He pointed to a large glass cabinet that would have looked more at home in a science laboratory. "And then we have the problem of acid."

"Acid?"

"Yes, from pollutants in the atmosphere and from the acids within the paper itself. Acid is one of the principal reasons for deterioration. The paper becomes brittle and weak, and there's little that can be done to save it. Papers made of unpurified wood pulp after the 1860s are especially vulnerable. Tragically, few of the artists who used that paper realised its impermanence. They bought it for cheapness. Only the rag-content papers of that era survive well, even if they have been sized with acid."

"So you got what you paid for, even then?"

"So it would appear."

"And the sort of papers an artist like Turner was using at his peak, the Whatman's and the linen-rag European papers, have they survived better than most?"

"Yes and no. It all depended how the artist treated them. Sometimes Turner abused his papers appallingly. It was almost as if he was punishing them. I have rarely known anyone to be so ruthless."

Charlie thought of Alan's attack on the paper taped to the easel of his Suffolk studio. *Ruthless.* Something cold slid through her mind. Forcing herself away from the image, she hastily changed the subject. "If the process of storage is so important and the climate the paper is kept in so vital, how can these kinds of works ever be put on display?"

"They aren't, for any great length of time. Many are allowed out of their cool, dark cells for only a few weeks in a year and then only in specially controlled conditions designed to protect them from harm. Some of the most highly prized artefacts are exhibited as reproductions. The originals are viewed only by special request. That way they can be preserved for future generations."

"Out of their cool, dark cells," Charlie repeated aloud, writing it down. "I like that. You make it sound like they're in prison."

The professor laughed. "Well, I suppose they are. And, if so, then I must be their jailer. Unless they behave themselves and I open the door, they remain locked away down here, never to see daylight or impart their colour and splendour to an unsuspecting public."

"And like all jailers," Charlie said, almost to herself, shivering in the chilly tomb of his working environment, "you're imprisoned here, too."

"That's very true," Walmsley agreed, winking, "which is why I do that." He pointed to the dangerous-sports logo on the mug she was still cradling for its residual warmth.

"Really?" She looked again at the cartoon of a man in free fall over a mountain. "I'm afraid I assumed that someone else had left it here."

"Not at all." He grinned. "At every possible opportunity, I hurl myself out of planes, scale mountains without a safety harness, snowboard, go hot-air ballooning and hang gliding."

Charlie laughed. "Frankly, I'm shocked. You just didn't seem the type."

"All of us need a little danger every now and again, Ms Hudson," he reminded her, his eyes dancing wickedly. "Isn't danger the only thing that reminds us that we're alive?"

STILL UNSETTLED BY her odd encounter with Sarah Matheson, and increasingly anxious about Alan's impending return, Charlie locked herself away for three whole days, transcribing and digesting all that Professor Walmsley had taught her. His voice was perfect as that of James Whatman, and his face became that of the great papermaker in her mind. With his unwitting assistance, she could finally see the one character who was pivotal to her book. Alan was Turner. He also doubled as Ruskin. All she had to do now was blend the three of them together seamlessly.

Next, she threw herself into compiling the glossary of papermaking terms for the front of the book. Lost to the outside world, she deliberately filled her brain to overflowing with the strange language of papermaking, or what Lori Hunter had called "white craft." Speaking each word aloud, until they seemed to take on a tempo all their own.

Double Pott. Pinched Post. Albert. Duke. Columbier. Best of all, though, were the words harvested from the complicated process of paper-making. These terms had a mysterious alchemy all their own. Abaca and alum, Badger and coucher, dandy-roll and flong, gampi, hog, kollergang, lignin, mitsumata, potcher, Silurian, slushing, and tribbles. Each of them created a magical waterfall of sound.

The more she listened, the more she stared at the words as they cascaded onto the flickering screen before her eyes, the more the little black letters pitched and fell, merged and mingled, until she no longer knew what she was writing or even thinking.

Time had no meaning, all other sustenance was unimportant. All that mattered were these weird and wonderful creatures drowning out the roaring in her ears.

27

CHARLIE COULD FEEL the sweat trickling down her back as she waited in the hot arrivals hall at Heathrow. Alan's plane was delayed by weather over France, and she'd been standing for over an hour, increasingly anxious for her first sight of him in weeks.

She wondered what she could possibly hope for. That by seeing him again, by looking into those fiercely intelligent eyes of his, she'd instantly know the truth behind Angela's damning accusation? That all her instincts would be right? And what if they weren't? What if she were to discover that secretly he was the sick monster the coroner's officer and even Nick believed him to be? What then?

The delay wasn't helping. Her back was a massed knot of nerves. Part of her wanted to run away—something she did so well—but another voice urged her to stay and face her fears.

"Trust your instincts, Charlie," she told herself under her breath as she waited. It was something her grandfather used to tell her time and again. She mustn't let anything undermine that.

She filled the hour watching holidaymakers in their suntans and straw hats arriving back to a drab October evening. Pushing their trolleys laden with luggage, duty-free goods, and local gifts they'd probably regret buying the moment they unwrapped them at home, she witnessed countless families being reunited, businessmen met by chauffeurs, husbands collected by wives. Shuddering, she hurried to the Ladies', splashed her face with cold water, and rubbed her hands under the hot tap until they turned purple. Pulling a rough paper towel from the dispenser, she dampened it and pressed it against her eyes.

How many airports had she'd flown into? How many flights had she taken? She remembered one manic trip to Central and South America when she'd notched up fifty-eight flights in forty days, after which she'd gone down with a case of pleuropneumonia that nearly killed her. Her double-size old-style British passport had become so full of entry stamps and visas from foreign climes that she'd had to apply for extra pages. In contrast, her burgundy EC replacement, issued a couple of years ago, was virtually empty. She preferred it that way.

"A good rule of thumb," Carrie had once told her as they tried in vain to get some sleep on the unforgiving plastic chairs at Kuwait's airport, "is that if you're visiting a place that requires a small paper stamp glued into your passport, you're almost certainly somewhere dodgy."

Emerging from the Ladies', Charlie strained to hear an announcement about flight BA186 from Rome, but the chatter amongst the new arrivals all around her drowned it out.

"Charlie? Charlie Hudson?" There was an unfamiliar voice at her shoulder. She turned warily to face an entire television news crew, fresh in from their latest foreign assignment.

"Wayne!" she cried in surprise, flinging her arms around the neck of a good-looking American reporter with whom she'd been to a dozen hot spots. "Wayne Tomchick, how the devil are you?"

The veteran anchorman gave her a hug that smelled of free champagne and aftershave, the distinctive odour of business class. "I'm terrific, sweetheart. How great to see you. What are you doing here? Um, sorry, where are my manners? Charlie, this is Pete the soundman, Kiwi the cameraman, Terry the researcher, and my editor Maxine. Guys, this is Charlie Hudson, the most fearless woman I ever met," he announced grandly.

"Oh, nonsense," Charlie chided. "So, where've you been?"

"Jerusalem. Peace talks. So-called. Nothing achieved apart from the usual suicide bombings and some great footage of an Israeli helicopter gunship raid on Nablus. What about you? Where are you hiding yourself these days?"

Turning again to his crew, Wayne explained: "Charlie was one of the *Tribune*'s best, until she quit. Nothing moved out there unless she knew about it first. Isn't that right, Charlie?"

"Why'd you give it up?" the young New Zealand cameraman asked bluntly. "Sounds like you were at the top of the tree."

Wayne's heavily lined face crumpled and he glanced apologetically at Charlie.

Colouring a little, she replied, "Oh, well, you know the trouble with being at the top of the tree is that, sooner or later, a branch breaks and you fall flat on your face."

Wayne made a strange noise in his throat and Kiwi sensed he'd put his foot in it, but didn't understand why. Everyone shuffled around on their feet. "Well, great to see you, Charlie," Wayne said, finally. "I'll get your number from the news desk and give you a call sometime." He kissed her cheek.

"Yes, do that," Charlie replied, knowing he wouldn't. "That'd be lovely. Bye."

She turned back to the incoming arrivals so she couldn't see the television crew walking away.

"Charlie?"

She spun round so fast she almost fell over. Alan was at her side, his tanned face beaming happily into hers. "Didn't you see me arrive?"

"No, no, I didn't," she said, rustling up a smile from somewhere. "Sorry, Alan. I was miles away."

DRIVING BACK INTO London from the airport in the dark, Charlie gripped the steering wheel and stared straight ahead, the lights of the oncoming cars on the wet road dazzling her. Alan's presence alongside her lifted the hairs on the back of her neck, but she couldn't decide whether that was the sexual frisson between them, or something else.

"So, how are you, Charlie?" he asked, his body turned towards her in his seat, his attention relentless. "Are you okay?"

"Of course. Why wouldn't I be?"

"It's just that we've hardly spoken these last few weeks. I was beginning to worry."

"No need." Charlie smiled thinly. "I've been terribly busy. I told you. Carrie came to stay and the book's been keeping me out of mischief."

"Good, because the only mischief you're allowed to get into from now on is when you're with me." He slipped a hand onto her knee.

Charlie forced a smile. "I'll look forward to that."

God, what on earth did she think she was doing? She felt an agony of confusion. Anxious to defuse the increasing tension, she switched on the radio and turned up the volume. Mozart. *Lacrimosa*. D Minor. She knew it well. So incredibly beautiful, it sometimes made her weep. Charlie summoned up an image of the great composer hunched over his desk by candlelight, the notes rushing from his brain to his fingers and down the scratchy nib of his quill. Flowing clefs and quavers, staves and minims, all preserved for posterity on great scrolls of buff-coloured handmade paper so that they could be treasured for all time.

So light she almost couldn't feel it at first, Alan's hand began to slowly trace a line up her leg. Acutely aware of its progress, she felt it slide beneath the hem of her skirt, and come to rest at the top of her thigh. There, his fingers played lightly with the soft fabric of her underwear. A wave of heat rushed through her and it was all she could do to stop herself crying out. Instinctively, she pressed her knees together and rolled down her window to let in some fresh air.

"Alan, I—" she began, but before she could say any more, his hand crept higher and higher and was soon peeling back the elastic of her waistband and sliding down behind it. His fingers felt unbearably cold against the flat warmth of her lower belly and she gasped. But it was a shiver of excitement that whispered across her flesh.

Gripping the steering wheel still tighter, she dared not look at him, dared not feel what she was feeling. Every muscle in her body tensed as she pulled the car over into the slow lane to avoid the heavy spray of a lorry. She slowed still further when his fingers reached their mark and plunged in.

"Alan, no, don't, I—I can't. . . ." Waves of pleasure rippled through her and, her eyes focusing desperately on the twinkling traffic ahead, she uttered a low groan and found herself, once again, utterly under his spell.

His breath warm on her neck, he was at her ear, murmuring her name. "Charlie," he whispered. "Show me how much you missed me."

The pleasure was becoming unbearable; Charlie fought to keep her eyes open, as the cars gradually slowed all around them. Ahead, she could just make out the first set of traffic lights. Through half-closed lids and a steamed-up windscreen, she watched the lights change from green to amber. By the time they were red and their car came slowly to a halt, her whole body was shuddering violently, slamming itself back against the seat, arms outstretched, knuckles white on the steering wheel. Deep in her throat welled a cry of such intense pleasure, that, when it burst from her lips, it sounded inhuman.

Almost animal.

ANGELA MUST HAVE been truly deranged. There didn't have to be another explanation. After all, Charlie couldn't explain why she didn't much like her own mother. No, Angela's tortured mind had somehow insidiously turned her against her father, and because of that she'd done everything to hurt and discredit him. Her final act—her defiant note—had been deliberately designed to cause him lasting pain. No wonder her own mother had called her a bitch. No wonder he never spoke of her.

Seeing Alan's home for the first time reassured Charlie still further. The elegant three-bedroom apartment with its large roof terrace in Onslow Square took her breath away. Pale carpets, walls, furniture, and curtains mirrored the perfect white stucco of the exterior. Floor-to-ceiling windows with shutters flooded the rooms with light. A low coffee table was piled high with large glossy books on everything from Venice to Sir

William Walton's Ischian garden. An exquisite orchid, its flowers yellow ochre with a pale blue beard, dominated the table. Charlie pressed her nose to the waxen petals, but realised, with a shock, that they were plastic.

Huge paintings adorned the walls, some of them Alan's but most by others—Lucien Freud, Pierre Bonnard, Giorgio Morandi. Others were less well-known, such as Ian Armour-Chelu and Margaret Thomas—Suffolk artists whose work Charlie knew and admired.

"This is wonderful," she told him, doing an impulsive pirouette to fully take in the room, a champagne flute in her hand. "I had no idea."

"I'm glad you like it," he said, threading his arms around her waist. He buried his face in her hair. "You smell heavenly. I think I missed that the most."

She turned to face him.

When his tongue touched her lips, Charlie tasted the champagne he'd just sipped. She stared deep into his eyes, willing him to seduce her again. Her need for him outweighed everything else. He'd awakened her from a long and lonely slumber and every time he touched her, she could feel new life—new hope—racing through her veins.

Tanned and lithe from his daily swim, he made love to her on the soft deep carpet of the lounge and again in the bedroom. Face flushed and his breath coming in rasping bursts, he was nonetheless smiling as he fell into a deep and restful sleep, oblivious to the silent tears she didn't seem able to prevent.

ALAN'S KITCHEN WAS clinically clean. A gleaming cream Aga took pride of place, far different from the battered enamel model she'd bought reconditioned from a warehouse and installed in her little Suffolk cottage. Charlie doubted if he had ever used his kitchen, and yet it was fitted with every conceivable gadget for the gourmet chef. Perhaps Diane, his second wife, had been responsible. Charlie had never met the elegant New Yorker, but Diane's photographs showed her to be an immaculately dressed blonde with a thin, finely sculpted face, her hair scraped back into a ponytail. Not the sort who would roll up her sleeves and make an omelette, as Charlie was doing the second evening after Alan arrived home from Italy, but certainly someone who wouldn't want her caterers to think she was anything other than a goddess in her own kitchen.

Bent over the polished steel counter, whisking eggs with a state-of-the-art electric beater, Charlie peered through the smoked-glass door of the eye-level grill to check on the asparagus. Alan had rung from his meeting at the Tate to tell her he'd be late, and had estimated his arrival at sevenish. It was 6.45 already and Charlie was fidgety. Perhaps she should have chosen a salad or something preprepared for this, their first meal together in his home. The phone rang again.

"Hello? Alan Matheson's home."

"Who's that?"

"My name's Charlie. I'm a friend of Alan's. Did you want him?"

The line went dead.

Charlie stared at the receiver and tried to think where she'd heard that voice before. She was wracking her brains when the telephone rang again.

"Hey there," Alan greeted her, in a defeated tone. "Look, I'm really sorry about this, darling, but something's come up. It'll be nearer eight before I'm home. You go ahead and eat. I hope you didn't make anything special."

Standing in his kitchen, apron around her waist, ear to the phone, Charlie found herself wondering if this is what it had been like to be Sarah Matheson, eating alone, waiting for her husband to come home. She'd never doubted for one minute that Alan could be infuriating to live with, but she hadn't expected this, not tonight. Shaking herself, she summoned her most serene voice and assured him it didn't matter.

"I'll wait for you, don't worry. Supper will keep. Come when you can."

Replacing the handset, Charlie's brain flickered into life. Sarah Matheson. That was who the first caller was. Oh, well, she didn't really blame Sarah for not wanting to speak to her.

She turned off the grill. Leaving a half-finished heap of Parmesan shavings, she abandoned the bowl of whisked eggs and chopped fresh herbs. Picking up her mug of coffee, she wandered into the living room. Kicking off her shoes, she trod softly around the carpeted room, studying the items Alan had selected to adorn his home.

Gilt-edged invitations on beautiful white paper were stacked above the pale marble fireplace, behind a row of photographs in silver frames. There was a disarming shot of Alan laughing with the Queen Mother while she was sitting for her portrait, and another of him with Princess Diana and Prince Charles, the latter in polo garb. Others showed him with Nelson Mandela, Margaret Thatcher, Mick Jagger, and Princess Grace of Monaco. Charlie noted, with a twinge, that Sarah had clearly been surgically excised from his carefully selected photographic record. As had his second wife. The only trace of Diane was a wisp of blue organza the wind had caught and wafted across his thigh in a shot of him outside Buckingham Palace after his knighthood, a photo which had—since their divorce—been cleanly cut in two.

Another photograph showed Alan relaxed and tanned, a young Angela by his side on what Charlie instantly recognised as the terrace of his Italian villa. Lifting that frame from the shelf, she peered into it for answers, hoping that something about Angela's expression, the way she stood next to her father in her bikini, his arm around her waist, her body half turned towards him, would reveal the secrets of her tormented life. But the teenager's eyes were hidden by her wraparound sunglasses, and there was nothing in Alan's that suggested anything other than a momentary pause for the benefit of the photographer. The only feature of note was Angela's pierced belly button, which sported a large gold ring.

The last framed photograph was a formal shot of Alan in front of a New York art gallery. Charlie lifted that one off the shelf, too, and stared intently at the devilishly handsome young artist with glossy brown hair and the unblemished skin of youth who was nonetheless recognisable as the man she now awaited. There was hope in that young face. Naiveté and hope. This was before life had dealt him the cruel blows that had silvered his hair and lined his eyes.

Tiring of the shelf, Charlie turned her attention to each of the paintings. As in Sarah's flat, above the mantelpiece was a delicate watercolour of his Italian garden with its symmetrical beds and venerable topiary. Tall cypress trees at the estate's edge cast long shadows across the garden, reminding Charlie piercingly of those languid afternoons when the sun began to dip over the hillsides of Montepulciano and Alan would break off from his painting to make love to her.

Perfectly lit and hung with a precision that defied logic, each painting in Alan's apartment was more pleasing than the last as the collection continued down the hallway towards the bedrooms. She recognised most of the signatures and noted that—apart from the one over the mantelpiece—there were far fewer of Alan's than she might have expected. Dramatically different from each other in every way, the paintings had nevertheless been collated in such a way as to complement each other perfectly. Thus, she found herself moving from a fragile watercolour of fading pink tulips on the finest art paper, to a bold Baconesque oil of an old man whose colours and textures somehow picked up where the watercolour left off.

Some of the works were lurid abstracts, their dancing whorls and screaming blocks of colour a vindication of Alan's argument that all artists are a little mad. Others were some of the finest portraits Charlie had ever seen, the tranquil faces of their subjects injecting a welcome touch of sanity.

This intensely private collection ended with a fine gouache of Alan's. Depicting a bowl of his Umbrian grapes nestling among green vine leaves, the deep mauves and blues of the bloom on the fruit's skin were exactly captured. Sipping on her coffee and treading thoughtfully along the corridor, Charlie couldn't help but feel cheated when she went to look for the next picture, only to find a closed door in its place. A spare bedroom, she assumed; Alan and she had spent the previous night in his, farther back. Reaching for the polished brass handle, she twisted it and stepped inside.

The room was in total darkness. Carefully negotiating the dark shapes of a bed, an armchair, and a dressing table, Charlie found the cord to the heavy drapes and pulled. The curtains slid open smoothly, bathing every-thing with a glow from the street lamp outside. Seeing a light switch by the bed, she turned it on.

A precisely angled spotlight on the ceiling sent a slanting shaft of whiteness directly onto the wall opposite the one against which Charlie now stumbled, transfixed.

Illuminated before her in all its horror was a vast watercolour, five feet square, depicting what could only be described as Hell.

A thousand naked torsos writhed in blood and black slime. Like eels. Several with limbs severed. Their eyes gouged out. Mouths open in screaming agony. A charnel house belched smoke in the background as emaciated corpses were heaped unceremoniously into its spitting fur-naces. In the foreground, on an unforgiving bed of brambles, women were raped and mutilated, young men buggered and defiled; animals tor-tured with hot irons. A bitch and her puppies, still suckling, were being hacked to death by a hideous creature, half man, half bird.

Deep in the centre of the painting, a naked woman, her twisted hair falling like a curtain across half of her face, was on her knees, cradling an infant. Its bloody umbilical cord was still attached to somewhere deep within her womb. Its crusty eyes were squeezed shut.

All that could be seen of the woman's face was her right eye, an un-usual shade of emerald green. And part of her mouth, smiling inscrutably as dark figures closed in on her, their murderous hands reaching for her newborn child.

28

*I*T WAS ALMOST nine o'clock by the time Alan Matheson turned the key in his lock and stepped guiltily inside his apartment. A faint smell wafted towards him. He felt childish pleasure at the idea of coming back to a home-cooked meal.

Hoping to surprise Charlie, he crept along the hallway and into the living room. From the kitchen he could hear a radio playing softly. Rounding the corner, a bouquet of bright yellow sunflowers in his hand to remind her of Italy, he was ready with a smile.

"Hey!" he said, but was surprised to find no one there. The worktops were cluttered with half-prepared food. A whisk stood upright in a bowl of congealing eggs; parsley, chives, and coriander lay ready on a chopping board; the grill door was open and he could see asparagus glistening in rows on a tray inside.

Wandering down the corridor towards his bedroom, he found that empty, too, as was the bathroom. Frowning, he again called out her name. About to turn back to the living room, he saw that the guest bedroom door was wide open.

"Charlie?"

She wasn't there, but Alan saw that the curtains had been opened. On the floor lay an overturned mug, its dark contents staining the cream carpet.

. . .

CHARLIE SAT ON the edge of her sofa gasping into a brown paper bag, trying to regulate her air intake as she'd been shown to do. Even if she'd wanted to, she wouldn't have been able to answer the incessantly ringing telephone. There simply wasn't enough air in her lungs to speak.

Slowly, her breathing became normal. Pulling at the buttons on her shirt, tearing the fabric, she ran to the bathroom and retched violently into the toilet bowl. Her mouth still sour and wet, she peeled off her outer clothing and stood under the shower, in her underwear, waiting for the stinging hot jets of water to cleanse her.

Forty minutes later, wrapped in a dressing gown, she slumped onto the soft cushions of her sofa, pink-skinned and struggling to compose her thoughts.

The panic attack had risen from nowhere, like a flock of startled seagulls inside her chest. It had been an age since her last one. But the grotesque painting in Alan's spare bedroom, with its scenes of torture, severed limbs, the dog and her pups, the green-eyed woman with an infant in her arms—it all seemed to point at her, to Rajak and its aftermath. And the distinctive signature on the painting could leave her in no doubt exactly who painted it: AM——Alan Matheson.

How could he possibly know so much about her? How could he see inside her head? Where had he witnessed that infernal place of the damned inside her? She shuddered at the thought. Or had he been sneaking furtively round in her past behind her back—just as she had in his? Had he left the painting there deliberately, intending her to find it? Knowing that her journalistic curiosity would get the better of her and she'd undoubtedly wander into that room? If so, how could he be so cruel?

The telephone rang again. The answering machine clicked in as Alan left another message.

"Charlie? Are you there? You're beginning to worry me. I'm about to call the police to report you abducted, so please, if you're there, pick up the phone."

Reluctantly, Charlie lifted the receiver.

"Charlie?"

"Y-yes, Alan, I'm here," she said in a voice hoarse from retching.

"For goodness' sake, I've been worried sick. What happened? One minute you were there and the next you weren't. Just a spilled cup and you vanished into thin air. What in heaven's name is wrong?"

Silence.

"Charlie?" His tone softer, he added, "Are you okay? Did something frighten you?"

"I saw the painting."

"What painting?"

"The watercolour in the guest bedroom . . . I—I saw it. When did you finish it?"

There was another, longer silence before he answered, and when he did his tone had become flat. "What makes you think it was mine?"

"Oh, come on, Alan. The initials, just as you always sign them. And I recognised your style. It's unmistakable. Those strong brushstrokes, the bold colours. Don't lie to me. It's just like those sketches of naked women I found in your Suffolk studio."

"Is that what made you run away?"

Charlie nodded but couldn't speak.

He sighed heavily into the mouthpiece. "I don't know what goes on inside your head sometimes, Charlie, and I'm not sure I want to know, but you must believe me when I tell you that I'd never deliberately do anything to hurt or frighten you."

"Then why did you paint that picture?" Charlie cried, tears pricking her eyes.

"I didn't."

"But I don't understand. I know the way you do people and animals, the technique, the paint. This is your work."

"Well, it isn't. . . . It was painted by my daughter. Angela. If you must know, it was the last picture she completed before she killed herself."

SUFFOLK HAD ALWAYS provided a retreat for Charlie, and it did so once again. Telling Alan that she needed some time alone, and begging him not to follow her, she ran away, like she always did when faced with something she couldn't handle. Cross with herself for this relapse in her progress, and locking herself away in her little cottage, she tried to bury herself in her work but found herself far too distracted.

Instead she'd stoke up the coal fire, pull on a warm woollen coat and hat, and wander out into the blustery afternoon. Past her beloved church now lit palely by a winter sun, she'd meander down the narrow lane, its hedgerows thick with berries, the air heavy with the scents of the season. On towards the sea whose waves she could hear crashing the moment she'd stepped through her picket gate. The cold slapping her cheeks, her hands buried deep in her pockets, she watched the seagulls wheeling overhead, buffeted by the North Sea breezes as she picked her way along the avenue of gnarled and ancient hawthorns on the cliff's edge.

The water was the colour of slate, churned into molten agate as the rollers swept in under pewter clouds, through which shafts of watery sunlight angled down. The smell of seaweed filled her nostrils. In many ways, this was her favourite time of year. She loved the wild loneliness of Suffolk and the isolation it afforded her.

There was rarely anybody about at this time of year, apart from the odd dog walker or a stoic "twitcher" watching the wading birds by the reed beds through binoculars. When they cried "hello," their voices were swallowed by the wind. The few people she did meet seemed an intrusion, and she resented them bitterly. How dare they encroach on her own private beach. For that's what it felt like. Hers. It had done ever since she'd first come here.

"I'm going to come here to live," she'd declared to the birds. "And be free." But how free was she really? Not of her past, not of Granddad or her parents, or Kosovo it seemed, and now unable to cut free from Alan, too. And what about Nick? Part of her, deep down inside, would always be shackled to him.

Her writing perhaps gave her the greatest sense of liberty, the chance to create literary portraits on a blank sheet of paper. That was surely her something beautiful, or the closest she'd come to it. Like creating a work of art, a painting. There wasn't much difference.

Painting. She shivered. She'd glimpsed something in Angela Matheson's depiction of Hell which had made her believe that its message was directed at her. But how could that possibly be? Angela had been dead for almost as long as Charlie had been alone.

Alan had once told her that everyone sees a painting differently. "Like those Rorschach ink-blot tests. Some people see fantastic butterflies, monsters, and demons. Others just see splashes of ink. It is all a matter of perception."

In Turner's *Crossing the Brook* Charlie had seen a dark symbolism in the archway of trees by the water's edge that would probably have left someone else completely unaffected. Would another person studying Angela's painting see similarities to his or her own life? Had Charlie ruthlessly singled out those aspects that had particular resonance for her? Or was it possible that her vision and Angela's had been identical, that two women—both tied to Alan—had somehow formed a link, transcending death and personal experience?

If Angela had painted that watercolour, then she had deliberately imitated her father's style. She'd even mimicked his signature, no doubt relishing the confusion she caused in doing so. Those long slanting letters—AM. Charlie now felt certain that it was Angela, not Alan, who'd painted the grotesques she'd found in his studio. Could it be that the demons Angela painted were the same that drove her to suicide? Had it been these monstrous apparitions she was running from all her life? And what of the squirming, bloodied infant in the painting? A little girl. Charlie pulled her Barbour even closer around her skin at the unconscionable thought of Alan sexually abusing his own daughter.

That photograph of Angela and Alan together—arms linked, her lean young body half turned towards him. Was it even possible that he could have taken Angela to the same places he'd taken Charlie? That he had touched her adolescent breasts and caressed her soft young skin? Shaking her head to dispel such twisted images from her mind, Charlie shuddered. She mustn't let these horrible suspicions Angela had so vindictively planted taint her own relationship with Alan. It was special. It needed to remain so. For it was something which had—for the first time since she'd left Nick, for the first time since Rajak—allowed her to really *feel*. How could she possibly turn her back on that?

THE TIDE HAD been high the previous night. Storms had lashed this part of the coast, and the ridge of sand and shingle had been pounded into submission by the relentless waves. Behind it, the cliff had crumbled in a dozen places, dragging even the most tenacious grass roots and small stunted trees to their doom. Every now and again, a cliff had not fallen away neatly, but formed an angled slope of sand and debris, flaring as it reached the ground, unearthing flints and stones, the bones of small animals, and minor geological treasures not seen for several thousand years.

Charlie realised she was probably only a mile or two from Pear Tree Farm, set well back from the Dunwich cliffs. Part of her longed to go on, to climb the steep path to the big comfortable old house and peer through the windows of the house Alan had made his country home. Maybe by being there, the place where Angela had spent so much time, she might be able to sense her restless spirit in those elegant rooms and finally understand it. Shaking her head angrily at her schoolgirl notion of ghosts and spirits, she decided against it.

The wind now whispered through the thin, dry reeds of the marsh beds and the tougher grasses of the dunes as she turned back. It seemed to Charlie that she was the only person left in the world.

STUMBLING BACK TO her cottage, she ignored the sunlight glinting on the waves and the flock of terns heading for the marshes that might, in another time, have made her stop and try to sketch them. Today, no notebook in her pocket and her hands numb with cold, she turned the key in the lock and brushed her damp hair back from her face to feel a wave of warmth from the little stove. The slightly acrid smell of burning coal filled the room.

Flopping onto a kitchen chair and pushing her books and notes to one side, Charlie examined the morning's post. There were the usual magazines and advertising pamphlets and a polite postcard from Nick, sent from Paris a few days earlier. *Revisiting some of our old haunts with a friend. Wish you were here. Nick. xx* So that's why he hadn't been in touch. He was probably there with Miranda.

Putting the postcard to one side, she picked up a thick white envelope. Her address was neatly written across it in fountain pen. Alan's handwriting. Holding the envelope, weighing its contents in her mind, she hesitated. Then, slitting it open cautiously, she tipped it upside down. A letter and a crumpled newspaper clipping slid onto the table.

> *Dearest Charlie.*
>
> *By the time you read this, I shall be back in Italy. I, too, sometimes need to run away. You have the capacity for great joy, I know that, but also for great despair—something I don't yet comprehend and am understandably troubled by. There are obviously matters we both need to resolve, privately and between ourselves. I cannot begin to express my growing affection for you and my wish that we may move forward, but yours is the next move. Our future happiness lies with you. A.*
>
> *P.S. I thought the enclosed might shed some light....*

Accompanying the letter were two obituaries of Angela that Charlie had already seen and a photocopy of a cutting from a newspaper arts report, nearly six years old. The headline read:

CONTROVERSIAL NEW ARTIST EXPLAINS HERSELF TO
HER CRITICS: ANGELA MATHESON, DAUGHTER OF
THE QUEEN MOTHER'S PORTRAITIST, TELLS
NEIL REYNOLDS ABOUT HER SINISTER WORK.

The article described Angela's penchant for horror and beauty in contemporary art and quoted her as saying:

"In Van Gogh's suicide note he said that only painting made his life bearable. Then he pulled the trigger. Virginia Woolf told her husband in her final note that she couldn't face the madness again, then she drowned herself. Our world is filled with war and pestilence, plague and death. We read about it every day, though we live our lives wrapped in cotton wool. Life is unbearable and art speaks of the insanity that allows us to bear it.

"When I pick up the brush and start to paint, the paper is daubed before I know it with the most monstrous scenes that come from somewhere deep within me. From the years of being wrapped in cotton wool, perhaps, or from the schizophrenia of denial. My father detests my work, and most of my friends believe I'm quite mad. Only my mother seems to understand what I'm trying to say, and she's been in therapy for years. But whatever your view, everyone agrees my paintings are compelling. They speak to each and every one of us about our most deep-rooted anxieties. I see myself as a role model for would-be schizophrenics everywhere."

The interviewer went on to detail some of Angela's most recent works, which were about to be displayed in the Whitechapel Gallery in East London. They included a vast watercolour of a Gothic headless horseman called *Lost,* an oil called *Just One More for the Road* of a convicted drunk driver about to be electrocuted, and a video entitled *Blood Ties* which featured a naked Angela spattering a wall with crimson paint. The article concluded with the artist giving a brief description of her current work.

"I think this is truly the best thing I've ever done. It's a visceral piece called *Hope Less,* and it depicts hell on earth, or at least hell as I see it. At the core of the painting, amidst unspeakable suffering and depravity, a young woman cradles a crying infant. New life amongst death. With murder all around. The contrast is so unexpected that it's shocking and—what people may not understand is—that's the whole fucking point."

CHARLIE SWIRLED BOILING water onto a spoonful of coffee granules. Sitting by the fire, cradling her mug, she read and reread the article Alan had sent her. This was the closest she'd felt to Angela so far. Hearing her words spoken aloud in her mind as she read them, seeing the images the young woman described, gave her a voice for the first time. She wondered why Alan had kept the article. Was he, too, listening for Angela's voice? Hoping she'd answer the question that must never be far from his mind— *Why, Angela, why?*

The clipping was, she knew, another piece of the jigsaw in the scattered fragments she'd so rashly collected. The photograph of Angela, the curtain of hair half hiding her face. Charlie's bewildering conversations with Dr North, Richard Dutton, and Sarah Matheson. There was so much she still couldn't make sense of. So many contradictions that didn't fit.

Dr North remembered little of Angela's death but that she'd kept her shoes on. Dutton's vindictive accusations, borne—Charlie suspected—of jealousy and spite, laid the blame firmly at Alan's door. Yet Sarah Matheson had suggested that Angela herself was responsible. And what had the girl's mother meant when she said that she'd had a lucky escape? Hadn't Lori Hunter warned her of the same thing?

Hunched by the stove, Charlie tried to detach herself from the situation, to look at it as if she were a journalist investigating a story about someone she didn't know. So far, all she had to go on was the suicide of a disturbed young woman who claimed to have been sexually abused by her father, and the odd behaviour of her mother, who'd herself been treated for mental instability.

The only link between the two women was Alan, a respected and ostensibly well-balanced artist who'd made a substantial success of his life despite great personal tragedy. There were undoubtedly elements of his character that could warrant cause for concern—his reluctance to discuss his dead daughter, the controlling side of some of his sexual appetites— but both could be explained rationally. If the police had truly suspected Alan had abused Angela, surely there would have been an investigation? Didn't the fact that they failed to publish her suicide note point to the fact that everyone, including the coroner, believed her allegation to be utterly false? Wasn't Angela just the tragic case of a young woman who, rejected by her father, had used her suicide to punish him from beyond the grave? And wasn't Sarah Matheson's odd behaviour entirely consistent with that of a woman whose daughter's life had ended in such circumstances, and whose marriage had crumbled as a result?

Most worryingly of all, what was it about Alan that seemed to drive the women he was involved with off the rails—Angela, Sarah, and, maybe, even her?

29

THE IRONY WAS THAT, despite the pressures weighing on her mind, Charlie had rarely worked so well. Her book was really beginning to take shape, with the tenets of Turner, Whatman, and Ruskin weaving seamlessly into each other and the history of paper. She'd managed to commit more than fifty thousand words to computer, and was surrounded by piles of books and boxes of notes that would help her write the next fifty.

Cloistered away in Suffolk, working for hours at her desk in her cottage by the sea, she'd lose all track of time and completely forget to eat, she'd be so immersed in her subject. Her current focus was on Turner's touching relationship with his father. The artist may have behaved questionably to his mother by abandoning her to the lunatic asylum, but to his dear "Daddy" he was devoted.

Indeed, the old man had lived with the artist for many years after he'd retired as a barber, stretching his son's canvasses and carefully tending to the younger man's precious paper, which was kept in special wooden solanders or chests. He also prepared the artist's palettes, cooked his meals, and cared tenderly for his riverside garden.

"My father is indefatigable and walks into London three times a week

rather than take the coach, " Turner told his friends in Charlie's imaginary conversation. *"It's what keeps him young and fit."*

Charlie thought of her own grandfather and his dogged refusal to give in to illness and old age. He'd pushed his aching body to its limits, digging manure into the flower beds, planting old-fashioned roses, carting his easel to the sea. He, too, would always walk rather than take a bus or a train.

When Turner's father died in September 1829 at the age of eighty-five, his son sank into a deep depression, and—painfully aware of his own mortality—wrote the first of many wills. Developing a penchant for alcohol and the numbness it brought, he became obsessed with death. Ruskin and his friends feared for him.

"There is a kind of madness which has descended over him like the swirling dark clouds he's so fond of painting," Charlie had Ruskin write. *"His friends despair of ever returning him to sanity."* Later, after Turner had been plagued with ill health and the loss of all his teeth, which made his mood plunge still further, Ruskin wrote that Turner's mind had failed *"suddenly, with the snap of some vital chord,"* and his soul *"crushed"* within him. He added, *"I saw that nothing remained for me to write but my friend's epitaph."*

Despite the best endeavours of those around him, Turner's art reflected his dark mood. He even painted a spectral horse, a human skeleton arched across its back, arms outstretched. Charlie thought of Angela's grisly picture, its skeletal figures begging for salvation, and crushed the memory.

Turner continued to find fascination in the battle of the elements. He had himself lashed to a ship's mast so he could experience firsthand a terrible storm at sea. Charlie listened to the wind howling down her own chimney, and decided Turner need never have ventured farther than East Anglia in November in his quest for tempests.

Her thoughts strayed, relentlessly, to Alan in Porto. What was he doing right now? Standing at his easel by the open window, she guessed. Painting while classical music filled the room. She could see his face, the intense concentration, the way his forehead furrowed when he frowned. She knew that he'd work on right through the day, stopping only when Maria summoned him for supper.

Dining alone on the terrace, with Lake Montepulciano glimmering distantly below in the failing evening light, he'd open a bottle of Brunello di Montalcino from his cellar and savour a mouthful of the tawny red wine before starting hungrily on the thick yellow ribbons of pasta that Maria made so well.

The first time Charlie had eaten homemade pasta had been with Nick, in a little trattoria in the Campo dei Fiori in Rome, on their first visit there years before. He'd been on the desk of the *London Evening News* then, and was considered the most eligible bachelor in the office. She was a junior reporter, learning her craft, flattered and grateful for the many indulgences Nick had shown her.

"*Buon appetito*," he'd said that night, raising his glass of *vino di tavola*. "Happy anniversary. Three months to the day since we met."

"Three months." He'd laughed, tucking into his *pappardelle con funghi*, his eyes intensely blue. "It seems longer, doesn't it?"

"I know. Thank you for remembering." She'd reached across and squeezed his hand.

"Hold that thought," he'd said, reaching for his camera as white doves flapped around the marble fountain behind her. She wondered if he still had that photograph of her. A glossy square of paper catching a perfect moment in time that no one could take away from them.

It was while making love to her in their hotel room later that night that he'd proposed to her. "Marry me, Charlie, and I promise you'll never regret it," he'd sworn, his voice thick with emotion.

And he was right. She never had. Poor Nick. She knew she didn't deserve his friendship, not after the way she'd treated him. Although she'd always known he'd been unfaithful to her during her long absences, it was nothing more than casual sex. At his core, she was certain, he was devoted to her. Like that loyal dog following his mistress across the brook in Turner's painting, her hat in his mouth, his big brown eyes pleading with her for some sort of reassurance she might never be able to give him.

Trust Alan to choose that painting. Even before he knew much about her, he'd sensed that something in that picture would touch a nerve.

• • •

CHARLIE RETURNED TO London with the chief purpose of visiting Turner's tomb in St Paul's Cathedral. There was some essential poignancy missing in her descriptions of his death and funeral—perhaps because Ruskin had been abroad at the time and hadn't chronicled it for her—that she now needed to recapture.

Walking up Wren's vast aisle to the domed apse, she listened to her footsteps echoing across the polished flagstone floor and the murmurs of visitors in the side aisles. She inhaled the heady scent of incense and burning candles and felt, as always in this hallowed cathedral, humbled. She'd been here a dozen times in the past; at memorial services and state funerals, private concerts and charity events, and its perfection never failed to move her.

Her favourite spot was directly beneath the great dome, looking up into its farthest reaches, the sunlight slanting in through small windows, giving the high open space a mystical, magical look. It was as if she were looking directly into Heaven itself. Sometimes, if she was lucky, the choir would be practising and she could close her eyes and be transported to a place of such serenity and peace that the memory of it would sustain her for days.

"When I die, I'd like a memorial service in St Paul's," she'd told Nick once. "I know St Bride's is officially the journalists' church and that St Paul's seems terribly grand, but it's the only house of God where I've ever felt completely at ease."

Visiting the cathedral again now, she relaxed as if she were in the company of an old friend. Not only was she in a place she loved, but she was paying homage to a man she now felt as if she'd known personally. She summoned to mind the details of Turner's state funeral, the pallbearers carrying his coffin up the aisle to Handel's melancholy Dead March from *Saul*, bathed by the resonant accompaniment of the cathedral's mighty organ. Five hundred mourners, dressed in black, attended, many in tears. For purists of watercolour art, the light had gone from the world with Turner's passing.

Standing by his full-length statue set on a pedestal in the south transept, she ran her fingertips over the chiseled letters of his name. The statue, sculpted by Patrick MacDowell and commissioned with the thousand pounds Turner himself had bequeathed for the purpose, depicted the artist in middle age with a caped jacket flung loosely over his shoulders, his head turned in profile towards the window, sporting fashionable sideburns and a prominent nose. In his lowered right hand he held a single brush, in his left a palette and four brushes.

His tomb lay downstairs in the crypt, a flat slab of grey granite set into the terra-cotta floor in a distant corner, far from the magnificent sarcophagi of Nelson and Wellington and Britain's illustrious heroes of war. Walking to it past the memorials to those who'd died in the South Atlantic and the Second World War, past the tombs of Generals Montgomery and Slim and Auchinleck, Charlie steeled herself for the voices of war in her head, but, to her surprise, they didn't come.

In a far chapel close to the tomb of Sir Christopher Wren and flanked by those of the artists Sir John Millais and James Barry, Turner's memorial read simply:

JAMES MALLORD WILLIAM TURNER, R.A.
DIED 19TH DECEMBER 1851. AGED 76.

Impulsively, she placed the palm of her hand flat on his final resting place and softly spoke the lines from the *Aeneid* that meant so much to them both. *"'I have lived my life and completed the course that Fortune has set before me, and now my great spirit will go beneath the Earth.'"*

STANDING ON THE broad stone steps of St Paul's, blinking in the bright sunlight, a sudden screech of brakes snapped Charlie back to the present day. BANG! A motorcyclist, who'd swerved to avoid an oncoming car, had been thrown from his bike and landed on the unforgiving pavement just yards from where she stood.

Motionless, she stared down at the man clad in black leather, his left leg skewed at an impossible angle. Frozen, she watched as others ran towards him, eager to help.

"Don't touch him!" Charlie shouted instinctively.

"Are you a doctor?"

Charlie shook her head. A chill crept into her heart.

The crowd parted, allowing her a clear view of the injured man's face. Somebody had removed his helmet. Unable to speak, twitching violently and gasping for breath, he lay looking directly up at her, his eyes wide with fear.

"For goodness' sake, get help!" someone pleaded as another knelt on the pavement and began loosening the injured man's leather jacket.

Galvanised into action, a young man did as he was told and ran off. A girl wailed lamely: "What should we do? Should we leave him until the paramedics get here?"

Charlie knew exactly what to do. She was fully trained in first aid, but her feet had sprouted roots that had planted themselves deep into the steps beneath her.

"This man needs an ambulance, now!" someone shouted. "Has anyone got a phone?"

Charlie had one. It was in her handbag. Next to the soap and her anti-sting syringe. If she could just unfurl her fingers from the fists they'd become and reach for it.

Someone else found theirs and dialed 999. Receiving instructions from the emergency operator, they did what a younger Charlie would have done, made certain the victim's airway was clear and resisted the temptation to move him. He was moaning, his body wracked with spasms that caused him to judder manically. His eyes had never left Charlie's. Was this his time? Was this his moment to die? Here? With her his mute witness?

"It's all right," Charlie wanted to tell him, to smooth his hair away from his forehead. His mouth worked strangely, opening and closing, his saliva dripping onto the pavement.

A cathedral warden in a grey-green uniform pushed through the crowd and spoke officiously. "The paramedics are on their way," he said.

Charlie heard herself scream, "He's going to die! You're all too late!"

But no sound came from her lips. She watched as the man drifted to the edge of unconsciousness and then slipped over.

If only she could move, if only she could go to him and slide his head onto her lap, she could stroke his cheek gently and reassure him until his eyes went milky. It wouldn't be long now. Feeling something rising within her, she squeezed her eyes shut, trying desperately to block the memory of the last time she'd held a dying man in her arms.

But the memory was too powerful and she was helpless in its grip.

Lebanon. The Gaza Strip. 1995. Danny, the Reuters cameraman with whom she's struck up a close friendship. Camera perched on his right shoulder, standing high on a rock above her, defiantly recording an Israeli tank firing randomly at unarmed Palestinians. The sudden noise of helicopter rotors above them fills her brain. The wind they create spits dust and grit into her face.

Above the din, a burst of gunfire. Charlie shrinks instinctively into the hole she's scraped for herself in the barren soil. She hears Danny swear and then watches as he topples, tilted by the weight of the equipment on his shoulder. He lands awkwardly on the rocks next to her, his camera shattered.

Despite the dark shadow overhead and the rotors still spinning dangerously near, she scrambles forward and pulls him to her. She pillows his head on her lap. The tangled contents of his stomach spill onto her boots and jeans. Feeling the blood seeping through to her skin, she rocks him in her arms as he writhes and screams his anger. She strokes his hair and croons his name. She begs him to live.

"Danny, I'm here. Stay with me, please, Danny...Danny!" She remains with him long after the helicopters have moved on. Long after his lungs rasp their final blood-flecked breath and his bladder empties onto her leg. The stink of urine mingles with that of blood. She cradles Danny in her arms and resists all efforts as people pull at her and attempt to prise him away.

"Don't—touch—him!" Arms flailing, not allowing anyone near in that dusty hellhole.

The tap on her shoulder now was from a City of London paramedic, his distinctive lime-green uniform blurred through the tempest of her memory. "Let us through, please, miss. We'll take over from here."

Charlie stayed where she was on the steps of St. Paul's, helplessly watching the medics do their best. His time has come, she wanted to tell them. This is meant to be. But they refused to give up, and when they applied the electric paddles of the defibrillator and warned everyone to stand clear, they seemed the least surprised of all when the man's frozen heart began beating again.

In the mêlée that followed, as they strapped him to a trolley and rushed him towards the waiting ambulance, Charlie remained rooted, hot tears dripping down her cheeks. Someone placed a tissue in her hand. She was absurdly grateful for the small kindness. They gently led her away.

"Do you want to go with him, luv?" someone else asked, pointing to the stretcher disappearing into the brightly lit rear of the ambulance. "Did I hear you say his name was Danny?"

Her mouth opened and closed silently. "No—er—no," she said, finally, wiping her wet face fiercely with the back of her hand. "I'm sorry. You're mistaken," she said, backing away. "I—I don't even know him. I don't know him at all."

30

*L*ONDON FELT COLD and damp. Charlie turned the key on a dank flat that smelled, inexplicably, of wet dog. She switched all the lights and the heating on. She hated winter, unless she was in Suffolk. Here, in the city, the low light of the mornings, the sheeting rain, and the wind conspired to lower her spirits. She could feel the scratchy beginnings of a sore throat and hoped she hadn't picked up some bug.

Red wine. That was what she needed. Château Musar, a fine claret-style red from the Bekáa Valley she'd first discovered in Lebanon with Danny. The two of them had shared many a bottle together on the terrace of their favourite restaurant, laughing and teasing and talking of all the things they'd do when they got home.

"I'm gonna have myself a pig," he'd announced one evening as the sun cast its tangerine light across the biblical landscape. "I'm gonna buy myself a porker and call him Yasser and treat him *real* good."

"Chickens," Charlie teased. "I've always wanted to keep hens. I love the idea of collecting fresh eggs each morning and whipping them up into creamy omelettes, washed down with scalding fresh coffee."

"Now you're talking, honey." Danny's blue eyes twinkled. "And how about a nice, lean slice of sizzling bacon to go with it, fresh from Yasser's rump?"

Danny was the closest Charlie had ever come to being unfaithful to Nick. With his blond hair, permanent suntan, and piercing eyes, he was a serious temptation. There'd been an instant chemistry between them, and he'd made his feelings perfectly clear. "I'm flattered," she told him the evening he'd kissed her and asked her to spend the night in his hotel room, "but I'm married, remember?"

"Oh, yes, that's right," Danny cried, mocking her. "And your marriage is so fucking wonderful that you leave the hubby home alone for months at a time. Do you seriously think he's sitting on his ass right now, twiddling his thumbs?"

"Probably not," she replied, her voice steely, "but even if he's screwing the arse out of someone, that doesn't make it okay for me to do the same."

Danny had never asked her again, although part of her desperately wanted him to, just for the comfort the chance to say yes would have given her in that place where all love and hope seemed to have died. Plenty of others did. She knew exactly how Danny dealt with his personal demons, and celibacy wasn't it. And when she stood, several months later, on the deck of that gently bobbing boat a few hundred yards off the glittering coast of Beirut, watching Danny's younger brother scatter his ashes into the Bay of St Georges, she wished more than anything that she had slept with him, after all. What would it have mattered if it could have brought a few hours of happiness to his foreshortened life? And to hers?

Pulling the cork from a bottle of Château Musar now, Charlie poured herself a glass and sat, still in her winter coat, at the kitchen table, waiting for the chill to leave her bones.

The telephone rang.

"Hi, Charlie, it's Nick. Just back from Suffolk?"

"Hmmm. Psychic? Or do you have a mole?"

"Carrie rang. She thought you sounded a bit distracted when you last spoke. She asked me to give you a call."

Charlie bristled. "You'd be distracted, too, if you had my deadline."

"So, you're all right, then? Er, I thought we might organise supper or something?"

"I'm fine, apart from a bit of a winter chill," she replied, deliberately ignoring his invitation. "Why shouldn't I be?"

"Oh, no reason. The book's going well, then?"

"Yes. I'm close to the final phase."

"That's great. See, I said you could do it."

"Thanks. How're things with you?"

"Good."

"Is that all? Just good?"

"Yes, well, no. Actually, life's been treating me pretty well lately. I can't complain."

Charlie nursed her wine. "Would Miranda and your trip to Paris have anything to do with that?" she asked, twisting her glass round and round in her hand.

Nick laughed. "I suppose so. She seems very keen, actually. She's even talking about moving in, if you can believe that!"

"Well, that is good, isn't it?" Charlie asked impassively.

"Yes, Charlie," Nick said cautiously. "I guess it is."

LATER THAT NIGHT, lying in bed in that semisleep state where memories and thoughts intertwine, her mind takes her back to the clinic and one of her therapy sessions with Dr Rees. She is sitting in her usual armchair, threadbare and coffee-stained, facing the picture window in his comfortable office that smells inexplicably of her grandfather's hair oil.

The psychiatrist is sitting a few feet behind her in a black leather swivel chair closer to the door, a seating arrangement they came to early on. Charlie didn't care to see his face and she didn't want him to read hers. In this seat, she can look out across the lawns at the front of the house and pretend she is only talking in her head.

"And how do you feel about Nick now?"

"I—I don't know," she says. "I'll always love him. But he's no longer part of my world."

"And who *is* part of your world?" the doctor asks.

"No one," Charlie says, shrugging. "There's just me in it."

"Wouldn't you like someone else to be in it with you?"

"Not now."

"Won't it be very lonely?"

Charlie shrugs again, but says nothing.

"Charlie? Won't you be lonely?" Rees tries again. In the reflection of the window she can see him taking off his spectacles and leaning forward to try and catch a glimpse of her expression.

"I've been lonely most of my life," she wants to say, but her lips remain sealed.

It is Dr Rees who first persuaded her to speak after her weeks of silence when she arrived at the clinic. In the beginning he asked her questions, hoping for answers. Finally, he rearranged the chairs like this and sat silently with her for the hour allocated for their session. The time passed interminably slowly, but one day, just as he was thinking of changing his strategy with her, she spoke.

"Did any of the puppies survive?" she asked.

"What puppies, Charlie? Where were the puppies? Can you remember?"

"Yes."

"What happened to them?"

"They shot their mother."

"Who, Charlie? Who shot their mother?"

"The men who came."

"What did they do next?"

"They took the women. And the girls."

"And then?"

"And then they came back for me."

With those few sentences, Dr Rees was finally able to find a way to Charlie's past. Her medical records told him the rest. Over time, he gently persuaded her that there was no shame in her mental collapse—rather that it was an inevitable consequence of what she'd endured.

"Your nightmares and the flashbacks are entirely to be expected, Charlie. Even embraced. It's the ones who don't have nightmares that I worry about. At least your pain is finding a way out."

Pain. She'd never known what pain was until she came to in that makeshift hospital after her rescuers had pulled her from under the wheels of the truck. The pain corkscrewed into her insides and gnawed away insatiably at her brain. Nothing the inadequate medical staff could give her in that primitive place even touched it. She writhed on the unforgiving metal bed until her body decided it'd had enough and allowed her to slip into the bliss of unconsciousness once more.

The next few weeks were enshrouded in fog. She remembered going into some sort of operating theatre, walls filthy, the air thick with flies. She recalled pleading for someone who spoke English before a grubby oxygen mask was lowered over her face.

She awoke in a stained gown, her head thumping like a sledgehammer, feeling completely emptied. It was as if something or someone had drained away her life's blood and left her, like the discarded papery carcass of an insect, weighed down by a blanket.

It was weeks before anyone came. Most had given her up for dead. Dressed as she was and without any ID, she wasn't immediately identified as the Englishwoman for whom Nick and Carrie, the Foreign Office, and her media colleagues had been searching all of Kosovo. The bloody corpses of Rajak had been discovered, photographed, and catalogued for posterity, but Charlie's body wasn't among those violated and discarded like rag dolls. Nobody knew where she was—until a weary doctor at the hospital mentioned to an American journalist in Pristina the unfortunate, mute young woman in his care.

By the time Nick and Carrie reached her bedside, it was too late. Her green eyes were blank. Her mind had caved in. Emaciated, dehydrated, and suffering from a raging infection after a series of botched operations, she was closer to death than life. But, worse than that, she'd lost all hope, and without hope, she simply couldn't fight anymore.

It was Dr Rees who taught her to believe that hope would return one day.

"And how do you feel about Nick now?" Dr Rees asks her again.

"I—I don't know," she replies. "I love Nick. I guess I always will. But he's no longer part of my world."

31

THERE WERE SIX new messages waiting on Charlie's answering machine when she returned from the shops the following morning. For the first two, the caller hadn't spoken. The third was from an art historian Alan had put Charlie in touch with, agreeing to a meeting.

The fourth was from her mother, inviting her for Christmas along with Fiona and her husband. It was an invitation Charlie was dreading. Christmas in that airless house, the five of them sitting around the dining table without Granddad, was something she'd never grown accustomed to and now, even after her mother's illness, she simply couldn't face.

The penultimate message on the answering machine was surprising.

"Hello? This is Sarah, Lady Matheson. I've been thinking about our last meeting and I'm afraid I was frightfully rude. I was wondering, could you come to tea on Saturday at four o'clock so that we can have that little chat you wanted? You know the address, of course. I shall be expecting you."

The final message was from Dr North. *"Charlie, it's Steve. I dredged up the file on Angela Matheson and refreshed my memory about the postmortem. You were right. There was something unusual I should have remembered. I'd rather not tell you over the phone, though. Give me a call."*

She found his number and dialed it straight away. His answering service switched in. "Steve? Charlie Hudson. It's six o'clock Wednesday. Sorry I missed you. Call me when you get this."

It was the following afternoon before he returned her call. "Hi, Charlie. You got my message, then?"

"Yes, and I'm intrigued. Look, I know this sounds crazy but where are you right now?"

"In the mortuary of Westminster Coroner's Court, about to start a postmortem. I won't be out of here much before seven, and then I'm flying up to Edinburgh tonight. I'm presenting a paper on forensic medicine in the morning."

Charlie's heart sank, then rose again. "Where are your notes on the Angela Matheson case? Are they with you?"

"Yes. They're in my briefcase. I was going to mail you a copy this afternoon."

"Okay. Stay where you are. I'll be there within the hour."

He laughed. "My patient and I aren't going anywhere for a while. Take as much time as you need."

PUSHING OPEN ONE of the narrow double doors that led to the main vestibule of the coroner's court, she was met with the scent of lilies and the sympathetic face of a grey-suited man with a clipboard.

"Can I help you, madam?"

"Yes. I'm here to see Dr North. He's expecting me."

"And you are?"

"Charlotte Hudson. I spoke to him on the phone less than an hour ago. He told me to meet him here."

"I think you'll find the doctor's a little preoccupied at the moment," the man said, impassively. "But I will go and tell him you're here."

He returned minutes later without his clipboard and with a less welcoming expression. "Dr North says you can either wait here for him or come through. I must warn you, he's halfway through the examination of a dead body." It was clear that he thought it most irregular for a strange woman to be allowed into the mortuary, and that he would most certainly be reporting the matter to his superiors. Charlie wanted nothing more than to run a million miles from the morgue, but she could tell, from this man's demeanour, that Dr North had won an important battle on her behalf. She responded accordingly.

"Thank you. I'll follow you through," she replied, forcing a smile.

Glowering with disapproval, he led her through a maze of doors, rooms leading into rooms, most empty. The final room, a small office with fading glossy posters of the Canadian Rockies on its walls, was choked with desks and office furniture. Two secretaries flirted, giggling, with three young constables while the officers typed up their reports with single fingers on ancient computers. When Charlie appeared at the door, the conversation stopped abruptly and their eyes followed her silently across the room. Respect for the dead and those who might be grieving penetrated even back here.

She smelled it before she reached it—the cloying odour of formaldehyde and sterilising fluid. Ducking under the arm of the coroner's lackey as he held open the door of the morgue, she entered a gleamingly bright, windowless room in which the pathologist stood over a woman's body on a table. A mask covered his lower face.

"Ah, Charlie! Come in. You're not squeamish, are you? I remember you sitting through a couple of these with me years ago."

Charlie shook her head, swallowing bile. *That was before,* she wanted to reply, *long before my far too intimate familiarity with the dead. Bodies and blood,* her mind kept repeating. *You're not good with bodies and blood anymore. Don't make a fool of yourself. Remember why you came.*

Focusing hard on the tiny folds of skin that crisscrossed Dr North's forehead as he bent over his task, an assistant by his side, she tried to ignore the muscle beneath her left eye which had begun to twitch.

"What's the case?" she eventually managed.

"Young woman, twenties I'd say, raped, stabbed, and dumped in an alley. Probably a prostitute from the look of her. Nothing too unexpected."

Charlie looked down at the woman for the first time; saw the hands lying loosely by her side, the broken red fingernails. There were surprisingly few bruises on her face or body; the dead girl looked quite intact apart from a neat puncture wound in her side, as if she'd been drained of all colour and lay, sleeping, on the slab. Her unnaturally blond hair cascaded from the table, nearly brushing the floor.

"I wonder whether she'd say it was nothing too unexpected," Charlie heard herself say.

Dr North ignored her remark and carried on marking out the corpse, circling small bruises and scratches in bold red strokes of a pen for the camera that was suspended above it. The soles of his plastic-covered shoes squeaked on the polished linoleum floor each time he took a step.

"So, what's so urgent about the Angela Matheson case that you had to race all the way across London to see me?" he asked, without looking up.

"You said you had something to tell me, that's all."

"But I didn't say it was that urgent. Why couldn't it wait?"

"I have an appointment with her mother in a few days. I wanted to be fully armed with the facts beforehand."

Steve North moved to one side while his assistant pulled the camera into place and started taking photographs. The great machine clicked and whirred and its lights illuminated the body even more cruelly.

"Why don't you take a look for yourself?" North said, closely supervising every frame. "My briefcase is over there." With a nod he gestured towards a battered leather case resting on a black plastic chair.

Charlie was grateful to turn her back on the lights, which were making her jump with every flash. Sitting, she placed the case on her lap and clicked it open. It was crammed with papers, police reports, and photographs. Looking up helplessly, she caught Dr North's eye.

"Sorry. I should be a lot better organised. What you're looking for is in a blue folder."

Reaching for it with her fingertips, she fished it out as if it were a vital forensic clue and set the case on the floor. Taking a deep breath, she flipped open the folder and stared down at a photograph of Angela Matheson lying naked on a mortuary slab. The curtain of hair that always hid her face was scraped back, to reveal a high forehead, arched eyebrows, and sculpted cheekbones. Metal earrings studded her earlobes on each side, and there was a small ring through one side of her nose. The one in her belly button was no longer evident. In the corner of her mouth was a fleck of yellow sputum. Her hair colour and general appearance were uncannily similar to those of the woman lying not ten feet away; for a moment, Charlie was stunned by the similarities.

She ignored the remaining photos and flicked through the interviews and police notes with the expertise of a journalist who knows she doesn't have long. She finally found what Steve North wanted her to find.

Scanning the postmortem report, following each sentence with her forefinger, she reached the end of the page and realised she was holding her breath. She squeezed her eyes shut and leaned back in the chair. If the waters were muddy before, now they were swirling with mire. Nothing could have prepared her for the irony of what she read, and the gamut of emotions it sparked within her.

"See what I mean?" Dr North glanced up from his hunched position over the dead woman's feet. The marker pen had been replaced by a scalpel, and Charlie knew she'd have to leave the room soon, very soon.

"Yes," she replied, struggling to appear less shocked than she was. "Do you have a photocopier?"

Within half an hour, having said a hasty good-bye, she was running back through the double doors of the court, a piece of paper clutched in her hand. "Taxi!" she cried, using it to flag down a passing black cab.

"Where to, luv?" the driver asked.

"East," she answered, breathlessly, rolling down the window urgently for some air. "Just head east."

Quarto

The size of book or paper given by
folding a sheet of paper twice; paper folded in
this way and cut into sheets

32

ISTRACTED BY THE EVENTS of the last few days, Charlie almost forgot her long-awaited meeting with Susie Ball, an art historian at
the Royal Academy. Rushing to make it on time, she barely did, arriving
disheveled and ill prepared.

She needn't have worried. Miss Ball set her instantly at ease. A blond
Texan in her late forties who gamboled into the room like a long-legged
colt, she had that devil-may-care attitude of many Americans that Charlie
secretly envied. The fact that she had become a leader in her field—
European art of the eighteenth century—was made all the more surprising by her nationality and relative youth.

"Call me Susie," she declared. "And, please, don't worry. It's usually
me apologising for running late, so I'm happy for the chance to be mag-
nanimous for a change!"

"Thanks," Charlie said with relief, flopping into a chair to catch her
breath. "Now, if you'll just give me a moment, I'll find the section I
wanted you to cast your expert eye over for me."

"Alan tells me you're working on a book together." Susie reached for
her glasses and perched them on the end of her nose in readiness. "On
paper and Turner?"

"That's right." Charlie smiled, sifting through the papers on her lap.

"And something he said to me made me go off at a tangent that I'd love you to confirm or deny."

"What?" Susie looked genuinely intrigued.

"Well, he said the British papermakers in the eighteenth century so superseded their European counterparts that British artists were actually able to steal a march on their rivals and thus lead the way in art for over half a century. In other words, it was the superior English paper that enabled artists like Turner and others to become so successful, as much as it was their own skills."

Susie Ball whistled and raised her eyebrows. "Contentious stuff! I can see why you'd want to check with someone. Alan and his paper, eh? That guy really is obsessed."

"So, is there any truth in what he says?"

Susie smiled. "I'm sure he believes it completely. I swear that man could sell sand to the Arabs." Seeing Charlie's expression, she added, "But of course, as always with Alan, there is an element of truth."

"But surely the European artists of the time had similar access to fine papers? The Italians had been making paper at Fabriano and Amalfi for much longer. And then there were the French and German manufacturers as well...."

"Of course. But none of them had yet mastered the manufacture of wove paper, which was developed by a mill in Kent called Whatman's, which I'm sure you've heard of by now. Wove paper was created by the weaving of a special wire cloth, you see, through which water could drain once the pulp was laid onto it. This far surpassed the earlier moulds, which were based on a grid system of rigid lines of raised wires on which the paper assumed the pattern of those wires. The new paper had a special quality, an innate smoothness that lent itself perfectly to watercolour painting and to drawing. It provided an ideal surface for this new means of expression. No one could argue against the fact that it was in Britain in the eighteenth century that watercolour painting reached new heights of brilliance."

"So, Alan is right? The paper really could have made a difference to the success of the art in this country?"

Susie nodded. "You only have to look at the evidence—Constable, Cotman, Turner... even lesser-known artists like Paul Sandby. Their refinements to the art of watercolour painting were pioneering. They were way ahead of their European counterparts in developing watercolour use for landscapes and taking it beyond mere flower painting or the colouring in of drawings. The one common denominator seems to have been the quality of the paper the British artists were using. It was a good fifty years before the rest of Europe caught up."

Charlie scribbled furiously, delighted by what she was hearing. Looking up, she said, "If I were to play devil's advocate for a moment, couldn't I argue that the skills of these artists might have developed naturally anyway? That they might have sparked each other's originality and thus prompted a growth in popularity of the new medium? That it had nothing at all to do with the paper?"

"Many art historians believe that, Charlie. They refuse to accept that the paper could have played such a pivotal role. They cite the works of Raphael and Dürer to support their claim. I think they fear that if they admit the paper itself is so important it might somehow diminish the genius of the individual artists. But the fact is that when paper conservators examine the works considered most important to this era—the English watercolours that really made a difference and so impressed Europe at the time—they are almost all on wove paper. And much of it was produced here by Whatman's. Alan may be obsessed with his precious paper, but he isn't alone in thinking that this must be more than mere coincidence."

"Wow! This is wonderful. Thank you."

Susie laughed. "Alan will be relieved I backed him up, I'm sure."

Charlie stopped writing and studied her tutor thoughtfully. "You sound like you know him pretty well."

Susie laughed. "I should. I'm his cousin."

"Really? He never said."

"Alan never says much about anything other than art. Haven't you noticed? He's always been like that."

"You must have known him all your life, then?"

"Pretty much, although my mom—Alan's aunt—took us to Dallas

when I was three, and I didn't come back for fifteen years. But it was Alan who persuaded me to read art at Cambridge and follow him into the family business, so to speak. I owe him a great deal."

"So . . . I suppose you knew his daughter pretty well, also?"

The expression on Susie's face altered. Her eyes glinted like the edge of a polished sword.

"Yes, I did," she replied evenly, collecting her glasses from her nose and dangling them from her long fingers.

"Tell me, what was she like?"

"Complex. Even as a child. By the time she was a teenager, her relationship with her parents was shaped by rebellion and, later, anger—especially towards Alan, for some reason I never understood. That whole awful business was devastating for him, and for Sarah, Angela's mother, of course. Neither of them ever really got over it."

"I know. Alan certainly finds it impossible to talk about."

Susie stared at Charlie in the same intense way as Alan sometimes did. "Well, he would, wouldn't he? What was it Arthur Miller said about betrayal? Oh, yes, I remember. It's the only truth that sticks."

33

CHARLIE ARRIVED OUTSIDE Sarah Matheson's door half an hour early and waited on a bench in the little square opposite, watching the time on a nearby church clock, her breath making clouds of steam in the crisp December air.

She didn't really know what she hoped to achieve by this meeting. Angela's face stalked her dreams. Whatever else Sarah Matheson was, she was direct and Charlie knew she wouldn't brush her questions aside, the way Alan had. But the woman had been through quite enough without Charlie turning up to harp on about experiences which must have caused her intense pain.

Yet some instinct deep inside, perhaps a journalistic one, told Charlie that Sarah Matheson held the key. She was the one person who could explain. To Charlie, Angela remained a mystical figure, half victim, half bitch, and Charlie never quite knew which persona she preferred. The bitch was the multipierced rebel who'd created that horrific self-portrait of Hell mocking her father, a wicked note in her hand. The victim was the sad-eyed girl peering out of the photograph Charlie had pinned to her office wall, someone who killed herself in that clinic only as a last, desperate act after years of abuse.

The parallels between her life and Angela's continued to dog Charlie:

the desire to paint as well as someone they loved and respected, their need to rebel despite an outwardly happy childhood, their attempt to end their lives after some sort of sexual assault, whether real or imagined. Even to the demons which seemed to haunt them both in Angela's painting. Charlie was increasingly convinced that only the lady hiding behind the curtains opposite could rid her of Angela forever.

At precisely five minutes to four, Charlie peeled off her woollen gloves and strode across the street to the imposing front door of the mansion block. Taking a deep breath as if she were about to submerge herself in water, she pressed the buzzer.

Sarah Matheson was dressed almost identically to the way Charlie had last seen her. The pearls, the cloying Chanel No. 5, the immaculate hands, the neutral designer dress, the tight skin of her manufactured face, and the ivory cigarette holder were as before. Her manner, however, was dramatically different. This time, a welcoming afternoon tea was laid out in silver on a small Japanese lacquered table. A three-tier cake stand displayed tiny sandwiches, their crusts carefully removed, stacked alongside scones and intricate chocolate confections—all, no doubt, purchased from the nearby Harrods Food Halls earlier that day.

"Please come and sit down, my dear, and I'll pour you some tea." Sarah Matheson took Charlie's arm and led her to a chair by the open fire. "I wasn't sure you'd even come after my appalling manners the last time we met, for which I can now only apologise." She stooped over the tea table but kept her blue eyes fixed steadily on her guest.

"Actually, it was I who was rude," Charlie replied. "I should never have come here uninvited. It was thoughtless of me to intrude on your private grief."

Sarah Matheson didn't answer. She was far too preoccupied with the precise art of serving tea. The finest leaves of Darjeeling, picked from a plantation owned for three generations by her father's family, had been infusing in boiling water for exactly four minutes. The tiniest dash of cold milk had been added to each pretty bone china cup with a small flourish of her wrist. Now, balancing a silver strainer over a teacup, she poured the steaming amber liquid from the pot. Lemon, which Charlie would have preferred to milk, was not on offer. Sarah repeated the exercise with her own cup. Finally, she lifted a second, much smaller pot, filled with hot water, and topped up the original teapot, before exhaling and settling back into her seat.

"Sugar?" she asked, waving her hand expansively at the table as if to indicate that her part in the ritual was over.

"Thanks, but no."

"A sandwich, then?"

Charlie selected a triangle of smoked salmon pressed between buttered brown bread and placed it on a delicate tissue serviette. Having nibbled dutifully at it, careful not to soil the perfect square of paper, she abandoned the offering.

The two women sipped from their cups and sat silently for a moment, studying each other. Charlie had chosen plum-coloured wool trousers with a cream silk blouse. Her hair was twisted into a smooth plait at her neck. She'd even dabbed on a tiny trace of lip balm in an attempt to look more sophisticated than she felt. When she'd left the house, she felt appropriately dressed, but here, in the elegant cosiness of Sarah Matheson's drawing room, she felt uncomfortably warm.

"Is the fire too hot for you?" Sarah inquired politely.

"No, no, it's fine," Charlie lied. Placing her cup carefully back onto the tray, she smiled at her companion and decided to take the plunge. "Mrs M—um, *Lady* Matheson. I know this can't be easy for you, and I'd like you to know that I'm in no way insensitive to your position."

"And what position would that be?"

"Well, what I mean is, you are Angela's mother and Alan's ex-wife. You must be wondering what right I, of all people, have to delve around in your past. I mean, especially as Alan and I are hardly even seeing each other at the moment. . . ."

A shadow fell across Sarah's features momentarily. "Oh, but you are, my dear. Alan was quite explicit in my conversation with him earlier this week."

"You spoke to Alan? In Italy? About me?" Charlie picked up her teacup again to occupy her hands.

"Yes. I call him every week. Old habits, I suppose."

"And h-he said we were together?"

"He made that perfectly clear. In fact, he went as far as to tell me he believed he had fallen in love with you."

Charlie swallowed against the constriction in her throat.

"He said that?"

"Yes, which is precisely why I invited you to tea," Sarah Matheson explained coolly. "To reintroduce myself to the future Lady Matheson."

Unexpected, Charlie's empty teacup slipped from her fingers, striking the table with a clatter, upsetting the silver spoon in its delicate sugar bowl and showering a cascade of white crystals across the lacquered table. Looking up, her eyes met Sarah Matheson's just in time to see the smile of triumph flare in them.

"I can assure you I have no intention of becoming the future Lady Matheson!" Charlie cried, trying to scoop the sugar into her hands. "I can't imagine why Alan would give you that impression. I—I'm still married, for one thing. Alan and I are barely talking at the moment and, as far as I can gather, he flew to Italy to get away from me." She regretted her admission instantly.

"Don't flatter yourself, my dear. Alan always spends the winter months there. The light is so much better than in England at this time of year. Regardless of what little problems you and he may be having right now," her hostess continued placidly, "the reason I asked you here, Charlotte—may I call you that?—is to find out a little more about you. As you may have gathered, I'm somewhat overprotective of my husband's interests. I wouldn't want Alan making yet another ghastly mistake. I'm sure you've heard about the unfortunate business of his last wife, Diane. Suitability is everything, isn't it? Now, and I'm sorry to have to bring this up, but my contacts tell me you've suffered from some poor health in recent years. May I ask from what? And may I assure you that nothing you tell me will go beyond these walls? I have myself been...unwell...for some years, and my daughter Angela—of course you know all about her ill health. So you can consider yourself in good company."

Charlie recoiled at the thought.

"You'll have to forgive me for pressing," Sarah Matheson continued firmly, "but I only want to know if your—condition—still requires any sort of treatment."

"No. No, it doesn't. I haven't seen or spoken to a psychiatrist in over two years." She felt as if she had left her privacy at the door with her coat.

Sarah Matheson sat waiting.

"I was a j-journalist," Charlie faltered. "I spent several years covering the sort of stories that would have unsettled the most levelheaded of people. Then I was very nearly killed in an incident which made me reconsider some of the experiences of my life. I consequently spent a short time in therapy."

She straightened. "I'm completely recovered. My only medical condition now is a severe allergy to bee stings, but that's hardly a matter for a mental health panel. I trust that has answered any doubts you might have about my *suitability*."

Sarah Matheson nodded her acknowledgement of Charlie's honesty. "Thank you for being so frank. You must realise, my dear, I only have my husband's and your best interests at heart."

"I can understand why you might be protective of Alan," Charlie retorted, "but why should my interests be of any concern to you?"

"The same reason my daughter's history should be of concern to you, I suppose," Sarah rejoined smoothly. "We both need answers, you and I."

She stood abruptly and reached for a cigarette from the box on the mantelshelf.

"If my daughter were still here, she'd tell you it was Alan who drove her to suicide." Sarah lit her cigarette from a tiny gold lighter and blew a stream of smoke into the air. "And in a way, that's quite true. Angela was a terribly muddled young woman, not so unlike yourself. She enjoyed, shall we say, a difficult relationship with Alan. Indeed, for much of her life, my husband and my daughter were at loggerheads. When she became ill, Alan had little or no sympathy for what he regarded as her attention-seeking behaviour."

"Was it? Attention-seeking, I mean?"

"Mostly," Angela's mother admitted. "Especially the arson attack on his studio. That was truly wicked. But as I think I said to you once before, my daughter could be . . . impossible when she wanted to be. Angela manipulated Alan to such an extent that when she finally took her own life, I'm sorry to say that it almost came as a kind of relief."

For the briefest of moments, the older woman had such sorrow in her eyes that Charlie had to resist the urge to reach out to her. Instead, she said impulsively, "That must have been terrible for you."

Sarah Matheson pulled away suddenly, visibly appalled by Charlie's sympathy.

Chastened, Charlie asked, "Why do you think Angela hated Alan so much? Didn't he spend time with her as a child? Didn't he teach her to paint? I'd have thought they'd have been close. Most fathers and daughters are."

"They weren't like most fathers and daughters. Yes, to begin with, they were close. They spent a great deal of time together . . . too much for their own good, perhaps. When he turned his back on her, to fulfil his demanding work and social obligations, she became unreasonably jealous. Almost like a lover. Their relationship was that intense."

"Lady Matheson," Charlie asked softly, "I'm so sorry to raise this, and I really hope you're not offended, but were you aware that Angela was pregnant when she died?"

Sarah Matheson's eyes clouded. Turning away, she moved to the floor-to-ceiling window, where she stood as if carved of wood. In the stark winter light her face was illuminated to such a degree that Charlie could see, more clearly, signs of her plastic surgery—cruel lines of tight, shiny skin behind her ears, around her eyes, and beneath her chin. But the harsh light also illuminated what she was so desperately trying to disguise—the furrows ploughed by years of loss and longing.

There was a silence of several minutes filled only by the murmur of traffic below while Sarah considered her answer. "Yes," she said, finally. "Yes, Alan and I knew Angela was pregnant."

"And did you ever find out who the father was?"

"No. Although I could probably make a guess."

"Was it someone close?" Charlie persisted.

Sarah Matheson's face drained of all colour. Once again, Charlie saw a glimpse of the wretchedness her daughter's death had caused her.

"No," she whispered. Ash fell from her cigarette onto the immaculate cream carpet. Turning away again, she said, "No one close at all."

Charlie sat uncertainly while her hostess composed herself by the window. Reaching for Sarah's half-empty cup and saucer, she refilled it with hot tea. "Here," she said, taking it to her. "Drink this. I'm sorry to have dredged all this up again. This is none of my business. It's cruel of me to ask you all these questions."

Sarah Matheson did as she was told, sipping from the lukewarm tea gratefully. "Thank you," she murmured, her face still turned to the window. "As you can see, I'm still very much in love with my husband."

"I think I always knew that."

Sarah Matheson pulled herself to her full height and gave Charlie a penetrating gaze. "I asked you once before if you loved him, and you told me you didn't know. Tell me, was that the truth?"

It was Charlie's turn to be silent. Thoughts of Alan flooded her heart. His unexpected protestation of love for her to Sarah, and how that made her feel; the agonies he must have gone through over his tragically rebellious daughter and needy wife; his secret inner pain that he had lost not only his child but his future grandchild, too.

"It was the truth then," Charlie replied. "But now I think I could learn to love him, in my own way, one day." Looking into the face of her companion, she added with surprise: "I really could love him."

34

WHEN CARRIE RANG Charlie to suggest that they meet up for a drink before she headed back to Manchester, Charlie was relieved. She really needed to talk to someone and the call couldn't have been better timed. She quickly took a shower, washed her hair, pulled on a sweater and a pair of jeans, and rushed out eagerly to meet her best friend.

Carrie was late arriving at the bar in Euston, by which time Charlie had ordered wine and was sitting at a candlelit table in the corner, watching for her. Giving her a smile and a wave as she came breathlessly through the door, Charlie stood and kissed each cheek as Carrie settled into the chair at her side, tossing a crumpled *Evening Standard* onto the table in front of them.

"That's better," Carrie said, rubbing her hands together. "It's bloody freezing outside."

"Here," Charlie replied, pouring out a glass of Merlot, "this'll warm you up. How was your Aunt Lily?"

"Mad. More eccentric by the minute. But underneath that grouchy exterior there beats a heart of gold. We had a surprisingly good time."

They chatted politely at first, Charlie bringing Carrie up to speed on the progress of her book, and Carrie explaining that she'd had lunch with

Nick earlier that day. "He's going to be running the paper while his edi-tor's skiing this Christmas. Secretly, I think he's thrilled. Not that he'd admit to it, of course."

"And Miranda?" Charlie asked dutifully.

"Still going strong, apparently," Carrie replied, less enthusiastically. "She's all set to move in and sort him out, I think."

"About time." Charlie laughed.

"What about Alan? How's all that going?" Carrie enquired, her tone guarded.

Charlie took a deep breath. "Complicated."

"How so?"

Charlie smiled and stared into her friend's face. "Where do I begin?"

"At the beginning? Nick told me you'd been to see the coroner's offi-cer in charge of Alan's daughter's case. For starters, you could tell me what you found out. You were quite upset, Nick said. He seemed to think it was important."

Charlie gripped her wineglass with both hands and took the plunge. "The coroner's officer said Angela left a note. But for some reason, the clinic and Angela's family and the court all agreed to cover it up."

"Cover what up, Charlie?" Carrie asked gently. "What did the note say?"

"It claimed she'd been raped. And it named the man who did it. Alan." Her words hung, static, in midair as Charlie re-examined them. Even though she'd owned the information for a while, it still shook her to vocal-ise it.

"Oh, I see." Carrie said it quietly. "And what do you think?"

"Well, it's all complete nonsense, of course!" Charlie cried. She low-ered her head and pressed it against her wineglass. Looking up, she weak-ened. "I'll be honest, Carrie, to begin with I didn't know what to think. I thought I knew Alan, and then everything suddenly seemed questionable. Now I'm certain it's all a lie. I'm convinced of it. I believe Angela just said it to hurt him."

"Why would she do a terrible thing like that?"

"I don't know. Not yet."

"Did this coroner's officer say anything else?"

"He said the cover-up came from the highest level. And that when he complained about the suicide note not being presented as evidence, he was threatened with demotion, or worse. Soon afterwards, they retired him, to keep his mouth shut. He said the Matheson family was extremely powerful. He believes a brother of Sarah's in the Home Office pulled some of the original files. He warned me not to get involved."

"And?"

"And I went to see the pathologist who conducted the case. He showed me the postmortem report. It said that Angela was pregnant. The feeling at the time seemed to be that it must have been Alan's child."

Carrie appeared to wait for the ugly charge to dissipate in the air before she asked: "Have you asked Alan about any of this?"

"God, no! Alan never speaks of Angela. If this whole nightmare was some kind of vicious, terrible lie designed to wound him, I can't possibly rake it all up again."

"So, what can you do?"

"I went to see Sarah, Angela's mother. She knows them better than anyone and she clearly doesn't believe it, either. In our hearts, I think we both know Alan couldn't possibly be that kind of man. That's all I need to know right now." She sipped at her wine by way of a full stop.

"What's Sarah like?"

"Sad. Immeasurably sad. Clinging to her youth and all the more sad for it."

"Was she friendly?"

"Not especially, and at first I was a little taken aback by her vehemence against her daughter. I didn't expect that, but I suppose I should have, in the circumstances."

"Why? What circumstances?"

"Well, Angela had been off the rails for years, according to some of the cuttings—sex, drugs, crime, theft. Sarah said her death didn't really come as a surprise. She even admitted she saw it as a relief."

"Which would explain why Alan's so reluctant to talk about her,"

Carrie mused. "There must be such unspeakable guilt in feeling relief that someone you love has taken her own life."

"I know," Charlie said. An image of her grandfather made her shudder involuntarily.

"But if Alan wasn't the father of Angela's child," Carrie added, clearly treading cautiously, "that still doesn't explain why Angela tried to hurt him by claiming he was."

"No. And there's something else, Carrie."

"What's that?"

"Well, if Alan wasn't the father of her child, then who was?"

THE ANSWER CAME to her in a blinding flash of revelation the following morning. She'd enjoyed her best night's sleep in ages, thanks in part to Sarah Matheson's ringing endorsement of Alan. Now she realised something else. If Angela's note really had accused Alan of being the father of her unborn child, then surely the police would have carried out a blood test and checked the DNA? Why on earth hadn't she thought of that before?

Fumbling for the light switch, she jumped up and looked for her personal organiser, scribbling down the telephone number of Dr Steve North on a jotter pad by her bed. Dialing it hastily, she swore aloud when she heard the answering service cut in.

"Steve, it's Charlie. It's—oh, God, sorry—just before seven on Tuesday morning. I really need to talk to you again. Please call me back when you can."

He returned her call two hours later, his tone decidedly guarded. "Charlie, are you stalking me? This is the third call in as many weeks. I'm beginning to get twitchy."

"I'm really sorry. I won't call again. I promise. I just need you to look something else up in that Angela Matheson file. Something I didn't get a chance to check. It will only take a couple of minutes and then I'll be off your back forever, I promise. Please?"

. . .

WHEN ALAN RETURNED from Italy and drove to his home in Suffolk four days later, Charlie was waiting for him. She'd taken a broom and swept her mind clear of all the ugly clutter and debris, leaving space only for the sparkling apology she'd rehearsed a hundred times. She had to make it up to him; she wanted to more than anything. There would be no more ugly suspicions between them. There would be no more talk of Angela, unless Alan chose to bring the subject up, which she very much doubted would happen. It was something that had caused him untold trauma and she, of all people, wasn't about to rub salt into the wound. Anyway, she'd found out all she needed to know. All that mattered to her now was their future.

She waited for him in his studio, let in by a reluctant Mrs Reeder. When Alan walked in, Charlie lay naked under a robe on the green velvet chaise. He rushed to her with the eagerness of a man half his age. Sarah Matheson had been wrong. It wasn't just lust that drew Charlie to Alan. No, there was something deeper. A meeting of minds. Alan used sex not as a weapon but as a method of communication. For him, it was as rigorous a process as painting, and equally sensual. When he trailed his fingers across her flesh, his breath heavy on her breast, it was as if he were tracing an outline across paper, his concentration was so intense.

He seemed to need to see her face, to watch her every response. He studied every flinch of muscle, every change in the texture of her skin. Like the true artist he was, he needed light, and he moved his grey eyes effortlessly up and down her body, returning time and again into her eyes. Most of all, he was the first man to make her feel beautiful again. The scars she was so terrified he would recoil from were, instead, a source of endless fascination to his artistic eye. He studied them minutely, kissing and caressing away the pain that had created them, allowing her to feel plea- sure in the sensitivity of their nerve endings rather than flinch away. That, almost more than anything, had made her realise she could love him.

Occasionally, he'd enlist help. A sable paintbrush with which to stroke her; a frozen cube from the ice bucket to tease up and down her skin; a droplet or two of wine from which he could sip. Her flesh memorised every place he'd been. Her mouth open, she received his gifts hungrily, gratefully giving herself up to him. She learned the satisfaction of watching him lose himself to sensations he could no longer control. The more they played with each other, the more he seemed to enjoy letting her take the lead. Their time together passed in a breathless haze, an oblivion of fulfilment and need that spoke of everything that needed to be said.

By the time they were sated at last, the Suffolk sky was streaked pink with the dawn. They lay, limbs entwined, Alan's breathing rapid and shallow, wrapped in a velvet throw, on the tatty chaise longue in front of the wood-burning stove.

"So, this is happiness," Charlie whispered into the intimacy of her soul.

THE FOLLOWING MORNING, after giant mugs of milky coffee and deliciously flaky croissants in the warm kitchen, Alan gave Charlie a gift. Finally agreeing to show her how much he'd accomplished of his painting for her book, he led her back to his studio, opened up the narrow wooden map chest he'd transported back from Italy, and placed the painting on his easel. Then he stood back to gauge her reaction.

The depth of colour and atmosphere astounded her. Using layer upon layer of colour washes, he'd perfectly recaptured the misty, hazy mood of the painting she'd examined in such detail at the Tate, Turner's *Crossing the Brook*.

"Ruskin once said of Turner that he painted with tinted steam," she murmured. "Because his watercolours were so evanescent and full of air. Now I see precisely what he meant."

Working first on the largest areas of paper, Alan had filled in the vast sky with its powdery blues and puffy white clouds and completed most of the detail of the panoramic horizon with its hint of buildings and a distant sea. The lofty green trees formed a focal point to the left of the picture; the cascading foliage hemmed in the right. Charlie peered closer to examine each delicate brushstroke of yellow, green, and brown, depicting the late summer leaves.

The bridge in the middle distance, with its graduated arches, formed a perfect line across the centre of the work, echoing the horizon and giving balance to the image. In the foreground, Alan had only sketched figures, the two women and the dog, and the boulders and rocks on the edge of the brook. But looking at it, Charlie could almost feel the water's coolness. She allowed her eyes to stray to the right, where the dark tunnel of trees had previously turned her blood cold. Now the untouched blocks of colour paled against the complexity and contrasts of the rest of the painting, and she realised with relief that Turner's trees, as captured by Alan, no longer frightened her.

"Oh, Alan! It's remarkable! Truly remarkable."

"Turner was once asked what his style was, and he replied: 'Atmosphere.' I adopted many of his own techniques to try to achieve just the right atmosphere," he explained. "First I toned the paper with my own washes to create Turner's colour harmonies, then I integrated them into the background to produce an illusion of depth, using a drier brush—like here—and here, for structures. Only as I near the completion of the painting will I use a fine brush for details."

"The water is glorious. I almost feel as if I could step into it."

He grinned. "Turner had an intimate grasp of surface and the way light plays on water. He was fascinated by the way reflections fragment shape and form. This painting was completed relatively early on in his career, and yet he'd already managed to achieve so much. His style relaxed with age into those wonderful formless, translucent works, but what I love about this one is its clarity, its freshness, the way the underlying washes seem almost to have been, as Ruskin said, steamed onto the surface of the paper."

"Was this particular picture well received?"

"Lord, no." Alan laughed. "One art critic at the time said it had a 'pea-green insipidity.' But it was always one of Turner's favourite works. He chose it, amongst others, to represent his work in some later engravings. It never sold, thank goodness, which is why it was left to the nation as part of Turner's gift."

Charlie stood looking at the painting, drinking in its beauty. "I think your version is going to be even lovelier than the original, Alan. This version of *Crossing the Brook* will definitely sell."

"Oh, no, it won't," Alan said, turning her to face him as he slipped his hands around her waist.

"Why not?" Charlie asked, smiling up at him.

"Because it's yours, my darling. I painted it for you and I'm leaving it to you in my will."

Staring up into his eyes, Charlie quelled a sense of foreboding deep within her. Not for the first time, she felt as if Alan had the power to stare right through her, into the darkness beyond, and she feared what he could see.

35

THE ANNUAL AWARDS CEREMONY for the Turner Prize was not the sort of event someone like Charlie would normally have been invited to. Tickets to Britain's most prestigious modern-arts prize, begun in 1984 in Turner's name, were as rare as hen's teeth. Celebrities jostled with artists for media airtime. This year, a famous pop singer was to present the award at Tate Britain, pushing the premium still higher. Alan was far too Establishment for the five-member jury who decide which of the "outstanding" contemporary artists of the year would receive the prize of twenty thousand pounds, but he was nonetheless invited annually, out of respect for his stature.

When he learned privately that the winner was to be Benjamin Quiller for his installation entitled *Work 567: The Flush*, an empty room with a stained lavatory that kept flushing itself automatically, he told Charlie he didn't think he could bring himself to attend.

"I feel like the boy in the fairy tale of *The Emperor's New Clothes*," he moaned, making her laugh. "Am I the only one who can see the nonsensical side of it? Everyone else is bowing and scraping to these pretentious young upstarts with their dreary ideas that say nothing of life. Lord only knows what Turner would have made of all this. I mean, the whole idea of calling the award after him was because he'd stipulated an annual prize for young artists in his will. But he expected *paintings*—proper works of art on paper or canvas that captured the soul and the imagination. Not soiled and sexual unmade beds with overfilled ashtrays, or incomprehensible videos, or someone who's a dab hand with sound systems or a lightbulb in an otherwise empty room. And they dare to do it in his name!"

"I know you don't have much time for modern art, but a lot of people do, including me," Charlie chided. "Anyway, I'd have thought you'd like this Quiller chap. He once exhibited a sheet of white A-four paper rolled up into a ball—well, at least it was paper! You really should put in an appearance. Besides, I'd quite like to know what it feels like to be seen on your arm in that kind of company."

And so, reluctantly, Alan had agreed. Charlie treated herself to a new dress, out of the advance to the second Rajak book she now knew she'd never write. She possessed only two other dresses, and neither would do. This was a stunningly simple design in raw black silk, cut on the bias, with tiny black beads fringing the hem. Slipping it on and examining herself critically in the mirror, she smiled back at her reflection.

Gone was the despair she'd wrapped herself up in for so long like a threadbare cardigan. In its place was a fresher look, softer and brighter. Since meeting Alan she'd gained a little weight, and her new curvaceousness suited her. With just the touch of his hand, Alan had made her appreciate herself once more. And oh, how she ached for those hands. Had she ever experienced sex as good as this before? Alan had performed a miracle and made her feel whole again—wanted and sexy and whole. She had been a girlfriend, and a wife. She was a daughter and a sister. But with Alan, for the first time, she was a woman.

Nick would undoubtedly be at the awards ceremony with his new literati friends and would probably meet Alan for the first time. The thought of the two men face to face filled Charlie with dread. Nick could be so spiky at times; she only hoped he wouldn't drink too much and cause a scene.

The Tate was buzzing when they arrived. A serried rank of press photographers was lined up outside, their flashlights popping. Alan, suitably sombre in dinner jacket and bow tie, stopped and posed at Charlie's side with the expertise of an old hand, a half smile on his lips. Charlie, meanwhile, blinked into the tidal wave of flashes. Alan squeezed her arm reassuringly and turned her deftly around, to give all the photographers a chance. He was clearly well accustomed to media attention, and she couldn't help but compare this performance to the day he'd grimly left his daughter's inquest, his hand held up protectively against the flashbulbs.

Inside the Tate were wall-to-wall celebrities, surrounded by swirls and eddies of more journalists and photographers. Alan disappeared to fetch them both a drink and left her standing on her own. Nervously, she looked around for Nick. He stood a good three inches taller than most and was usually easy to spot. She couldn't see him. Perhaps he hadn't arrived yet.

To her dismay, she was cornered instead by Nick's editor. Jake Burton and Nick had been at Cambridge together. When Jake became the youngest editor in what was still euphemistically referred to as "Fleet Street," he'd wanted Nick by his side. Grateful as she was for his patronage of her husband, Charlie had never liked Burton. He was too scheming by half; after she and Nick had split up, Jake had dropped all pretence of liking her, either.

"Nick's one of the best," he'd told her back then. "And if your raddled female brain can't figure that out, then you're even more insane than we all thought you were."

They'd not spoken since, and fortunately encountered each other rarely. But with Sir Alan Matheson as her escort and Charlie now a successful author, she'd apparently taken on new stature in Jake's eyes. Flanked by his cronies, he ambled over with them in tow.

"Charlie Hudson! How good to see you," he cried. "Come. I'd like you to meet some people."

For the next ten minutes she was unable to extricate herself from introductions to the newspaper's political, foreign, and social editors, the director of the National Gallery, the latest MP who'd deserted New Labour, and the head of a lobbying firm which conducted polls. When the small talk was just about exhausted, Jake bared his fangs.

"So, how are we, then?" he demanded in his most patronising tone. "Still crazy after all these years, eh?"

"*We're* fine," Charlie replied, acidly, wondering when Alan would reappear. "And how about you, Jake? I see you've somehow managed to hang on to your job."

Jake turned to the befuddled MP at his side. "Charlie had a bit of a breakdown a few years ago," he announced in his effeminate voice. "Had to give up her job at the *Tribune*. Went off to live in the sticks and has written a book about—well, what *was* it about, Charlie?"

Before Charlie could reply, she heard a familiar voice at her side. "It was about the catastrophic rape and destruction of an entire nation. It was about greed and power and evil. If I were you, I'd read it. You could learn a great deal about the human condition." With that, Alan grasped Charlie's elbow and led her firmly away.

Rescued, Charlie smiled up at her lover gratefully. "I didn't know you'd read my book!"

"I wanted to know more about the enigmatic woman I was dating."

"And?" she asked, suddenly anxious for his approval.

"Alan, how are you?" a voice interrupted. A familiar stab of perfume spiked the air. Lori Hunter, Charlie's Cambridge guide to the history of paper, stood before them, elegant in a tight red silk dress, her long blond hair piled up on top of her head. She held a small fan, delicately folded out of intricately patterned paper, which she wafted expertly against the closeness of the night.

"Lori, how nice to see you again," Alan responded warmly. "I believe you've met Charlotte Hudson?"

"Yes, of course." Lori smiled, extending one of her long hands. It lay cold and lifeless in Charlie's.

"It's been ages, Alan," Lori continued, her eyes restive. "I've missed you."

"Good." Alan's expression remained impassive. "I like nothing better than to hear I'm being missed."

Lori blinked, no doubt trying to decide if he was mocking her. "Perhaps we could have dinner sometime?" she suggested, adding, "if Miss Hudson doesn't mind."

"No, not at all." Charlie kept her tone friendly.

"Well, perhaps Charlie should join us." Alan seemed to be enjoying the discomfort he was causing. "I'm sure she has plenty more questions to ask you about paper."

"I—I, er, well, yes," Lori answered, clearly confused. She glanced at Charlie but looked away again hastily when she saw the pity in her eyes. "I'll give you a call," she told Alan, backing away, almost upsetting a tray of canapés being circulated by a waiter. "Oh, sorry, sorry." And with that she melted away into the crowd.

"Oh, Alan," Charlie cried. "That was cruel. You could at least have been civil."

"I *was* civil, Charlie. I just wasn't very polite."

Before she could protest, he'd wandered off towards some people he knew and was beckoning to her imperiously. "Charlie, my dear? I'd like you to meet the Patrons of New Art."

Charlie forced her facial muscles into something resembling a smile, and stepped towards the waiting group.

PERHAPS IT WAS the champagne, Jake Burton, the presence of Lori Hunter, or just the heat and smoke of the room, but by the time the evening was drawing to its finale, Charlie felt unreasonably nettled. So much so that when she saw Nick across the heads of the crowd, she groaned aloud.

Slipping from Alan's side, she darted through the double doors leading to one of the side galleries. She was disappointed to discover several others had the same idea, and the large rooms were bustling with people attempting to escape the crush and the hype. Finding her way to the areas she knew best, those that housed tall cabinets containing some of Turner's personal effects, she pressed her nose to the glass and stared long and hard at the artist's boxes, paints, even the round-rimmed spectacles the great master had used. Turner had perhaps worn those very spectacles when he'd painted *Crossing the Brook*. Charlie could almost imagine them resting on the artist's bulbous nose, the glass liberally speckled with paint as he daubed flamboyantly onto his canvas, breathing life into his works.

The room bore testament to the fact that, for many, Turner was still the greatest British artist of the nineteenth century. Few others would merit such dedicated space. Not for the first time, she wondered what had drawn her to him in the first place, aside from her grandfather's passion for his work. A shared sense of the tragic, perhaps? So many of Turner's paintings were epic—shipwrecks, plagues, storms, burials at sea, the burning of Westminster, avalanches, snowstorms, and, lest she forget, even skeletons on horseback.

One of her favourites was called *Shade and Darkness—The Evening of the Deluge,* and she headed for it now. In the Clore Gallery, she stood in awe at its feet, compelled once more by its power and intensity. Completed just eleven years before Turner's death, the controversial work depicted the night of the Great Flood. Swirling whirls of black and brown paint filled the composition with a tremendous sense of foreboding as the energy and power of the ensuing flood built up, threatening to engulf those hapless men and animals who weren't in the sanctuary of Noah's Ark. The work was almost an abstract. At its core once more lay a tunnel of white, just as in *Loss of an Indiaman,* with all its despair. Turner had even written a poem to accompany this painting, called *The Fallacies of Hope.*

Charlie read its opening lines, printed beneath the masterpiece.

> *"The moon put forth her sign of woe unheeded;*
> *But disobedience slept; the dark'ning Deluge closed around . . ."*
> The Fallacies of Hope.

Angela's painting had been called *Hope Less.*

Was hope a fallacy for those tormented by their art? Was she helping Alan heal as much as he was helping her? Did he hope that Charlie might save him from the same madness that destroyed his daughter and so permanently damaged his wife? What hopes did Charlie have—could she have—for him? Wasn't the theme of all these works of art the inevitability of Death? The futility of hoping for anything more than that? Was that why she loved Turner so? Because for him, the answers always lay in Death?

Her unhealthy fascination with her own mortality had shaped her life for as long as she could remember. By the time her grandfather faced his final, painful months of silence, she was actively willing Death to take him. She knew only too well the relief Sarah had spoken of feeling when Angela had killed herself. And the guilt. The night Granddad hastened that dark embrace, abandoning her, he had come to her in a dream. There was a light in his eyes and a smile on his face that had been absent for so long she'd almost forgotten it. Seeing him that way, she felt nothing but joy.

"He's happy now, really he is," she'd told her mother firmly as they waited for the ambulance to come and take Granddad away. "He came to say good-bye to me in a dream last night, and he was happy."

Marjorie Hudson looked up at her daughter with distracted eyes and let out a rasping sob. "Why didn't he come and say good-bye to *me*?" she'd wailed. "Why did it have to be you?"

Now CHARLIE WANDERED over to the glass case that held Turner's death mask sculpted in alabaster and held her breath. The funeral directors her mother had chosen had combed her grandfather's thinning grey hair the wrong way across his forehead and done his shirt up too tight, so that the skin at the top of his neck folded uncomfortably over the collar.

To Marjorie's horror, Charlie had reached into the open coffin and angrily unbuttoned his shirt. The releasing of the pressure had softened her grandfather's face but made him seem suddenly less structured, as if the tiny button had secretly held everything in place.

The effect was similar with Turner. Gone was the dignity provided by the wooden false teeth that had given him so much discomfort in life. Instead his lips sagged over his exposed gums. His eyes were closed, his cheeks caved in, his appearance sad and sallow. Completed by Thomas Woolner, the mask was displayed with a short note written by the sculptor about the moment he'd seen his subject in death.

Dear old Turner. There he lay with his eyes sunk and his lips fallen in . . . on his calm face were written the marks of age and wreck, of dissolution and reblending with the dust. This was the man whose worst productions contained more poetry and genius than most laboured efforts of his brother artists . . . nor was it without emotion or with a dry eye that I gazed on so sad a sight.

"I thought I might find you here." Alan's voice, so close, startled Charlie and she spun round. Slipping his hands around her hips he pulled her to him, finding her mouth. In his, she tasted champagne and smoked salmon, inhaled linseed and aftershave. But the nicotine, which clung to his clothes and hair from the cigarettes that seemed to be enjoying resurgence among the arty set, made her gag.

"Can we go home now?" Her voice sounded strange, even to her.

"Yes, if you want to," he murmured, his face buried in the soft folds of her hair. "They haven't announced the award yet, though."

"I don't care. I just want to get out of here. Please," she pleaded.

"Is everything all right? I thought you wanted to come to this."

"I did. But now I'm here, I want to go. Put it down to the vagaries of women, if you like."

Alan frowned. "Would Lori Hunter have anything to do with your mood, by any chance?"

"What mood?"

"The mood you've been in ever since she came up and spoke to us."

"I wasn't aware that you'd noticed, you were so busy putting her down."

"What did you want me to do? Invite her back into my bed? She meant nothing to me, and yet there she stood, trying to imply to you that she had. I put her in her place, that's all. I thought you'd be pleased."

"Pleased? Why on earth would it please me to see you behave like a complete pig? She clearly thought a great deal more of your relationship than you ever did, and it would have cost you nothing to be kind. She was helpful to me and she obviously bears me no malice. I can't understand why you had to be so heartless."

Alan sighed and ran his hands through his hair. He tugged at his bow tie.

"I really don't understand women. If I'd been over-friendly, you'd have accused me of flirting. Because I gave her the brush-off, I'm now a chauvinistic villain. If this is to be our first public row, Charlie, then please let's make it about something important."

"Oh, okay!" Charlie cried. "You mean something *really* important, like your daughter? Or the fact that you've never had the guts to tell me the truth about her? That you've left me to try and figure it all out for myself like the sneaky journalist that I am, to agonise over the details I couldn't possibly understand?"

Seeing his shock, she rushed on, without thinking of the consequences. "I know everything, Alan. I know about Angela's suicide note, and I know she accused you of abusing her. I even know about the baby. I've spoken to the pathologist and the coroner's officer and I know the DNA test proved the baby wasn't yours."

Alan stood before her, the blood drained from his face, expressionless.

Too late, Charlie realised her mistake. "Alan, I..." she began, but he raised a forefinger to his lips and pressed it against them. Then, without a word, he turned on his heel and walked briskly away.

Charlie watched him leave and wondered if she should go after him. By the time she'd decided she should, he'd disappeared through the double doors and back into the overheated room where the award was about to be announced. The throng inside was virtually impenetrable, all faces turned to the podium where the night's celebrity announcer had taken the stand. Charlie threw open the doors and rushed straight into the broad chest of Nick, spilling his champagne down the front of her dress.

"Oh, Nick, God, I—I'm sorry," she said, brushing herself down, and peering past him for a glimpse of Alan.

"I thought I saw you slip in here." Nick's eyes were brimming with good humour as he pulled her to one side. "Where's the fire?"

Charlie gave up Alan with a sigh. He'd probably be hurrying down the front steps and hailing a taxi by now. Seeing Nick's expression, she attempted a smile. "Sorry. I didn't mean to be rude. I was just trying to catch someone before they left."

"Sir Alan Matheson?"

The slight slur as he said Alan's name told her all she needed to know. His breath smelled of a combination of whisky, champagne, and a woman. No doubt, he'd sunk a few before leaving the office, drunk far too much free champagne on an empty stomach, then screwed the life out of some bimbo in the lavatory. She could picture the girl now, skirt hitched up, sitting on the basin, while he lunged into her, her arms bruising under his grip. The soft white flesh of her own arm pinched as he gripped her, more to steady himself than to keep hold of her.

"I thought I recognised Matheson," Nick said. "I saw him stomping towards the door. I tried to introduce myself but he just brushed past me, a look of thunder on his face. What happened? Did you two fight?"

Charlie refused to reply.

"Come on," Nick said, "I think we both need a drink."

Transferring his grip to her elbow, he manoeuvred her roughly through the crowd into the packed bar. Looking at the queue in despair, he said: "This is hopeless. Let's grab a taxi and go somewhere else. Are you hungry? I'm famished. How about Rosa's?"

Charlie nodded, feeling like a piece of seaweed drifting with the tide.

"Great," Nick replied, grinning that stupid drunken grin of his. "Because I've got something really important to tell you."

36

I WANT A DIVORCE."

The words came rushing out before they'd had time to sit down at a table in the window or take their coats off. Charlie listened to them, feeling like a piece of wet paper suspended in a vat overflowing with water. She could hear it in her head: drip, drip. Any second now and she, too, would slip over the edge. Or maybe become so waterlogged that she'd sink to the bottom, helplessly.

All around her, the restaurant's old-fashioned interior was filled with lovers and theatregoers, regulars and stagehands. Rosa, with her flaming hair and faded Sophia Loren looks, was taking orders at a large table noisy with American tourists. The barman was almost hidden behind the raffia-covered carafes of red wine he was stacking onto the bar.

"Did you hear me, Charlie? I said I want a divorce." Nick leaned forward and spoke, too loudly. "Miranda wants—we both want—to get engaged. And we can hardly do that while I'm still married to you, can we?"

Charlie stared at a couple in the far corner. Their fingers interlaced, their eyes shining in the candlelight. Happy people, so close she could almost touch them.

Twenty minutes, she estimated with a flicker of panic. She just had to get through the next twenty minutes and she'd survive. If she could manage to stay in the present, then she wouldn't drown. Silently, she urged Nick not to go on, not to say the words dripping away inside her skull.

"I know this probably comes as a bit of a shock." Nick's eyes met hers, then darted away. "And I'm sorry. But there's no easy way of asking you, and I thought it best just to spit it out and get it over with. I mean, it's not as if we didn't both know it would happen one day, when one of us met somebody new. We're only not divorced now because neither of us could be bothered to get round to it."

"Is that the reason?" Charlie asked, softly, her throat aching with sorrow. "I often wondered."

"Look, this isn't easy for either of us. Whatever anyone says, divorce means failure; it marks the end of something we both thought was for life. But you made it perfectly clear three years ago that you needed to be free of me, and when you did I reluctantly let you go because that's what you wanted. Divorce hasn't mattered before, but now I've met Miranda, everything's changed."

"Everything's changed," Charlie echoed.

"I've finally met someone who makes me feel good about myself again. Who's helped me forget," Nick blundered on, sobering fast. "Losing you was the worst thing that ever happened to me, Charlie. But, in your very own words, I had to move on, which is what I'm trying to do. Please, try to understand."

Just fifteen minutes to go, Charlie figured, staring at the clock on the wall. As the waiter lit their candle, Rosa rushed over to them, arms outstretched. "Nick! Charlie!" she cried, kissing each of them three times on the cheek. "How wonderful to see you. How's my favourite couple?"

"Never better," Nick replied. Picking up the menu and using it as a shield against Charlie's eyes, he added: "Please, Rosa, bring us a bottle of house wine. I'd kill for a bloody drink."

CHARLIE COULD TASTE nothing, feel nothing; just the water slopping around in her brain. She twisted the wide ribbons of pasta round and round her fork until she grew bored and pushed her plate aside.

"Charlie, talk to me," Nick pleaded, in between bouts of shoveling spaghetti angrily into his mouth. A dribble of meat sauce ran down his chin. "Don't let's spend the whole evening in silence. This is crazy."

"Crazy?" she said, looking up, suddenly aware of the role she was expected to play. "You're right. This *is* crazy, and I'm the craziest one of all." The sounds of the people all around them roared now like a sea in her ears.

Nick shook his head, stung by her fury. "Look, what was I supposed to do? Sit home waiting for a call from you whenever you happened to be in town? So that I could hear about your new lover and your unique collaboration and know all the time that you were fucking each other senseless? You hardly let me near you when you came back, and yet Matheson had everything handed to him on a plate. How do you think that made me feel? I'm only human, you know. Flesh and blood."

"Flesh and blood." Charlie felt the water seeping into every recess of her heart.

"Miranda's young and talented and fun to be with. She makes me laugh. I'd forgotten what it was like to have someone to wake up with every morning. And, God knows, I didn't have it often with you." He, too, pushed his plate aside. Sauce spattered the tablecloth. His eyes were blazing.

"I need time," Charlie said finally. "There's no hurry, is there?"

"And why shouldn't there be a hurry?" Nick replied, throwing his napkin onto his plate. "Why shouldn't I want to do something impulsive, after all these years of hanging around, and for what? You know nothing about me." Sticking his finger between the collar of his shirt and his neck, he slid it around to loosen the tightening gap.

"I know you better than you think," Charlie said quietly, staring at his neck and trying to banish a foul memory. *Five minutes.* She just needed five minutes more. "I can't make a decision about this just like that."

Nick clicked his fingers to attract the waiter and signaled for the bill. Tossing a crisp fifty-pound note onto the table, he stood and pulled on his jacket.

"Miranda said you'd be difficult about this and she was right," he said, in a tone Charlie had heard before. It usually preceded his roughest love-making, when the only way he knew how to vent his anger was to grip and bruise and force.

"The reason we're in a hurry is quite simple," he added, coldly. "Miranda's expecting a baby. I was going to tell you, but not just yet. I'd have done anything for you not to have found out now, like this, but you would keep pushing, wouldn't you?"

He glared down at her. "My lawyer will be sending you some papers in the post. Just sign them, Charlie. Sign them. Then we'll both be free."

THE NEED TO see Alan was like a hunger that ate away at her. Only the presence of his fingers against her skin would keep the water from rushing in, and slow the sinking of her mind.

Running from Rosa's in a daze, she hailed a taxi and, sitting on the edge of the seat, dialed Alan's number breathlessly. After three rings, his voice mail cut in.

"*Hello, this is Alan Matheson. I'm either away or on the other line, so please leave a message after the tone.*"

"Alan? It's Charlie. I'm so, so sorry about what I said tonight. Please. I need to see you. To explain. I'm in a taxi. Phone me as soon as you get this. I'll be waiting outside your house."

He hadn't replied to any of her calls by the time the cabbie pulled into Onslow Square forty minutes later, so Charlie sat tensely on the backseat staring up at Alan's darkened windows, willing him to come home while the meter ticked like a metronome and the cabbie sat happily reading the sports pages. She closed her eyes, forcing herself to imagine what would happen when Alan did return. The only room they wouldn't have gratify-ing, wanton sex in was the one where Angela's painting had been. Charlie wasn't strong enough to see those images again. Not yet.

But thirty minutes later, there was still no sign of Alan. By midnight she realised, with panic, that he might not be coming back at all that night. Twisting a strand of hair round and round her forefinger, she reluctantly decided to go home and hope he'd be waiting for her there. "Damn him!"

she cursed under her breath, as the cabbie pulled out into the Brompton Road.

By the time she reached her apartment, she'd left two more messages on his voice mail. *"Alan, it's Charlie. Please. Come over as soon as you get this message. I need you. Desperately."*

Her final message said: *"Alan. Where are you? Please come. Don't let's end the night like this. I must speak to you. It's urgent."*

She was turning her key in the lock of her front door when she heard the distinctive clackety-clack of another taxi pulling to a halt outside. Taking a few steps up the steep stone stairwell, she peered through the wrought-iron railings to see a tall figure paying off his fare. She raced to open the gate for Alan as he walked across to see her, his face a closed book.

"I don't know why I'm here. What's all this about?"

Charlie silenced him with a kiss. His lips were cold but his mouth warm. Instantly, it plugged the leak, the constant drip, drip. "Nothing," she said, her breath rising like steam. "I just had to see you."

Taking a few steps back down into the darkened stairwell, she grabbed his hand and pulled him towards her. Reaching inside his long cashmere overcoat, she grappled with his belt and unzipped his dress suit trousers. Her fingers fumbled at the task as her mouth found his once more.

Pressing her against the wall, Alan ran his hands down under her coat and dress and lifted them. As his fingers felt the bare flesh at the top of the stockings she'd worn as a secret reward for taking her to the Tate, he let out a small cry. His hands were freezing and it was Charlie's turn to gasp. Pulling open his shirt, she watched as he peeled silk from her shoulder and sank his mouth into her breast. In the catlike movement he so loved, Charlie wrapped one and then the other leg around his hips. Clasping the firm flesh of her buttocks, he reached deep within her, his neck arched in pleasure, her own head pressed back hard against the wall.

Nothing mattered. Not Nick, not Miranda and their baby, not Angela, not even Charlie's own past. All that mattered was this, the oblivion Alan brought her with his body, the pleasure that rippled through her each time she allowed him in. She closed her eyes against the deluge.

37

*H*OURS LATER, IN the perfumed warmth of her bedroom, Alan lay in her arms like a shipwrecked sailor. His still weight across her chest, his hair was plastered to his head and his face closed in sleep. She watched him breathe, studied the slow rise and fall of his chest, and allowed her eyes to roam down the landscape of his flesh, down the ridged valley of his stomach to the tight, dark forest below.

Resisting the urge to rise silently and take a shower, Charlie mentally listed the reasons for not replacing the smell of him on her skin with essential oils. Part of her never wanted to wash again, and the power of that important revelation filled her with happiness as she drifted back to sleep.

HER DREAM TAKES her to Paris. She smiles, relieved. This is a happy dream. Her thirtieth birthday. Nick has arranged everything. Carrie and Stuart, her boyfriend of the time, are waiting for them at their favourite restaurant. After a lunch of oysters and langoustines, washed down with fine wines, Nick presents Charlie with a beautiful bracelet. She unwraps the package and lingers over the crinkly gold paper. Afterwards, they wander together down the Left Bank. Full and happy, they stop to look at the bookstalls and take photographs of each other by the Pont Neuf.

But in her dream, when she looks into the muddy waters of the Seine, the happy memory ends without warning. She sees dead bodies, scores of them. Men, women, and children, all floating facedown in the turgid river. Bloated corpses, their skin white and waxy, flesh rapidly decomposing. Nick and her friends have vanished. Now she is running, desperate to get away.

She is abruptly alone again and in Iraq. At a wadi, almost dry, just a quarter of the width of the Seine. A truck full of soldiers shelled weeks before. The truck slowly sinking into the soft mud. All that can be seen are the upper torsos of the corpses who never escaped from the burning metal. Jammed together like sardines. The bridge is gone. The only way for Charlie to cross—to flee the terrors pursuing her—is to walk across on the helmets of the dead men.

Strands of hair sticking to her neck with sweat, she steps as lightly as she can. Each time her foot comes into contact with a slippery helmet, the decaying flesh beneath it collapses. Bodily fluids squirt and a noxious stench assails her. Moving hastily, teetering precariously, arms outstretched, she almost loses her footing. Terrified of falling and sliding feet first into a slippery soup of rotting entrails, she swallows bile.

"Keep going!" someone behind her yells, in a voice not so unlike her own. "You're almost across."

Come on, Charlie. Crossing the Brook.

SITTING UP IN bed, her heart hammering against its cage of bone, Charlie snatched frantic lungfuls of air as she fought to dispel the fetid stench still lurking in her throat and nostrils.

Crossing the Brook. The words had stolen into the secret chamber of her nightmare like a lover and lain down beside her. She was still intoxicated by them, her head thick with sleep.

Something about the painting reminded him of her, Alan had said. A woman wading across a river, trying to reach the other side. What had he seen within her that led him to believe she was up to her knees in water? That she had already been much deeper but was now nearly across the brook? In her nightmare, she was also trying to cross something, with terrible consequences, but the painting had saved her. Could it really be a metaphor for her entire life? And what of the loyal dog, following behind with her hat? Was that Nick, still trying to protect her, even now? Or was it the spirit of her grandfather? Hadn't she been wading through a swiftly flowing current ever since Granddad had abandoned her midstream when she was eighteen? She'd let the current take her, and now she was swimming desperately against it.

It was only just light, the dawn breaking pink and rosy over the rooftops opposite; the melodic hum of traffic in the Mile End Road two streets away suggested the rush hour was well under way. Sliding carefully out from under a sleeping Alan, his face flat against the mattress, Charlie pulled on a T-shirt and walked into the bathroom.

Switching on the light above the sink, she peered into the glass. She, too, looked like a victim of a shipwreck. Her cheeks were pale and her eyes sunken. Her hair was unruly and her lips bruised. Her skin still tingled pink from the bristle on Alan's chin. Elsewhere it felt tight and damp. Dragging a brush across her scalp, she splashed her face with water and brushed her teeth, before tying her hair in a loose knot at the back of her neck and wandering barefoot into the kitchen.

When the water in the kettle boiled, she poured hot water into a mug of brown granules and watched them swirl around and around until they dissolved.

"Is that for me?" Alan asked, as he watched her from the doorway. Charlie turned. Her lover stood in navy-blue boxer shorts, his face still crumpled with sleep.

"Sure," she replied, reaching for a second cup and clicking the kettle on again.

He took a seat at the little table, his hands cradling the mug, and stared up at her. "Thank you," he said, and she knew he was expressing gratitude for more than the coffee.

Charlie sat opposite, sipping gingerly from her mug. "I owe you an apology," she began. "I said some really stupid things last night. I guess I drank too much champagne."

"It's okay. It's my fault. You're right. I should have told you everything from the start, and then you'd never have felt the need to find out for yourself." Looking up, half smiling, he added, "You are a journalist, after all."

Charlie reached for a teaspoon and stirred milk into her coffee.

"I was," she answered, staring into the mocha-coloured liquid. "But I went too far. . . . You're not the only one who's been keeping secrets, and I suspect we both did so for the same reasons."

Alan didn't reply.

"I only want to help you, to understand," Charlie continued. "Don't you see? Angela's death is part of you, part of your life that's a complete mystery to me. Until I find out what happened, why she did what she did, what you went through, what you *think* about it deep down inside, then I won't really know you at all."

And when she knew, when she'd shared his pain, Charlie wanted to add, then maybe she'd feel brave enough to share some of hers.

"A week after Angela's death," Alan told her, "when I was still so terribly numb, I discovered that she had been four months pregnant. I'd had no idea. It came as such a dreadful shock. We'd lost not only her but her unborn child."

"Who told you?"

"The police. They thought I knew."

"And you never suspected? The pregnancy didn't show? Didn't Sarah say anything?"

"Not a word, although I later discovered that she'd known all along. That news lodged in my head like a maggot. I couldn't spend another day with Sarah after that. I can't forgive her for not telling me. I can't help but feel that if only I'd known about the baby, I might have behaved differently, done something else, somehow been able to stop Angela doing what she did."

"Do you know who the father was?" Charlie whispered. The DNA report Dr North had read out to her proved only that Alan wasn't responsible. No one else had been tested.

"We never knew for sure," he answered. "Probably that long-haired art student she'd been hanging around with, smoking dope. I think his name was Tony. He certainly seemed the most upset at her funeral."

The name Tony rang a bell somewhere deep inside her, but when Charlie tried to listen, the ringing stopped. "Tell me, Alan, why do you think she killed herself?"

She spread her fingers wide and pushed them across the table towards Alan's. His silence was almost as painful as his words, but she felt compelled to keep him going.

"One joint too many, one tranquiliser over the odds. Anger. Hate. Fear. Who knows? She'd inherited her mother's nerves. Her paintings were becoming so dark and sinister. Something finally pushed her over the edge, but I never found out what."

Or who, Charlie thought. "Why would she accuse you of abusing her?"

"I have absolutely no idea." His voice was steady.

"Was there ever any suggestion of it before? I mean, could she have misinterpreted something you'd done or said in the past?"

Alan massaged his temples. He sighed. "Angela and I were best friends until she turned sixteen. I taught her how to ride a bike and a horse. How to paint. We sailed, we went to Italy, we laughed all the time. We had a very special relationship whenever we were able to spend some time together which, sadly, became increasingly rare. But the minute Angela started to become a young woman, she seemed suddenly unstable, wildly unpredictable, even vindictive. She became this complex mix of dependency, love, cruelty, and desire. She directed all her rebelliousness at me and yet seemed unhealthily close to her mother. I used to feel as if she and Sarah were ganging up on me.

"Angela would paint for hours in the studio, only to destroy all the work she'd done. The sketches you found of those hideous women were from her imagination, not from life. I didn't much like them but I did tell her I thought they showed promise. I only hid them so she wouldn't rip them up. She'd run away from home to go to all-night raves with her friends, and then she'd return in tears, begging forgiveness. At nineteen, she and I had a silly row over something; after that, she virtually severed all communication. Her hostility frightened me. Then, on her twenty-first birthday, she broke into my studio. She doused it in petrol and lit a match. Dozens of paintings were lost, work I could never redo. How could I forgive her for that? I sent her away, to get proper, professional advice. In the end, I couldn't help her."

"Perhaps no one could."

"Yes, but I was the one who locked her away," he insisted. "I never took the time to find out why she'd become what she was. I didn't even try."

Charlie rose to comfort Alan, but he shook her away. Picking a mandarin from a bowl on the table instead, he began peeling it with steady hands. Charlie was mesmerised by the action. His lean fingers, the beauty of his movements. But inside her head, something was hammering like a water pipe. Not for the first time, she wished she kept some aspirin in the flat.

Alan separated the mandarin segments and offered one to her and she slipped it between her lips. He watched avidly as she savoured the explosion of flavour, refreshing the bitter dryness of her mouth. Doing likewise, he gave her a thin, tired smile that signified the end of the small ritual. Now it was her turn.

Charlie had always known she couldn't leave the weight of the past behind her. But she wanted Alan to slow down, to savour his last few minutes of not knowing the truth. If she could have had one wish, it would be that the two of them could be frozen in time, sitting together like this, peeling mandarins in the winter light, their bodies still smarting from their lovemaking.

But she knew the time had come to reveal everything that was stuck to the flypaper of her brain.

"Sartre once said that hell is other people," she began softly. "Well, I guess my hell started in other people's wars. When I was a journalist, I saw many things no one should see. I compiled a mental video collection that would never get past the censors. But like all journalists, I believed I was immune...until Kosovo."

Trembling, she continued. "You know I had an accident. You've seen the scars. It was at a place called Rajak. I was on assignment there for a news feature when the Serbs returned. I watched...I saw...men being

marched to their deaths. I hid in a cellar. With some other women. But...
the Serbs found us."

Alan sat waiting, listening, his hands steepled over his mug. Few people really know how to listen, Charlie realised, to sit still and silent and
wait for the next sentence, not come to the rescue or merely wait their turn
in the conversation, planning their own contribution. But Alan did.

"Before the accident—I mean, *immediately* before...I was...I was...
taken, d-dragged— There were men. Creatures with no regard for life.
For women. Even for dogs." She crushed the spherical peel of the mandarin in her hands, releasing a pungent citrus vapour, and stared down at it.

"They...they did things. They made me....I wasn't able to fight them
off....They'd done the same to others. Even the children, and the old
women. And then they shot them all...."

A tear glittered on her eyelash. She waited to regain control of her
voice. To stop the water flooding in.

"I—I knew....I knew what would happen...what was happening. I
knew I had to escape. Somewhere, somehow, I found the strength...I ran.
I was running. I couldn't hear anything but the blood in my ears. My
clothes were...I was...and then the truck hit me...."

Her voice trailed off as her throat closed protectively around the
words.

Still Alan sat, silently, watching her without embarrassment. Without
pity. It gave her the courage to go on.

"The truck was driven by some local Albanians. They'd heard the
gunfire. They'd come to help the villagers, but there was no one left to
help. Only me."

The pain of surviving still stung.

"I remember nothing of what happened afterwards. There was a gun
battle...I was rescued...they drove me to a hospital. When I awoke, I
was empty. I couldn't feel my legs and I was completely empty...."

Tears slipped silently from her eyes and she rubbed them away angrily
with the heels of her palms.

"Nick—my husband—he came. And Carrie, my friend. They were
frantic, they'd been looking everywhere for me. They put me on a plane,

then in another hospital. I couldn't speak. Couldn't feel anything. They sent me to a clinic. I wanted to die ... and, Alan, I tried to. In a clinic, just like Angela, I tried to end it all."

His shoulders stiffened but still he didn't look away from her.

"Nick took me to Suffolk. To a friend's cottage by the sea. That's when I realised I could never go back. Not to Kosovo, to wars, or to Nick. He tried to keep hold of me, but the current was too strong. I had been slipping out of his hands for some time, but Rajak pulled me under."

Her hands had become fists. Charlie released the mandarin peel and let it roll onto the table.

"I sought sanctuary by the sea. I wrote. I completed my account of what happened to the people of Rajak, without elaborating on what had happened to me, and then I tried to put it all behind me. I took up painting again. I began to think about writing a very different kind of book. And then I met you."

For the first time in her stammering tumble of words, Charlie met Alan's eyes directly.

"I never thought I'd be able to let a man near me again, until you. For a time, you seemed too good to be true, but then I found out about Angela's suicide and Sarah's breakdown. And I saw that painting. Suddenly there was madness all around me once more. Not just with Turner and his mother, but with you, too. I was terrified, Alan. I feared I was slipping under again. I needed to decide whether or not to continue seeing you, to risk further pain."

Alan lifted one of her hands to his face and held it gently against his cheek. For the first time, Charlie could see his tears just beneath the surface.

"There's something else," she murmured, stroking his face with her fingertips. "The baby, Angela's baby, was important. And the one in the painting—I can't have children, Alan. It's physically impossible, after ... what happened. The accident put an end to all that for me. Children, I mean. I—I just thought you should know, that's all."

Alan nodded, his eyes flickering sympathy at last. Charlie saw it and quickly pulled her hand away.

"I still have so many ghosts to exorcise, Alan. In truth, I may never be free of them all. If you're prepared to be patient, and not rush me, I would very much like to carry on seeing you. You've been so great for me, you really have. You've made me stop feeling like damaged goods. But you have to know: You can't fix me. Perhaps nobody can. And if you can't handle that, or if you want more than I am able to give, then I think perhaps we should end it now, before either of us gets hurt."

Only the ticking of her grandfather's clock in the hallway broke the silence.

Alan watched Charlie's downturned face, waiting for his chance to speak. Finally, he reached across the table and clasped her hand, forcing her to look into his grey, grey eyes.

He spoke with quiet conviction. "Charlie. I'm fifty-six years old. I've had two marriages and my fair share of sadness. I have everything I could possibly want materially, artistically, but I don't have anyone to share it with. You're a lot stronger than you think you are, and you've already taught me so much about courage and strength and hope. It really doesn't matter to me what strange parallels there are in our lives or what terrible circumstances brought us together, I'm just glad they did."

Charlie willed more tears not to come, but they dripped down her cheeks anyway. Alan came to her, enveloping her in his arms. "Sssh," he soothed, kissing her face. "Don't cry, Charlie darling. Please, don't."

"I—I don't know what to say."

Alan held her chin in his hand and sealed her mouth with his kiss. "Don't say anything, then," he told her. Taking her hand, he led her back to bed.

38

$\mathcal{N}$IGEL ARMSTRONG WAS LOSING patience. He'd been asking Charlie for some early chunks of her manuscript for weeks and she'd refused until now, jealously guarding her new creation, afraid to give up even a small part of it, for fear of his criticism and possible rejection.

"I can't give you an appraisal of how the damn thing's going unless you let me see some of it," he complained. "Besides, there's the other book on the Balkans to be thinking about. Your publishers are getting decidedly twitchy."

Charlie hadn't yet broken the news to Nigel that her second book would never be written. Perhaps she'd just return what was left of the advance in his Christmas card. Right now, she had more important matters weighing on her mind.

Nigel wasn't the only one awaiting Charlie's manuscript. Her new editor was even keener to see it. Not that her chosen subject matter was of widespread interest or expected to be a runaway bestseller, but a recent flurry of excitement in the media about the firm's new author and the man she'd been linked to in the gossip columns had elevated her to a position where people might buy the book just to find out more. The publisher's art directors had readily agreed to use Alan's painting for the jacket, delighted to have a unique and accomplished work by one of the country's greatest living painters for which they were not expected to pay a penny.

"Charlie, daaaahling, you're a genius," her editor had enthused, never using one vowel when three would do. Self-effacingly describing herself as "mutton dressed as leopard," Lola Lewis's rather brassy exterior hid a heart of gold and a mind as sharp as a razor. There was nothing Lola hadn't read, done, seen, eaten, drunk, or endorsed. With a face that betrayed her age but a body as lithe as a woman fifteen years her junior, she'd been hugely enthusiastic about Charlie's book from the outset.

"Sleeping with the nation's favourite artist was a masterstroke, if you'll excuse the pun," she said in a voice that spoke of a thousand cigarettes. "The review of his new painting will take up more column inches than the reviews of your book. It'll certainly make people pick it up in the shops. You're such a dark horse!"

Lola had, along with the rest of the nation, learned of her new protégée's bedroom secrets via the gossip columns. Charlie's presence on the arm of Sir Alan Matheson at the Turner Prize ceremony had sparked widespread interest. The article which caused Charlie the most trouble was in one of the tabloids:

You read it here first. Europe's most eligible artist may have been withdrawn from auction. Dishy Sir Alan Matheson, 56, who bewitched the Queen Mum when he painted her centennial portrait, spends much of his time these days in the company of Charlie Hudson, 42, erstwhile journalist and author, whom he proudly unveiled at this year's Turner Prize ceremony. Ms. Hudson left the *Daily Tribune* six years ago "tired and emotional" and has rarely been spotted since. Fresh from his divorce from the voracious New Yorker Diane Colvin—following the suicide of his daughter and sad decline of his first wife—Sir Alan might be interested to know that his new companion is still married to none other than Correspondent assistant editor Nick Lambert, tipped to be the next editor of the *Sunday Times*. Lambert, in turn, is currently dating reporter Miranda Davies, named last year in divorce proceedings by the wife of Sir Freddy Collier, erstwhile proprietor of the *Sunday Sentinel*. It seems that once the marital confusion is over, Ms Hudson will have a title, Mr Lambert will have his editorship, and Sir Alan and the gorgeous Miranda may both have served their purpose.

The morning the article was published, Charlie had dashed out to buy some coffee and returned an hour later, ruddy-faced and humming, to hear the telephone ringing. Hearing her mother's voice, her heart sank, but she needn't have worried. Marjorie Hudson wasn't badgering her about Christmas again. Perhaps she'd finally accepted her daughter's insistence that she intended to spend it alone in Rhubarb Cottage. No, Marjorie had other things on her mind.

"Charlie! I've only just heard! Irene Vale rang to tell me. Your father and I are delighted. I can't believe you haven't told us. Sir Alan Matheson, eh? Now, that's what I call a catch! No wonder you want to spend Christmas in Suffolk!"

The next call, a few minutes later, was from Charlie's father, presumably made from his study while her mother was regaling her neighbours with the news.

"Hi, rabbit," he said, almost in a whisper in case his wife should walk in unexpectedly. "Just wanted to make sure you're okay about all this. Expect you didn't want your new relationship blurted out this way."

After that, Charlie stopped answering the phone. The next call was from Carrie, also checking that she was okay. *"I'll try you on the mobile,"* her friend said into the machine, when Charlie didn't pick up. *"Don't worry, I'm sure no one will have bothered to read this rubbish."*

There was no call from Nick. He must have seen the article, must have wondered at it. Perhaps Miranda had forbidden him from making contact after their stupid row.

THROWING HERSELF INTO the final push for her book, Charlie chose to ignore the growing clamour of those wanting to know more about her personal life. Despite her journalistic background, she felt very strongly that this was nobody's business but her own.

Fortunately for her, the process of writing enthralled her. And being an author was utterly different from her previous life, filing copy on the hoof, shouting into a satellite telephone or sending reports across the ether on her laptop computer. This, by contrast, was methodical, systematic, and painfully slow. All she needed was time alone to pull all her material together in this, her final surge, edit out the irrelevant parts, and inject the necessary coherence and fluidity that would make the book both readable and entertaining.

This task required supreme presence of mind, something she could truly summon at will only in her cottage by the sea. There, she could lose herself to another world, seeing and hearing nothing but the text unfolding before her on the computer screen.

Fortunately, Alan understood completely. When he was painting, he, too, wrapped himself in a dark cloak of concentration. Once he re-emerged, he seemed emotionally and physically depleted for several days. As if his life's essence had been drained and bled onto the paper or canvas. What happened after that mattered little. He hardly cared if the painting was sold or not, whether it remained stacked in his studio or hung in the National Gallery. All that mattered was that it was done. He'd set himself a task and achieved it, at times better than others.

Charlie craved the same solitude when she was working. She loved nothing more than to write in intensive bouts, sometimes all night, between walks on the beach watching the high seas and foam-flecked waves of the December tides. Alone with her thoughts, answerable to no one, she was able at last to find tranquillity.

Her final piece of research was designed to give voice to James Whatman on the romance and history of watermarks, or papermarks as they were sometimes called. Alan had lent her half a dozen books on the subject, which now lay across her desk, bookmarked or open, detailing the hundreds of historic patterns and styles. The mystic symbols known as watermarks, she discovered, had been around almost as long as paper itself. Originally devised, like hallmarks on silver, to detail the history and date of manufacture, some dated back to manuscripts written in the time of the ancient Greeks.

It was the Italians in the thirteenth century who took watermark production to new heights, creating beautifully artistic designs of animals and plants that soon became coveted for their prestige. The very wealthy would commission their own distinctive watermarks in much the same way someone might have their linen monogrammed or a bone china dinner service decorated with the family coat of arms. Watermarks became vital in the constant quest to deter counterfeiters, adding authenticity to anything from bank notes and postage stamps to tickets, passports, and financial documents.

Charlie read aloud from one of Alan's heavy tomes, chasing the words across the page with her finger and imagining Whatman speaking them to a visitor to his mill.

Watermarks are created by literally stitching an emblem to the fine wire mould used in the handmade papermaking process, or by embedding or raising the wire in the shape of the desired design into a large cylinder called a dandy-roll, which is applied to the paper while drying. In "line" watermarks, the design appears as a clear impression lighter than the rest of the paper, where the pulp settles onto it and becomes thinner. In "shadow" or "chiaroscuro" watermarks, the design can be more complicated, with tonal depth, using different heights of wire, to create lights, darks, and an almost photographic image as the pulp settles and then dries.

In older, handmade papers, the watermark usually appears just once on each sheet; whereas in machine-made papers, it can often be repeated many times on each sheet and in a continuous pattern. The beauty of watermarks is that, because of the nap and texture of the paper, they can only be seen when they are held up to the light.

Looking up, Charlie stared at her cherished sheet of handmade paper, given to her by Marco at the Fabriano paper mill and now, pressed between two thin pieces of glass, hanging in the window. She admired once more the design, a circle around three arches of the oldest bridge in Fabriano, straddling a fast-flowing river, and a blacksmith working with a fire and bellows.

"Watermarks can only be seen when they are held up to the light," Charlie repeated, as she typed out the words that made up that sentence. The watermarks were there all along, strong and true and beautiful, woven into the very fabric of almost every sheet of fine paper, yet interfering in no way with whatever purpose the paper ultimately had. Unless they were illuminated in some way, unless someone took the time and trouble to lift them to the light, they went largely unseen.

Light, as always, was fundamental. Without its bright illumination in the darkest recesses, these things of great beauty to be left behind would lie undiscovered, unadmired. How true that was of life. Of everything she had come to learn about art and Alan and of the human spirit.

THERE WERE, SHE discovered, a surprising number of people who collected watermarked paper, enthusing excitedly about their latest finds on Web sites and in a variety of magazines on the subject. Collectors hoarded anything from old cigarette papers with the name of the company woven within them to official documents, bank notes, cheques, and train tickets. Vast archives of watermarks existed throughout the world, as universities and private individuals painstakingly logged and photographed every one, adding them to a worldwide database for researchers and students. Charlie was staggered by the international interest in a subject she'd believed was of fascination only to her.

She flicked through page after page of archive images of ancient watermarks, amazed by their variety and complexity. One French dictionary of watermarks produced in 1907 listed more than sixteen thousand different symbols. There were prancing unicorns, running dogs, harts wearing studded collars, spreading oak trees, hands grasping quills, crossed keys, turreted castles, giant scissors, vast wheels, ringing bells, and fleurs-de-lys, plus countless different initials, intricate geometric designs, and bold heraldic crests on shields.

In some cases, different symbols denoted different sizes of paper: a jester was used to depict foolscap, for which it was named. Elsewhere, there were hidden meanings, a sort of subliminal advertising for a time when a unicorn meant moral purity; an eagle, royalty or authority; a circle, eternity; and a clover leaf, the Holy Trinity. Sometimes, the watermarks were believed to secretly carry religious or political propaganda, known only to their medieval creators. Some were symbols of secret brotherhoods, their marks like invisible ink, registered only by those who knew what to look for. All of George Washington's personal paper carried a phoenix watermark, denoting resurrection.

Few areas of paper collecting were unaffected by the passion for watermarks. Philatelists prized stamps that carried a watermark, because they represented the relatively short period when that was done. Fakes were common, and the only way to tell a genuine watermarked stamp was by dipping it in lighter fluid, which didn't affect the ink but mysteriously revealed the hidden watermark. Similar processes were used for dating and authenticating works by some of the world's greatest writers, Caxton's early papers, Mozart's music manuscripts, precious works of art, or historical documents of national importance. Whole symposiums were held just on the subject of watermarks and how to authenticate them.

She was fascinated by the unscrupulous practice by some European papermakers of appropriating some of the British watermarks, leading to forgeries and untold problems for historians and artists. The value in forging something like a Whatman's watermark was obvious. The name of the mill had become synonymous with quality. A fraudulent papermaker could charge far more for an inferior product.

She wondered if Turner had ever been so duped. Allowing her imagination free rein, she created a scene where the artist stood holding some paper up to the light before he bought it from an art shop in Venice, believing it to be something he trusted, before parting with several heavy coins from his leather pouch.

Envisioning him later at his easel on the banks of the Lido, she described the moment he realised his mistake—the moment he started preparing the paper for paint. *"What the—? This isn't Whatman's! The devil take the man who sold me this!"* Returning to the art shop in anger, she had him rail bitterly at the unscrupulous Italian merchant, demanding his money back and vowing to be far more cautious in the future.

State-of-the-art forensic techniques, she learned, were now harnessed to identify such forgeries. Those experts whose everyday work normally consists of identifying fake bank notes, concert tickets, or passports, were often thrilled by the arrival in their laboratories of some historic work of art whose every fragile characteristic they could scrutinise for a few hallowed days.

With the meticulousness of a pathologist, such experts probed and photographed, dissected and disseminated every fragment of information they could from the inert object laying on the slab before them.

And just like a dead body, like the lifeless corpse of Angela Matheson whose dead infant's DNA had vindicated Alan from the grave, Charlie couldn't help thinking, their genetic makeup and inherent qualities bear silent witness.

39

*I*F CHARLIE HAD HOPED for a romantic reunion with Alan when he came up to Suffolk to join her for the weekend, she was to be disappointed. She'd never seen him so angry. The veins in his neck bulged as he paced the floor of her cottage, stopping only to berate her once more.

"I can't believe you sloped off to see Sarah when my back was turned and never even told me about it," he said of his recent discovery, the one she hadn't found the courage to broach with him yet. "And *twice*! What right did you have to go and see her?"

"I didn't *slope* anywhere!" Charlie protested, hugging a cushion defensively to her chest as she backed into a corner of her sofa. "Sarah invited me to tea at her apartment, which I accepted. I only didn't tell you about it then because, because—"

"Because you knew I'd forbid it!"

"No, because I suspected you'd be unreasonable," she shot back. "Which you are being. Plus, you didn't even know I knew about Angela back then. How could I possibly explain talking to Sarah?"

"But if you wanted to know about Angela, why the devil didn't you ask me? Surely you knew I'd tell you eventually?"

"I didn't ask you because I didn't want to hurt you. I could tell how painful the subject was."

"But you didn't mind hurting Sarah?"

"No, I mean, yes, of course I didn't want to hurt her, either. I simply thought that it might be easier talking to her about it."

"Easier for whom?"

"Listen, Alan, I don't know why you're so upset. Sarah and I had a perfectly civilised tea together. And no one got hurt."

Alan rounded on her, his eyes blazing. "Oh, didn't they?" he sneered. "Well, it might interest you to know that the only reason I found out about your visit was because Sarah's psychiatrist—whose bills I pay—called to inform me she'd asked to go back under his supervision the morning after your last visit."

Charlie could feel the colour drain from her face.

"Well?" Alan demanded.

"I—I'm so sorry, Alan. I had no idea. She seemed perfectly fine when I left her, honestly. She was a little strange when we talked about Angela, admittedly, but by the time I said good-bye she was completely normal."

He ran his hands through his hair and perched on the arm of the couch, shaking his head. "You simply don't understand, do you, Charlie? I've spent most of my life protecting Sarah from this sort of thing. The last person I expected to go and stir this all up for her again was you."

Charlie reached across and laid a hand on his arm, but he withdrew it immediately. "Alan, I'm so sorry," she repeated, aware how insubstantial her apology sounded. "I had no idea. I thought Sarah was fine. Truly, I never meant to hurt her."

"You always think you know everything, Charlie, but you don't. You don't know anything at all. I expressly forbid you from seeing my wife again, do you understand me?"

Charlie nodded and allowed the silence between them to calm him. She did not protest that Sarah was no longer his wife. When his breathing had slowed, she reached for him again. This time he didn't resist.

"Sarah's lucky to have you," she said, and meant it.

Alan's eyes were soft with sorrow, but they looked straight through her, as if seeing something in the far distance. "When we first met, she was such fun to be with. I'd never come across anyone quite so vivacious."

He took a sudden sharp intake of breath, as if the memories that had rushed in to fill the empty spaces in his head pained him. "She desperately wanted a family. We tried for some time, but she lost the first two babies. That was when she suffered an emotional dip so catastrophic as to render her speechless. Clinical depression, the doctor said. It was only then I realised just what I had signed up for."

"Poor Sarah. Surely having Angela made things better?"

"Not at first. Not until Angela started to have her own emotional problems. Sarah seemed almost relieved that someone else knew what it felt like to sink so low. She was suddenly not alone. The doctors treating Angela wanted her removed from Sarah's care for that reason, but both refused. In the end, I think they spent so much time alone together that they fed off each other's paranoia."

"Oh, Alan," Charlie murmured. Pulling him down onto the sofa, she held him tight as he lay huddled in her arms. Kissing him, she whispered, "Don't say any more, darling. It's okay. Everything's going to be okay."

HER LETTER TO Sarah Matheson was brief but to the point. After all that Alan had told her, she felt she simply had to write and apologise. Having discarded the first three drafts, she finally settled on the wording and pulled out a piece of her best Fabriano writing paper, giving in to the temptation to first hold it up to the light.

Her fountain pen poised, she took a deep breath and wrote carefully in her gentle, looped handwriting.

> *I'm so sorry.*
> *I never intended to cause you any pain.*
> *Forgive me.*
> *Charlotte.*

Sealing the envelope with its delicate powder-blue lining, she copied out the Knightsbridge address, licked a stamp, and walked to the village postbox set deep into a moss-covered wall.

Alan need never even know, she told herself.

Blotter

Unglazed absorbent paper used for

soaking up excess paint or ink

40

I'D LIKE TO VISIT Angela's grave if you have no objection," Charlie told Alan the following morning, as she sat with him in her little kitchen, drinking coffee and watching him devour a plate of bacon and eggs. She'd lain awake half the night listening to the rain and thinking about the intense sadness of his daughter's life.

No longer a mythical figure in her mind, Angela Matheson had finally become truly mortal to Charlie. Like her mother Sarah before her, Angela was nothing more and nothing less than a deeply unhappy young woman who simply hadn't been strong enough to swim against the tide. Hiding behind a curtain of hair, and a façade of toughness epitomised by her re-belliousness, multiple piercings, and drug taking, she had been, beneath it all, frightened and lonely. There but for the grace of God, Charlie thought. . . .

Alan stopped chewing and stared up at her speechlessly, his expression blank. "Then by all means do so," he told her coolly. "But don't expect me to accompany you. It is not somewhere I choose to spend any time."

After stopping at a florist in Southwold to buy a bunch of crimson roses, Charlie made the short drive alone. She arrived at the church of St James in the coastal village of Dunwich in the middle of a downpour. The sky pressed heavy and low upon her, billowing charcoal clouds ominously to the east squaring up against giant grey cumuli rising to the west. Sleet and snow were forecast.

Stepping from her car under the lee of an umbrella, Charlie sheltered her small bouquet as she wandered around the graveyard until she found a row of new headstones lined up beneath a venerable flintstone wall.

A slender oblong of pale Carrera marble, with a raised section at the head, bore a small slate square.

ANGELA MATHESON. 1976–2000

There was no mention of her unborn child. A small circular symbol, not unlike a watermark, was carved in the centre, depicting a sun rising on the horizon. Beneath, a quotation was engraved in what looked uncannily like Alan's sloping handwriting. Charlie bent to read it through the slanting rain:

Sadness flies on the wings of the morning
and out of the heart of darkness comes the light.

She recognised it at once. Giraudoux. *The Madwoman of Chaillot.* Charlie wondered at the choice.

Discarding the patterned paper the roses were wrapped in and scrunching it into a tight ball, she reached for a small tin vase that lay in a specially fashioned hollow beneath the slate. Looking around for a tap to top up the rainwater that had half filled it, she spotted one in the opposite corner. She hoped it wasn't as temperamental as the one at Granddad's grave, which regularly spluttered rusty water all over her shoes.

Great sheets of rain began to sweep in from the sea. Hurrying across the graveyard to the tap, head down, flowers and vase in hand, she was startled to find a young man standing there when she reached it. His matted, spiky hair was glistening, his clothes saturated and dripping. He'd clearly been exposed to the bad weather for some time. He stared at her with a hostile expression.

Charlie didn't know what made her say it, but the name flew from her lips. "Tony?"

The young man's wide-set eyes, one with an unusual splash of yellow, lost their hard glaze. "Do I know you?" he demanded, a drip of water hanging off his large, sharp nose. With his fleshy mouth and narrow eyes, Charlie thought how cruel fate could be, to give someone such an unfortunate juxtaposition of features.

"No. I'm a friend of Alan's. Sir Alan Matheson...Angela's father."

"How did you know it was me, then?"

"I guessed. No one else but the father of Angela's baby would hang around a graveyard in this weather," she replied, her eyes locked on his. "Anyway, I recognised you from your photograph in the paper, after the funeral. You swung a punch at Alan, didn't you? Some of the papers reported it, and Alan said you were the most upset among Angela's friends."

The young man glanced nervously over her shoulder. "He's not here, is he? I told him I'd kill him if he ever came near her again."

"No, Alan's not here. I came alone. I wanted to bring her some flowers." She waved the roses and the little vase and gestured towards the tap.

Tony seemed to accept her explanation without question. "Angie was the best thing that ever happened to me. She thought I was beautiful, she did. She didn't care what anyone else thought. She said she wanted to paint me and nobody else for the rest of her life. I come here just to sit with her, to talk about us, and the baby. It was a little girl, you know. She'd have been six next May."

"Yes, I know," Charlie said softly, reaching out and placing a hand on his arm. "I'm so sorry."

"It was his bloody fault!" he cried brusquely, sniffing and wiping the snot from his nose on the back of his hand. "If it wasn't for Angie's father, they'd both be alive."

"I'm not sure that's true, Tony," Charlie said, choosing her words carefully. "Angela was a very sick young woman. She might have killed herself at any time. Alan did all he could to help her."

"No, he bloody didn't!" he cried, pulling away from her. "He made her sick in the first place, with all his interfering. Dirty old man. I ought to knock his block off." From deep within his chest he summoned up a ball of yellow phlegm and spat it onto the sodden grass.

"That was all part of Angela's sickness, don't you understand?" Charlie soothed. "She didn't know her own mind. Things became confused. She accused her father when she didn't mean to. Had no reason to."

"Oh, yes, she did!" Tony shrieked, recoiling, looking at Charlie contemptuously. "You don't know bloody nothing. You don't know what he was like. She told me."

"Please try to understand," Charlie pleaded. "All of this was in Angela's mind. There was never any basis to her allegations. The police said so. It was a fantasy."

"That weren't no fantasy." He shook his head vehemently. "I know what he did to her. I know how he made her do what he wanted."

"What do you mean?"

"She told me, and anyway, I saw him!" he cried, stabbing an accusing finger into the air. "I bloody saw him, the dirty bastard! I caught him with Angie in his studio. She didn't have no clothes on, and he was messing with her." Frightened now, he suddenly took off, shouting his abuse as he ran. "He's a bastard, a fucking bastard, that Alan Matheson, and I'll get him! I'll show him!"

As Charlie watched him run, the roses slipped from her fingers, their bloodred petals strewn across the wet grass.

IT SNOWED ON Christmas Day. Flakes of ice danced in the sea breeze outside her bedroom window to add to the brittle white covering already on the ground. It should have been perfect, alone in Suffolk with Alan. It might have been but for her encounter with Tony.

As if sensing her unease, Alan had been especially attentive. After tea and toast by the log fire in her little lounge, they'd spent the morning in bed. Deep under the duvet, he'd lowered himself to kiss her. Her hands on his shoulders, unable to resist, she opened her eyes just enough to watch a dying wasp—surely the last of the year—stagger sleepily across the window ledge as she blinked away her tears.

Later, sitting by the fire drinking champagne as their small turkey cooked in the Aga, they draped themselves in their dressing gowns and the duvet they'd dragged down the twisting oak staircase with them, to exchange gifts.

"This is for you," Charlie said, handing Alan his present wrapped in delicate green tissue paper. "I hope you like it."

He smiled as he put down his glass and peeled back the paper. Hidden inside was a tooled leather set of Adrian Bell's Suffolk trilogy—*Corduroy*, *The Cherry Tree*, and *Silver Ley*. The volumes were similar to the set on her shelf above him, the limited editions that he had so admired on his first visit.

"Charlie! These are wonderful! You know how much I covet yours. Thank you." He kissed her tenderly.

"Merry Christmas, Alan."

Beaming at her, he rose to his feet. "Close your eyes."

Charlie did as she was told, feeling the flames from the hearth warm her face.

She could hear rustling as Alan approached. "Now, hold out your hands."

Something flat and square was laid in her hands. Opening her eyes, she looked down at a package wrapped in pretty gold paper and tied with a white ribbon. Attached to one corner was a tiny card, cut, she noticed instantly, from a sheet of his Whatman paper. Opening it, she read the inscription.

FOR MY CHARLIE. ALAN. xx

Sliding a fingernail along the package, Charlie carefully opened the paper and pulled out a deep, gilded frame. Turning it over gingerly, she stared down at an exquisite watercolour of Rhubarb Cottage.

"Oh, Alan, this is too much!" she whispered, overwhelmed. He must have come to her cottage secretly and painted it from across the lane while she was away. She imagined him working away at it in his studio, returning to Rhubarb Cottage now and again to check details and light. "Thank you!" Rising to her knees, she reached for him across an ocean of guilt and regret.

"Merry Christmas, darling," he said into the tousled folds of her hair. "I hope that from now on, we can put the past behind us and start again."

"Of course," she said, swallowing, her gaze avoiding his.

"So you're no longer upset by what that silly young boy told you at the graveyard?"

"No, of course not."

Alan held her chin in his. "You do believe me, don't you?"

"Yes, Alan," she replied, staring at him levelly. "Why wouldn't I? Your explanation is entirely plausible."

"It's more than just plausible, Charlie, it's true! I've told you over and over, Angela was stoned out of her mind on drink or drugs or God knows what that night. She went to my studio specifically to wreak havoc."

"To wreak havoc, yes, but naked?"

"Oh, she was always throwing off her clothes," he replied defensively. Charlie thought of the Cornish sketches; a young girl so at one with nature. "Ask anyone. She loved the freedom of it, and the shock her nudity always generated."

He grimaced with the weariness of repetition. "When I walked into the studio that night, she was semiconscious and completely incoherent. God knows what she'd taken. I checked her pulse and planned on calling the doctor from the house. I'd just reached for a robe to cover her up when Tony burst in and found me standing over her. The silly young fool ran off before I could explain."

Charlie smiled with relief. "I'm sorry, Alan. This all makes perfect sense. I was silly to even listen to what he said."

"Good." Alan's smile didn't completely light his face. "Then, please, darling, let's never speak of this nonsense again."

. . .

TWO DAYS AFTER Christmas, Charlie told Alan she needed to spend a week alone concentrating exclusively on her book.

"I'll see you on New Year's Eve," she promised, ushering him out of the door and pretending there was nothing more on her mind than the impending final stages of the project they'd been working on together since late spring.

"Well, if you get fed up and want some company, give me a ring."

"I will. But you of all people know what it's like, working on the final stages of something as important as this. I can think of nothing else."

He smiled uneasily. "I'll never be very far away." After a pause, he added: "And I do hope I've eliminated all your doubts."

"Yes, Alan, of course you have. Now go."

"Good," he replied with obvious relief. "Bye, darling."

Closing the door on him, Charlie leaned heavily against it.

41

CHARLIE'S HEAD WAS LIKE an attic, she decided, full of cobweb-covered treasures and boxes of junk. Some of the treasures had lain untouched for years, waiting to be rediscovered one day by their owner. Alongside them lay boxes of things not loved enough to be brought out into the open, but important enough in their own way to be given house room.

Sifting through them now, she sensed that it was time to roll up her sleeves and sort everything out once and for all. Those overflowing boxes marked "Angela," "Sarah," and now "Tony" needed to be brought down the precipitous stairway of her brain and sealed tightly before being returned to storage forever.

Her meandering train of thought was interrupted by the telephone. It was Carrie, checking up on her. "Hi, what are you up to?"

"Oh, I'm in the attic," Charlie replied, absentmindedly. "There's a lot I need to sort out."

"Well, come down quick and turn on the television. Nick's on."

"I don't have a television here. What's he doing?"

"*Question Time*. Jake's away skiing and Nick's standing in as editor. He's being given a serious grilling about his newspaper's stance on asylum seekers by Germaine Greer."

"Good old Germaine." Charlie laughed. "Go, girl." Feeling sudden sympathy, she added, "Is Nick holding his own?"

"Sort of. He looks like he's seriously regretting agreeing to it. But he's managed to make some reasonable points."

"God, I haven't seen him since he asked me for the divorce. Does he seem okay?"

"Fine, and anyway he won't need that now, will he?"

"What?"

"The divorce."

"Why not?"

"Miranda's left him. I'm sorry, I thought you'd have heard."

"No, no, I didn't. Jesus, poor Nick. What happened? I thought it was all going so well."

"So did he. But being acting editor means he has to be in the office night and day. Miranda went off to some swanky hotel in Shropshire with a gang of friends, furious that he couldn't join her. On Christmas Day she told him she'd met someone else and, by the way, wasn't pregnant after all."

"Oh, my God! So she lied about it, do you think?"

"Probably. She's got quite a reputation around the office, according to some friends of mine there. She thought she was onto a good thing, but now she's found someone better."

"Who?"

"Martin Stone," Carrie replied.

"What, *the* Martin Stone? The property tycoon?"

"Yes. She interviewed him for an article a month or so ago and apparently spotted the potential. You have to admit, drop-dead looks, his own Caribbean island, and a country estate the size of Surrey does rather beat Nick's modest assets."

CHARLIE CALLED NICK later that night. After his grilling on live television and three large Scotches, he sounded like he was feeling decidedly sorry for himself.

"Have you rung to gloat?" he asked miserably.

"No, I rang to see how you are. Carrie told me about Miranda."

"She was never even pregnant, Charlie. I think now she may have made the whole thing up. What a sucker I've been."

Charlie remained silent for a moment, trying to think of a response. "Are you going to be okay?" she finally asked.

"I dunno," he replied, his voice cracking. "You and Carrie are the only people I can talk to and neither of you gives a toss."

"You know that's not true."

"I'm probably keeping you from your book," he said, his voice slurring. "Or have you finished that now?"

"I'm delivering it in a week or so." She was still shaken by the prospect of being free of something that had consumed her so utterly. Frowning, she noticed another wasp meandering its way across the sill of the window, the other side of the glass. There must be a nest somewhere, shutting down for the winter, the queen preparing for hibernation, while the worker wasps were left outside to die. She'd have to get someone in to deal with it.

"Well done," Nick said, his voice dull. "When will it be published?"

"Next spring."

"Oh." Then he said suddenly, "I once wanted to be a father almost more than anything in the world, but the truth is, Charlie, it was always your child I wanted, not Miranda's. When I found you in that hellhole, when I realised what those bastards had done to you, what they'd taken away from us, I thought I'd never get over it. But I did.... We both did."

Charlie held her breath. Dear Nick. How hard that must have been for him to say. She had to admit, when he'd told her that Miranda was carrying his child, it had seemed so unfair, another woman having her husband's child, the baby Charlie had been robbed of.

"Do you think I was selfish not to want Miranda's child?" Nick's voice rasped down the line.

"Nick, you don't know the meaning of selfish. She's a fool. Give yourself time. Someone perfect is just waiting around the corner for you. Just wait and see."

• • •

CHARLIE DIDN T KNOW why, but the next morning she woke up feeling as if she could take on the world. What was it about Nick's news that had lifted her spirits? Relief? A somewhat sadistic pleasure that Miranda wasn't carrying his child after all? Or was it just that she was days away from finally completing her book?

Hurrying to pull on some clothes, she laced up her walking boots and almost ran to the beach, the bright winter's day lifting her with every step that brought her closer to the sea. Blythcove looked magnificent. The beach was deserted and the sea was as placid as a millpond. Way out in the distance, so far into the sunlight that she had to shield her eyes to stare at it, a little fishing boat trawled up and down, hungry seagulls wheeling and circling in its wake. A single black cormorant rose from the water closer to the shore, a silvery trail of droplets falling like diamonds from its webbed feet.

Taking greedy gulps of air into her lungs, she spread her arms wide and arched her neck into the watery glare of the December sun. Allowing herself to fall backwards onto the soft sand dunes, she stared at the sand martins high above her and watched, mesmerised, as they ducked and dived, chasing each other and catching flies. How unique this place felt, how soothing to her soul. After the mayhem and madness of the past few years, only here in the land of giant skies and wild birds could she find real peace. Italy was glorious; London was a necessity; but Suffolk was home.

Alan was right, she was strong. Until very recently, she hadn't appreciated quite how strong. And she felt stronger now than she had in ages. She thought it had taken the last of her resources to pull her back from the brink after Rajak, but she was wrong. Now she bet she could even make herself think of that place and force herself through the pain of memory.

"Go on, then, prove it," a voice in her head taunted. "Let's see how tough you really are."

She closed her eyes and dug her fingers deep into the sand as she finally allowed the memories to flood in, one by one.

• • •

THE NOISE OF cotton ripping as the front of her shirt is torn away. The smell of nicotine on their hands, the taste of it in her mouth. With every blow that rains on her, she gasps in new surprise, shocked by the speed and vicious power of the fists slamming into her soft flesh.

The blows come so furiously that each new gasp fills her bronchioles with air until her lungs feel as if they will burst. Exhaling in a momentary pause between punches as her chief assailant alters his position for better purchase, the release takes her to a level of pain she'd never experienced before. Blood and air fill her mouth and lungs.

"God...Please...No!" she hisses, as her body folds protectively into itself and she crumples to the ground.

Her attackers deftly switch weapons. Where knucklebone and sinew had impacted with her soft tissues before comes shoe leather hardened by sweat and blood and rain, capped with toes of reinforced steel.

Her mouth open, she is beyond pain as her spleen ruptures and her kidneys take the brunt of a new blow. Mercifully, she slips into a state of semiconsciousness where everything is coloured red.

Tiring of their violent sport, the men chuckle in anticipation as they unfurl her body and pin her down. Now she won't try and struggle anymore. Somebody yanks off her boots. Her head is filled with the men's noise and smell as her bruised limbs are manipulated into position. Vile flashes of reality keep her from the oblivion she desperately seeks.

Glimpses of yellowing teeth. Foul, warm breath on her cheek. Strange words in her ear. The rhythmic jerking, and the weight of them, one after another, heavy on top of her. When it is finally over, they are distracted momentarily by their self-satisfaction and their need for a cigarette.

One of them pulls out his pistol and wipes the blood off it on his trousers in readiness to place it against her temple, as he did with all the rest, their bodies staining the earth all around her red.

Knowing that she has just one last chance, and summoning reserves of strength and adrenaline she wasn't sure she possessed, she makes a sudden dash for freedom. Gunfire rakes the ground next to her as she stumbles and falls.

She is barefoot in the woods. Her heartbeat pounding in her ears, she can feel every pained attempt to catch her breath, can hear the furious men scrabbling in the dirt behind her. And she can also hear something else, something loud, something very near.

The truck driver is driving blind in the night, hoping to surprise the marauding Serbs. His vehicle is full of armed young Muslims, praying they are not too late to save Rajak. Leaning on the horn, the driver switches on his lights just in time to see the young woman directly in his path, a few feet from the hood.

Demented with pain and terror, and bare-breasted, Charlie raises an arm to shield her eyes from the sudden glare, squinting up at him in those final few seconds. A few feet away the driver sees six or seven men, guns raised, clothes in disarray.

She knows they are almost upon her. But she also knows they won't make it.

In that split second before impact, she looks straight into the driver's eyes and smiles up at him in triumph.

THERE THEY WERE, the sand martins. Familiar. Friendly. Safe. She'd made it. She'd cheated Death. By being in the right place at the right time. It wasn't her turn. Not yet. But she'd looked Death in the eye, she'd seen it closer than any of the other moments of her life, and instead of being afraid, she'd laughed in its face.

Jumping to her feet, she dusted herself off and hurled a pebble she'd been gripping tightly in her hand, far into the waves.

"I'm alive!" she yelled at the top of her voice, startling the birds as her cry drifted up towards them and evaporated. Setting off at a trot, she started jogging along the beach, leaving soft footprints behind her, increasing her pace until she was running so hard and so fast that she was almost falling over herself with every step and leaving deep gouges in the surface of the beach.

Breathing greedy gulps of salty air, she stopped and fell to her knees, joy spilling from her eyes.

42

NEW YEAR'S EVE was an event Charlie had dreaded for much of her life. There was something about the passing of an old year and the birth of a new one that blew a cold wind right through her. The words of "Auld Lang Syne" pricked at her eyes, reminding her as they always did of her grandfather. For Charlie, midnight was an unhappy place.

She told Alan nothing of her trepidation, but he quickly picked up on her reluctance to join in with his planned celebrations.

"I think I'll just stay home, if that's all right," she'd told him quietly when he'd first mentioned them. That's how she'd spent the last three New Year's Eves—alone in her beloved cottage, a fire crackling in the grate, a book on her knee, and a glass of cognac at her side. In wild and windswept Blythcove, she'd hear no fireworks or champagne corks popping. Not there would she be interrupted by the cries of people wishing each other Happy New Year, or the striking of Big Ben. No, sleepy little Blythcove was the only place she ever wanted to spend that particular night.

But Alan had been at his most insistent. "But darling, you *have* to come. It's a Matheson tradition. Old Year's Night is a custom that dates from my earliest years here—a party at Pear Tree Farm for all my Suffolk friends. I need you by my side, Charlie, please."

"Oh, couldn't we just curl up together and have a quiet dinner?" she pleaded. "I could make something lovely and we could drink some of your special Italian wine. I'd really much prefer it."

"We can do that the night before, or as many nights as you like afterwards," he promised with a smile. "But on New Year's Eve, I want you to help me uphold a few important traditions. And perhaps begin a few new ones, okay?"

At his insistence, she'd invited Carrie, Lola Lewis, and Nick. The latter had balked at coming, but Charlie had persisted. "I need you here," she'd pleaded, "you know how I hate all this. And anyway, you can be Carrie's date for the night."

Carrie had jumped at the chance. "I really want to meet your Alan," she'd told Charlie. "And it'll be wonderful to see Nick again. It's been way too long since we all went out together."

"I think Alan's feeling rather nervous about the whole thing," Charlie confessed.

"Why, for goodness' sake? Nick's hardly the aggressive type. He's not going to have a problem with this, is he?"

"It's not Nick that Alan's frightened of meeting, Carrie!" Charlie cried. "It's you."

Despite the comforting presence of her dearest friends and her new feeling of invincibility, Charlie suspected that with the passing of the year, old ghosts would still leap out to catch her unawares. They always did.

SHE GREW JUMPIER as the day wore on, but as Alan rushed around, organising the caterers and the lighting technicians, the florists and the wait-staff, he barely noticed. The weather was unusually mild, warm even, and Charlie had hoped they'd be able to enjoy a long, languid lunch together in his sunny dining room to calm her nerves.

But their meal was, instead, an unusually hurried affair. As they sat at one end of the table, the French windows open to the lawns, Mrs Reeder thumped a reheated cottage pie in front of them. "You'll have to help yourselves," she announced moodily. "You're lucky it wasn't soup and sandwiches today."

After serving them both with a large silver spoon, Charlie sat back down in her chair and studied Alan's face. Nettled to be away from the cocoon of Rhubarb Cottage, she was spoiling for a fight. "You love all this, don't you?"

"What?" he said, looking up from his plate.

"All this fuss and bother. And for what?"

"What's the matter, Charlie?"

"I can't honestly see the sense in wasting all this money and effort on a few people you barely know. It's—it's—ostentatious."

His frown deepened. "Ostentatious?" He picked up his fork and scooped a mouthful of mashed potato onto it. "Good word."

Infuriated that he hadn't risen to the bait, Charlie was about to protest further when one of the young men in charge of the fireworks came rushing into the dining room.

"Sorry to interrupt, Sir Alan, but I'm afraid you're needed outside. There's a problem with the big Catherine wheel." He waved an arm anxiously towards the garden.

Pushing back his chair, Alan dabbed his mouth with his damask napkin and nodded his excuses to Charlie. "Forgive me," he said, with a half smile, "but ostentation calls." Turning on his heel, he walked off without even a backwards glance.

CHARLIE WAS JUST stepping out of the shower a few hours later when Alan wandered into the bathroom with two glasses of champagne. The party was due to start soon.

"Here, drink this." Raising his glass, he added: "A toast. To a successful joint venture and a brilliant Old Year's Night. Congratulations on finishing your book, darling."

Wrapping herself in a plush cream bath towel, Charlie took her glass.

"Thank you. Turner, Whatman, and Ruskin will be with the publishers next week, so it's up to them now to argue their case. There's not much more I can do. And as for tonight, I suppose I'll just have to cope."

"You will," Alan murmured, brushing her damp shoulder with his lips and inhaling the lemony scent that curled up from her skin. "And I think what you need to do most of all is relax."

He grabbed a handful of her towel and pulled her resolutely towards him. Charlie knew, with the keenest anticipation, what was to follow. Placing his glass on the bedside table, and putting hers next to it, he wrapped her in his arms and kissed her mouth hard. Charlie reciprocated as the two of them fell backwards onto the bed. Her towel fell open, revealing her soft, pink body.

"Oh, Charlie," he whispered, burying his face in her wet hair.

They moved slowly, biding their time, allowing each other to succumb, watching each other in the large gilt-framed mirror on the wall at the foot of the bed. And when they'd finished, breathless, they took a shower together, the perfumed oils she so loved soothing their chafed skin. Toweling herself down again afterwards, Charlie felt a profound sense of calm. Alan was right. This was a special night—the first time they would be seen together as a couple by Nick and Carrie—and, despite her misgivings, she wanted it to go well.

She'd decided to wear the dress she'd bought for the Turner Prize party. Alan had offered to treat her to something new, but she'd resisted.

"There's no point," she'd laughed. "Nobody here apart from Nick was at the Tate, and he was too drunk to notice."

Alan, red in the face from his recent exertion, zipped her in. Staring over her shoulder at her reflection, he declared softly, "I could make love to you all over again." Then he kissed the downy skin at the back of her neck.

Her hair piled up into twisted snakes, Charlie warned into the glass, "Don't look straight at me or I'll turn you to stone."

"Too late," he replied, reaching for her hand and placing it firmly between his legs.

• • •

LOLA LEWIS WAS quite beside herself. Not only was Charlie Hudson about to deliver her long-awaited manuscript, but Sir Alan Matheson had invited her to his country home on New Year's Eve for an exclusive preview of his painting for the jacket. Ever since that magazine article had appeared about the pair of them, interest in Lola's pet project had soared within publishing circles. *The Bookseller* had run a piece; everyone suddenly wanted to take Lola to lunch and find out if the gossip was really true. Now she was getting a chance to meet the great man himself.

As always with Lola, the clothes she chose to wear reflected her mood. Tonight, she was in skintight tiger-print Versace that left little to the imagination, set off with a Tiffany diamond cross. "If Liz Hurley can have one, then I don't see why I can't," she'd protested, justifying the purchase to a girlfriend before taking the plunge.

By the time she arrived, as arranged, an hour before the party officially began, she'd smoked an untold number of cigarettes and sunk two large gin and tonics to steady her nerves. Standing in the open doorway, she held out a hand weighed down with gold bangles and false red fingernails.

"Charlie, darling," she crooned, "how lovely to see you again. And Sir Alan," she added, taking his hand in both of hers and looking adoringly into his eyes, "may I say what a great pleasure and privilege it is to meet you at last."

Charlie had already spoken so fondly of her new editor that Alan was guaranteed to like Lola immediately. Charlie knew he'd sense her natural worth beneath the thick veneer of makeup. Now, as he summoned her into his studio and carefully unveiled his homage to *Crossing the Brook*, repositioning a spotlight to illuminate it, they both knew she wasn't faking her response.

"Sir Alan!" Lola gasped. "I had no idea! It's exquisite." Standing back, she took in the full effect of the colour washes and the delicate handling of the paper and paint.

Charlie stood beside her, studying the glorious work of art Alan had created especially for her, its slow evolution keeping pace with their relationship. When he had first shown her the completed work earlier that day, she'd been rendered speechless. Her eyes feasted on the contours of the idyllic landscape that Turner and now Alan had so masterfully re-created. She admired the way he had framed the view on either side with the trees which led the gaze to the pale far horizon, much as a landscape gardener would do to create distance and space.

Seeing the painting in its entirety—the gentle gradations of colour, theme, and light lovingly layered brushstroke by brushstroke onto the ultimate paper—Charlie realised that it depicted a kind of Utopia, a mythical, perfect place far removed from reality. It was a place of retreat for those who found reality too difficult to deal with. People like she had once been, perhaps.

What had once made her shiver now filled her with pride. Her comprehension of the painting's inherent qualities and subtleties was complete. Staring at it again, she shook her head in wonderment at the talent and vision that lay behind it. No one who could create something that sublime could be anything other than fundamentally good.

Lola was equally mesmerised, as Charlie's enthusiastic talk of the importance of Whatman's suddenly made sense.

"Why, Charlie!" she exclaimed. "It's a masterpiece!"

"Isn't it?" Charlie agreed with a smile. "We're very fortunate."

"Indeed we are, my darling," the older woman gushed. "I can't wait to show it to the art director. He'll *die*!"

Alan laughed out loud. "My paintings have evoked many different reactions, but the idea of actually killing someone with one is, I think, one of the greatest compliments I have ever been paid."

Lola all but melted back onto his green velvet chaise longue.

"Where on earth did you find Alan, Charlie?" she said breathily. "He's simply too good to be true."

. . .

WHILE ALAN GAVE Lola a guided tour of the principal rooms of the house, champagne flutes in hand, Charlie wandered into the kitchen. The rear rooms were buzzing, staff in white blouses and black trousers running back and forth with platters of canapés and trays of drinks.

"Is there anything I can do?" Charlie asked Mrs Reeder, having found the housekeeper emerging, harassed, from the walk-in pantry, a whole ham in her hands. "I know it's probably too late, but there must be something."

Mrs Reeder eyed her suspiciously and shook her head. "If anything goes wrong now, it won't be nothing to do with me," she puffed. "I've done all I can to make this a success, only I don't suppose for one minute he'll bother to thank me."

"I'll make sure he does." Charlie watched her slap the ham down onto a large oval dish. "I know he's very appreciative. We both are."

"It's not been easy, organising this lot." Mrs Reeder waved her hands at the room full of people. "I'm no spring chicken. It might have killed a younger person." To Charlie's horror, her face crumpled and she began to weep.

"I'm sure Sir Alan will be most grateful, Mrs Reeder. Please don't upset yourself needlessly—"

The old woman dabbed her tears on the corner of her apron and sniffed noisily. "It's not him," she said, her eyes glistening. "It's what happened this morning, over in Dunwich."

Charlie wondered what she was talking about. "Really?" she responded absently, reminding herself that she really ought to go and check her hair and makeup before the guests began to arrive.

"His mother was a friend of my daughter, Beryl," Mrs Reeder prattled on, shaking her head at the memory. "He was a good boy, despite the way he sometimes looked. He took care of his mum even when he went off to college. He always sent money home."

Charlie's hand was on the housekeeper's arm, and she felt her fingers tighten involuntarily.

"He was that upset when Miss Angela died. He never really got over it. His mum's been worried sick about him."

Tiny hairs on the back of Charlie's neck bristled and she continued to stare at Mrs Reeder's mouth opening and closing.

"But he seemed to be a bit better lately. Said he was even thinking about going back to college. To study art."

"Tony," Charlie said, in a voice not quite her own. "You're talking about Tony."

"Yes, of course," Mrs Reeder said testily. "Tony Rogers. Did you know him?"

"No," Charlie said, transfixed by the deep creases around the old woman's lips. "I mean, I only met him once. Last week."

"Well, he was a good boy, despite everything," Mrs Reeder declared, her eyes filling again with tears. "And to end up like that."

Charlie had to remind herself to swallow. "Like what?" she finally managed through the roar.

Mrs Reeder stared at her, realising for the first time that she couldn't have heard the news. "Dead," she said distractedly. "They found him this morning. I'd have thought Sir Alan would have mentioned it. Hanging from one of the yew trees in St James's churchyard, a suicide note in his pocket. Just a few feet from Miss Angela's grave."

DOWNSTAIRS, CHARLIE HEARD the first guests arriving as she sat forlornly at the dressing table. Looking at herself in the glass, she saw not the willing young accomplice Alan usually made her feel, but an older, harder woman halfway through her life, a hundred tiny spears jagging her nerves.

Death. So here it was again. Tonight. In this house. Tony was dead. She hardly knew the boy, and yet the news stabbed at her heart. Those eyes, with the unique splash of yellow, would never see another Suffolk sunrise. Angie, he'd called her. His Angie. To him, Angela had been warm and kind and loving. She'd looked at him and seen only the beautiful person beneath the skin. Had told him she wanted to spend the rest of her life immortalising him in paint.

Charlie wished now that she had run after him in the graveyard, and made him believe the truth about Alan. But she'd been too cowardly. Now it was too late. Tony had decided to join his Angie and their baby in that perpetual embrace. Meeting her at the graveyard on that rainy day had nothing to do with it, Charlie told herself sharply, even if the note in his pocket suggested as much.

"I'll show you," it said, according to Mrs Reeder. The last words Tony had spoken about Alan that day in the graveyard.

Worse than the shock, which had sliced through Charlie so keenly, was the news that Alan apparently knew of the boy's death and hadn't told her. He'd never even mentioned it, or seemed the slightest bit upset. How could that be? Wouldn't he have at least been saddened that his daughter's boyfriend had ended his life similarly? Would he not have considered canceling the party?

Staring at herself in the mirror, Charlie shook her head. Why would Alan cancel? What did he care about Tony? As far as he was concerned, he was a scruffy young tearaway who'd made his daughter pregnant and then continued to accuse Alan of unspeakable crimes after her death. He'd probably be relieved that he was out of his life for good. Charlie would just have to accept Tony's death as another sad suicide and leave it at that. The journalistic instinct was way too strong in her. Trust was something she seemed to have mislaid somewhere along the way.

"Stop it," Charlie told her reflection crossly, standing and smoothing the silk of her dress with sweaty palms. "You're not to blame. He was an impressionable, vulnerable young man who couldn't face life without the girl he loved, that's all; couldn't face yet another anniversary. It's a terrible tragedy, but it has nothing whatsoever to do with you. Or with Alan."

Picking up a gossamer scarf in the same ruby red as her garnet earrings, she threw it across her shoulders, cleverly veiling her cleavage. Taking a deep breath, she turned the handle on the oak bedroom door and stepped out onto the galleried landing.

The hubbub below was increasing as more and more people arrived. Her ears filled with the noise, but it was muffled as if she could only hear it distantly, under water. Carrie and Nick were driving up together after he'd put the first edition to bed and would, she knew, be late. She couldn't wait to see them. Their familiar presence would act as a life raft in the increasingly choppy seas of her mind.

Below, through the waves, she could hear Alan's distinctive laugh and the clinking of cut crystal. Her right hand on the polished wood handrail, she descended as gracefully as her legs could take her down the stairs to meet the gathering throng.

43

THE PARTY WOULD undoubtedly be considered a triumph by everyone who attended. From Mrs Reeder, anxiously supervising the dozens of white-jacketed caterers overrunning her kitchen, to the effusive guests who crowded around their illustrious host, the evening would be the only topic of conversation in this part of the county for weeks.

Charlie had little appetite but was able to lose several valuable minutes to herself in quiet appreciation of a holiday table groaning with delights. The centrepiece was a huge side of beef, its thick pink slices splayed out on a platter in the shape of a fan. There were two whole hams and a sixteen-pound turkey, meat and fish pâtés, and a game pie of rabbit and herbs. Alan had ordered Cromer crabs from the excellent fishmonger in Halesworth and a platter of smoked prawns and oysters from Orford.

Desserts included a huge raspberry trifle, chocolate profiteroles, meringue pavlovas, and thick pear and almond flans. Cheeses of every description slumped on slates decorated with fig leaves, and vast bowls of black grapes adorned almost every surface to satisfy the Italian tradition of eating twelve grapes before the witching hour.

The champagne was free-flowing and few passed it up, least of all Charlie. Alan introduced her to guest after guest, clearly showing her off, and she mingled resolutely with the county set, and the London set with county homes, and all the other sets whose only common denominators seemed to be frightening intellects and unspeakable snobbery. As the sounds of the sea lessened in her ears, one face began to meld with another.

Feeling swamped, she turned away from them all and wandered out onto the terrace, softly lit by candles and moonlight. Despite the unseasonable warmth of that day, there was now a chill breeze and she drew her scarf around her shoulders. The fresh air sobered her a little, and she inhaled deeply. Several couples were already outside, leaning against each other and listening to the string quartet just inside the door playing songs from the twenties and thirties. Shivering, she recognised "Goodnight, Sweetheart" from her grandfather's favourite Al Bowlly LP.

Cradling her champagne flute, Charlie lowered herself wearily onto a wooden Lutyens bench and gazed across the garden, cleverly lit with coloured spotlights, illuminating the ice crystals just beginning to form on each blade of grass. Across the fields were the twinkling lights of the village. Just a short distance away on the other side of the house lay the sea. She inhaled again, the cool night air slowly clearing her head.

Looking back inside at the party in full swing, groups clustered together to gossip, or gathered around the buffet, she longed to see a face she knew amongst the crowd. Charming as all these invited friends of Alan's seemed to be, she didn't really belong amongst them. Alan's world was so very different from the one she'd carefully carved for herself in Blythcove. Watching the way he was in company tonight and remembering how strange he'd been at the Turner Prize ceremony—she was beginning to realise that she was only really comfortable with him when they were alone.

Sarah Matheson would have been completely at home here tonight. So, too, she suspected, would Diane Colvin, Alan's waspish second wife. Was Charlie foolish enough to think she could ever fit in to his way of life as effortlessly? Beguiled by the physicality of their relationship, overlooking their glaring social and intellectual differences, had she deluded herself into thinking that she could ever really become a permanent fixture in his high-profile life?

Someone once told her—was it Danny?—to imagine her life without Nick, and see if she preferred the life she imagined to the one she really had. It was a dangerous enterprise and one that had cost Nick dearly. If she were to walk away from Alan tonight, how would her life look then? Once she'd stopped missing making love to him—oh, the aching void that would create—what would she be left with?

Under Alan's expert guidance, her reawakening was almost complete. By releasing her senses, he had led her out of a choking, suffocating darkness. Could she hope for anything more than that? Could anything good ever come out of such a tormented history as theirs? Surely their relationship was founded on little more than intense desire and shifting sands, while all around tides of madness and death washed over them?

And what of Alan's needs? He wanted more, she could tell, and not just a society wife who could perform at functions like tonight's. Yet she didn't honestly know if she could ever give herself completely to someone again. Maybe it was too soon; her wounds were too fresh. Perhaps in time, she could. But what if he tired of her before then and found someone else to share his bed? Wasn't that what he'd always done in the past? Run from the people who hurt him, just as she had? What if she gave herself completely, only to be hurt again? Could she survive the pain? Wouldn't it be better to walk away now, to protect herself from the inevitable? Closing her eyes, she could once again feel the water slopping against the inside of her skull.

"So there you are." Nick's voice floated towards her like a lifeline. Opening her eyes, she saw him hand in hand with Carrie, and noticed, as he bent to kiss her, that he never once relinquished his grip.

"Hiya." Carrie smiled, similarly reluctant to let Nick go.

Carrie had never looked lovelier. Gone were the ubiquitous jeans and white T-shirt. In their place was an off-the-shoulder dress of crimson velvet. "I scrub up quite well, don't I?" She grinned, as Charlie looked her up and down appreciatively.

There was a new glow to her friend's face and a flushed, excited expression in her eyes. Glancing across at Nick, Charlie saw it mirrored there. For the first time in years, it seemed, his jaw wasn't clenched in anger. Perhaps Nick's someone perfect was a lot closer than she'd thought.

"How was the journey up?" she asked.

Carrie blushed and Nick shifted uneasily. "Fine," he said, unable to meet Charlie's eyes.

"We've been catching up on old times," Carrie interjected. "It's been great."

"So I see."

"How's everything here?" Carrie asked, clearly anxious to change the subject.

"Couldn't be better," Charlie replied, quelling a hiccup. "I've been drinking my way to oblivion and playing devil's advocate with myself."

"About what?" Carrie asked, looking at Nick in an expression of shared concern.

"Oh, nothing important," Charlie said, waving her hand at them dismissively.

Suddenly a figure stepped from the shadows into the light. Striding across the terrace he extended his hand. "You must be Nick. I'm Alan. Thanks for coming. Good to meet you at last."

Nick faltered slightly at the first proper sight of his wife's lover, but took Alan's hand and shook it cordially. "It's good to meet you, too. I've heard a great deal about you." Turning to his date for the night, he introduced Carrie.

From the moment Carrie and Alan set eyes on each other, there was a spark between them that bordered on the flirtatious. Carrie was open and friendly and generous in her praise of his lovely home. He, in turn, had nothing but good things to say, telling her how fondly Charlie spoke of her.

"I understand you first met when you worked together on the *Tribune?*" Charlie overheard him asking her, as the pair wandered farther along the terrace. "And became best friends."

"More like sisters," Carrie admitted.

"I'd love to hear more about it sometime," Alan said. Lowering his voice but not enough so that Charlie couldn't hear, he added, "Charlie so rarely talks about her time as a journalist."

"Well, why would she?" Carrie said, giving nothing away. "That was all an eternity ago. In another life."

THE CLOSER IT came to midnight, the more unsettled Charlie felt. Carrie and Nick disappeared inside to eat, and from the terrace, she heard the chatter inside grow louder as the waiters filled everyone's flutes to the brim.

Alan found her alone and topped up her glass himself. Inside, the excitement rose to a crescendo; a few seconds before the witching hour, there began a noisy countdown. "Ten, nine, eight, seven..."

"Happy New Year, my Charlie." Alan kissed her tenderly, his eyes on fire.

"Alan, I..." she began, but stopped herself. Now wasn't the time to speak.

Putting down his glass, he reached into his pocket and withdrew a small blue box, pressing it into her hand.

Charlie froze. She opened her mouth to protest, but as she did so, he placed a finger firmly against her lips.

"I don't expect an answer now," he told her. "Open this only when you feel ready. Until then, keep it safe, darling."

Before she could say a word, he turned back to his house, his glass raised to toast his guests. "Happy New Year, everybody!"

Watching him go, Charlie caught sight of Nick and Carrie, standing by the window. They were silhouetted against the light, their bodies locked together in a passionate embrace.

44

CHARLIE WAS CURLED UP in her own warmth, wrapped in a blanket in front of a fire at Rhubarb Cottage, checking her manuscript through for the last time. Nigel Armstrong already had an advance copy, but it wouldn't do any harm to give it one final read-through before she shoehorned the pages into a large padded envelope and despatched it to the London offices of Lola Lewis.

Staring at the words leaping up at her from the paper, she tried to focus on their rhythm and intent. Turner. Papier-mâché. Whatman. Ruskin. *Crossing the Brook*. Paper conservation. Watermarks. All placed in time and space, their voices rising from the pages in a beautifully orchestrated, harmonised chorus; each character lending colour and vibrancy to the information he was imparting. Everything was finally there, in the right order, and the myriad fibres and strands had meshed together well in the figurative vat she had created. But her eyes kept straying to the flames licking at the applewood logs in her grate, and her mind kept wandering from the purity of what she had created.

The events of New Year's Eve had done little to clear her mind of all that debris she was planning on getting rid of. Now it wasn't just thoughts of Angela and Sarah Matheson who cluttered her head. They were joined by Tony, Carrie, and Nick. And Alan, of course. The catalyst. For Alan was the reason they had all come to some sort of personal epiphany on Old Year's Night.

Angela had blamed Alan for the deficiencies of her life. She'd punished him by taking her life and attempting to heap the blame on him. Poor, broken Sarah, less vehemently perhaps, concurred—and yet couldn't help but love him still. Tony was filled with hatred for Alan right up until the moment he threw away his young life, as if it were nothing more than a worthless scrap of paper. Carrie and Nick, always so distrusting of Alan and yet brought together at his behest, ironically had him to thank for finally finding comfort in each other's arms. And Charlie. Had Alan shaped her future, too?

Yet, through it all, Alan remained, it seemed, untouched, unassailable, and somehow always just out of reach. The glimpses of his inner self that he'd permitted Charlie to see had been only that, she realised now, mere glimpses. Oh, there had been much tenderness and kindness and even generosity of mind, spirit, and body. He'd been courteous and charming and urbane. He'd even given her a ring. But the mystery that lay at the core of his life—the real secret of his relationship with Angela—seemed locked away as securely as the contents of his vault.

Maybe that was how he had always been. Maybe that was what drove the women who loved him to madness. The frustration of never being able to get really close; of always being denied the intimacy he seemed emotionally unable to give. There was more to know, Charlie felt sure. So much more to understand about him. There had to be. But through fear or loyalty to the dead or something else she didn't yet comprehend, he preferred not to share his secrets.

Secrets. How she hated secrets. She'd been plagued by them for much of her life. Granddad was her secret as a child, her secret weapon. Without his lavish favouritism, she might have had the colourless childhood of her sister, tinted only with the monochrome hues of her parents. Keeping the secret of her grandfather's suicide had been a heavy burden for a grieving teenager. But Marjorie swore them all to secrecy, fearful of what people might think.

Then, with Charlie's work as a journalist, came the secrets of the dead and dying, the maimed and brutalised. Despatched to tell their stories, she could only scratch at the surface; only give a sanitised, inoculated version of the horror. The public wasn't ready for the real, raw truth. And by the time she left her last assignment, and Kosovo, she had her own terrible burning secrets seared into her soul, secrets she believed could never, ever be told.

On the table next to Charlie was the ring box Alan had given her three days earlier before he returned to pressing business in London. It had taken three days to summon up the courage to even open it, for fear that by doing so it would become a Pandora's box of her own making. The diamond solitaire inside was exquisite, square cut, set on a fine platinum band, but she knew she couldn't possibly accept it. Snapping the lid shut, she hoped that nothing had escaped from the box that might cause her any future regret.

THE KNOCK AT her door was so timid that Charlie scarcely heard it at first. When it came again, she unfurled her legs and, setting down her reading glasses, approached cautiously, as she was not expecting visitors.

The sight of Sarah Matheson on her doorstep snatched a breath from her lungs. Alan's ex-wife seemed utterly incongruous in her rural surroundings, especially with a thick fur-trimmed coat draped around her shoulders and a gleaming black Jaguar ticking over in the narrow lane behind her. Charlie stared at her, speechless.

"Hello, my dear." Sarah smiled politely. "I do hope I'm not disturbing you. I've come for a few days' break from all the London parties and Alan mentioned that you were up here, too."

Stepping in through the door uninvited, she cast an expertly critical eye over the cosy interior of the cottage until her eyes alighted on the Tiffany box on the table and remained locked there. "I wonder," she continued, staring intently at the ring. "As we're both alone tonight, would you do me the very great honour of being my dinner guest?" Dragging her eyes away at last, she told Charlie, "Nothing too fancy, I'm afraid. I've asked Mrs Reeder to roast us a chicken and prepare some vegetables. It will be ready at eight. I do hate dining alone, and I'd be so grateful for the company."

Charlie faltered for a moment, thinking of Alan and her promise never to see his ex-wife again. She thought of the note she'd sent to Sarah and wondered if the older woman considered her own invitation the most appropriate way to respond to Charlie's apology. Finally, she thought wistfully of the simple supper she'd planned for herself in front of the fire—cheese, salad, some crusty bread, and a few glasses of Rioja.

"Of course," she replied, unable to resist the expectant look on her visitor's face. "Of course I'll come, Lady Matheson. See you at eight?"

NICK COULDN'T QUELL the feeling of uneasiness. Something wasn't right. He'd had this sensation before, when Charlie was on some of her worst assignments. Months later he'd discover that the bristling hairs on the back of his neck and the fluttering in the pit of his stomach had coincided exactly with Charlie's proximity to danger. Now that she'd finally given up that crazy way of life, he'd never expected to feel it again, and yet here it was, back again—tap, tap, tapping away at his insides.

Standing in the middle of the City Road outside his office, waiting for a taxi in the rush hour, he was miserably cold, his mobile phone battery was dead, and he wanted to get home and try Charlie's number once more. He knew he'd only be content once he'd heard her voice.

When he still couldn't raise her at the cottage several hours after dark, he told himself he was being irrational. He drank two beers, persuading himself that this was nothing more than a stupid anxiety attack, probably brought on by the unnerving sight of Charlie staring directly at Carrie and him after their impulsive midnight kiss on New Year's Eve. Thinking of that, he dialed Carrie's number and asked if she'd heard anything.

"No, nothing, not since the party. Oh, Nick, she saw us, didn't she? Is that why she hasn't been in touch? We never meant to hurt her."

"I know," Nick replied, his mind elsewhere. "Don't worry about it, Carrie. I just hope she's okay, that's all. Listen, I'll call you later once I've heard from her."

Only after he'd left two more messages on Charlie's answering machine, one on her mobile, and tried her London flat once more, did he reluctantly dial a fourth number.

Alan picked up the phone at his Onslow Square apartment.

"Hi, Alan, it's Nick . . . Nick Lambert."

"Oh! Nick! Hello."

"I—er—I was wondering, is Charlie with you? I can't seem to reach her at the cottage. Is she back in town yet, do you know?"

"No, I'm afraid not. As far as I know she's planning on staying up there until the end of the week. Come to think of it, I haven't spoken to her since New Year's Day." Pausing before deciding to explain, he added, "She asked for some time to herself. You know how she needs her solitude."

"Y-yes, yes, I do," Nick replied, unsatisfied. "But if she should get in touch in the next twenty-four hours, could you possibly ask her to call me? I need to talk to her. . . . It's quite important."

"You wouldn't have called me unless it was," Alan observed. "Is everything all right?"

"Fine," Nick replied, staring at the lie. "I just need to make sure she's okay."

"Why on earth wouldn't she be?"

"Oh, no reason. Just get her to call me, okay?"

"I will," the older man replied, in such a way that Nick could tell he, too, was now concerned.

45

CHARLIE SIPPED THOUGHTFULLY at her glass of red wine and watched Sarah Matheson post a forkful of chicken breast between her pumped-up, heart-shaped lips. To make their supper together less formal, Sarah had asked Mrs Reeder to place Charlie immediately to her left while she took her place at the head of the long dining table. It must have been a very long time since Sarah had sat in this position, but she gave every impression that she had never left it.

Charlie yearned for the familiar cosiness of Rhubarb Cottage. The silences between sentences were getting longer. She'd already used the bathroom once to waste time washing her hands, even though she no longer felt the urge. She wasn't sure she could slip away again so soon.

"I didn't know you liked being in the country," she offered finally, a morsel of sage and onion stuffing on her fork.

"I don't," Sarah replied succinctly, sipping from her own glass of white wine.

"Then why are you here?"

"To see you."

"Oh." Charlie couldn't think of any other response.

Sarah put down her fork and reached for her cigarettes. "I thought you might want to talk to me again," she said, lighting one. "About Angela?

About Alan and Angela and Tony? Surely you do. Isn't that why you accepted my invitation?"

"You know about Tony?" Charlie asked, staring into her companion's face for clues. "I didn't think you'd have been told."

"Of course I was told. His mother telephoned me the day her son's body was discovered. We've known each other for years. She didn't want me to hear it from anyone else."

"Oh, I am sorry."

"Don't be. I never really liked the boy. My daughter was far too good for him."

Charlie didn't know how to respond.

"Tony's mother said he met you a few days before," Sarah said. "At Angela's grave. Is that right?"

Charlie fought not to squirm under her intense gaze. "Yes. I went there to pay my respects. He seemed—upset."

"Well, come, then," Sarah prompted, smoking viciously. "Aren't you dying to tell me what he said?"

"I'm not sure we should be talking about Angela, or about Tony. Alan wouldn't like it."

"Alan wouldn't like it," Sarah repeated, then laughed. "But Alan's not here."

"I know, but he doesn't even want me to see you. He said you'd been unwell."

"Well, I'm better now."

"I know, but, well, maybe you won't be tomorrow."

Sarah Matheson leaned back in her chair. Her facial muscles, already pulled tight by surgery, creased into myriad thin lines, like concertina paper. "I promise I won't tell Alan. There now, does that make you feel better?"

In the ensuing silence, Charlie finally rose to the bait. "Very well, then tell me what Angela was really like."

"Miserable," Sarah replied promptly, suddenly intently serious. "My daughter had an endless capacity for unhappiness, from the earliest age."

"Have you any idea why?"

"Perhaps," Sarah replied enigmatically, blowing smoke into the air. "But it wasn't for lack of anything. She had all she could possibly want."

"What about love? I mean, sometimes parents don't know how to show it."

Sarah Matheson tensed. "I know it's the vogue to blame the parents for every child's problems these days, but I can assure you, Angela was very well taken care of. She went to the finest schools, had Alan at her beck and call for much of her early life, and never wanted for anything."

Charlie acknowledged the warning shot across her bow and took a gulp of her wine. "I didn't mean to imply that you were in any way to blame. I was just trying to understand what might have made her so unhappy."

"Alan," Sarah replied, this time without hesitation.

"Why do you say that?"

"Because it's true."

"Yes, but why did Alan make her unhappy? I mean, what did he do to upset her so?" Charlie arranged her sentence carefully to distract her from the familiar sound of water rising in her ears.

"It's what he didn't do," Sarah replied. "You must have realised by now, my dear, that my husband is an extremely focused individual who really only cares about his work. Everything else, and I mean *everything*, takes second place. Angela and I came a very long way down the list."

"Sarah, why did you really come here tonight?" Charlie asked suddenly, pressing her fingers against her temple.

"I wanted to find out how much you know." Sarah's voice was steady but Charlie wondered what lay beneath it as she knocked ash in precise little taps from her cigarette onto her half-empty dinner plate. "I also want to stop you from doing anything foolish."

"Like what?"

"Like marrying Alan. He's almost certainly proposed by now." Reading Charlie's response, she snorted. "I thought so. I saw the ring box. Oh, he's so predictable! He asked me on Old Year's Night, you know, and Diane, too." Her lips curled at the name of Alan's second wife.

The thought of becoming just another Matheson statistic repulsed

Charlie, but she felt the need to press Sarah further, despite her increasing sense of alarm. "And why would marrying Alan be a foolish thing for me to do?"

"Because it just would!" Sarah snapped. Drawing herself in, she added, "He made me unhappy. He made Angela unhappy. He even made Diane unhappy. Eventually, he'd make you miserable, too." As she spoke, she ground her cigarette butt, stained with lipstick, into her half-eaten chicken breast.

"Yes, but *how* did Alan make you all so unhappy? I don't understand."

"He takes what he wants. He gives nothing back."

"But wasn't he enormously busy back then, trying to make a name for himself?" Charlie's muddled brain tried to reason its way out of the corner she was relentlessly being backed into. "I mean, it must have been such a struggle in the early days—you without a penny and Alan trying to raise a family on an artist's income?"

"I see you've done your research."

"I—I just saw something in an old newspaper."

"No matter." Sarah dismissively pushed her plate away. "The feud with my family was a long time ago, and, anyway, it worked out all right in the end."

"You mean with your inheritance?"

"That, and the fact that I got my husband back." Seeing Charlie's evident confusion, she elaborated. "Alan left me not long after we lost our second baby. He walked out one day without explanation. I was devastated. A black cloud descended over me and I didn't know how to lift it. I desperately wanted to try for another baby. I simply had to get him back."

"So what did you do?" Charlie asked, trying to ignore the worsening pain in her head.

"I went to see my father." Sarah's forehead furrowed at the memory. "We hadn't spoken for years—I didn't even attend my mother's funeral."

"What did you say?"

"I lied," she answered, her ice blue eyes fixed on Charlie. "I told him I was pregnant with Alan's child. I begged him to reconsider his decision to disinherit me."

Charlie couldn't imagine Sarah Matheson begging for anything. "And his response?" she asked.

"He caved in, as I knew he would. He wrote me a cheque and promised more when his grandchild was born. Within three months, Daddy was dead. He left me everything and Alan came back to me. Shortly afterwards, Angela arrived."

"I see," Charlie murmured, not really seeing anything very clearly at all. "And Alan came back because ...?"

"The money, of course." Sarah sighed, a long-suffering parent explaining something to a child. "Don't you see? He was broke. Once the inheritance was mine, Alan really had no choice but to come back. It would have been the end of him as an artist otherwise. He might have still painted, but without my connections, my money, he'd have been nothing."

"And Angela?"

"What about her?"

"You said you'd lied. But you must have been pregnant because Angela was born soon afterwards."

Sarah's eyes flickered just long enough for Charlie to see the truth. The final pieces of the jigsaw Charlie had puzzled over for months fell into place with a satisfying, but terrifying, click.

"It wasn't that you weren't pregnant," Charlie said, softly. "The lie was that the child was Alan's! Alan wasn't Angela's father. That was what the DNA report on Angela's unborn child must have proved. It was supposed to show whether he was the father. What it also proved was that he wasn't even *her* father!"

"So you *do* know everything." Sarah nodded, seemingly satisfied. "The pregnancy was a means to an end, that's all," she said, her face empty. "Whatever else Alan may be, he is a gentleman. He would never have left me in the lurch. The baby and the inheritance guaranteed his presence for a few years more."

"And then Angela grew up," Charlie said. "She became a sexual creature. She used her sexuality to flatter the man she believed to be her father."

"She was a little whore," Sarah hissed. Pushing her chair back, she stood and topped up both their glasses. "Always giggling with him. Whispering. Flirting. Excluding."

She reached into her handbag and pulled out a bottle of pills. She unscrewed the lid and tipped some into her hand. Throwing her head back, she swallowed them with a slug of wine and offered the two remaining yellow tablets in her palm to Charlie. "Here, take these. They'll help numb the pain of what I'm about to tell you."

"No," Charlie said, pushing away her glass of wine.

Sarah shrugged her shoulders and returned the bottle of pills to her handbag. She moved towards the window, her hands clasped together, as if formulating the right words in her mind.

Charlie sat turned dumbly towards her, numbly waiting for the news she now realised she'd somehow anticipated all along. Just when she'd thought all was steady beneath her feet, she felt the waves crashing to the sand all around her.

"I used to make excuses for them," Sarah began, her voice steadier. "I put it down to the fact that they'd always been exceptionally close. Even when Angela was much younger, she'd often slip into Alan's side of the bed at night. I'd find them in the morning, wrapped together like spoons, Alan completely unaware that she was there."

Charlie's mouth was dry.

"I'll admit that I didn't enjoy being left out," Sarah continued, remorselessly, "but I accepted the unique bond between a father and daughter, especially when I wasn't always completely myself."

She turned and stepped a few paces towards Charlie, scrutinising her.

Charlie sat holding her breath, waiting for the words she now knew were designed to break her.

"Then, one night, I woke with a frightful headache. I needed a pill, but they'd all been locked away. I put on my dressing gown and slipped downstairs. I saw the light on in Alan's studio. I crossed the courtyard and opened the door."

Sarah's voice bubbled through the water in Charlie's ears, but was still clear enough to paint a vividly painful picture.

Afraid to exhale, she could see it all—the cold, grey lustre of moonlight illuminating the courtyard, the artificial light coming from the studio. Dark shadows fringing the corners, drawing the eye inexorably to the centre of the frame, to the stable door partially open, a thin shaft of light escaping from within.

She was at Sarah Matheson's side; she could feel the weight of gravity as she pulled open the heavy door. She saw what Sarah saw. What Tony had seen. Their visions became one.

A SCREAM FILLS her skull. The images laugh at her, lurid and vile. They twist and writhe in blood and guts and bile, gouging and tearing at each other and her eyes with their fingernails, the demons in Angela's painting, the half crescents in the flesh of the naked women, the dying infant, the mutilated girl, the dog with the hat.

Everything melts horribly into one: paints and papers, oils and grease, a congealing mass of festering flesh and burning bodies as the ground spins wildly beneath her.

And, all the while, the waters keep rising.

46

$\mathcal{A}$LAN MATHESON WAS NOT usually a man to do things on impulse, but Nick's call had disturbed him more than he cared to admit. By the time he put down the telephone after failing to reach Charlie for the third time at the cottage, he'd made up his mind. Quickly packing an overnight bag, he reversed his Mercedes out of the underground garage and pointed it northeast.

In hindsight, presenting Charlie with an engagement ring may have been a little premature. It may have upset her much more than he'd realised. She'd certainly seemed quiet the last time they spoke. There was a flatness in her voice, a tiredness which at the time he'd put down to the strain of completing her book. It had been three days since then and he hadn't heard another word. Maybe he should have called sooner. Perhaps she'd suffered some sort of relapse. Even though it would be late when he arrived, he'd be extremely relieved to see her.

The journey was long and frustrating, as he found himself stuck behind a slow-moving convoy of trucks on the A14 heading for the port of Felixstowe. With classical music filling the warm dark space within his car, he forced himself to relax and listen to *Dido and Aeneas*. The remarkable Queen Dido, abandoned by the man she loved, her only salvation suicide. Their tragedy woven into an extraordinary opera by Purcell. Dido as painted by Turner, *Leaving Carthage on the Morning of the Chase*, the year before he completed *Crossing the Brook*. The similarities between the two paintings uncannily striking. Tall trees to the left, lower ones on the right. The gentle sky of blue and yellow hues. Groups of people in the foreground; the eye drawn always to the middle distance.

Once again a pastoral scene, a fantasy of peace and light and harmony upon which to rest the eye and feast the soul. Yet, like *Crossing the Brook*, there lay within a story of epic proportions, a hint of tragedy behind the idyll. Dido was, at the point at which Turner painted her, deliriously happy and completely unaware of the great sadness that lay ahead. In *Crossing the Brook*, Alan sensed similar tragedy. This painting, he felt, represented a journey, a rite of passage. For Turner it was full of longing for the classical lure of Italy, a place he was to visit soon afterwards. His journey meant leaving behind England and the sad memories of his dead mother and sister.

For Alan, and maybe for Charlie, too, the work represented a watershed, a point at which the shades of the past were finally left behind. In a near-religious rite of cleansing, in wading across a stream away from the darkness, a new journey was surely beginning. Behind them both, in the shadows beyond the woods, lay death and madness, lost love and suicide.

Suicide. His poor troubled Angela, whose eyes had dulled in her final months, her fiery, rebellious spirit all but extinguished. She was broken. Had he broken her? Or was it her art? Either way, she'd hardly even bothered to put up a fight. And now Tony, young and foolish, cursed by Nature, was with her in whichever hell she'd chosen for herself.

Was Charlie able to see a way of going on after all she'd been through? Or had his offer of marriage somehow tipped her backwards? He'd overlooked all the warning signs with Angela—was history going to repeat itself to punish him? Pressing his accelerator pedal to the floor, he drove on with the foolhardiness of fear.

By the time he pulled his car to a halt outside Charlie's darkened cottage just before midnight, he was desperate to see her, to hold the warmth of her in his arms. Ignoring the cold night air that sucked the breath from his lungs, he ran towards the house, opened her little garden gate, rushed up the herringbone brick path, and knocked on the door. Listening for signs of life above the wind, expecting to see a light flicker on inside, he waited, the cool air chilling his skin.

But there was no sound, no light. He knocked again. Lifting the flap of her letterbox, he peered into the gloom and shouted: "Charlie! Charlie! It's me, Alan." Still no answer.

After his interminable journey, disappointment tasted bitter. Looking around and realising that her car was missing from the driveway, he wondered where she could be at this late hour. Had they passed each other as she headed back to London? There was nothing for it at this time of night but to head wearily to his country home. He'd try to locate her in the morning.

To his surprise, Pear Tree Farm was ablaze with light. Candles spluttered in the dining room, and lamps were on in just about every upstairs window. Confused by tiredness, he sat in the warmth of his car for a moment, wondering what it could mean. Surely Mr and Mrs Reeder weren't using his home secretly while he was away? As if about to plunge into icy water, he took a deep breath before opening the driver's door and stepping out.

The porch was unlit and he fumbled with his key. When it finally found its mark, he turned it and leaned into the heavy oak door to open it, only to find his way barred by the safety chain which had been pulled across inside.

Then he had a sudden flash of inspiration. "Of course," he muttered crossly. "Charlie." He'd given her a key so she could use his library. She must have driven over and stayed too late and decided to spend the night. It'd be Charlie who left all those lights on. She didn't like the dark. Looking around in the blackness, he spotted her car parked beneath the large walnut tree at the edge of the drive, confirming his theory.

Delighted at the thought of seeing her after all, he tugged on the wrought-iron pull handle that jangled a Victorian bell deep within the building. For a long time, nothing happened, so he rang again. One of his cats slunk by the coach house leading down to his studio. By the time he rang the bell the third time, he was beginning to feel the cold creeping up through the soles of his shoes.

"What do you want?" a loud voice challenged from the shadows. Alan spun, half frightened out of his wits.

"Er—hello?" he said, stepping forward so as to get a better look. The beam of a flashlight blinded him. Raising an arm to shield his eyes, he could just make out the dark silhouette of a man holding a garden fork.

Arthur Reeder stood guard in his dressing gown, a piece of frayed string tying it around his ample girth. Behind him, her hair bristling with curlers, stood his redoubtable wife.

"Sir Alan?" Arthur growled, suspiciously.

"Yes, Arthur, it's me. I've just driven up from London, but I can't seem to get into the house."

"You've got company, sir," Arthur grunted unhelpfully, lowering his weapon. "She arrived this afternoon."

"Yes, yes, I know. But she's locked the front door from the inside. Do you have a key to the back door?"

Mrs Reeder whispered something to her husband and the two of them stepped forward into a circle of light from an upstairs window. "She's probably locked that as well," Arthur commented. "Very cautious, these Londoners. Didn't you get any answer at the front, then?"

"No. Any idea how we can get inside? How about one of the windows?"

"They ain't locked, sir. They never are. This is Suffolk."

"Then, can you please help me get inside before we all catch our deaths of cold?"

By the time Arthur had lifted the heavy sash window in the drawing room, climbed in, and ambled round to the front door to undo the chain, Alan was frozen to the marrow. He stood hugging himself in the hallway as Mrs Reeder switched on the hall light.

"Mrs Matheson!" she called up the stairs, her voice rising hoarsely at the end in the age-old Suffolk manner. "Mrs Matheson! Are you there?"

Alan shook himself to get warm and looked askance at her. "She's not Mrs Matheson just yet," he reminded her swiftly.

"No, not *her,*" Mrs Reeder corrected him, her hands deep in the pockets of her pink candlewick dressing gown. "It's the first Mrs Matheson who's here. She arrived out of the blue this afternoon, full of herself, barking orders and causing a right old kerfuffle. It was her who invited your girlfriend over to supper tonight."

Sarah? Here? Inviting Charlie to dinner? Alan would never have believed it unless the God-fearing Reeders were standing in front of him, nodding that it was true.

But suddenly, all the colour leeched from his face. And then he ran.

Alan made it to the landing in a matter of seconds. He saw a light shining under the door of Angela's old bedroom, ran towards it, and flung it open, causing it to crash against the wall.

Sarah sat in a green silk dressing gown at a delicate writing table, her ash blond hair brushed free from its usual confines. In her hand was a sheet of paper. When she looked up, it seemed to take her several moments to even recognise him.

"What are *you* doing here?" she asked, frowning.

"I might very well ask the same of you, Sarah," he said, striding towards her. "I came to see Charlie, but Mrs Reeder tells me you had her here to dinner tonight. What are you up to?"

"Nothing," she said, carefully rearranging her features and setting down the paper in her hand. "I came here for some peace and quiet, and—and when I found out Charlotte was up here, too, I—I thought it would only be polite to ask her over."

Alan stood over her, fists clenched. "The last time we spoke, you accused Charlie of being a lunatic and a gold-digger. You said she'd made you ill with all her questions and you never wanted to see her again. Why the sudden change of heart?"

"I—I realised I'd been a little harsh," Sarah countered. "I realised you cared for her more than I knew. I thought that maybe I should be more forgiving."

"And were you?" Alan asked, towering above her. He could feel the veins pulsating in his neck.

"Completely," she promised him, nodding. "We had a very pleasant supper and then she went home."

"Then why is her car still in the driveway? And why isn't she at her cottage?"

"I—I forgot. I drove her home after dinner. She was quite tired, you see, and a little upset."

"Upset? Why would she be upset? What did you say to her, Sarah?" Taking his ex-wife by the shoulders and shaking her violently to her feet, he shouted into her face, "What did you tell her?"

"Nothing," Sarah insisted. Pulling away, she stepped a few paces back and turned away.

"Sarah? Tell me what's going on!"

When she turned back her expression was quite different. It was Alan's turn to step away, suddenly afraid of her eyes.

"You're too late," she said softly.

"What do you mean I'm too late? Sarah! What have you done?"

"It was her fault. She knew too much," she said by way of reply, shaking her head crossly. "She was far too inquisitive for her own good. Before long, she'd have found out about Angela as well."

Registering the horror in Alan's eyes, her face twisted into something new, and she rushed towards him. "I had to do it, Alan. To protect you, don't you see?" she pleaded, her hands on his chest, a tiny bubble of saliva in the corner of her mouth.

Disgusted, he pushed her away. He had to find out what happened, but he also knew he had to handle Sarah very carefully. Taking a deep breath to steady himself, he placed both hands firmly on her shoulders. "Now stop this, Sarah. You're frightening me. I need to know where Charlie is. Tell me!"

Pulling herself to her full height, Sarah stared up at him defiantly. "I told you, Alan: you're too late. You shan't be marrying her, after all."

Reaching down and picking up the piece of paper she'd been examining when he came in, she showed it to him. "But don't worry. I've thought of everything, or rather she did. She even wrote this note. That's what gave me the idea in the first place."

Uncomprehendingly, Alan stared at what was in Sarah's hand, instantly recognising the distinctive writing paper Marco had given Charlie at the Fabriano paper mill. Its envelope, still on the table, was lined in powder blue.

I'm so sorry.
I never intended to cause you any pain.
Forgive me.
Charlotte.

"What? Where did you get that?" Alan felt his knees give way and he slumped back onto the bed, staring up at her in disbelief.

"She sent it to me, after you told her how upset I was. As soon as I saw it, Alan, the very minute I opened that envelope, I knew exactly what I must do. I knew you'd forbid her to see me, so I came here instead. All I had to do then was tell her the truth. Oh, and get her drunk enough not to put up too much of a fight."

Deep within him, Alan's mind lurched. Something was telling him to run, to find where Charlie was and flee with her, but his legs felt leaden. Reaching out, he grabbed a handful of Sarah Matheson's flimsy dressing gown and pulled on it.

"Please, Sarah," he murmured. "Please. Stop this nonsense. I don't understand."

Her immaculate hands prised his fingers from the green silk. Cupping his hand over her breast, she whispered, "Make love to me, Alan. Please make love to me. I need you, darling. Love me."

Alan listened helplessly, his face grey.

Sitting down on the bed next to him, her hand on his thigh, Sarah smiled and stroked his leg. "Now it'll be just you and me again. There's nobody left who knows. No one else knows the truth about you and Angela."

Alan's breath was coming in rasps. All he could smell was Chanel

No. 5. All his eyes could focus on was the row of pearls around Sarah's neck—her wedding-day pearls—worn even over her nightclothes.

"Knows what about me and Angela?" he moaned. "Sarah, what are you saying?"

"Oh, it's all right, my dearest darling," she said, leaning her head on his shoulder and moving her hand higher. "I understand completely. I know what Angela could be like. I don't blame you for wanting her, not when I'd foolishly turned you from my bed. But it's quite different now. *I'm* different."

Standing suddenly, she flung open her dressing gown to reveal a diaphanous negligee underneath. "Look at me, darling," she cried. "Look at me, I look just like Angela now!"

Alan jumped up, pushing her away in horror. "But I didn't want Angela! I never laid a finger on her, I swear! What are you saying? Oh, my God, Sarah—is that what you really think?! Have you always believed her lies, all this time? How could you?"

Sarah looked at him longingly, her eyes bright. "It doesn't matter what I think, darling. The point is that there's just you and me now. There's nobody left to interfere. Not Angela. Not Charlotte. I've seen to that."

"Charlie! Where's Charlie!" He gripped her by the shoulders and shook her. "Oh, my God, Sarah, what have you done?"

Reaching into the pocket of her dressing gown, Sarah retrieved a small empty syringe. "Do you know what this was filled with, Alan?" She grinned at him with childish excitement. "Wasps' venom. I get it from my doctor. It causes an allergic reaction in the soft tissues around my mouth, creating this perfect pout."

Leaning forward, she pressed her wet lips hard against his.

He jerked away, disgusted.

"The warning on the packaging is quite clear." Sarah smiled. "It must never be used on anyone who suffers from an allergic reaction to bee stings. It could cause a fatal anaphylactic reaction."

"What? But—Charlie! How did you know? Oh, my God!" A frisson of terror ran through him. He felt as if a hand was tightly squeezing his heart.

She waved the Fabriano notepaper in his face. "The verdict will almost certainly be accidental death. The poor girl was stung by a wasp in your studio and not found until the next morning. But just in case there's ever any doubt, I'll keep this little suicide note of hers in a safe place."

The pain in Alan's chest and rocketing down his left arm was so severe that he could no longer focus. He'd had this before—angina, the doctor said—and it had always passed, but until it did or until he was able to slip one of his pills under his tongue, he knew he wouldn't be able to make his escape.

"Sarah!" he cried, fighting for every breath and slumping back onto the bed. "You must listen to me—Angela was insane—she lied to you as well—I never touched her—I swear.... I don't, I don't know what you've done—but you were wrong. You were so, so wrong.... Oh, my God!"

Sarah's face fell. Still clutching Charlie's note, she dropped heavily on the bed next to him.

"But Angela told me everything," she reasoned, shaking her head against what he was saying. "She gave me every graphic detail. How you would come to her in the night. How you would touch her. Oh, Alan, that really broke my heart. That's why I persuaded her to take all those pills in the end. I had to get rid of her and the baby—your baby. I had to. Surely you understand?"

"Sarah!" Alan gasped. "Listen to me, please...you must listen to me.... I don't care what you did before.... I don't want to know....but find Charlie, Sarah...please...find her. Save her. She's not involved in this.... She carries an antidote.... It will be in her handbag. Sarah, do this for me. If you love me. Please!"

He fell sideways, clutching his left arm and praying for someone to come who could save them all.

Bending over him, stroking his silver hair and staring down at his face, Sarah kissed him tenderly. "But Angela told me, Alan. She *told* me. It had to have been the truth. Or I would never have needed to protect you. And Charlotte, she believed it, too. I told her everything, just before I jabbed the needle in her neck."

Bent double now with pain, Alan let out a long, lonely cry.

The last thing he saw as Sarah knelt over him was her expression faltering, then cracking into a series of irreparable fissures.

"Alan?" he heard her whisper, far far away. "Darling?"

BACK IN THEIR bed, in the tiny cottage adjacent to Pear Tree Farm, Mr and Mrs Reeder were just drifting off to sleep again when they were awakened by a noise, a strange, primal scream, coming from the main house.

It sounded like the cry of an animal, howling in pain.

Folio

A single leaf of paper that has been folded in two

47

NICK COULDN'T REMEMBER the last time he'd seen so many flowers. St Paul's Cathedral was filled with everything from white lilies to red roses; the air was heady with their scent. Tributes and messages from friends and colleagues adorned every wreath. The elegant mahogany coffin, just out of reach, was bedecked with a cascade of sunflowers. They glowed luminous yellow in a brilliant shaft of sunlight that poured onto them from the south transept window.

The organist was playing Handel, a sombre piece entirely in keeping with the mood as, one by one, grey-faced friends and relatives shuffled into their seats behind him, coughing and fidgeting and wishing that the service would start. Glancing over his shoulder, Nick met a hundred eyes, including those of Mrs Reeder and her husband, and a few faces he recognised from the New Year's Eve party. A few rows back sat Jake Burton, on crutches and looking suitably solemn. To his left, resplendent in a large black feather hat, was a woman Nick had never met until today. Lori Hunter.

Turning away from the penetrating gazes, he blinked up into the great dome above him, framed as it was by gilded mosaics of angels and cherubs, the perfect symmetry of the arches meeting the perfect round of the dome. High, high above him, above the statues and the first row of windows, around which ran the whispering gallery, looking deep into the heart of the beautifully painted fresco, he saw the mystical, magical light in the pinnacle of St Paul's, a place which Charlie had always said reminded her of Heaven.

Lowering his eyes, he looked to the right and saw, just a few feet away from where he sat, the white marble statue of J.M.W. Turner, palette and brushes in hand, his sightless eyes gazing distantly at an exquisite stained-glass window. Turner. Charlie's Turner. The artist she'd so admired. The artist Alan Matheson had most tried to emulate. The poignancy of his presence, here and now, was almost too much for Nick to bear. Hanging his head, he interlaced his fingers so tightly that his knuckles showed white through the skin.

"Are you all right?" Carrie asked, squeezing his arm.

"Fine," Nick lied. "I'm so glad you're here."

Beyond her sat Charlie's parents. Marjorie Hudson, clad in black from head to toe, an ebony walking stick at her side the only indication of her recent illness, had fixed her expression into one of stoic endurance.

The dean of St Paul's climbed the few steps to the pulpit and cleared his throat. "Friends," he began, his rich baritone voice echoing across the cathedral through the speakers placed discreetly on either side of the flower-filled nave. "We are gathered here today to remember someone very special, someone who touched all of our hearts, a person whose life was so cruelly cut short...."

The service was a fitting memorial. Purcell's *Dido and Aeneas* was played at both the beginning and the end. "*When I am laid in earth...remember me,*" a member of the choir had sung movingly. An old school friend read the words from Virgil's *Aeneid* that Charlie admired: "*I have lived my life and completed the course that Fortune has set before me, and now my great spirit will go beneath the Earth.*"

The wording on the note accompanying the cascading sunflowers sent to Alan Matheson's funeral read:

"*Thank you for saving me, Charlie xx*"

The blooms would always remind her of Villa Girasole, and the happiest times she'd ever spent with Alan. If only they'd stayed in that Umbrian haven, maybe things would have been different.

Nick and Carrie had visited Charlie at her London flat earlier that morning to make sure she was certain about her decision not to attend the funeral.

"Positive," she'd replied firmly, her face pale with sadness. "It would only become a media frenzy and I don't want to spoil Alan's day. Please, you two go as my representatives."

They'd left her in the capable care of her sister. Fiona had traveled down from Derbyshire, the two women on the brink of a new and more forgiving relationship. As Charlie mystifyingly told her, they'd crossed the brook.

Carrie had helped Fiona tuck Charlie under a blanket on the sofa and had promised she and Nick would call as soon as the funeral was over. "I won't miss a single detail," Carrie had assured her.

Charlie knew she could rely on them to describe everything that happened. They had already been so helpful, filling in the gaps in her memory about the events that terrible night at Pear Tree Farm. She had no idea Alan had driven up from London, looking for her. She could remember little after supper with Sarah. She'd had to ask Nick what happened, and only then did fragments of her own memory fill in the cracks.

"Alan arrived and rushed upstairs when he heard Sarah was there. About ten minutes later Mr and Mrs Reeder heard a scream. They ran back to the house," Nick had told her.

"I remember that scream," Charlie remarked, her mind confused. "It was like nothing I'd ever heard before."

"They found Alan, cradled in Sarah's arms. There was nothing they could do, Charlie. Sarah was in a daze. It was all the Reeders could do to prise her away from him. Then, suddenly, as if possessed, she jumped up and ran down to Alan's studio."

Carrie picked up the story they'd gleaned from the police officers and paramedics. "The old couple followed Sarah, and found you collapsed on the studio floor, close to death."

"All I remember is Sarah screaming my name, over and over. She kept asking me the same thing. 'Charlotte! Where is it, Charlotte? Where is it?' I could no longer speak. I thought I was drowning. Then she tipped the contents of my handbag onto the floor, and found the syringe. I don't remember anything else after that."

Nick nodded. "Sarah saved your life, Charlie. She gave you the Adrenalin shot. She held you across her lap, and rocked you until the ambulance came."

Charlie listened intently to Nick's words, which no longer roared like the sea in her ears.

"She told the police everything when they arrived," Carrie explained. "They said it was as if she was recounting something that had happened to someone else."

"She was so jealous of Angela's relationship with Alan that she tried to turn her against him," Nick continued. "Even when she told Angela the truth, that Alan wasn't her real father, Angela refused to believe her. So, Sarah began to secretly feed her daughter the powerful mood-enhancers that had been prescribed for her. Washed down with alcohol or mixed with cannabis, Angela became delusional."

"Which is probably when she created those extraordinary paintings," Charlie murmured. "And started to believe her mother's lies."

Carrie took up the thread. "Sarah wanted Angela to go away forever, to leave her and Alan alone. But when Angela told her she was pregnant, Sarah was convinced, in her jealousy, that the child must be Alan's. Even poor Angela began to believe it. The two women fed on each other's despair. On Sarah's final visit to Angela at the Norwich clinic, she slipped her some extra pills. Somehow, she persuaded her that she and the baby would be better off dead."

"And the note?" Charlie asked, feeling as if she was nothing but skin stretched over bone.

"Angela wrote that after Sarah left her that day. The police had no choice but to investigate," Nick explained. "That's when Alan finally learned the truth. The report confirmed that not only wasn't he the father of Angela's unborn child, but that he wasn't even Angela's father. Alan realised then what Sarah had done to get him back in the first place. That's when he left her."

"But he never once betrayed Sarah, or Angela," Carrie reminded Charlie. "He never told you or anyone else what they had done to him. He protected them both till the end."

"What finally killed him?" Charlie's voice was barely a whisper.

"His heart," Nick replied. "He'd been on angina medication for over a year, but he left London in such a rush that night, he forgot to take it with him. He'd been warned not to put himself under any stress. But when Sarah confessed that she'd not only facilitated Angela's suicide but had also murdered you, his heart quite literally burst."

Charlie remembered Alan's prophetic vow to die once all his paper was gone, his breathlessness when they made love, his face aflame with exertion. His hands. His mouth. Something deep inside her ached with sudden longing.

"Poor Sarah. I don't think anyone ever loved Alan as much as she did."

"Sarah made it quite clear that Alan loved you very much, Charlie," Carrie said. "That's why she saved your life. It was the last thing he asked her to do."

THE NEWSPAPERS COVERED the funeral and the events following Alan's death in exacting detail. Some of the obituaries had been far from kind. Sarah Matheson still had friends in high places who clung to the view that her shabby treatment by the artist had led inevitably to her unfortunate mental collapse. Carrie and Nick kept Charlie from as much of it as they could, but they couldn't protect her from the inquest, where she gave evidence in a remarkably clear voice about what she could remember of Sarah Matheson's state of mind that fateful night.

Taking her place in the witness box in a stuffy coroner's court in Ipswich, Charlie watched as the reporters' pens flew across the lined pages of their notebooks, faithfully recording her every word. It was a job she'd once done, in a previous life. She wondered what they made of her now, this lone survivor, recounting events that left nothing but pain and devastation in their wake.

Charlie knew what the verdict would be before the inquest even began. There wasn't enough evidence for unlawful killing; Alan had died of natural causes. Sarah Matheson may have tried to kill Charlie, but she had also saved her life. Her mental collapse now complete, she was incapable of giving evidence herself. Sectioned under the Mental Health Act, committed to the permanent care of the doctors who'd been treating her for so many years, she'd never again return to her elegant Knightsbridge flat with her late husband's painting of an Italian villa over the marble mantelpiece.

CHARLIE WENT WILLINGLY to Carrie's house to convalesce, no longer afraid of Manchester and its memories. She found herself sleeping surprisingly soundly at night and well into the mornings. The two friends spent the afternoons walking and talking and, in the evenings, stayed in by the fire, indulging in some fiercely competitive games of Scrabble.

"Words," Charlie told Carrie, smiling. "I can always lose myself in words."

Only when the media spotlight had swung round onto another hapless subject did Charlie decide to slip quietly back to London, much against the wishes of her friend.

"Why don't I come and stay with you for a while, just until you find your feet?" Carrie suggested.

"I know where my feet are, thanks. If you want to come to London then do so, but I think it's Nick you should be spending time with, not me."

Carrie stared at her best friend. "Does it bother you?" she asked tentatively. "I mean... we could stop right now if it did."

"No," Charlie replied, honestly. "It doesn't. In fact, I'm relieved. You have my blessings, and all my love. I can even provide the engagement ring when the time comes. I have just the thing."

Carrie flung her arms around Charlie's neck and kissed her cheek. "Oh, thank you, Charlie! You know I've loved him forever."

"I know that now." Charlie smiled back. "And you'll be perfect together. Really."

"What about you? Will you be all right?"

Charlie nodded slowly. "Yes," she said with the quiet conviction she'd only recently acquired. "Yes, I will."

48

CLOSING THE DOOR of her London flat behind her, Charlie kicked off her shoes and trod softly into the lounge. Turning on a lamp, she wandered into the kitchen and clicked on the kettle. Within a few minutes, it had boiled and she made herself a coffee. Sipping at it through the steam, she closed her eyes and leaned against the wall, enjoying the comfort of the liquid's bitter warmth.

Wandering back into the book-lined lounge, mug in hand, she flopped onto her sofa. Glancing at the answering machine blinking at her from a side table, she ignored it and stared instead at the proposed jacket for her new book that Lola Lewis had just sent her. *Paper Chase* by Charlotte Hudson, with a foreword by Sir Alan Matheson, R.A., the title read. Beneath it was a reproduction of Alan's beautiful painting. The publishers planned to rush it through the presses in double-quick time and release it as soon as possible to cash in on the public fascination with the life and death of Sir Alan Matheson.

Never in his wildest fantasies could Nigel Armstrong have hoped for such a PR dream. Although he'd never actually said it, Charlie could tell that both he and Lola Lewis thought her involvement with the scandal of the year a pure masterstroke of marketing. Her book would be a surefire bestseller, they assured her.

•   •   •

THE FOLLOWING MORNING, the taxi arrived dead on time. Opening the door for her, the driver couldn't help but notice the woman's understated elegance. The face devoid of makeup, the simple clothes under a dark grey overcoat. He thought she seemed sad yet dignified. A widow, perhaps.

He gladly accepted his passenger's generous tip, promising to wait.

"Any idea how long you'll be, luv?" he called, as she was about to step inside to the ornate marble lobby of the City's most venerable bank.

"Not long," Charlie replied, stepping inside.

Walking purposefully, she crossed the intricate mosaic floor and approached one of the cash desks. After a brief exchange with the cashier to whom she handed a letter, a bespectacled man with a receding hairline emerged from a side room. He shook her hand warmly, opened the envelope, read the short letter inside, and then escorted her through a locked security door. It swung shut behind her with a bang.

SHE TURNED THE small key in the lock of the large, flat safe-deposit box. The key turned easily in her hand. Taking a trembling breath, she lifted the lid on the small steel coffin and closed her eyes, half afraid of what she might find. The cool air from within drifted up towards her, bringing with it the special scent of what it had been keeping safe and dry for many years.

Paper. Linen rags. Pulp floating on water. The pressure of stone. The heat of the drying lofts. Each sheet a miniature work of art, an icon of beauty with an integrity that no mark on its surface could ever improve upon. Is a sheet of paper ever truly blank, Charlie wondered, or is it complete in itself?

Opening her eyes, she stared down at the contents of the box. Her fingers lifted the thin wooden board that had once weighed down the last sixteen sheets of Alan's precious vintage paper. Gone were the waterproof wrappings and the acid-free white tissue paper. In their place lay a single folio of Whatman's paper, neatly folded in two.

Gingerly retrieving it, Charlie leaned back in her chair and closed her eyes again. Taking another deep breath, she opened them and stared down at the creamy white sheet. With a deft motion of her thumb, she flicked it open. The writing was unmistakable. The letter was dated December 27, the day Alan had left her alone at Rhubarb Cottage to finish her book. Less than a week before he gave her his ring.

> *If you're reading this, my Charlie,* the note began, *then I'm gone and you now know that all the paper has gone, too. I used to think there would be nothing else worth living for when that happened, but then I met you.*

Gripping the paper to steady herself, Charlie read on.

> *My life has been full and not always happy. But one person, more than any other, has given it more meaning than I could ever have imagined. You said it was I who healed you, but, in truth, it was you who healed me all along. For that reason I'm leaving you not only* Crossing the Brook—*as already promised in the will lodged with the solicitor who sent you my letter asking you to come here—but also my London home and Villa Girasole. Pear Tree Farm is to be left to Tony Rogers's mother. I thought it was the least I could do.*
>   *Sarah has already been adequately provided for. Angela is dead. If not to you, then to whom? Please accept this. It is the only way I can tell you what you mean to me.*
>   *I love you, Charlie. I did from the moment I met you.*
>   *Alan.*

It seemed a lifetime ago since she had first sat here next to Alan, virtual strangers on the brink of a relationship that would change both their lives so dramatically. Even then, she'd sensed his power—infuriating, invulnerable, intoxicating. But how could she ever have guessed how truly cataclysmic his influence would be? So much had happened to her since that day that she would barely recognise the tense young woman who had shivered at the mere scent of paper.

Charlie finally allowed the tears to come. Then, taking Alan's note, she refolded it and placed it into her pocket, before closing the lid on the box. Standing, she hurried from the bank without looking back.

RHUBARB COTTAGE FELT chilly and damp; she quickly lit a fire. The flames lapped at the slivers of kindling and licked hungrily at the dry fruitwood logs Charlie had placed on top. Pulling herself up to admire her handiwork, her left hand inadvertently brushed the painting of her cottage, hanging above the fireplace. She stroked the watercolour lightly with her fingertips, her eyes thoughtful.

Turning her mind away, she busied herself, emptying her shopping bags and restocking the fridge. From a shelf, she took down a glass vase and filled it with a generous spray of yellow daffodils, placing it on the low oak table in front of the fireplace. How Alan would have enjoyed painting that, she thought. Perhaps, one day soon, she'd try.

Pulling on her boots and a scarf, not even bothering to change out of her overcoat, she walked out of the front door. Stopping to admire the abandoned wasps' nest that had been carefully placed in the porch by the handyman who'd removed it from her loft, she knelt and examined the way its delicate layers overlapped each other in a fine scalloping pattern of yellows and browns, like the scales of a river fish.

"The nest of a common paper wasp," the garrulous workman had informed her as he emerged from her attic with it on a stick.

"They make it by chewing wood fibre, you know, scraped from trees, fences, telephone poles, even buildings. Then the clever little bug mixes it with his saliva and makes a sort of pulp. He crafts the nest from it, using his legs. When it dries, the pulp forms a tough, durable paper that bonds together to create this."

Apparently encouraged by her silence, he continued. "Each winter, when all the workers and the drones have been killed off by the cold, a new, young queen emerges from hibernation beneath the ground and sets about beginning a new colony in the spring. The old nest is almost never reused. Did you know that it was by looking at how the wasp made its home that the ancient Chinese first came up with the idea for making paper?" he'd concluded, triumphantly.

"Yes," Charlie replied at last. "Yes, I knew that."

As SHE PICKED her way down the path to the beach, past the old tarmac road and its precipitous cliff edge, the strong sea breeze whipped her hair around her face. The seagulls and sand martins wheeled overhead as if welcoming her. She was pleased to note that she felt nothing but happiness at being back. She refused to allow anything to taint her pleasure in this magical place she called home.

Strolling across the sand under a crystalline sky, she looked back at the footprints she'd left and carried purposefully on, making more. Stopping in her tracks a few paces farther, she reached down with care and picked up a large white pebble, smoothed and eroded by the forces of nature, a perfect hole in its centre, turning it over and over comfortingly in her hand.

Head down, she searched for more, picking at the stones and the flotsam and jetsam thrown up from the previous night's high tide. There were lead fishing weights, pieces of orange netting, all manner of driftwood, crab claws, fish heads, and the battered plastic floats that prevent a boat from crashing against the harbour wall. Farther up the beach, she came across a small glass bottle, its top screwed tightly on, its contents unclear. Rubbing away the sand, she saw it held a scrap of paper rolled tightly inside.

"Thrown into the sea on December 9, 2004, from a cross-Channel ferry by Henry John Guy, aged sixteen," it read. In a spidery scrawl along the bottom it gave his address near Guildford in Surrey.

Charlie remembered walking on a Cornish cliff top with her grandfather, carefully writing out a similar note and folding it hopefully into a bottle.

"Throw it as far as you can, Granddad," she'd urged, as he took the bottle from her outstretched hands and hurled it manfully into the waves. In a way, she'd never stopped waiting for that bottle to come back, for someone to reply to her childish missive. She'd watched for the postman every morning for a year, but no answer ever came.

Looking back along the coast as a flock of Canada geese flew overhead, their bugle cries honking, she could just make out the wisp of smoke trailing up from the chimney of her cottage. Inside, she knew, it would already be warm and cosy. She'd make a pot of tea and some hot buttered toast. Thinking of it gave her a sudden rush of hunger.

Waiting for her on the low table next to her sofa were several biographies of a man who had long fascinated her, the English architect Sir Edwin Lutyens, and a scrawled draft of the research needed for her next book: a historic novel about his remarkable work in New Delhi, provisionally entitled *Spires and Minarets*. She already had an opening paragraph burning away inside her brain; she could hardly wait to fly out to India and get started.

Screwing the lid back on the bottle, Charlie determined to enter into a correspondence with Henry John Guy later that afternoon. It would take only ten minutes. The time it used to take her to wash her hands.

She slipped the bottle into the pocket of her overcoat. As she did so, her fingers touched something else. Lifting it out, she stared hard at the folded piece of paper Alan had left for her in the vault.

Tightening her grip, she reached for it with her other hand. Tearing the paper in two, she watched as the handmade deckle edges crumbled. Sandwiching the pieces together, she tore it again, into four, then eight. Her jaw set, her expression determined, she carried on rhythmically, relentlessly, until the note was no more than a hundred tiny fragments in her palm.

Inhaling deeply, Charlie raised her arms slowly above her head, and turned into the wind. Opening her fingers one by one, she released the fragments piece by piece, allowing the breeze to carry them out across the waves.

Only when every last scrap of paper was gone, and her pocket contained only the treasures of the future, not the relics of the past, did she finally allow herself to exhale. Turning away, she looked into the far distance and strode off resolutely along the shore.

Author's Note

I am gratefully indebted to a number of scholars whose work on Turner and paper has informed and inspired me. Chiefly the indefatigable Peter Bower for his many excellent books and articles on Turner and his papers, and Silvie Turner for her joyous *The Book of Fine Paper*. The British Association of Paper Historians for its superb Web site. Also Anthony Bailey for *Standing in the Sun, A Life of JMW Turner*; Guy Weelen and Graham Reynolds for their respective books, both called simply *Turner*; and Ian Warrell for *Turner: The Fourth Decade, Watercolours 1820–1830*. Last, but by no means least, Anne F. Clapp for her informative *Curatorial Care of Works of Art on Paper*.

All the characters in this book are fictitious and any resemblance to actual persons, living or dead, is purely coincidental.

About the Author

TAYLOR HOLDEN, as Wendy Holden, was a respected journalist for *The Daily Telegraph*, where she covered wars and events around the world, including Northern Ireland, the U.S., Eastern Europe, and the Middle East. She has co-written several autobiographies of remarkable women, including Goldie Hawn's recent *New York Times* bestseller. She lives in Suffolk, England, with her husband and four dogs. This is her first novel.